D0126942

FAITH'S REWARD

a novel

Tammy BARLEY

WHITAKER
HOUSE

FAITH'S REWARD
Book Three in The Sierra Chronicles

Tammy Barley
www.tammybarley.com

ISBN: 978-1-60374-110-1
Printed in the United States of America
© 2011 by Tammy Barley

Whitaker House
1030 Hunt Valley Circle
New Kensington, PA 15068
www.whitakerhouse.com

Library of Congress Cataloging-in-Publication Data

Barley, Tammy, 1969–
Faith's reward / by Tammy Barley.
   p. cm. — (The Sierra chronicles ; bk. 3)
   ISBN 978-1-60374-110-1 (trade pbk.)
   1. Married people—Fiction. 2. Marriage—Fiction. 3. Family secrets—Fiction. I. Title.
PS3602.A77557F35 2011
813'.6—dc22
                           2010038084

1 2 3 4 5 6 7 8 9 10 11 12 **ധ** 18 17 16 15 14 13 12 11

Acknowledgments

As always, my sincere and deep appreciation goes to Terry Burns, literary agent extraordinaire, and to all the wonderful folks at Whitaker House, for their tireless dedication in assisting me to entertain, to inspire, and to take readers on great adventures of the mind and heart. You are the best.

Dedication

To my big brother, Tom,
who turns pale as a limp sock at the sight of needles
yet would have donated a kidney.
I love you, bro.
And to all blood and organ donors.
You are heroes.

Faith is being sure of what we hope for
and certain of what we do not see.
—Hebrews 11:1

Do not throw away your confidence;
it will be richly rewarded.
—Hebrews 10:35

Chapter One

January 1865
Honey Lake Valley, Northern California

Jake?"

Jessica Bennett jolted upright in bed, her hand trembling as it searched the cold sheets in the darkness beside her. Her fingers brushed Jake's equally cold pillow, then the soft fur of the cat that huddled on it, the only trace of warmth in the place where her husband had gone to sleep beside her. *"Jake?"*

Wind rattled the windowpane with nearly enough force to crack it. The wintry cold had seeped through the glass and turned the bedroom to ice. Jess hugged her flannel nightgown firmly to her and sat still and alert, straining to hear over the storm for any indication of movement in the house, either upstairs or down. She heard no thud of boot heels on the plank floor, no jingle of spurs to suggest any presence inside the house but hers.

Judging by the thick darkness, dawn was still hours away. Though she and Jake had worked until sometime after midnight, until they were both exhausted, he must have rested in bed until she had fallen asleep, but no longer than that. Once he had been certain she and the baby within her were at rest, he must have gone back to work and joined the next shift of cattlemen who fought to keep their horses and cattle alive, digging them out of the snow and providing hay to stimulate their bodies' heat.

The misty darkness abruptly grew darker, closing in around her.

Then, blackness.

An image flashed through her mind—she stood in boot-deep snow under a gray sky, a Henry rifle gripped in her hands. At her sides stood two of the cattlemen. More than a dozen Paiute Indian men stepped forward to stand alongside them. She recognized one Paiute who worked at the ranch. The others were strangers. Their faces revealed fear, and resolve. In front of her, perhaps five paces away, stood thirty or more renegade white men who, as one, reached their hands to their holsters, drew their guns, then took aim at Jess and the Indians. Jess cocked the Henry rifle, pressed the butt to her shoulder, and sighted down the barrel at the cold, glittering blue eyes of the man who aimed the bore of his revolver at her. Though fear burned like liquid fire beneath her skin, she firmed her grip, shifted her index finger from the rifle's trigger guard to the curve of the metal trigger. And pulled.

An explosion rocked Jess, tearing her back to the present. Shaken, she waited for the effects of the premonition to ebb, and focused on palpable images as they came to her: Her pulse, pounding like rapid drumbeats just beneath her ears. Her breath, passing though her parted lips in deep gasps, drying her throat. She swallowed. A chill permeated her flannel nightgown. The scent of forest that clung to the pine log walls filled the bedroom. The storm…. A second explosion!—No, not an explosion. It was the windowpane, pounded by the wind. Something trickled down her temples, rolled onto her cheeks. Startled, she swiped at it with her fingers. Dampness. Sweat. Nothing more. Sweat misted her forehead as well. She dried it with her sleeve and forced her breathing to calm.

Jess felt beside her, then remembered. Jake was gone. He hadn't gone to sleep the night before.

In one movement, she flung the covers aside and reached toward the end of the bed for the union suit she had purchased two months before, shortly after she'd realized she was expecting a child. Leaving her flannel nightgown and stockings on, she stuffed her feet into the woolen legs of the union suit then stood and buttoned it up to her neck, using her thumbs and fingertips to feel the buttonholes and shove the buttons through. Jess hurried to the pegs on the wall near the window and felt for one of Jake's flannel shirts. Her hand brushed one, then a pair of his trousers. Frustrated with not being able to see, she grabbed both garments and flung them onto the bed then rounded it to Jake's side, where she felt along the surface of the tall chest of drawers until her hands connected with the oil lantern they kept there and finally the matchbox. After three strikes, a flame flared to life, and she lit the lantern then replaced the chimney with a glass-on-metal *clink*.

Winter buffeted the window once again. Jess ignored it. Moments later, dressed and belted, she slid her feet into her cowboy boots, then stuffed the extra fourteen or fifteen inches of Jake's pant legs into the boot tops. Just as rapidly, she plaited her hip-length brown hair and secured the bottom with a leather thong.

She grabbed up the lantern, threw open the bedroom door—the place where she first saw her tall, handsome Jake standing when she was brought to the ranch, she recalled with a sudden lightness in her heart—then hurried out onto the landing and down the stairs, her boots and the steps gilded by a wide ring of golden lantern light.

The fire in the hearth had burned down and gave off little heat. Jess set the lantern on the mantel and pulled her weighty sheepskin coat from its peg near the front door, then tugged it on, followed by her woolen hat, scarf, and gloves.

The premonition had shaken her more than the other few she'd experienced before it, but what truly unnerved her was the certainty that had woken her—something had happened to Jake.

Jess lifted the iron latch that served as a door handle. The front door blew in and struck her in the chest. Resisting the wind, she held tightly to the door as she stepped out onto the covered porch and pulled the door closed, straining against the force of the gales.

On the porch she huddled deeper into her coat, thankful it hung to her knees. Squinting against the wind, she scanned the ranch yard and glimpsed dots of orange that flickered ahead of her and to both sides, lit torches that were barely visible through the snowflakes being driven through the night and against her cheeks and chin. Most of the torches appeared to congregate near the smithy, ahead of her and to the left.

Jess descended the two porch steps and moved toward the smithy, leaning into the wind. Her nostrils stuck closed, and she was forced to breathe through her mouth. If Jake had walked in this direction and broken a path through the drifts, she was unable to distinguish his tracks in the blackness. Already her toes and fingers tingled in sharp pain as if rubbed by frost.

One of the orange torches blew out. A moment later, another torch relit it. The man who held the relit torch shifted the flame away from the others, toward the ground. Its fire burst to nearly thrice its size, then gradually settled back to its original mass. The men must be using kerosene to keep them lit. On the wind, the faint smell of smoke drifted to her.

She pushed on and lifted one booted foot after the other over the snow as she forced her straining muscles to move as quickly as she could make them go, feeling oddly off-balance due to her inability to see.

A torch broke away from the others and wended its way in her direction, no doubt carried by someone bringing hay for animals to eat so they could produce their own warmth. She and Jake had done the same, beginning late the previous afternoon, when the storm had given its first whispers of the violence to come, and continuing until midnight, scattering hay about the ranch's main compound. But now the snows made foraging impossible. The men who gathered near the smithy must have found another way to protect the animals.

The light of the single torch grew brighter and nearer, and she altered her path to move toward it. Orange light revealed Taggart's surprised round face as his eyes met hers, his hairy eyebrows, mustache, and beard frozen white with ice and snow.

Jess leaned close to his ear and shouted over the storm. "Have you seen Jake?"

"He's tendin' the fireplaces in the buildings!" he yelled back and jerked a wool-clad thumb over his beefy shoulder. His fingers held a coiled lasso. "He told the men to string a rope corral from the smithy to the cookhouse to the bunkhouse, and back to the smithy. We're searchin' for the beasts and bringin' them over, hopin' the heat from the buildings will keep the critters from freezing."

"By 'beasts' do you mean the horses?"

Taggart shifted the torch, apparently in mild impatience to be under way. "No, the cattle."

Jess's eyes searched the darkness and found a distant square of light emanating from the cookhouse window. Jake must be warm near the fires, or at least he remained so while inside, between jaunts from one building to the next in the deathly cold. Still, she couldn't throw off the conviction that something was horribly wrong. "What about the horses? Without them, we'll lose the ranch!"

"Jess, there's no time for explainin', though the boss knows about the horses," he assured her above the scream of the wind. "He ordered us to wrangle the horses to the barn and stable."

Jess nodded and held a glove over her nose, wishing she had a way to warm her face.

"Ye should be sleepin'," Taggart chastised her, "but since ye're here, we need ye." He took her arm and turned her to face the outskirts of the ranch. "We're able to drive the horses—a couple of the boys are on horseback doin' just that—but the cows are the problem. They turned their backsides to the wind and lowered their heads to stay warm, but the snow is coverin' them, and their breath and body heat have turned the snow into a casing of ice around them. They're suffocatin'. Come on!"

Within her, Jess's stomach sank in dread. She kept up with Taggart, step for step. They wended their way east past the ranch house and toward the Paiute village in the same manner he had approached her, occasionally changing direction from left to right as they continued forward, searching for cattle trapped in ice.

"Ye see? There!" Taggart held out the torch and headed toward a large mound half buried in a drift. The beast moaned, a pathetic plea that was nearly swallowed by the howl of the storm.

Jess thought the cow was merely covered in snow, but as she neared and touched its side, her glove stuck to ice.

Taggart kicked low to break the ice, again, then again, until it gave way with a dull crunch. The cow, with its first full breath, gave a loud bawl.

Desperate to help, Jess rounded the animal and kicked from the other side. Her toes stung unbearably with each blow, so she turned her boot and kicked with her heel. The frozen casing gave way.

Taggart secured the lasso around the cow's neck and rapidly pushed off the rest of the snow. "Can ye take her to the rope corral, Jess, then come find me again? With two of us working together, one can break the cows free and the other can lead them to the buildings."

Immediately, Jess took the end of the lasso from him. "If you wander too far, I won't be able to see your torch."

"Ye will. The wind's still a fury, but the snows are dyin' down. See?"

Jess realized he was right, though she was still forced to squint. *Thank You, God, that the snows are dying.* "I'll hurry back."

She had to pull to encourage the cow to move, and had to keep pulling against its wont to stop and hunker down. At the rope corral, she exchanged brief nods with the ranchmen there, then lifted the looped end of a rope from an iron post to lead the cow through to join the others. Jake's idea was working. The cow nosed its way into the warm press of livestock and lowered its head to eat from one of the bales of hay. Though she paused to scan the open spaces between the buildings for Jake, she didn't see him.

For the next several hours until sunrise, Jess helped the men rescue cows mired belly-deep in the snow, pausing only to gulp hot coffee kept in constant supply by the ranch cook and her longtime friend, Ho Chen.

Gradually, the snow had slowed until it resembled falling dust, but it wasn't until dawn, while she led yet another cow into the corral, that she finally saw Jake. He was making his way toward the ranch house, hunched over, coughing uncontrollably, and was supported by two of the cattlemen, Seth and Lee.

The last of Jess's strength bled from her. Jake had passed between extreme heat and cold, into hot buildings and out into the frigid storm, all night. She knew what such extremes did to miners who descended shafts to work in the hot steam more than two thousand feet beneath the surface of the Comstock, then later emerged up into arctic gales. Countless numbers of the miners died. From pneumonia.

"Lord Almighty," she breathed, and ran toward the house. *Never again,* she promised God, *never again will I doubt the instincts You gave me, if only You will let Jake live.*

Chapter Two

Jess shouldered the front door closed against the force of the wind, then dropped the bar in place to secure it. The two cattlemen had Jake halfway up the stairs to the bedroom. "Seth, Lee, bring Jake back down. He needs to be by the fire."

Jake waved an arm, evidently struggling to catch his breath so he could speak. "Jess, I should be in the bedroom. Take me up, boys."

Both grasped the banister to lift him to the next step.

"No, Jake, you *want* to be in that freezing bedroom, where no one will see you ill and your pride won't suffer. You *should* be near the fire. I'm sorry, but you'll just have to manage. Seth, Lee," she ordered, "bring him down."

The two men exchanged a long look. With his free hand, young Seth Griffin rubbed the thumb of his glove over the downy whiskers on his cheek, his eyebrows raised to Lee's dark brown Indian features in silent communication. Apparently they chose to go against their male inclinations, which dictated that men must suffer in privacy, and sided with safety, knowing the danger of contradicting a woman. With more brute force than grace, Lee went up one step while Seth went down one, and the three broad men in bulky sheepskin coats turned around.

Jake glared at Jess between coughs that were turning his face red. She ignored the glare as she struggled to shove the massive, pine-framed leather sofa across the wood floor and nearer the stones of the hearth. She was far more concerned with Jake's survival than with his unwillingness to appear infirm to the other men of the ranch.

While the cowboy hat on Seth's head and the rabbit skin hat on Lee's bent together to ease Jake to the sofa, Jess swiftly hung her gloves, coat, hat, and scarf on their pegs then gathered twigs from the woodpile. She rolled back her sleeves then knelt at the hearth, laying kindling on the still-warm coals. When the twigs ignited, she added larger sticks and blew on the flames until the fire grew. The nearest doctor lived a two days' ride from the remote ranch, she reflected—longer if he wasn't immediately available—and the death of her little brother, Broderick, had proven that doctors' knowledge of cures for pneumonia was limited. As were their options. Jake needed help now. "Seth," she said urgently, lifting her voice to be heard above Jake's relentless coughing, "please send Ho Chen. Tell him to bring anything he thinks might help Jake's cough. And, Seth? Tell everyone to use the back door to minimize the drafts."

The tall youth gave a sober nod, then headed into the short hallway under the staircase, turned left into the dining room, and exited through the back door.

Jess added more sticks to the fire. Already the heat was driving the chill from her fingers and toes. "Lee?" She glanced over her shoulder at the sinewy Paiute man with the steady gaze. "Do you or any of the other Paiutes have medicines that can help?"

Jake held in a cough and laid a warm hand on Jess's arm. "They have to see to the horses and cattle. Let's not take them away from that until we have to."

Still crouched with sticks in her hands, Jess spun on the balls of her feet to look up into the steady, whiskey-brown eyes of the man she loved. Steady, she knew, to mask his concern for her. Beneath the brown brim of his hat, the creases at the outer corners of his eyes scrunched together as he turned his head to cough. Darkly sun-bronzed even in winter, his face was an arresting fusion of roguishness and virility, from his habitually unshaven, hard-muscled jaw, to his angular nose and mouth, to the thick, nearly black hair that her fingers always joyed to feel. Jake Bennett was all man. And he was her man. Though he was alarmingly ill, he was concerned not for himself, she knew, but for her and the challenges she would face without him in the hours and days ahead. Her concern, however, was for him. "Jake, you've almost certainly come down with—"

"Pneumonia. I know."

"*Pogonip*," Lee said, his face grim as Jake's shoulders jerked in a persistent fit of coughing. "White death. It has brought this." He remained calm as always, but clearly regretted completing his thought. "Jess, no one can survive it."

"Some *can* survive it," Jess countered, her sudden glare shifting between Jake and Lee. "And Jake *will* survive it. Debating that fact is a waste of time. Now, Lee, do you or any of the other Paiutes have medicines that can help?" she repeated.

Though Lee's ears probably stung from her reprimand, the doubt vanished from his onyx eyes. "I will ask," he assured her, then strode from the room. A moment later, the back door closed.

Jess thrust her branches into the fire, then went into the kitchen and returned with a small iron pot. She placed it on the hearth and filled it from the nearby water bucket. Lifting the filled pot by its handle, she hung it in the fireplace. "This will have to suffice until Ho Chen can bring a larger cauldron." A glance at Jake told her that a fever had taken hold. His neck and face were flushed, and he shook with chills as he peeled out of his wet outerwear. "Simmering water will force hot moisture into the room," she explained. "I learned that years ago from the doctor who tended my little brother before he died. It helped Broderick, though not enough to save him."Broderick was just a baby, Jess," Jake said between chattering teeth, responding to the tremor of fear in her voice. "Weak, and born three weeks early, you once told me. I'm a big, strong man, and I have you and your Hale tenacity to get me through this."

She'd started up the stairs to collect blankets, but paused and shot him an admiring look. "Bennett tenacity," she corrected.

He began to chuckle but was seized by another onslaught of coughing.

At the top of the stairs, Jess turned right and strode into the room where she had slept when Jake first brought her to the ranch. Immediately she set to work stripping woolen Indian blankets from the bed. Then she stopped and let them fall back to the bed.

This was the first moment she'd had to herself since the premonition had jolted her awake hours before. Since that vision, she'd been terrified—for Jake, for the Paiute people and the cattlemen, for the horses and cattle, and for the ranch itself. This was their livelihood. It was the place where she and Jake had fallen in love, and all the people who worked here depended upon it for their food, work, and very existence. Together they'd battled Indian haters twice before, but never as many as she'd seen in the premonition—thirty men standing ready to kill the Paiutes and determined to do it. Unable to maintain her guise of confidence, Jess leaned tight fists on the bed and dropped her head to one of her arms. The beautiful Paiute people, the cattlemen, the ranch, and Jake…they were all she had. They were all she loved.

Jake.

The day her brother, Ambrose, had left their family's home in Carson City, Nevada, to fight in the War Between the States, she'd told him that she would never marry. She had seen too many wives' hopes destroyed by their husbands' selfish wants and ambitions, and she'd told Ambrose that she could never live her life under some man's boot heel, that she'd make her way on her own.

But then she'd met Jake. The life she and Jake shared was different. In every way, they were right for each other. They shared the same longed-for dream, and they worked endless hours side by side to turn a played-out cattle operation into a successful horse ranch. Together they had brought Thoroughbred stallions all the way from Iowa to breed with the other horses they owned, to add speed to the endurance of the Morgans, and to that they would add the hardiness of the wild mustangs they'd caught and green broken. She and Jake shared the same love of the Paiute people, of the Sierra Nevadas, whose northern foothills stood less than five hundred paces behind the back wall of the ranch house, and of Honey Lake Valley, which stretched out beyond the ranch to the north and east. She and Jake both felt driven by the same need to see justice in the unjust West, and they both believed in the same fights that were in desperate need of being fought.

Jess rubbed her forehead on her sleeve, absently comforting herself from her fears of the next battle that she had envisioned, in which she stood alone, without Jake.

After the previous premonitions, Jake had told her that the visions were not, in fact, the curse she'd believed them to be, but rather God's way of preparing her for tough times to come, and a reminder that He would be right alongside her. She had yet to learn if the visions revealed eventualities she would remain powerless to prevent, or if there might be some way she could alter the outcomes.

With fitful movements, Jess resumed tearing the blankets from the bed.

Jake's constant faith in God had bolstered her own trust in Him. *Lord above, I love that man*, she thought as she carried the bundle of blankets to their bedroom, where she set them down and began to pull more blankets from their bed. Jake inspired her, teased her, and subtly, constantly, showed her his love. He was rare, and wonderful. And he had pneumonia.

Why did Jake continue to work when he knew he was becoming ill? He must have known he wasn't feeling well the night before, and even the day before that. Jess's fingertips tingled. She recalled touching him before they went to sleep—before *she* went to sleep. His skin had felt warm to the touch, a little more so than the usual heat he emitted. And he had begun to cough. Why didn't he have one of the men take over for him? Immediately the answer came. Jake would never allow another man to become ill in his place. It was his personal code of honor, understood and shared by nearly all the cattlemen she'd met in the West. She loved that about Jake and had adopted the code herself. Cattlemen rarely backed down from what was right, no matter how difficult that proved to be. It was the way God had knit them together.

Jess pressed her lips together almost painfully, and let her head fall back as she searched the beams of the steeply sloped ceiling high above for answers to Jake's illness and to her other heartaches.

Since the day they started working together to try to save the ranch, they'd had nothing but setbacks. A band of Union sympathizers moved like ghosts beyond the reach of the law, invoking fear and apprehension in the region as they waged silent attacks against the Southerners who now lived here, often burning the Southerners' homes, as had happened to Jess's parents' home. While she and Jake were away from the ranch buying the Thoroughbreds in Iowa, the government's local land office had sold half of their land, which she and Jake desperately needed, and their new neighbor, Hank Beesley—a good man, praise the Lord—had built his house before their return. Last summer, they had battled a drought that had cost them severely—they had lost several horses and cattle. Most recently, Jess had learned that her father had left her more than ten thousand dollars when he died, but that it had been taken by an unknown person or persons from the bank. It was money that would save the ranch in the event of another year of drought. And now she and Jake faced another setback—pneumonia.

That's *all* it was, she told herself. A setback. He *would* recover. She refused to even think of the possibility that he could die. Hot tears stung her eyes as they took in the pine ceiling above her, which Jake had laid in place with his two strong hands, the same two hands that had built her a washstand she'd needed, as well as a jewelry box for her keepsakes.

Somewhere, in the region of her heart, she felt sharp, debilitating pain.

It drove her to her knees. In prayer.

I know You love each of Your creatures so much that You even know when a sparrow falls from the sky. I am not going to ask You to save Jake's life. Jake's breathless, ragged coughing arose from the main room downstairs. *Her* Jake, she thought. The man who filled her heart. Jess pressed her clenched hands knuckles-first into the bed and continued determinedly on. *Lord, I am going to thank You now for already saving him, in the event I forget to thank You for it later.*

❖◆❖◦❖◆❖

Ho Chen's round, yellow-brown face looked thoughtful as he leaned his short frame over the hearth and lowered a towel into the steaming iron pot. He turned with small, patient movements toward all who'd gathered, his long, neat, black braid of hair hanging precisely down the middle of his back. Though Jess had never asked him, she had often thought that he must be somewhere between forty and fifty years old. Whatever his age, he had gained great wisdom, and Jess very much needed that now.

Jake sat up against one arm of the sofa with his legs stretched out toward the other arm, shivering beneath several Indian blankets. He didn't resist when Ho Chen pushed back his blue flannel sleeve and took hold of his wrist.

"Cold sweat," the Chinaman observed. "It is not good sweat. Miss Jessie, you have parchment?"

Jess released her grip from the back of the sofa and retrieved a sheet from the desk in the corner. Ho Chen rolled it into a long funnel, pressed the large opening to Jake's chest, and listened through the narrow end. The parchment cone bent near the middle each time Jake jerked with coughs, but still Ho Chen listened. His narrow eyelids closed as he concentrated.

"Does chest hurt?"

"A little, when I cough," Jake admitted.

Finally Ho Chen stood upright and spoke gently. "Your lungs make sound like onion's dry skin when it is folded. And your heart beats very fast. Miss Jessie? You will need to make much tea to help with cough."

Jess gripped the back of the sofa once again. "We have no tea, only coffee."

"Jess, I have a mint plant at my house." Their neighbor, Hank, pushed himself up from the leather chair he'd been sitting in at the end of the sofa, already buttoning his coat. "Mary planted mint and some herbs in pots before she died. What else do you need, Ho Chen?"

"Medicinal plants are not easy to find in January," Ho Chen answered in his hampered English. "Most begin to grow in March or April. I do not think you have herbs such as *xie bai san* or *banxia houpo tang*?"

Hank chuckled, his merriment deepening the ever-present pink in his cheeks to a shade that matched the apples he grew. "Not that I know about." He gave Jess a warm, fatherly wink and thought for a moment. "What I've usually found is that if you eat and drink plenty of the healthy things God grew, the sickness often takes care of itself. Few of last summer's vegetable plants bore up under the drought, but I do have several jars of tomatoes that Mary canned."

"Parsnips are good," Ho Chen said. "Do you have?"

"No, I don't have parsnips, but I'll bring the mint leaves and tomatoes."

Jake forced himself not to cough. "Hank, can you bring some honey? I remember my ma giving me spoonfuls of it for sore throats back when I was too small to rope anything bigger than the neighbor's dog."

Jess and Hank both chuckled at that.

"I have plenty of honey, my friend. I'll be right back."

Hank bustled toward the back door, adjusting his knit hat lower over his nearly bald head, somehow injecting warmth and enthusiasm into even that simple act. Once again, Jess thanked God for him.

Steam began to rise from the pot in the fireplace. Jess's gaze followed a ribbon of the vapor all the way up to where the chimney stones disappeared through the roof high above. It would take time for steam to permeate the room, she knew, even though she'd closed the upstairs doors to keep the steam contained to the main area.

"The boss, he needs chili peppers, amigo," Diaz told Ho Chen, his silky black mustache curving in a grin. "Enough to make that cough run for cover."

"Chili pepper is good idea," Ho Chen agreed. "And there is much in cookhouse. Have garlic and cayenne pepper also. Will make hot chili soup to steam away cough and chills from inside. Also will make garlic paste for chest to help with breathing." Ho Chen lifted the dripping, steaming towel from the pot and wrung it lightly over the pot. Turning, he gestured for Jake to open his top shirt buttons, then laid the hot towel over Jake's chest and throat.

"Give the boss whiskey," Taggart recommended from the other chair, his hairy orange eyebrows, mustache, and beard lifting as he bent toward Jake with an impish grin. "If ye've got to be sick, man, ye might as well enjoy it."

Seth chuckled, a little nervously, Jess thought, for the youth continued to pace behind her, the jinglebobs on his spurs clinking with an uneven rhythm, his face as tight as unworked leather.

Despite the humor behind Taggart's suggestion, Ho Chen considered it as he ladled onion broth into a mug and gave it to Jake. "Irish solution may help, but whiskey may also dry lungs and bring more cough. Mr. Bennett drink tea instead. Too bad we do not have dandelion greens. Dandelion help also."

Seth's jinglebobs quieted. A little self-consciously, the youth slid his fingers into his pockets and rocked on his feet. "My third-grade teacher said that word came from the French folks' word for lion's teeth because that's what they thought those jagged leaves looked like."

Taggart knuckled his hat brim back and rolled his pale blue eyes in Seth's direction. "So ye say. What French word?"

Seth lifted his thumbs in a shrug. "I think it might have been *dent-de-lion*, or something close to that. She said for us who spoke English, it would translate like 'tooth of a lion.' She liked to talk in big words, so I never understood much of what she said, but I thought this bit was neat, so I remembered it. Nowadays we just put them French words together and call it a dandelion."

"Ye're sayin' *dent* is 'tooth'?" Taggart said, lowering his head dubiously.

Diaz smiled broadly, exposing two perfect rows of gleaming white beneath his mustache. "To my people, is *diente*."

Seth's mud-brown eyebrows stretched upward. "Oh, like in *dentist?*"

"Pay them visits often, do ye, lad?"

"I've heard of them," Seth said, evading the question and drawing good-natured chuckles from the cattlemen.

Jess shifted her weight. She appreciated Hank's cheerfulness and the men's attempt at levity, but she knew they were all trying to lighten the gravity of the situation, and that gravity began to weigh heavily on her. Men died from pneumonia. Even strong ones. And the only solutions they had available to them were onion broth, chili soup, tea, and steam.

The back door opened and just as quickly closed. At Lee's appearance, her hopes lifted. If anyone had a solution, it would be the Paiutes. They had survived in the Sierra Nevada region for generations.

Lee gazed at Jake and Jess both. "I asked all the Paiutes. We have no herbs. If we did, we would give them."

"Thank you, Lee," Jake managed, his shivers appearing to ease beneath the hot towel. "I know you would. And I wish you had them available," he added, the corner of his mouth quirking in the crooked grin Jess loved. "Ho Chen is going to force-feed me chilies and smear me with garlic."

Lee gave a quick smile, but Jess grew anxious, desperate. She was in danger of losing Jake, and there was nothing she could do to stop it. Until now she'd held hope that Ho Chen or one of the Paiutes would know of some cure, some sure way that American doctors had not yet discovered, to help Jake, but they knew of nothing. Nothing! She couldn't accept that. One of the Indians in northern California or Nevada had to know of some medicinal cure, had to know of some way to help. She'd seen her Paiute friends occasionally add unusual plants and roots to their food or brew them into teas to help heal a sore throat, a fever, a chill.

A chill. Hadn't Ho Chen's wife, Lily, given little Mattie some concoction back in November, or December, was it? She grabbed on to the idea with the same fervor with which she'd clenched the sofa. "Lee, what about the plant that Lily used to help Mattie a few months back?"

Lee shifted and looked uneasily to Jake, as if reluctant to answer. "Jess, Lily used the last of it, and we haven't been able to get more because of the snows."

"More? Where would you go? Lee, I know you know. Would you go to a shaman? Where does he live? Lee? Lee, tell me where he lives!"

Jake glanced at her with fevered, red-rimmed eyes, but he remained the ranch owner and her husband. "Jess, you can't go—"

"Lee, where is the shaman?" When Lee looked to Jake, Jess strode forward to force his gaze to her. "If you don't tell me," she growled, "I'll ask Lily, Nettle, and Spruzy, and they will tell me. You're only wasting time."

His face as taut as Seth's, Lee stared over her head for a moment, then met her gaze. "He winters near Shaffer's Station."

Shaffer's Station. That wasn't far. There and back in less than a day, even with the snow. She'd take Cielos, Jake's huge, long-legged stallion. He'd make the best time over the drifts. And she'd take plenty of hay bundled in a buffalo robe—the hay to feed Cielos, the buffalo robe for extra warmth should the snows grow heavy again. She wished she could take Jake to the hot springs there, but any benefit of the waters would be undone by the chill of the air. Mentally readying herself for the journey, Jess moved past Lee, Diaz, Taggart, and Seth. She retrieved several gold coins from the desk drawer and secured them in the spare drawstring pouch they kept beside the leather bag partially filled with coins. She scratched the deduction in the ledger, then shut the drawer.

Lee laid a hand on her arm. "Lily offered smudge sticks. They may help."

Briefly, Jess considered that. "Thank you, Lee, but they might do more harm than good. The smoke could make Jake's cough worse." She tossed him a smile and hurried toward the stairs.

Jake struggled to rise, giving her pause. Ho Chen surprised Jess by placing a hand on Jake's chest and holding him there. Apparently Ho Chen knew that Jake wouldn't survive without help and, despite the risks to Jess, had sided with her.

Jake flashed Ho Chen a look of surprise at his quiet insistence, but Jess knew that Jake respected the small man's wisdom as much as she did. He settled back and handed his mug of onion broth to Ho Chen.

Jess and Jake exchanged long looks brimming with determination—hers to leave and find the shaman, and his to prevent her from going. Despite his pallor, he looked menacing.

They'd engaged in verbal duels of will enough times before that Jess knew Jake was concerned for her safety, and that of their unborn child, and that Jake knew she wouldn't relent on an action she believed was right.

Finally Jake's glower faded. "I don't want you to go."

Jess curled a hand over the bottom end of the banister. "I know. I'm going anyway."

"I know."

❦

Jake watched as Jess rolled down her sleeves and buttoned them at her wrists as January's winds battered the wide front window behind him. She shook back the long chestnut hairs that always worked loose of her braid and swept the sides of her oval face in a way that made him wish he was alone with her and not shaking with chills so that he could place his hands where the hairs had touched. He loved the determination that shone in her sage-hued eyes like green fire. That same determination deepened the peach tone of her skin, and firmed the curve of her lips…lips the near-red of rose petals.

He ached to kiss her, and to protect her. He'd lost his first wife and their baby daughter to outlaws' guns years before, when Olivia took Sadie to visit her mother without him, believing they would be safe. This place, this life, was harsh, and he would rather die than lose his Jess. But if he died, Jess would be forced to live years more without him, unprotected, building their dream alone.

She stood like a bottled tempest in his flannel shirt and his trousers, which were gathered with her belt at her tiny waist. She was slender, yes, but the Almighty had given her a spine as solid as a branding iron, and the passion of twenty soldiers. Jake had seen Jess battle fear with anger and action before. The anger fed her courage, and it had gotten her through situations toughened cattlemen had called impossible. She was summoning that anger now— he could hear it in her deepening breaths and see it in the tilt of her chin.

"Do you think I'm just going to sit here and watch you die?" she asked.

"No, I reckon I don't."

She lifted a brown eyebrow, curved like a sparrow's wing. "And?" she prodded, her mouth softening as she no doubt read the answer in his sigh.

"And if you were lying here instead of me, I'd be riding out into the snows to get help for you."

A measure of tension eased from Jess's shoulders as she walked toward him. Ho Chen and the cattlemen moved away to give them a little privacy. "We're getting better at this," she said, emphasizing her silky, southern belle accent in a way that deepened his breath and, unfortunately, brought about another round of coughs. She removed the cooling towel from his chest to reheat it in the pot, which billowed steam. "We didn't waste half an hour debating the matter before you saw my side of it."

"I always see your side of a discussion, Jess. But the reason why the Almighty puts two folks into a marriage is so that one can think of what the other hasn't. What?"

Jess smiled a little and shrugged. "I love how you call God 'the Almighty.' How you say it with the same ease that you call your father 'Pa.'"

"I also call the Almighty 'Pa' when I pray. That's what He wants us to call Him. Dad."

Jess's green eyes turned misty, and she bit her lower lip as if that thought hadn't occurred to her before and had touched her.

"I've seen you fight fear and challenges with anger, Jess. When we first met, I didn't understand that. Since then, I've seen how much you draw on it to accomplish whatever's in your heart to accomplish. I understand it now, and have for some time. I just need you to understand that I may be aware of dangers or challenges you may not have considered."

Something flickered in her eyes, but she instantly bricked it over. "I know that."

Now what was that about? Her fingers trembled as she wrung the hot towel over the pot. A few drops of water fell to the flames beneath and hissed. "Jess? What are you not telling me?"

She faced him squarely and placed the towel over his chest. Her eyes locked with his. "I'm going now. I refuse to wait to see whether everyone's remedies help or not." She hesitated. "I'll be home before nightfall, Jake. I *will*. There is no such thing as 'can't'."

"There is no 'can't'," he agreed, knowing it but for once regretting it. The Almighty had done miracles for them before, he reminded himself, and He would again. With God, there was no "can't." Even so, there was such a thing as good sense and taking precautions. The Almighty expected folks to help themselves some, too. "Take Taggart and Seth."

The two cattlemen nodded and headed toward the dining room and the back door.

"No!" Jess firmly shook her head. "I'm going alone."

Quick as a snake's strike, Jake's hand clamped onto her arm. "If they don't go, you don't go."

Her green eyes shot fury, and beads of sweat dotted her face. For some reason, she seemed terrified for them to go with her, yet she and Jake both trusted the cattlemen with their lives. Taggart, for all his joking, had a sharp eye and always watched out for her, and Seth could use the gun at his hip with accuracy almost as deadly as Jess's, and she knew it. What was she afraid of? "They'll be all right. Trust the Almighty, Jess. Trust Him." He tightened his grip on her arm in gentle reassurance, then released her.

Sweat popped out on his own forehead. The towel was working. He was beginning to feel hotter than sunburned lizard skin.

Jess took an abrupt step back, toward the stairs.

Jake looked pointedly at the flannel shirt and trousers. "What do you think you're going to wear?"

"I think I'm going to wear sheepskin coats, mine with yours over it," she rejoined. "And I think I'm going to sweat puddles into my boots. That's what I think." She gentled her voice. "Both the baby and I will be fine, Bennett."

He gave a weak chuckle. "You only call me 'Bennett' when you're mad at me."

A couple of the cattlemen laughed softly. Apparently they'd overheard that comment...and everything else.

Her rosy mouth curved into a genuine smile. "You must like the sound of it to prompt me to say it so often."

The men laughed outright at that. Jake shot them his best ranch owner's glare. It must have fallen short. They grinned at him idiotically.

Jake returned his gaze to Jess. In the few seconds he'd looked away, her jaw had firmed with purpose.

"How many times have you saved my life?" she asked.

The chills grew worse, shaking him. "A few."

"And you'll live to do so again."

"Take one of the Henry repeating r-rifles," he said, frustrated that he couldn't speak right, frustrated that it was his place to protect her, and that his ability to do so was nullified by an illness. "Those sixteen shots you can take before having to reload may make the difference if you're attacked. I want you back safe, love."

Jess gave a quick, decisive nod. "I'll take both."

Chapter Three

Taggart, Seth, and Lee—who insisted he serve as their Paiute guide to the shaman—gathered their clothes, bedrolls, and provisions and ate a quick breakfast. Meanwhile, Jess, already bundled in two sheepskin coats and woolens, saddled Cielos, tied on the bunch of hay that was secured against the elements in a buffalo robe, as well as the two Henry repeating rifles, fully loaded. And left.

The horses and cattle had been fed and seen to, so all the ranchmen were sating their appetites in the cookhouse when she rode out. No one saw her leave.

She loped Cielos across the three hundred and twenty acres of the ranch, knowing every stone and rabbit hole on their land, which they'd had to fence in the summer before. Three hundred and twenty acres was all they had left after the government land office had sold the other half of the six hundred and forty acres Jake had worked years to pay for and the government officials had stuffed their own vest pockets with the money. *The way tarts stuff their blouses*, Jess thought irascibly as she pushed the northern gate closed behind her. She knew Hank's land just as well as their own, since it had once been theirs, and the land of the neighbor who'd bought the remaining acreage on the far side of Hank's property, which had been theirs as well.

But here, in Honey Lake Valley, she knew the land far less and reluctantly walked Cielos to keep the stallion from injury. Powerful, sleek, and black, he lifted his massive hooves over the snows like a locomotive churning up powder and rapidly put distance between them and the ranch. Jess firmly held a gloved hand to the reins to deny his inclination to run.

As best she could while wearing thick layers of sheepskin, Jess shifted in the saddle to study the ranch, which rapidly grew smaller in the distance. Beneath the blue snow and green pine peaks of the Sierra Nevadas, the stables, barn, smithy, and cookhouse looked like a set of child's blocks, and the horses and cattle looked like cleverly carved and painted miniature toys. The post-and-wire fencing that surrounded the ranch was nearly buried in weeks' worth of snowfall; the tops of the posts and top fence wire were all that remained visible. Though her eyes probed against the bite of the wind, Jess saw no people moving about, no one scanning the valley looking for her.

She turned forward in the saddle again and guided Cielos around a lone desert mountain to put it between the ranch and its view of her. She had perhaps half an hour's start ahead of Lee, Taggart, and Seth, a distance she determined to increase. She knew she could, since she rode the largest horse of the ranch.

The mountain was one of countless lone forms that dotted the desert like sombreros or the upended hulls of ships, which she was often tempted to ride around to see how many minutes it would take her, but which she had little time to do. She estimated that without the snow, she could circle one in twenty minutes at an easy walk. Now the red earth of the mountain was hidden by thick, low clouds and layers of frosty white. Jess put another such mountain between her and the ranch and patted Cielos on his warm, muscular neck for moving so fast.

When Jake had told Taggart and Seth to ride with her to the shaman, images of the premonition had reasserted themselves like evil wraiths dancing around her. Jess had told Jake no, but he had insisted. If she had told him about the vision and why she wanted the men to remain at the ranch, he would have tied her wrists and feet like a yearling calf about to be branded and left her that way while he gradually succumbed.

She guided Cielos north toward Shaffer's Station with a mounting sense of foreboding that the revelation—and the gunmen—waited for her there.

Warm, liquid sweat trickled, thick as blood, beneath her hat and scarf and down through her hair.

God is here with me, she told herself, over and over. *God is here with me.* Then a Bible verse came to mind: *"Greater love hath no man than this, that a man lay down his life for his friends."* She would face this battle alone, just she and the Lord. And she prayed He would enable her to change the outcome.

Jess remembered the line of renegade white men who, as one, drew their guns, then took aim at her and the dozen Indians—one of whom she now knew had been Lee—and two cattlemen—Taggart and Seth.

Cielos continued north at an alarmingly rapid pace, though, thankfully, Jess was still alone. She knew that she might not be able to alter the outcome of the premonition, but it was a certainty that if she faced the threat alone, three fewer people she cared about would be harmed.

Despite her worry, she smiled faintly. Her last battle alone, she recalled, had become her first one alongside

Jake. Had that been only two years ago? Mentally, she counted. Two years, indeed.

It had been February 1863, almost three years after Ambrose had left her and their parents in Carson City and moved back to the States to keep the Union Army out of Lexington, Kentucky, and Greenbriar, the home of the Hale family for three generations. War hostilities had spread to the West, and a group of nine Unionist men in Carson City had overheard her Southern accent and concluded she was a Confederate sympathizer. They'd attacked her just before dawn, right on the streets of Carson City.

The sudden presence of Jake and four of his ranchmen—all of whom had looked fully able to take on twice their number, along with anything else that might get in their way—had inspired her attackers to back away. One of those four ranchmen had been Taggart.

Jake had taken her for a ride that day. He had recognized in her the same need he possessed deep in his soul—to be away from the crowds and concerns of the city, to run a horse who loved to run, and to drink the wind that flowed past one's face and over the red earth and green sage desert that rolled endlessly along the foot of the mighty Sierras.

As they rode, they had been accompanied by the cattlemen—whom she'd learned were men of few words and unspoken honor—and, for the first time in a long while, she had felt safe. And free. Free of the contention between Unionists and Southerners who had moved west. Free of the blasted war.

But the war against Southerners in the West had spread to remote regions. It had encroached on people even as far removed as Honey Lake Valley, as had another war, the one renegade white men launched against the Paiutes, especially ranch Indians, out of prejudice and hatred for taking "white men's jobs" and "white men's pay."

There was too much hatred. Too much judgment without thought. Too much placement of the desire of a few above the needs of many.

Winter frost nipped at Jess's cheeks as she let her gaze travel the smooth, flowing desert of pure white that rolled away from her for miles in every direction. It was beautiful. No, unforgettable. But if the pure, endless white were never broken by the yellow-faced flowers of spring, or the rich, deep brown earth of summer, then, she reflected, the land would never benefit from the balance of God's creation that set off each detail of His handiwork as unique, with its own unforgettable color and character, specially chosen by Him.

How long? she wondered. *How long before people trouble themselves to look past the bad so that they can see the good?*

Jess glanced behind her again, glad that she still saw no one following, though by now the three men had likely set out.

She and Jake had battled such prejudices and injustices together, but now she was on her own. And beginning to sweat puddles into her boots. For more reasons than one.

Jake had taken hold of her wrist before he permitted her to go. She'd had to resist the urge to jerk her fingers away in shock. Jake's fever made his skin feel like she'd touched white-hot coal. Just as the three cattlemen had to stay away from Shaffer's Station, she had to keep moving toward it. Jake needed whatever help and knowledge the shaman could provide.

Oddly, she wondered just how many whites had died of illness, seething with hatred toward the very Indians who might have known of a cure to save them.

❖◈❖

Jess slowed Cielos and removed her hat, purposely letting her long braid fall so that the men of the small Paiute village who slowly approached her with bows, arrows, and guns in hand would see it and realize that she was a woman and not an outlaw or someone bent on causing harm. She called out a greeting in Paiute—the only words of their language she spoke. The men looked fierce wrapped in skins, their faces hard, their black eyes glittering at her. Cielos they appraised with more regard, and she hoped they both would make it home. Jake had raised Cielos from a colt, and man and horse had become one in spirit.

The icy wind dug its talons into Jess's scalp, and she pulled the hat back on. They knew she was a woman. She didn't need to risk catching her own illness by leaving it off any longer.

She stepped down and held tight to Cielos's reins. "I am wife of Many Horses," she told them in simple English, her voice loud but tremulous as she spoke the name that many of the Paiute people called Jake. "Is there any among you who knows my husband?"

Two of the men parted. A tiny, ancient Indian man stepped between them and raised his gaze to hers. Beneath his rabbit skin hat, the elder's leathery, wrinkled brown face considered her.

Jess's mouth fell slack. "Stone Bird?"

"It is good to see you, Jessica," he said.

Jess's thoughts raced. Jake had hired Stone Bird to pose as a deaf, enfeebled man at the ranch the summer before, when Jake had suspected that one of the new cattlemen he'd hired had become a threat to Jess. Stone Bird's sharp hearing and attentive eyes had saved her life.

In the small circle around her, the other men's gazes remained alert as they closely watched her movements—she did have two Henry rifles strapped to her saddle, she reminded herself—as well as kept an eye on the direction she had come from. Several of them had, however, eased their grips on their weapons. Stone Bird spoke to them, and they stood aside, opening a path for her to the cluster of large, dome-shaped wigwams of woven sticks. Several round, brown faces, some wary, some curious, looked on from within the structures' arched doorways, where they pulled aside skin coverings that kept out the elements.

Stone Bird led her toward what she surmised was his dwelling at the far side of the others. "Why have you come, Jessica?"

"Jake is very ill," she said plainly. "He has pneumonia... sickness brought about by *pogonip*," she explained, and Stone Bird nodded. "Ho Chen—you remember Lily's husband?—he has some food remedies, but Jake needs more. He has fever and chills and a terrible cough that makes it difficult for him to breathe. Lee said a Paiute healer lived near Shaffer's Station, and the man at the trading post directed me here."

Stone Bird watched her face and listened as they pushed through the snow, but he said nothing.

"I have money, gold coins, to purchase medicines," she said, growing desperate. Taggart, Seth, and Lee wouldn't be far behind, and a few of the men at the trading post had given her looks that had magnified her sense of foreboding. "I need help from your shaman, and I need to leave again as quickly as I can."

Stone Bird stopped and shifted his eyes in silent command. In response, four of the Paiute men mounted bareback horses and rode away from the village in four different directions. Guards, she realized.

"I don't want to put you or any of the People in danger. Please, Stone Bird, can you tell me if the shaman is here?"

"I am sorry to say that he is not, though I wish he were. He returned to Pyramid Lake just before the big snow began to fall."

Jess turned toward Cielos in frustration, then turned back, gazing out over the snow that looked as blank as her mind felt. She forced her thoughts to focus. Pyramid Lake. That was half a day's ride in midsummer. Shaffer's Station was only an hour from the ranch over clear desert but had taken nearly four times as long to traverse. That meant that a journey to and from Pyramid Lake would take four days, and the people there were far more protective, far more hostile, than those at this camp. In four days, Jake could be…gone.

"Stone Bird, did the shaman leave your people any herbs or medicines?" Jess smoothed a gloved hand over Cielos's black neck, attempting to calm herself with the gesture. If Stone Bird said no….

Stone Bird tilted his head, very much in the manner of a bird, considering. "He did. We have very little to share, Jessica, but, yes. We will share what we are able."

Suddenly Jess found herself holding on to the muscled neck for support, and hot tears of relief pricked inside her nose. "Thank you, Stone Bird. I'm sure that even a little will help."

Rather than continuing to his dwelling, he led her toward a wigwam, where a thin Paiute woman with wide cheekbones had gazed out at Jess. Jess felt both light and weighted at the same time, her heart soaring within her while her legs labored to lift her boots each step through the snow.

They stopped at the doorway, and when the woman pulled aside the animal skin, Stone Bird spoke to her in Paiute. Then he tied Cielos to a stand of sage that thrust up through the drifts a few feet away. At Jess's frown, he reached a gnarled hand from inside his fur wrapping and gently patted her arm. "The horse will be safe here, Jessica. The People know he is yours. Come."

Jess looked south toward the ranch, then southeast toward Shaffer's Station, puffing clouds of vapor into the stillness. No white men stirred in either direction.

If she hurried, she might just avoid the terrifying outcome of the premonition.

Even as that lovely thought lighted on her mind, the premonition's images surged in her mind, the evil wraiths' dance frantic. *Flash.* A line of thirty or more renegade white men. *Flash.* Their hands reaching to their holsters. *Flash.* Taggart, Seth, and Lee beside her. And Stone Bird, and others.

Unbidden waves of heat arose from the area around her heart, dreadfully aware, thickening, pulsing.

At Stone Bird's urging, she ducked, following him into the wigwam's black, smoky maw.

❖❖❖❖

Jess's eyes gradually grew accustomed to the low, flickering orange light of the fire. She attempted to make herself comfortable, as she did when visiting the homes of her Paiute friends at the ranch, but this woman's strange, accusing stare, and the red light that danced in her eyes and the hollows of her cheeks, made that endeavor most difficult.

Even Stone Bird seemed unaccustomed to the woman. His hesitancy added to the sickly, warm sensation swirling inside of Jess.

Quietly, he began to speak to her. Jess recognized the Paiute words for Many Horses. He gestured with the back of his hand in her direction, and Jess surmised he was explaining that she was the wife of Many Horses. Jess nodded, but the woman's stare had lowered to the fire. She didn't look at Jess.

Several achingly long minutes passed while Stone Bird argued with the woman, who clearly refused to part with the herbs Jess needed. Jess listened for any sounds that penetrated the low, curved roof and stick walls, knowing that every moment brought the premonition nearer. If she didn't leave in the next few moments, she knew the People would be in danger.

Outside, words were exchanged, though she couldn't identify the voices or the language being spoken. Fearful, and warring violently with her instinct to hide, she swept her eyes over the baskets, pouches, and jars that lined the curved wall behind the unbending woman, and found no place that would conceal her or end the battle she'd inadvertently begun when she had asked for directions to the Paiute village at the trading post. Jake, she decided, would forgive her for failing him, but neither of them would forgive her for failing the Paiutes or bringing harm to them.

In a burst of ferocity, before her fears could change her intent, Jess ran out the door, pulled a Henry repeater from its sheath, and pushed past the shoulders of the Paiute men grouped together.

And stood in boot-deep snow under a gray sky, the Henry rifle gripped in her hands. At her sides stood Taggart and Seth. More than a dozen Paiute Indian men stepped forward to stand alongside them. She recognized Lee. The others were strangers. Their faces revealed fear, and resolve. In front of her, perhaps five paces away, stood thirty or more renegade white men, two of whom she recognized from the trading post.

As one, they reached their hands to their holsters.

The man in front of Jess spit a wad of tobacco into the pristine snow. "Are these vermin ranch Injuns?" he demanded of Taggart.

Jess's muscles burned and twitched as she searched for a way to stop the vision from playing out.

"Ye're not lookin' at vermin or ranch Indians, either one," Taggart replied, his typical amusement strong, though his Irish accent had broadened, and the vein in his neck throbbed. "These lads are…reporters, for *Harper's Weekly*," he announced, "and they've come west to photograph and tell the tale of the most hog-ugly man in existence. Now that they've seen that lad down on the end, they'll ask him some questions and then get headin' back east."

A few of the gunmen looked down the line and chuckled, while the man on the end turned red in anger.

"Quiet!" barked their leader, standing across from Jess, and the momentary buoyancy dissolved, even from Taggart.

As one, the thirty men drew their guns, then took aim at Jess and the Indians. Jess cocked the Henry rifle, pressed the butt to her shoulder, and sighted down the barrel at the cold, glittering blue eyes of the man who aimed the bore of his revolver at her.

In that fraction of an instant, Jess denied the events as they continued to unfold, prayed for strength…and struggled to undo what had yet to take place.

In that same instant, though fear burned like liquid fire beneath her skin, she firmed her grip, shifted her index finger from the rifle's trigger guard to the curve of the metal trigger. And pulled.

❖◦◑◦❖◦◐◦◦❖

Jess cocked the Henry before the first man fell, then shifted her aim to the next man.

The remaining toughs had jerked at the *boom* of the discharge, but none of them had fired. Their leader's body made a whispery sound as it sank deep into the red-spattered snow.

From the corners of her eyes, she glimpsed, stretching out to both sides, two cattlemen and more than a dozen Paiute men, their rifles held or arrows fixed, steady, aiming.

A voice several paces behind Jess called out an order to drop weapons, and a wave of federal-blue uniforms surged forward between them—a dearly welcome blur of hundreds of gold stripes and thousands of gleaming buttons of brass. The soldiers from Camp Smoke Creek! One of the four men Stone Bird had sent must have reached them.

A man—a captain, judging by his stripes—identified himself to the renegades and all others present as Almond

Wells. Lee, Stone Bird, and a few of the other Paiute men spoke to Captain Wells while his men made arrests.

Jess felt herself lower the Henry rifle, felt Taggart look over her head to Seth.

Taggart blew out his breath. "Well, I need to change into clean britches. How about you?"

Seth laughed. He sounded relieved.

Jess swayed toward Taggart and collapsed.

Chapter Four

Jess's eyes opened. Above her stood the fierce, chiseled brown face, piercing eyes, and long, unbound black hair of a wild Indian. Lee. Had she woken to find this face above hers years ago, when she was still a young, genteel Southern girl living on an elegant horse farm near Lexington, Kentucky, she would have seen him as no less threatening than the angel of death.

He extended a brawny hand toward her. Jess took hold of it, and he helped her to her feet.

"Are you all right, Jess?"

She still felt wobbly, as if someone had pulled the muscles from her legs, and then the bones. Lee held her against him, his arm firm against her back, as she nodded and gripped a handful of his buffalo-skin wrap to hold herself upright. "I'll be fine...in a minute."

Taggart poked a finger at her collar. "The boss'll be plenty mad when he sees ye were nearly shot."

Jess looked up at him blankly, feeling now like someone had removed her brain, as well. "What?"

The orange eyebrows and blue eyes lowered to indicate the rolled sheepskin collar of Jake's coat that she was wearing. Jess tucked her chin and craned her neck so she could see. Helpfully, Taggart placed his brown-gloved finger behind the pale tan wool, revealing a small, neat hole.

Jess strained her mind, trying to recall seeing the renegade's gun jump, or hearing the sound of its discharge.

"His gun fired the same moment as yers. Good thing yer brother taught ye how to shoot straight. That man wouldn't have given ye another chance."

Suddenly she felt unbearably heavy and crumpled against Lee. He caught her as she fell and helped her to sit in the snow. Kneeling, Lee studied her face and looked into her eyes. A round face appeared beside his, likewise gawking. Taggart's.

"Yep, she's still in there," he announced. "C'mon, Jess. We have to get those medicines and get back to Jake."

Yes, Jake. He'd be so very pleased to find out she'd confronted thirty men *and* been shot at. Oh, and that she'd known before leaving the ranch that the confrontation was going to happen.

Jess dropped her head into her knit gloves, cheerfully debating the notion of an extended journey abroad, but suddenly felt two pairs of large hands on her arms, hoisting her to her feet.

Taggart and Lee stepped back to reveal young Seth looking anxiously down at her. Beside him, Stone Bird moved forward, his frown curving the deeply cut wrinkles around his mouth. He bent down, lifted the Henry repeater from the snow, brushed the snow and ice from it, and handed it to Jess. That done, he started back toward the cluster of dwellings.

Captain Wells approached their small group and, seeing Jess, tipped his hat. "Gentlemen. Ma'am. Are any of you hurt?"

"We are not harmed," Lee answered. "Most of those men are the ones who attacked us at the Bennett Mountain Ranch last winter and drove us away."

Seth nodded and stood by Lee. "I remembered them too. Remember that one with the powder burns on his chin and the scar under his eye?"

Captain Wells exhaled and perused the land around them, as if a great weight had been removed from his shoulders and he was free for the first time to enjoy the sights that God had placed there. "Then you are to be congratulated. We've been looking for these men for the past couple of years. Are you two the only ones who can identify these men?"

"Well, there are others at the ranch," Seth told him. "Our neighbor Hank saw them, other cattlemen—"

"Will and Doyle," Lee put in.

"Right, and Ho Chen and the other Paiutes."

"If that becomes necessary, we'll question them then."

"Seth and Lee are men of honor, Captain," Jess said. "If they say they recognize these men, then these are the men."

"Thank you for that, ma'am. If you two will spare me a few minutes, I'll ask you to identify as many as you are able to. The rest we'll arrest on the charge of assault with intent to kill. Those you identify will face two charges, minimum."

Seth and Lee followed the captain to where the soldiers held the men. Grasping Taggart's beefy arm for support, Jess indicated the wigwam where the Paiute woman lived, where Cielos stood tethered. Together they moved toward it, and the steadiness gradually returned to Jess's limbs.

As they approached, Stone Bird stepped from the doorway, and the woman, though still scowling, followed.

"Jessica, she has the medicines you need." Stone Bird urged the woman forward with the back of his curved, gnarled hand, waving it toward her.

The woman's eyes settled on Jess, gazing, probing. She raised her fist to Jess. In it she clutched a small burlap sack, which may have at one time held a few pounds of flour or sugar.

"Thank you," Jess said. She removed the thread of sinew that held the top shut. In the bag were several large, dried leaves shaped like elongated spades with a light, block-like pattern that reminded her of the markings on a snake's skin.

Bending close, the woman tapped the leaves and spoke in Paiute. "Plantain leaves," Stone Bird translated. "To calm the cough. Boil them to make tea. Jake should drink four cups each day." Next the woman prodded slender peels of bark and spoke again to Stone Bird. "It also calms, and heals," he said. "Jake must drink two cups each day, but she warns not to drink more than two cups. It can slow down the heart." The third plant the woman indicated was bright yellow, a root. She studied Jess again, though she spoke to Stone Bird. "Make tea to ease headache. She says that she has seen all three help cure the sickness Jake has."

"Stone Bird, please tell her thank you." Jess pulled two gold coins from the pouch in her pocket and pressed them into the palm of the woman's mitten.

The woman took them but continued to consider Jess. With great care, Jess retied the length of sinew around the burlap, then pushed the bag deep inside the pocket of her coat, where it would be protected by Jake's coat, layered on top. When she finally raised her eyes to the woman, the woman spoke through Stone Bird again. For once, Stone Bird appeared uneasy to reveal her words.

"Jessica, she says that you know things, that you see things others don't see."

Jess's gaze shot to the woman, stunned.

"She says that when you fear what you see, remember to hold on to your strength."

Captain Wells and the soldiers rode at an easy pace toward their fort, with the men who'd confronted Jess, the cattlemen, and the Indians, walking weaponless in the midst of them.

Jess pulled off a glove and stroked Cielos's neck as the Paiutes went about their daily activities, perhaps a little more lighthearted than before, now that one of the threats against them was no more.

She slid her hand lower, along the smooth, satiny fur that shimmered like a pool of ink over the horse's chest, then lower, to feel the fur between his front legs. The muscles beneath were no longer warm, but cool.

Drawing on her glove, Jess moved to the saddle and untied the buffalo robe from it. She spread the robe containing the hay before Cielos, and the horse ate ravenously. A glance over at Taggart, Seth, and Lee revealed they were likewise seeing to their own horses. Had Cielos and the other animals still been warm, Jess would have insisted they start back to the ranch immediately. But the horses needed food for the warmth it brought, or they could freeze before they made it back.

Jess stood by Cielos, reliving all that had happened since she arrived at the Paiute camp. Though the soldiers had thrown the body of the man over a saddle and taken him with them, the shower of blood remained on the snow, and the Indians made no effort to remove it. She understood, though she wasn't sure if she'd want to see the blood until another snowfall came and covered it.

In all, she decided, she had had enough of the premonitions. Since she first arrived at the ranch two years ago, her occasional intuitions had grown more pronounced, until one day images flashed into her mind, images of places she hadn't seen. With them came strong reactions to what she was seeing, reactions that she often wished she could tear from her mind, but couldn't.

Jake had once told her that God allowed her to see what lay ahead so that she would be assured of His presence and His help in all things. Well, she supposed Jake was right about that. God had kept her safe today. He had kept all of them safe, all but one, who'd intended to kill her, and then almost certainly the others after her. Holding the Henry repeater, she'd possessed the biggest threat, and he'd attempted to gun her down. He had been the second man she'd shot to prevent herself or someone else from being murdered. The cloying guilt of knowing that she'd shot twice in defense, and killed twice in defense, was tempered only by the memory of her brother's words when he'd taught her how to shoot. When you pull the trigger, Ambrose had said, don't think of what will die, but think of what you will enable to live. The War Between the States had been imminent, and Ambrose had known he would be caught up in it, and that she might, as well. He had no idea that while he continued to fight in the East, similar fights were taking place in the West. Ambrose could help change the outcome of a battle, but the battle Jess fought was against her own visions of what was to come, and she had no ability to change the outcomes she saw.

What would she do if a vision came to her that was truly awful? How would she bear up under it without losing her mind?

Already she had had enough. She wanted nothing more to do with her "God-given" sense. While Cielos finished his hay, she prayed that God would take away all visions of events to come.

⬦◈⬦◈⬦

Though Jake attempted to hide his grimace of distaste—*Cattlemen don't show pain*, Jess thought, ruefully amused—his eyes watered like snowmelt in May. The blend of teas the Paiute woman had given to her smelled horrible. She had no desire to sample it.

"Bitter?" she asked.

Jake lowered the mug and stared into it with a mild frown. "A little."

From the mantel Jess retrieved the jar of honey Hank had brought, poured a generous stream into the mug, and handed Jake a spoon. "Better?"

He sipped cautiously and sighed. "Better. Thank you, love." For a full minute neither of them spoke, while they waited for his hoarse coughs to pause.

For want of something to do, Jess added another log to the fire, though it was unnecessary. Ho Chen had brought a larger cauldron to steam the room and had supplied Jake with an equally large pot of meaty, spicy chili, she saw. Apparently Jake had refused the garlic paste.

Night had fallen, and the room was nearly dark, so Jess struck a match and lit the lantern, turning the golden flame to low.

Finally Jake quieted and gradually caught his breath. Keeping her back to him, Jess turned the wheel on the lantern, raising and lowering the wick, watching the tiny spade of fire likewise wax and wane.

"What happened, Jess?" he asked gently.

When she turned to him, he moved his blanket-wrapped feet to rest them on the low sofa table and patted the place beside him in invitation. Since they were alone for the night, she joined him on the sofa. If the pressure wouldn't worsen his cough, she thought, she'd lie against him. Curl into him. She needed to feel his embrace, to know she was safe. And forgiven. But that would come only after she told him all that had happened. At least, she hoped he would be able to forgive her.

Jake Bennett always perceived more than Jess revealed. Even as ill as he was, he paid attention. And cared. With his free arm, he pulled Jess against him and let her nestle there.

"Now tell me what happened, love."

Jess watched quiet flames embrace the log she'd added to the hearth. Trying to focus on the shifting peaks and valleys of orange and yellow rather than on the happenings of the day, she told him everything, even about the premonition, holding nothing back.

Jake didn't react as she spoke, except that he stopped taking swallows of tea. He continued to hold her, and asked occasional questions when he sought clarity on a matter. When Jess had nothing left to say, she continued to rest against him, loving his nearness, though dreading his response. He said nothing but almost certainly thought over all she'd said. She realized his fingers were caressing her arm, and her dread began to pass, and the deep weariness from two nights without sleep slowly pulled her in.

Jess's breathing became slow and even, and her right arm rested limply across his leg. It was the arm that had been burned in the Hale house fire, Jake recalled. Now, two years later, it bore permanent scarring from the burns. The same arm bore another scar, from a cut she received less than a year ago, when the horse she'd been riding was shot as a deterrent and fell on her. She'd suffered bruised ribs for weeks.

Jake coughed, unintentionally waking Jess.

"What are you thinking?" she murmured, settling against him again.

"I was thinking how hard this life can be. I once said that you weren't raised for ranching or for the harsh conditions in the West, and you weren't. But this *is* who the Almighty meant you to be.

"For months I feared things happening to you like what happened today, and I feared that such things would either harm you or drive you to seek a less harsh life, and I tried to prevent you from leaving the ranch, and I held you so tight that you weren't able to breathe. You faced your fears today, and you didn't let those fears stop you from doing what was right. Because you did, those men who have been terrorizing ranch Indians have been caught, and a lot of folks—Paiutes and ranchers alike—will have some peace now." Jake battled down a spur of anger and admitted the truth to them both. "If I'd been well, I would have been with you. I wouldn't have tried to keep you from going, no matter what your vision revealed." He looked down at the top of her head and kissed it. "You didn't come to the ranch to be caged up but to be free." He resumed caressing her arm, loving the softness of it, of her, underneath which was a core as solid and unshakable as the Sierras themselves. "Fear is one of those ploys that the devil pulls from his nasty little bag of tricks. If he can make a Christian fear, or doubt, or find excuses, then he prevents good from being done, and he wins. Yet the Almighty didn't give His people a spirit of timidity, but a spirit of power. For either of us to deny the strength He gave us is to deny the Almighty a victory."

Jess tipped her head back to look up at him. Firelight flickered in her beautiful eyes like nuggets in a gold pan. "Are you saying you've finally accepted that I'm headstrong?" she asked, smiling a little.

"If the Almighty gave you a spirit of power, I'm not going to be the one to tell you to listen to the devil instead."

"But?"

He sighed. That started him coughing again. When he stopped, he said, "But I will ask you to talk with me before you act, to be certain you're—*we're*—acting with good sense and are being as safe as we can. Both of us."

"I'll do my best, Bennett."

"And before you ask, love, no, I don't believe you were anything but careful with the baby. I expect that the baby is part of why you were tempted to hide, to keep it safe. Neither of us is going to raise a child who will hide while harm comes to others, or hide from any fear." He recalled what she'd just said. "You called me Bennett," he teased. "Does that mean you're mad at me?"

"No." She burrowed sleepily against him, a tease in her own voice. "It means I'm just a little annoyed."

Though her eyes fell closed, she smiled. Lord above, he loved her.

Her eyelids parted again, and she watched the fire. "Jake?"

"Hmm?"

"I need to ask your forgiveness…for not telling you about the vision. I thought if I told you, you wouldn't let me go."

Jake sighed again. "You're right, I wouldn't have let you go. But since you did, and the Lord saw to it you're back home safe, I'll trust that He has His purposes. As I said, if I hadn't been ill, I'd have gone with you."

Jess shook her head. "You wouldn't have let me go."

"Maybe not." For a moment, he sat still, feeling their hearts beating in rhythm as one. "But when the Lord sets you to running in the future, I won't be pulling back on the reins."

"You'll be running beside me?"

"I'll be running beside you."

❖❖❖❖

Gray early-morning light dispelled the shadows in the bathing nook and bedroom, except for those that rested around the edges of the walls where they touched the floor. Jess had loved the natural warmth and pine beauty of Jake's bedroom, their bedroom now, from the first moment she saw it.

Sinking lower into the froth of bubbles and hot bathwater, Jess lay her head back against the edge of the galvanized tub and gloried in the simple pleasure of liquid warmth and steam as she let her gaze settle where it would. The bathing alcove around her was barely bigger than a closet, its three wood-plank walls lined with a rancher's arsenal of defense—the Remington revolvers, Henry rifles, spare gun belts, stacked boxes of ammunition, and empty tins they used to practice their aim.

Bullets and bubbles. She smiled to herself at the irony. It was home.

Home. Memories of her previous home in Carson City came to her. A stately, large white two-story befitting the owner of an imports store that was frequented by mine owners and bankers who had made millions from the silver ore of the Comstock. The house had boasted silver knobs on every door and floor-length velvet drapes on every window. Richly colored Turkish rugs had carpeted the parlor. The long table in the dining room had been lavishly set with etched silver candlesticks and serving trays, hand-blown Venetian stemware, and hand-painted china edged in gold. Over the wide front staircase that rose to the bedrooms upstairs had hung the prized crystal chandelier that originated in a fifteenth-century castle in France's Loire Valley, and that Jess's father had purchased to surprise her mother. Black walnut armoires and four-poster bedsteads had filled the bedrooms upstairs. In the servants' rooms, the furnishings had been mahogany. To Jess, it had been more museum than home.

Then one night, the outside walls had been doused with kerosene and set ablaze, and a Confederate flag had been pointedly staked in the yard.

Jess thumped the back of her head against the tub's rim. In two years, little of her rage had dimmed.

Both her parents had died, as had Emma—Jess and Ambrose's baby sister, whom Ambrose had longed to meet but never did. Ambrose had left to fight in the war before Emma was born, and she'd died in the fire at ten months of age, and even now the war raged on. The blaze had also taken the life of Emma's nanny, Elsie Scheuer, who had been Jess's dear friend. Jake and his men had been in town that night, purchasing supplies for the ranch, and Jess and Jake had been walking together several houses away when they saw the fire. At a command from their boss, a few of the ranchmen on horseback had carried Jess away to the ranch after she had collapsed.

Jess sighed. She'd hated Jake for that at the time, and for not allowing her to try to save her family. When he'd returned to the ranch several days later, she had been exploring his house and the view of the mountains through his bedroom window, and then she had turned. He'd stood in the doorway, his face ruggedly handsome with two days' whiskers roughing his jaw, and his whiskey-brown eyes gazing into hers.

Part of her lower arm bore the faint scar caused by the heat of the inferno that her house had become. Jake, however, bore a scar that extended from his shoulder blade to his ribs, caused when the house began to fall, when he had gone in to try to save her father, who had hoped to save her mother and Emma.

Jake had tried to save her family. She loved him for that, but that was who Jake was—a man who would face a fire rather than face defeat or allow loss to come to someone else. She also loved that he'd sifted through the smoking rubble the next morning for her family's remains and then buried them. He could have left it to the law to do, but he'd done the macabre task for her.

She'd been on her way to a ball the night of the fire, and the jewelry she had been wearing was all she had left of her family and that life—diamond and sapphire earrings that had belonged to her mother, an inlaid rose-and-vine-patterned comb, and an emerald pendant Ambrose had given her for her sixteenth birthday. When Ambrose left for war, Jess gave him the green satin cording that had held the pendant at her throat. He had pinned it in his pocket as a keepsake.

Jake had crafted a jewelry box to hold her treasures. It resided there, in the dressing table at the end of the bed, along with the letters her brother wrote to her from the war.

Jake had done so much for her, and more than once had risked losing everything for her. Perhaps that was why she'd left the red gingham curtain open that normally closed off the bathing alcove. She wanted to see their room, everything Jake had built, everything he had crafted for her.

At his request, she had slept in their room rather than downstairs near him, to be sure she and the baby rested well in a space heated sufficiently to remind her of a warm summer night. After she left to find the shaman, the main room had been well heated by the fireplace, and Jake had had all the bedroom doors opened to be sure she would be warm in every room of the house.

Jess sent up a prayer of thanks that Jake was still resting. The teas might be bitter, but Jake had managed to sleep for a couple of hours without coughing.

Her thoughts still clinging to images of the fire, Jess sent up a second prayer of thanks, that the arsonist who'd been paid to set it had been found, and that God had seen justice done. The person or persons who had helped Miriam Van Dorn to hire the arsonist had not been found, she reflected, and for the better part of two years she'd wanted to hunt down those responsible, but God had shown her that vengeance was His, and that He brought about justice in His own good time.

The Lord, and this land, she mused, smoothed out the impatience in a person, the same way that a river smoothes out stones.

She wished Him the best with smoothing out hers, shook the water from her hands, and grabbed a towel.

Chapter Five

Jake grimaced. "This tea is awful. You want me to recover and live just because I make better coffee than Seth does."

"Week-old coffee thick with chunks is better than Seth's," Jess countered, enjoying a sip of Jake's roasty, homemade brew. "Now quit fussing and drink your lousy tea."

"I brought more honey and mint," Hank's voice called out, and then the back door shut. Hank emerged from the dining room, pink of face and bearing gifts. "Aah, is that Jake's special brew that I smell?"

Jess took the honey jar and basket of mint leaves from their neighbor. "Isn't Jake sweet? He makes it for me even when he's ill." Her hands occupied, she pointed an elbow toward the coffeepot that nestled in the glowing orange coals of the fire. "Help yourself!"

In the small kitchen behind the fireplace, Jess stripped the leaves from the stems and rinsed them in a bowl of water, her fingers trembling. Bracing her hands on the countertop, she forced herself to be calm. Jake had spooned the ground coffee into the pot for her, yes, but that was all he'd had the strength to do, and he'd shaken with chills and stopped several times to cough. Jess took several slow, deep breaths. *I trust You, Lord,* she prayed. *I trust You.*

Back in the main room again, she added the leaves to the pot she and Ho Chen kept filled and steeping in the hearth, then poured a scant teaspoonful of honey into Jake's cup, hoping to make it last. When Jake raised his eyes in almost boyish hope, struggling to hide his misery, she added a dollop more then placed the jar on the mantel.

"I brought something else," Hank said. He blew into his coffee and drank a few swallows, his smile altering almost imperceptibly as he considered Jess.

"What?" Jake asked, his voice raw.

Hank's smile swiftly broadened to triumphant. "Ho Chen sent along garlic paste for your chest." He pulled a small jar from his coat pocket and set it on the sofa table with a sprightly snap.

Jake rubbed a hand over his face. "That's good news?"

Jess patted his shoulder. "Don't be surly, Bennett. Ho Chen said it would help."

Jess's stomach grew leaden as Jake struggled to catch his breath, and she felt the need to breathe for him. He didn't comment about her calling him "Bennett," she realized. Feeling her jaw tremble, she looked pleadingly to Hank. Hank was at least thirty years older than her own twenty-two years; in all those years, hadn't he learned of some way to battle an illness, even one as bad as this?

Hank set his coffee mug on the table and rubbed his hands together with a fair amount of zest. "If you're looking for a better idea, my friend, I suggest we try Taggart's suggestion, as well as the garlic paste. Together they'll steam your nose, throat, and chest, inside and out."

Jess lowered herself to the chair beside Jake. "But won't whiskey dehydrate him and make his cough worse?" If that were possible.

"No," Hank said. "With that simmering pot of water filling the house with steam, and the hot towels you keep putting on Jake, he'll have plenty of moisture. Also remember that he's been drinking tea continually since last evening. We'll add some honey to the whiskey, and the honey will help his throat even more."

Jess pressed her hands together between her knees and worriedly buried them in the red wool of her skirt. If Jake's cough grew much worse, he wouldn't be able to breathe. She dearly wanted to share her concern with Hank, but she didn't want Jake to overhear the words.

Hank gave her his gentle, fatherly smile, seeming to understand. "If it doesn't work within an hour or so, Jess, he can always set it aside."

Her fingers reached for Jake's hand. It was shaking, hot with fever, and damp...clammy, not the healthy damp that Ho Chen said meant the fever was breaking. "Jake?" she asked softly.

Jake's hand tightened briefly around hers. "I'll give it a try."

❖❖❖

By mid-afternoon, Jess gave up all pretenses of teasing and lightheartedness. She latched on to all she had left— her fierce determination—and forced Jake to swallow more chili and cayenne, more tea, more honey, and to withstand the garlic paste, steaming towels, and layer after layer of blankets that held him fairly immobile on the sofa. She suspected it was more the fear he must see in her eyes than her bullying and demanding that compelled him to take every bite and sip.

The whiskey should have put him to sleep. It hadn't. It *had* made him even more tired, but the relentless coughing kept jolting him awake. By late evening, he began coughing up mucus tinged with blood.

For the next five hours, every time Jake opened his eyes, Jess poured tea down this throat. He opened his eyes less and less as he grew too weak and too exhausted to respond to her.

Now, at two thirty in the morning, Jess paced behind the sofa, praying with all her might, while hot tears scalded her cheeks as she watched the man who filled her heart struggle for every breath.

The words the strange Paiute woman had spoken through Stone Bird echoed in her mind: *"When you fear what you see, remember to hold on to your strength."*

Jess slammed the heel of her moccasin on the floor. Why did all her premonitions show her a future problem? Why did they never show her how to fix a problem?

She pushed her hands through her hair. *What is my strength?* she thought. As she struggled for the answer, she recalled what Jake and Ambrose and others had said of her.

God and determination. And *anger.*

"Taggart!"

The portly Irishman jumped from his bedroll near the desk, instantly on his feet, struggling to be alert. "What do ye need? I'm here."

"Wake up Ho Chen. Tell him to heat as much water as he can and to keep it coming. Then get Doyle. Bring him back with you...and one of the cauldrons we use for laundry!"

Taggart stuffed his hefty arms into his coat as he hurried toward the dining room and back door.

Jess ran up the stairs two at a time and into the middle bedroom. The large bathing tub had been drained and wiped dry—had that been only the morning before? Not waiting for help, she pushed aside the small washtub she usually used and wrestled the large one from where it stood tipped on end against the wall. With both arms and her chin bracing the heavy tub, Jess lowered the upper end to the floor. She half-lifted, half-dragged the unwieldy thing as she backed toward the door, pausing frequently to tug aside the hem of her skirt, which kept getting trapped beneath it. Never had she been so thankful for the assistance Jake or one of the other ranchmen had always provided in moving it.

She reached the short upper hallway, her hip bumping into the stick-and-branch railing, sharply reminding her of the injury to it the previous autumn.

Sweating now, Jess looked over the railing and down at Jake. She wiped a sleeve across her forehead and realized she was watching Jake's chest to be sure that it rose again.

In fresh desperation, she battled doorway, railing, her hem, and shadows, and hefted and tugged the obstinate tub fully out into the upper hall. Turning it at the top of the stairs went much easier, and she backed down, one step at a time, letting the tub slide while holding firmly to its rim to keep it from swinging out of control.

When she reached the main floor, she tugged it close to the sofa table, shoved the sofa table toward the front door, then pulled the tub in its place between the sofa and the fire. Another swipe of her sleeve across her forehead, then she wrung the wet towel over the cauldron, and used it to remove the garlic paste from Jake's chest.

She longed for him to comment about the foul substance, to jest, but he merely breathed, barely moving at all.

Jess wiped the exhaustion from her eyes then blinked hard, trying to focus on the open collar of Jake's shirt.

Two days' whiskers darkened his jaw and cheeks. She looked up at his swollen, red eyelids and silently begged God that Jake would live to shave again.

Her teeth dug into her lip with enough pressure to keep her awake, keep her moving. She set her eyes again on Jake's collar, then his flannel shirtfronts, and began to work them across his shoulders and down his arms.

His shivers increased as she pushed him to one side and pulled his arm free of the sleeve. She tugged the blankets high around his chin and began to listen for Taggart and Doyle's return as she removed Jake's socks.

Finally, the back door opened and then shut. Taggart and Doyle entered the main room. Doyle's strong arms hefted one of the giant iron cauldrons she and the Paiute women used for washing the ranchmen's laundry. He set it on the hearthstones, directly in front of the blaze. Taggart carried a lengthy pair of tongs and two buckets weighed down with what Jess knew must be the potato-sized stones that the Paiutes used for heating liquids from inside a vessel.

"Thank you both!" Jess took one of the buckets from him and immediately began placing the stones straight into the coals of the fire, under the burning logs.

Taggart did the same, then Doyle grabbed up the buckets. "Jess, I'll be back with snow to melt," he told her, then left.

"Ho Chen and Lily're both in the cookhouse doing the same as we are. Ye plannin' to give the boss a bath?"

"No, to bring up his body temperature and force him to sweat."

"Aye, I see. The heat'll cause him to sweat out the sickness, then?"

"I hope so. If a human body can't live long at a high temperature, then perhaps germs can't survive it either. And I'm betting that Jake has more determination to survive the heat than the germs do."

Taggart cautiously bent over him. "Is he still with us?"

Jess grunted, frustrated at his lack of delicacy. Didn't he have the slightest notion what this was doing to her?

"Help me remove his shirt and trousers, Taggart. He's too heavy for me to budge. We'll have to worry about finding him a dry union suit later; he's going into the tub in the one he's wearing."

A sudden draft curled through the room as the back door opened and closed, so they paused before removing Jake's blankets and clothing. Doyle stamped the snow from his boots and then entered, followed by Eli Payton—a tall, middle-aged willow of a man with sunken cheeks and a dark mustache and beard that hid nearly all of his face and neck. Both men gripped two buckets of snow in each hand, eight buckets total. Jess took the first bucket and dumped the snow into the cauldron. The cauldron's iron sides were already hot, and the snow sizzled where it touched.

She dumped bucket after bucket, her fingers stinging with pain as she used her hand to pull out the snow that clung to the bottom edges.

As Taggart had, Eli and Doyle stared somberly down at Jake. They stood side by side waiting for the buckets, the older man tall and lanky, the younger even taller and as powerful as two men. The willow and the telegraph pole, Jess thought absently, pushing several loose hairs back from her face.

"You're wearin' out, gal," Doyle said. "You need to get some rest, for you and that baby."

Jess rubbed her eyes for a long moment and then looked up at him, feeling every hour of the nearly two days that she'd been awake. "I will. But first I need to make sure the baby's father lives to see him or her, don't I?"

"I reckon so." Doyle bent to give her arm a reassuring squeeze. "I'll bring more snow."

Eli followed him out, both men carrying empty buckets.

When the door rattled closed, Taggart helped Jess to remove Jake's shirt and trousers, and then she fastened the open buttons of his union suit.

In all their shifting and jostling, Jake's eyelids remained closed.

❧❦❧❦❧

By setting the hot stones in the cauldron with the tongs, Jess melted the snow nearly as fast as the men could carry it in. When the stones she'd added lost their heat, she returned them to the fire and placed hot ones into the water. Scant minutes later, the cauldron was full of melted snow.

With her persistence in stone-heating the water in the ranch house fireplace, plus the persistence of Ho Chen and his Paiute wife, Lily, doing the same in the cookhouse fireplace, the water was ready to add to the tub in less than an hour. Doyle, Taggart, Eli, Ho Chen, and Lily brought buckets of water over from the cookhouse and poured them into the tub. Jess added hot stones directly to the tub to restore the warmth that had been lost in the frigid wind.

The men moved toward the hallway and in quiet voices scheduled the following day's ranch duties and care of the horses and cattle. They also planned to rotate in a well-rested man to replace Taggart, so that Jess would continually have someone at hand should she need assistance while tending "the boss."

Lily scooped up a bucket of water from Jess's cauldron and poured a hot, vaporous stream into the tub while Jess dunked her bucket in the cauldron and did the same.

"Thank you so much for your help, Lily," Jess said. Though Lily was only a handful of years older than Jess, the short, plump Paiute woman possessed a comforting, motherly way that made her a favorite of the cattlemen, whom she doted on, and she was equally loved by her two young daughters, Mattie and Grace.

Lily touched a soft, cool hand to Jess's cheek. Her smile brightened her creamed-coffee skin and hazel eyes—features inherited from her father, who'd been a German trapper—and sent a single ray of sunshine into Jess's heart.

"I am glad to help you, my sister," Lily said sincerely. "And do not fear. Your Jake will be all right."

When the tub was nearly two-thirds full and the water the temperature of a hot bath, Jess and Lily set the buckets aside, and the men hefted Jake from the sofa and lowered him into the tub. Jess watched the water level shoot higher and held her breath as she waited for it to spill over and soak the floor, which would cool and then chill the room. She let out her breath as the water hugged the top edges of the tub. Doyle was already moving, dunking a bucket into the tub and removing excess water.

Taggart and Eli made themselves comfortable on the sofa as they continued to hold firmly to the shoulders of Jake's union suit so he wouldn't sink under the water.

Using the tongs, Jess pulled more hot stones from the fire and carefully added them to the tub so that they wouldn't touch Jake and burn him. She glanced up at the people looking on. "I am so thankful to each of you for all the help you've given. It must be four o'clock or so, a few hours until dawn. I'd appreciate two of you staying, but the rest of you should get some sleep." She gave them a smile, then added another stone and listened to it clang softly against the bottom of the tub. When no one moved, she looked up again. "I'm sure he'll be all right," she said. *He has to be.*

Doyle glanced at the others. "The boss will be fine, Jess, but we need to be sure you're going to be all right too. We can see to the boss. You and your chil' are the ones that needs to get some sleep."

"I appreciate that, Doyle," she said with a soft smile at the big man, "but you have to know that I won't leave Jake." Jess added another stone. She would have to keep the water as hot as she could stand to touch it for as long as it took for the fever to break.

"I know you won't." Doyle gestured to Ho Chen and began to move the bulky leather chair beside him over to the tub while Ho Chen did the same with the other chair. Still holding on to Jake, Taggart and Eli relocated to the chairs, leaving the sofa vacant. Doyle flashed a decisive grin of his own. "Now you can get some rest and stay right with the boss too."

Jess wasn't sure if she was going to laugh or cry. She was so weary, she suspected she might do both. With a sigh, she rested the tongs on her knee and let her head drop onto her arms. As soon as she did, fragments of a dream flitted through her mind, and she vaguely heard the tongs hit the floor. Then she was being lifted, by Doyle, she supposed, and she felt the sofa beneath her, then the weight of blankets over her, then Lily's soft, cool hand on her forehead.

"Sleep, my sister," her voice said.

<hr />

At a rough, rasping sound, Jess opened her eyelids against their longing to stay shut. Taggart's blue eyes winked at her as he dropped another hot stone into Jake's tub. The sound came again, and Jess looked to the back of Jake's head. His shoulders lurched with the coughing.

Her eyes teared. She hadn't realized that she hadn't heard that sound in quite a while. Until now. The change had come, she calculated, not long after he'd tried the whiskey and honey. It had helped his cough, and it had enabled him to sleep deeply.

Pushing herself up on her elbow, she looked from Taggart to Eli, whose face above his beard was tired but no longer showed grave concern. Neither of the two men was holding on to Jake, she saw. Jake was sitting up—well, leaning—on his own.

Jess lay down again, her cheek to the cool leather of the sofa. She reached her fingers to his dark hair, which was hot and damp with sweat, but which still felt as wonderful as ever to her touch.

Pulling her hand back under the blankets, she closed her eyes and, with added hope in her heart, again allowed sleep to take her.

<hr />

Quiet voices dredged her up from the heavy arms of Morpheus. Jess smiled inwardly. If she was thinking in such terms as the myths she'd learned years ago in school, then she was still tired. Even so, she forced herself to sit up.

Doyle had claimed the chair where Taggart had been, and Diaz now sat in Eli's place. Seeing her gaze, the Spaniard paused his whittling and touched his knife to his sombrero in a respectful salute.

Plying the tongs, Doyle leaned to remove a few wet stones, then added hot ones from the fire, which the men had kept burning high.

Jake was sitting more than leaning now, she saw. She pushed her blankets to one side and scooted to the front edge of the sofa. Her throat was so tight that although she tried to speak, she couldn't. Instead, she reached out a hand and slipped it over Jake's shoulder and partway down his chest. His skin was no longer clammy but sweating freely. A good sweat. He wasn't coughing, and his breathing had deepened.

With her thumb, she caressed his neck. She didn't care that Doyle and Diaz could see her eyes tearing up.

All at once she felt off balance; then, she realized the two ranchmen had grabbed the front sofa legs and were pulling her closer to the tub. When the sofa stilled, her skirt was bunched against the galvanized tin.

Doyle resumed adding stones, and Diaz continued carving the chunk of wood. Jess slid her arm further around Jake's chest and laid her forehead against his neck.

Jake's hand lifted from the water, and the wet heat of it curved around her own.

Though she tried to hold it in, Jess cried softly into Jake's neck. *Thank You, God!* she prayed, and then she smiled just for Him. *I guess I didn't forget to tell You "Thank You," after all.*

"When can I get out of this confounded tub?" Jake growled. "I've been in here for hours!"

Jess added honey to a mug of tea, stirred, neatly tapped the spoon on the cup's edge, and thrust the tea into his hand. "Not until I say. That's when."

Doyle had left to be sure the horses and cattle had been seen to, so Jake shot an insistent glare at Diaz. He idly inspected his carving, blew away a few loose shavings, and spared Jake an uninterested glance. "Whenever the *Mariposa* says so, boss."

Jake growled again and gulped a swig of tea.

Diaz shook his head and grinned. His teeth flashed white, made brighter by the silky black of his thick mustache and goatee. "The *hombre*'s like a bear with his foot in a trap, eh, *Mariposa?*"

Jess smiled back, as much amused by the bear analogy as she was touched by the name Diaz had always called her, *Mariposa. Butterfly.* It was the same nickname her brother, Ambrose, had called her for as long as she could remember. His little green-eyed butterfly.

"This wool itches," Jake muttered.

The back door slammed and Taggart sailed in, hearty as an Irish brigantine. "At least that garlic stink is gone, boss." He plunked into the empty chair with a sigh of profound contentment and tossed his knit hat and gloves onto the hearth to dry. "After that stench, ye're doin' well to still have friends." With both hands, Taggart briskly scratched his orange beard as if relishing the sensation. "We milked the cows, boss, but it's so cold out there, they're givin' ice cream." He laughed out loud at his joke.

Jake turned his glower toward Taggart. "Will you get me some dry clothes so that I can get out of this?"

Taggart glanced at Jess's mute gaze, then raised a hairy eyebrow to Jake. "Are ye completely mad? I'd rather try to stuff a buffalo down a rat hole. Jess," he said, gentling his voice, which elicited an eye-roll from Jake, "it's fixin' to snow some more. Ho Chen said to let ye know he's keepin' supper warm for ye should ye decide to come over to the cookhouse and eat."

"Thank you, Taggart. Can you kindly tell Ho Chen that I'll stay in tonight and eat his wonderful chili with the surly boss here?"

Jake speared them each with a glare. "Did you plan this in advance, or are you improvising?"

With a hoot of laughter, Jess bent and nearly kissed Jake full on the mouth before she stopped herself. She and Jake did not permit themselves to show affection in front of the men, at least not in most circumstances. The ranchmen were bachelors, every one, and their lives were difficult enough without a married couple reminding them of a kind of closeness they didn't have.

Jake apparently knew what she'd intended, and he grinned the crooked grin she loved. Then, "I miss my hat," he grumbled.

With that, she realized that his gruffness was fabricated, at least in part, played out in front of the men. Jake's smile dimmed, but a pleasant warmth came from his eyes, a warmth that said he looked forward to being well again…and alone with her.

Jess sent back the same look and went to find him some clean, dry clothes.

Chapter Six

Jake watched Jess flit up the stairs like a filly in spring and wondered where expectant mothers found such energy. She'd slipped out of bed at dawn, helped the men to feed the horses and cattle, left again to collect firewood, which she'd brought in, and then restacked the woodpile between the fireplace and the front door. After dinner, she'd swept fresh snow off the front porch, nailed a loose floorboard back in place, stuffed fresh straw into every bedsack in the bunkhouse, helped Ho Chen and Lily prepare supper for the men, washed the dishes herself, then swept the front porch again and built up the fire for the evening.

At the top of the stairs, rather than turn left into their bedroom, she'd gone straight into the middle bedroom, which he'd used for storage since little Sadie had died, and now he heard shuffling and dragging.

He continued to sand the dresser that had long needed to be reconditioned. Once he refinished the outside and repaired the broken drawer, Jess would be able to use it for the baby's things. From where he sat on the floor behind the desk, he could just glimpse a yellow flicker of her skirt or another part of her in the lantern light as she buzzed about the room like an entire swarm of bees. If he recalled right, Olivia didn't start nesting until the last few months before Sadie was born. Jess had only just stopped wearing the braided leather belt he'd made, and at four or so months along, her middle was only slightly rounded. She still had plenty of time left before the birth, he mused, and he'd kept all of Livvy's larger-waisted dresses and all of the baby clothes and things—who would he have given them to?—so there was little that Jess needed to do to prepare for a child.

Jess was busy working for no good reason. That meant that there was something wrong.

Jake ran his hand over the area he'd sanded, feeling for rough patches and slivers. Satisfied there were none, he began sanding old paint from the next area with patient, steady strokes.

As best as he could recollect, in the past three weeks that he'd been recovering from pneumonia, Jess had worked just as steadily, though not briskly. She'd scheduled the men's tasks at first light, overseen the care of the animals throughout each day, and in all other ways seen to the care of the ranch while he'd gradually recovered from his cough. She'd taken time to bring him meals, chatted pleasantly with him while they ate, and brewed tea whenever he needed it.

But his cough was nearly gone, and while he wasn't yet working outside with the men, this morning he'd begun joining them for meals again, and had taken over scheduling the men's tasks. Instead of taking advantage of the extra time that afforded her, Jess had finished breakfast, then set her feet to the floor like a whirlwind. Her smiles had been bright…just a shade too bright, he reckoned.

Jake stood and dusted off his hands just as the orange cat jumped up onto the dresser top. The cat leaned shamelessly into Jake's fingers as he rubbed its neck, purring like a plucked fiddle string. Jess had never been one to talk about a matter that troubled her until she was good and ready to. There were times he wished she was as plain about her thoughts as the cat was about its own, but he wanted to be there for her just the same.

At the top of the stairs, he leaned against the doorjamb. Jess held a stack of old papers and books and thumbed through the loose pages, tossing most of them into a crate. She shot him a quick smile, then carried the books past him and into the bedroom at the front of the house, which she'd slept in when she first arrived at the ranch. She stepped past him again, hands empty, gathered up a large basket of yarns, and carried it downstairs. Anticipating her next goal, he grabbed up the loom and brought it down to the main room for her, then set it along the wall behind the sofa, beneath the painting of Jess's mother and the painting of Jess and him, which Hank completed last autumn. Jake stared at it in appreciation. The man was a gifted artist, but he wanted to live away from the city, among the ranch folk, and he'd planted an orchard and raised bees for honey. Jake understood him well. When the Almighty created the world, He'd planted a garden, knowing man would want to work in the outdoors.

Upstairs again, Jess worked to clear a corner. Jake helped her move aside the crates. "Jess, in these crates are the clothes Livvy wore while she was expecting, and baby clothes too."

"Thanks. I know. I've gone through them."

When he saw she intended to lower to the floor a bunk that had been stored on end, he kissed her hair and lowered the weight of it himself. Using an old towel, Jess cleaned the dust from the bunk, then resumed her work.

"You shouldn't be helping me, Jake." Her green eyes briefly touched on his. "It'll start you coughing again."

With her forearm, Jess pushed loose hairs back from her face as she unfolded a bedsack. Though she shook it, no dust came from it. Looking satisfied, she refolded the fabric and hung it over the foot of the bunk. She pushed the crates of clothing neatly under the bunk for easy access. With the same towel, she dusted off two small tables and stacked the sewing box and materials there. Finally she stepped back and surveyed what she'd accomplished. The room was organized, and ready for a little occupant.

Jake smiled at the thought, but then Jess grabbed up a broom, upended it, and industriously began pulling away the few spider webs that hovered at the tops of the walls, climbing atop the bunks and tables to reach them. If she didn't calm down, Jake thought, she was going to exhaust herself and make herself sick.

"Jess, what's the matter, love?"

❖❖❖

At his question, she hesitated in her task, then she continued sweeping at cobwebs. *How does he know?* she wondered. *How does he* always *know?* She loved having a husband who cared about her so much that he noticed when she was troubled, but sometimes it unnerved her that he knew her so completely. The only time she'd been able to keep a matter to herself was when he'd been sick and feverish with pneumonia.

"Jess?"

Oh, no. He was using that voice, that deep, gentle, masculine voice that made her want to tell him her worries, that made her believe he could solve them. But no one could solve this, only God.

From behind her, his hands slid down her arms to her hands and, with her, lowered the broom to the floor. "It might help to talk about it, love." He pulled her back against him and lowered his smoothly shaven cheek to nuzzle hers. He smelled so good—like leather, and horses, and man. The best smell there was.

She hated to tell him half-truths, but even more, she hated to worry him. He had already lost one child. "March isn't far off," she said. "The mares will start foaling, and the baby's due at the end of June. I figured if I didn't get things ready now, I'd be holding a baby before I had another chance."

"Mmm-hmm."

She felt his warm mouth touch lightly to the underside of her jaw, and his arms tightened around her. Her head tilted to the side of its own volition, and his lips brushed teasing, whispery kisses along her neck that made her stretch upward like a cat. It had been weeks since he had felt well enough to be close....

She let the broom fall, and reached her hands up and back to caress the soft skin at the base of his throat, just inside his flannel collar. *How can a man with muscles as hard as steel have skin so very soft too?* she wondered.

"Jess."

"Hmm?" She ached to rip the intrusive buttons from his shirt. Instead, she curled her fingers into his hair.

Then he was turning her, unbraiding her hair. She rose up on the toes of her moccasins, pulling his face down to hers. He kissed her cheek...the tingly place beneath her ear.

"What's the matter, love?" he cajoled softly.

"Not a thing." She *could* sew his buttons back....

"There was something wrong before," he murmured.

Jess rubbed her forehead against his. "I don't want you to be sad."

His thumbs lifted her face, drawing her gaze to his brown eyes flecked with gold and emanating strength, then his lips met hers. His lips did wonderful things. His hands did wonderful things in her hair.

"I won't be sad, Jess. Whatever it is, we'll fix it together." With the sure step of a lead dancer, he began moving her backward toward the doorway.

"Someone could come in."

"Nope. I placed the bars over the doors before I came up."

"That was nice of you." She kissed the soft place at the base of his neck.

"Hmm."

At the doorway, he bent to blow out the lamp. Soft, gray light hovered about the windows like clouds, lending to the house the feel of a pine forest hidden at the top of some desolate mountain.

Jake's warm, strong arms enveloped her. He pressed her back against the wall and nuzzled.

"Tell me what's wrong, love."

Jess was no longer certain why she didn't want to tell him. She pulled her arms free and eased her hands behind his neck and down, between the back of his shirt and his skin. "At the Paiute village...the confrontation with those men...it scared me more than I've told you." His firm fingers kneaded soothingly along her spine, from top to bottom, making her glad that she had one. "I've had nightmares," she whispered, and her fears began to choke her. "My mother miscarried twice. She lost two children."

Jake rested his chin on top of her head and continued kneading. "And she gave birth to four."

The words surprised Jess. She hadn't thought of what her mother did have, but only of what she had lost. Still…. "Broderick died of pneumonia."

"We may have found a way to help overcome pneumonia."

Jess smiled into Jake's shirt. "We can't give a baby whiskey."

"Taggart would."

Now she laughed. "Yes, I guess he would. Even so, we're not sure which of our attempted remedies truly helped. All we know for certain is that the whiskey helped you to sleep."

Jake moved his hands to massage her shoulders, his touch intoxicating. Jess realized she was glad she had shoulders too.

"I know what helped," Jake said. "You prayed."

"How did you know that?"

"James five, verse fifteen. *'The prayer of faith shall save the sick, and the Lord shall raise him up.'* When you prayed, you believed and didn't doubt. That's why He pulled me through."

Jess let her arms fall and dangle from her shoulders. At least she hoped her arms were still there. For all she knew, they were lying on the floor. Jake's thumbs were rubbing fabulous circles into her shoulder muscles. Surely she still had muscles, didn't she?

"I also think He didn't want you to be a widow," he murmured. "In Deuteronomy, I believe, I read that the Almighty has a special place in His heart for the fatherless and widows."

"Since He's everywhere, He must have a really big heart," Jess thought, then realized she'd said the words.

"He does, at that," Jake agreed. "Circumstances of all kinds are tough when a lady has to face them alone, especially out West, I imagine. Perhaps that's one of the reasons why some folks feel so close to God out here— because He stays close to those who need Him most."

"Makes sense." The side of her face was smushed against his chest—actually, she realized, her cheek was the only thing holding her up—but she was too content to care if her words sounded muffled. The Lord had saved Jake, and he was still here to smush her face against. That was all that mattered.

Except for her fear of a miscarriage. Her mother had suffered through two of them with no adversity to cause either one. Jess was living in the West, where few laws prevailed, and she'd nearly been shot that day near Shaffer's Station. Thanks be to God that only Jake's sheepskin coat had suffered damage. Even so, "I still have nightmares, Bennett. About the standoff with those gunmen."

"I'd be concerned if you didn't have nightmares about the standoff, love. If it didn't scare you, that would be because you didn't care about yourself and our child. I'm certain the others who were there have had nightmares too. It seems that dreams help us overcome such things. They remind us that we survived it.

"You care so very much about those you love, Jess, and you're fiercely loyal. You're going to be the type of mother that all the other kids will wish they had for themselves."

"Thank you." Jess raised her hands to Jake's sides— apparently her arms were still attached—and soaked in his strength. She couldn't tell him the rest. She couldn't tell him her other fear, that unless they found who had stolen her father's money and got the money back, the ranch wouldn't survive another year. The previous three years' drought had cost them most of the animals they would have otherwise sold and earned a profit from. Because of the recent snows, the animals would have grass this spring, but due to their losing half the land in the government land sale, they wouldn't have enough acreage to feed the animals through next winter. The half of the land that had been sold was the land where they'd harvested their winter's supply of hay, and now they would have to buy the hay. In addition to all of that, they had to pay and feed the ranch workers. The problem existed because of her. She had encouraged the purchase of the twenty Thoroughbred stallions—only six of them had survived the drought—and she had brought about a costly months-long trip to the States. It was her fault, but Jake, being the man of honor that he was, would accept the fault as his own, and it would hurt him terribly. *She* would hurt him terribly.

He had once teased her and told her that she was a lot of trouble. She had laughed at the time. She wasn't laughing now. He was right. She was a lot of trouble. That drove her to want to track down her stolen inheritance, so that she would be a blessing to Jake rather than a liability.

The ranch was all they had, and it was all they loved, that, each other, and the Lord. How would they be able to care for a child in the midst of a depression if they lost their house and their means of survival? How would the people of the ranch live without their jobs and homes?

Jake moved his hands to the sides of her face. Again she felt his strength. Jake knew all this, she reminded herself, except for her fear that, at some point, they might not be able to care for their child. Because of the land sale. Because of the drought. Because of her choices.

Jake began moving her backward as before, toward their room, his hands growing more purposeful. She needed his touch. She needed him to fill her with love, to make her forget.

His lips. Where were his lips? Ah, there…beneath her ear….

They were in their room, spinning in the stillness, and Jake was closing the door.

She left her fears on the other side of it.

❖◈❖◈❖

The first gift arrived at dawn.

It was on the front porch, in the bassinet. Jake had made the bassinet for Sadie, then Jess had shared it with Lily's daughters, Mattie and Grace, to play with. Now they had given it back. Inside the tiny, almost doll-sized bassinet was a pair of impossibly tiny moccasins.

Jess sank to her knees, almost afraid to touch them.

They were deerskin, with fringes around the ankles, brightly colored beads sewn to the tops, and slender leather lacings. Jess picked them up. The pair of them fit, side by side, in the palm of her hand. The bottoms were abraded. Both Mattie and Grace had worn them as infants. And now Lily had given them to her.

Jess delayed feeding the animals so she could go thank her friend.

❖◈❖◈❖

In the barn that evening, Jess stretched her back, then brushed the last bits of hay from her skirt. Carefully avoiding the open edge of the hayloft, she followed young Will to the ladder—slats of wood nailed to the wall—then descended after him, one story below, to the barn floor. There they grabbed pitchforks and helped Diaz move the hay they'd dropped down. With few words to break the mutually enjoyed silence, they fed the expectant mares and yearling calves that they kept in the barn out of the snow and wind. Watching her Spanish friend, Jess frowned. Diaz walked with a limp now, she reflected, and had since the summer before when the horse he'd been riding collapsed in the heat and fell on his leg. The broken leg had mended, and he said that it didn't pain him at all. The break had earned him a new pair of fancy boots—and he said it gave pretty ladies a reason to fuss over him. She smiled at that, then went to hang up her pitchfork as Will and Diaz left, carrying out the leftover hay to give an extra treat to their favorite horses.

The iron nails where the pitchforks hung protruded from a large crossbar that helped to support the barn wall from the inside. Immediately above her pitchfork's empty iron nails, perched on top of the crossbar, was a hand-carved wooden horse. She recalled the grinning black mustache, the salute with the blade of a knife. *Diaz.* Jess laughed and pressed her hands to her face in delight.

Their child's first toy.

❖◆❖◆❖

Jake looked up from the nearly finished dresser. The orange cat was curled up in one of its drawers, which Jake had left on top of the desk. Jess laughed. "I should ask Hank to make us a painting of that."

"You should see the painting he did make us."

"What?"

With a smile as bright and smug as the one he'd worn when she'd first told him she was expecting, he took hold of her hand and led her up to the middle bedroom, the baby's room. The bassinet rested on the floor beside the bed, the tiny moccasins still in it. Above the bassinet, at her eye level, Jake had pounded three new nails into the wall. Now she understood his smile. Inside her, her own heart skipped to a lighter rhythm.

On the center nail hung a painting of warm, jewel-toned colors. She recognized it at once. She had seen it last summer, in Hank Beesley's house next door. It hadn't been finished then. She stepped closer and let herself take it in. The painting beautifully depicted two Paiute girls—Mattie and Grace—standing on different rails of the ranch's corral, the older girl wearing the tan and blue calico dress Jess had sewn for her, the younger girl in the tan and green dress. The sisters were petting the nose of a horse with palomino coloring. Luina.

The first sight the Bennett baby would see would be the ranch his or her parents loved, and two of the wonderful people who helped to make the land a home.

Jess couldn't stop smiling. She leaned against Jake's side and shared a hug with him. Finally her gaze shifted to the other two nails. "What are those nails for?"

Jake chuckled. He nodded to the table where she'd left the sewing things.

A tin cup sat on the table's surface in the center of a small, child-sized lasso. Jess looked up at his grin, at the wrinkles at the corners of his eyes.

"Will made the lasso himself."

"And the tin cup?"

Jake threw back his head and laughed out loud until his eyes teared. The laughter started a cough, but it quickly passed. "Guess."

She shook her head. "I don't know."

With his thumb, Jake wiped his eyes. "It's from Seth. He said he wanted to give the child his or her first cup of coffee."

❧❖❧

During the next weeks, more gifts for the baby appeared at odd times and in unusual places. The morning Jess prepared to wash the ranchmen's laundry, she walked into the workshop to gather up the laundry tub, washboard, and soap. As she reached for the tub, she saw, folded neatly inside it, an infant-sized blanket of black and red flannel. Deeply touched, Jess ran her fingers over the soft fabric. Small, precise stitches bound two layers together around the hem. After a moment of trying to place where she'd seen the flannel before, Jess remembered. It was from the new winter shirt Taggart had bought last autumn.

No wonder she'd washed it only once. Taggart had cut it apart and sewed it into a blanket. With a smile, Jess wondered just how much the other men had heckled him while he'd sat up nights, sewing.

One Sunday afternoon in late March, after Eli Payton and a few of the other men spent their free weekend in town, Eli dismounted in the ranch yard a few feet from where Jake and Jess were coiling the rope they'd used to corral the horses during the snows. Eli opened his saddlebag and pulled out a book of Brothers Grimm fairy tales, which he thrust into her hands. "My ma used to read their stories to me," he said, then stared from Jess to Jake and back again. Without another word, he led his horse to the corral to unsaddle him.

Days passed. As she often did when it was Jake's shift to stand watch, Jess rose in the middle of the night to accompany him. Together they stepped from the front porch onto the ground, which was still muddy from snowmelt. Overhead, winter's clouds were dissipating. Between the fragments that still drifted across the sky, brilliant white stars once again were visible. Black-Eye, the tall, well-humored Paiute man who'd had first watch, waved from the corral and headed toward his village, which sat on the east side of the ranch. Jake waved back then took Jess's hand in his, his large fingers holding her slender ones, and they started toward the corral. Jess loved these nights with him. They were the only times they were free to enjoy the ranch and be close to each other, because the ranchmen were asleep in the bunkhouse, and the Paiutes in their village. Abruptly, Jake's head turned toward the smithy, then Jess noticed that the door was outlined in pale, yellow light.

"Doyle must have left the lantern burning," Jake said.

Jess knew just how unlikely it was that Doyle would forget something so important, but she didn't answer as they walked over.

Jake rolled the smithy door aside. Doyle had left the lantern burning. In fact, by the smell of sulfur that tinged the air, he'd lit it within the last five minutes. He's also lit a candle. Jess could just see the flame flicker…beneath a boot-high Indian tepee fashioned of thinly hammered iron. Tiny holes had been punched through the metal all around, through which "stars" flickered on the smithy walls and ceiling.

Jess beamed up at Jake. "Doyle made a lantern for the baby," she said.

She had feared not being able to provide sufficiently for the baby. With so many people already watching out for him or her, their baby would have plenty.

And he or she would have love.

Chapter Seven

Every Sunday morning, Jake and Jess read a few chapters of the Bible together with all the ranch people who wanted to join them in the cookhouse. When they were done, they prayed. Like warriors who had full confidence in the King who led them. They fervently thanked the Lord that no further attacks against local ranch Indians had occurred since Shaffer's Station. They asked the Lord's blessing on the ranch, trusted Him for the rainfall they desperately needed, and asked Him in His mighty power to end the assaults against Southerners who now lived in the West, to spread peace throughout the nation, and to bring an end to the War Between the States.

This was the only time Jess saw the men with bare heads. The moment they said "Amen," all hats went back on.

Afterward, as had become their custom since Jess had lived at the ranch, everyone either stayed for coffee and conversation or went his or her own way to enjoy a day of minimal chores. Some participated in games, while others simply rested. For those ranchmen who couldn't read, Jess penned the letters they dictated, then addressed them to be sent to their families, most of whom lived back East, in the States. In the ranch house, Jess also wrote to Jake's father and brothers in Illinois, and to her own brother, Ambrose, silently praying that her letter would get through the battle lines and reach him.

Around mid-morning, with most of their free day still ahead of them, Jake pushed the sofa all the way to the back wall, then carried in several pieces of wood that he'd cut, shaped, and sanded, along with a crate of tools. In the middle of the floor, he carefully arranged the pieces of wood in a mysterious order known only to him. That step complete, he lifted a devastatingly handsome black eyebrow at Jess, his gold-brown eyes alight with anticipation. He was beginning the final stage of his latest project—the two rocking chairs he had first mentioned building before winter had set in. Jess had known when he'd mentioned the rocking chairs that Jake never just "mentioned" anything. Whenever her husband said he'd do something, he carried it out. Now Jess could see the curved armrests and the rockers the chairs would be attached to, the two seats, and the various support spindles for the chairs' arms, legs, and backs. When finished, they would be beautiful.

Jess sent Jake an answering smile from her seat beside the wide front window, then bent again to her own project. With scissors, she cut another inch-wide strip from the clean rag—it had been a blanket at one time, she thought. That was one of many good ideas she'd learned from the Shaker people in Kentucky years before. The Shakers wasted nothing. New fabric became clothes, blankets, and towels. Old clothes, blankets, and towels became rags. Old rags they wove, with yarns of dyed wool, into rugs to soften and warm their floors. This was her gift for the baby. A soft rug for his or her bedroom floor, to crawl on, to play on. To grow up on.

Taggart knocked on the open door and stuck his head in.

"Come in all the way," Jake invited.

Taggart slapped his hands together and rubbed them vigorously, peering from Jake's project to Jess's. Evidently taking more interest in Jess's, he waddled over, hitched his britches up over his paunch, and inspected her work.

"A rug, for the baby's room," Jess explained.

"For the baby? What'll ye use when the cat starts spitting hair balls on it?" Blue eyes twinkling, he guffawed.

"Taggart?" Jake said.

The Irishman pasted a look of boyish innocence on his face and spun. "Aye, boss?"

Jess smiled behind his back. Taggart rarely failed to make her laugh. Still, she was mighty tempted to use the wickedly sharp scissors to prick his backside.

"You came in here for a reason?" Jake reminded him.

"What? Oh, aye. Two of the mares have started to foal."

There was a heartbeat of stillness, then Jess shrieked in delight, jumped up, and threw the rag and scissors onto her chair. She almost knocked Taggart over on her way out the door, Jake close on her heels.

"They're in the stable!" Taggart called after them.

Jess tried to run, but at a sudden pain, she pressed a hand to her side and slowed, still laughing. *Two foals!* Jake stopped too, his smile just as wide as hers. She waved him on. "The baby doesn't want me to run. I'll be right there."

Apparently Jake didn't care who was watching. He bent and swooped her up in his arms, then continued jogging toward the stable.

Two hours later, all the people of the ranch had missed dinner, and no one cared.

Three wobbly-kneed foals—twin chestnut mustang-Thoroughbred colts and one white mustang-Morgan filly—tried their first steps in the hay, beside their mothers.

Jake and Jess shared a gaze of pure happiness. A year ago, they had owned eighty horses and foals. The drought and other challenges had claimed all but fifty-six. Every one of those fifty-six had come through the winter, and about twenty-five of them were expectant mares.

The ranch would survive, Jess thought. Somehow, all the people together, with a few more blessings from God, would see to it that the ranch survived.

"Mother?" Little Grace, about seven years old, looked like a Paiute cherub as she knelt in the straw and joyously tugged on Jess's sleeve. Jess loved the Indians' custom of calling their close friends "brother" or "sister," and those older than they whom they cared about "father" or "mother." Those simple words provided families—genuine families—for those who didn't otherwise have them. "Mother, you once said that when you were a child, you named the newborn horses at your father's ranch."

Jess smiled, encouraging Grace to continue her thought, but she did not correct her or explain that her father, Isaac Hale, had owned a horse farm in Kentucky, rather than a ranch. "That's right, I did. My brother Ambrose and I named them together."

Grace's large, dark eyes glimmered with hope. "May Mattie and I help you name them?"

Mattie, older than Grace by four years, looked on, her young face stony and bitter due to a hard life, the murder of her father, and the abuse of some cruel white men. Her mouth had softened at the sound of Grace's request. Jess had come to know that that softening meant interest.

Jake gave her a wink over the girls' heads.

"I'll certainly need your help," Jess told them. "After naming so many foals, I'm not sure I could come up with new names on my own."

Each of the girls tentatively suggested a couple of names. Then Taggart, Diaz, Seth, and even Eli joined in from where they sat or leaned around the stall, offering their own ideas, many of the names based on favorite horses they'd owned or ridden, and accompanied by tales of this horse's speed or that one's mettle. Finally the girls decided on Rose for the white filly—Taggart insisted his first name, Rosemont, was a highly respected family name among the Taggarts—and chose Sheik and Trouble for the colts.

Seth frowned comically at Taggart. "Rose *and* Trouble? How come you get two horses named after you?"

"We could have named one after ye," Taggart countered, "but the girls decided Spindleweed sounded a mite uncomplimentary."

Grace tugged on Jess's sleeve again, then also looked to Jake. "Could you come with us to tell Mother and Aunties about the foals?"

"Sure I could," Jake answered and helped Jess to her feet. "It's a fine day for a walk."

Grace bounded ahead along the stream that led to the village. Her black, bobbed hair fluttered, and her tan-and-green calico dress rippled behind her in a strengthening wind. Diaz had dubbed her *Mariquita*—Ladybug—and the sweet name fit her well. She had grown since the previous summer, Jess observed, in more ways than one, as had Mattie.

Diaz called Mattie *Valentía*. Courage. Mattie was that, and she was fiercely protective of her little sister. She walked sedately but with a quicker-than-normal pace in her tan-and-blue calico, not allowing Grace to leave her sight. Mattie spoke a little more often than she once had, and her mouth softened occasionally, as it had in the stable. This ranch was a good haven for overcoming past sadnesses, Jess knew. The ranch and the people in it. This place had helped Jake and her—and others, she knew—overcome their own griefs. It was part of what bound them together.

They couldn't lose the ranch, Jess decided. It was special. Rare. A place mightily blessed by God.

⬥◗◐◗⬥◗◐◖⬥

"You have that look," Jake said, and Jess lifted her gaze to his. The coincidence of the brewing storm clouds above and behind her gave him a chuckle. Lord above, he admired that about her. She was the strong woman he would always want by his side, one who would never cower from doing what was right. Though sometimes that determination of hers meant trouble. He had learned the subtle changes in her expressions long ago. Storm clouds or not, he knew what the steadiness in her green eyes signified, and what that tilt of her chin meant. "That look says you're planning for battle."

Jess's rosy lips curved into a smile. "No, just planning. Or trying to." With both hands, she pushed back the long hairs that the wind whipped into her face. "It's a relief to see water in the stream again, though I wish the snowmelt had filled it more than half full."

Jake nodded toward the huge, low gray clouds that rolled toward them. They filled the western sky, dark and heavy with rain. "If you wait an hour, you may get your wish."

She paused, looking behind them. "It's so good to see, after going three years without. In truth, I'm not sure I've seen clouds like that since before I left Kentucky." Her lovely mouth tightened. "I spoke with Hank this morning. He heard in Milford that part of General Sherman's army has pushed Wade Hampton's cavalry back, and that another part is closing in on Johnston's men. He also said that if General Lee is pushed back much father, he will be forced to abandon the capital at Richmond. Both the Yankees and the Confederates are putting up a furious fight." She sighed. "At least they're finally getting rain there too. The drought must be terrible for the men fighting."

"The war can't last much longer, love," Jake said, answering the question she didn't ask. "I'm sure Ambrose is fine."

Beneath her hat brim, her green eyes narrowed in thought. They were only a shade darker than the gray-green sagebrush that dotted the desert around her. "I'm sure he is too. Hales are too stubborn to die." She smiled, then tipped her head. "What do you suppose Seth is doing?"

Jake followed her gaze. Young Seth leaned against the corral, one hand set casually on his hip below his gun belt. He looked north past the post-and-wire fencing that encircled the ranch. Tips of bunchgrass coming up through the earth had begun to turn Honey Lake Valley a light green. "Taking in the view, I reckon. The girls are waiting for us. We'd better keep walking."

"If the war ends," Jess mused as they continued along the creek, "maybe then the attacks against Southerners around here will finally be over." She grunted. "I wonder what life will be like when we no longer have gangs of thugs to fight."

"There'll always be outlaws, and men who want to steal horses, ours or someone else's. And men who feel gratified when they cause someone else to deal with the troubles they stir up. There will always be some wrong to fight, Jess," he said. "Well, maybe not always, but sometimes." He glanced down at her. "In between, we'll have peace."

Dull thunder rumbled in the distance.

Jess laughed softly. "The last time I heard a sound like that, you and I were out this way trying to outrun a herd of wild mustangs."

"Our herd now," he said. "With foals on the way. That reminds me. We'll need to brand the yearlings soon, both horses and cattle. In a few weeks, when the cows fatten up from all this grass, I'm going to take all but twenty of the cattle to sell. A couple of the boys will go along to help drive them. We'll keep the others here to breed new calves, and for milk, butter, beef, and so on." He looked over his shoulder and realized that Jess had stopped again. She was looking intently southeast, toward the foot of the Sierras. "What?" His own sharp eyes searched the foothills for movement that might indicate the presence of outlaws or—

"The mustangs."

His heartbeat kicked up a notch. A fresh herd of mustangs would mean profits for the ranch that they badly needed. "Where?"

She tilted her face up toward his. "Not new mustangs. The first mustangs. When they were running wild, their hooves on the earth sounded like thunder. The herd stampeded straight toward the Paiute village, and the cattlemen couldn't turn them, remember?"

"Yes. You rode to the village like your tail was on fire. You got everyone into the cave, and they were safe." He waited for her to explain, not sure where her thoughts were headed.

"Not a cave. A mine tunnel." She waited for him to mentally connect the ends, elation bursting from her face.

Jake had no idea what she was talking about. "You'll have to help me along, Jess. I don't—"

"A mine, Bennett. You once said that before you bought the land, men worked it. For *gold.*"

"Whoever it was left before I first got here. If they'd found anything worthwhile, they wouldn't have abandoned it."

The bright pink in her cheeks didn't dim in the least. "There could be a dozen reasons why the miner or miners left and didn't come back. They could have run out of money to fund the dig, or supplies. They could have hired on in Virginia City or Gold Hill, at one of the big mines that are paying well. They could have fallen from a sickness, even pneumonia."

"Jess, I've had a good look in there, and I took lanterns along so I could see every inch. The shaft goes about forty feet deep into the mountain, with one crosscut. No veins, no nuggets."

He could see the wheels turning behind her eyes, and he knew she wasn't listening. Mentally, he sighed.

"We've seen gold flecks along the riverbanks." She laughed. "I know, it isn't quite a river, but it'll look like one once the water rises. Others have found gold around here, Bennett. We've both heard the stories."

Bennett again. Mildly agitated, Jake strode a few paces, then walked back. When she said "Bennett" like that, it meant she was determined. "Jess—"

"We don't have to send the men on roundup because the ranch is all fenced in now, and the horses and cattle have plenty of grass—at least they do for now—so the men'll have more time to spare." Her eyes, still expectant, hadn't left his face. "I interrupted you," she said. "I apologize. Please continue."

"The stories we heard—"

"But *think* of the possibilities, Bennett! If we found gold, even a little, it could be sufficient to get us through until next year. If the rains don't come again after today, or if they don't produce enough grass for the animals, the gold—if we find enough—will buy plenty of food to last us until winter. And while the men dig, you and I can go to Carson City and see if we can find out who stole my father's savings from the bank."

Fairly certain that she would think up another point in her favor, he hesitated before answering. She pulled off her hat and began pacing as he had, fully absorbed in her thoughts.

She dragged a hand through her hair, mussing her braid. Then she held out her palm, holding back anything he might have said. "Bennett, I know what you're going to say. You're going to say that the men hired on to work the animals, not to dig in a mine."

Jake crossed his arms and braced his booted feet wide, finding some satisfaction in knowing his wife so well.

"What we'll do is ask the men if they want to work the mine. We'll pay them the forty dollars each month they normally earn, plus...."

He saw her change from Jessica Bennett, ranch owner, to Jessica Hale, former bookkeeper and daughter of a successful business owner, in less time than it took an eagle to snatch a fish from a lake with its talons. She chewed her lower lip, her eyes seeing inward, as she calculated.

"...fifty percent of whatever they dig up. We can schedule shifts, just like we do with their other tasks."

Tipping back her head, Jess gazed up at him through thick, dark lashes, easing into a smile intended to melt him like candle wax. It irked him that her look did just that. He stood his ground. And he would continue to stand it, so long as she didn't—

"Jake?" she cooed, lifting her little minx fingers to his sides. They began caressing.

Oh no. *Lord, help me.*

Her fingertips worked their siren song around to his back. He could bear it. He *could.*

"Jake, what would it hurt to try? If it doesn't work out, there'll be no harm done."

Beneath his hatband, sweat popped out on his forehead. Her fingers. He *loved* what she was doing with her fingers. They continued lower, easing his tension, drifting over his muscles. They reached his gun belt, then moved higher again, with feathery, light caresses that coaxed more purposefully as Jess realized she was winning.

"No harm done," she said again, this time in a throaty purr. "The men might even have a little fun, gettin' to hunt for gold, and one of them might strike it rich. Now, how could that be a bad thing?"

Absently, Jake wondered if she knew that her Southern accent grew more pronounced when her mind was set on a matter…if she knew that her voice brushed soft and pleasing as the skin of a peach over his senses. He should feel unmanned by her manipulations, but quite the opposite was true. He felt like the most blessed man alive.

She pressed her womanly curves against his body, only slightly impeded by their child within her. He burned for her.

He'd never allow her to lure his agreement about a matter he was staunchly set against, but for a matter like this where he could bend, he'd gladly let her entice him over to her viewpoint.

That way, everyone was happy.

Seeing the answer in his face, she smiled and kissed him. Still grinning, she observed his eyes while she toyed idly with her hat strings. "You were always going to say yes, weren't you."

Jake calmly lifted a shoulder. His back still hummed in contentment. "I usually say yes to your requests, but I especially liked the delivery of this one."

They grinned shamelessly at each other. Jake saw Grace bobbing in place underneath the cottonwood trees, waiting for them, Mattie stoic beside her. "The girls are waiting for us," he said.

Jess's gaze dropped to his mouth. Her own lips lifted, almost imperceptibly, toward his.

Though his insides groaned with wanting time alone with her, he nevertheless started them both toward the cluster of wigwams, already counting the hours until nightfall.

❖◈◦◈❖

Overhead, the sky rumbled. Fat raindrops plopped onto Jess's modestly rounded middle, and her uplifted face, and her hair. She didn't put her hat on, or duck under the cover of the cottonwood leaves. She opened her arms and spun in circles, her hat swinging gaily at the end of her hand. *God is so good!* she praised Him inwardly.

Nearer the trees, Jake tried to grab her hand to pull her under, chuckling at her antics. Jess evaded him. She hadn't stood in the rain in years, and she wouldn't cheat herself out of enjoying it now.

"Come join me!" she invited the girls. "This is God answering our prayers!"

Grace, already giggling, threw her arms wide and leapt toward Jess. Jess bent to catch her hands, then waltzed her around the tree where Jake leaned and smiled. Mattie stepped forward, a small, quiet grin on her face. All three joined hands—Jess's amusingly pale among the brown—and spun like a wagon wheel on its side, until they nearly fell over from dizziness.

The rain grew heavier, darkening the sky. Reluctantly, Jess waved the girls toward their home, plopping her hat on Grace's head as the little girl hurried past. Grace clutched it in place and ran inside their large, dome-shaped dwelling. Mattie hurried after, her eyes as bright as pebbles in a pond, her cheeks rosy with color. Then Lily was kneeling in the doorway, urging Jake and Jess indoors. Jess stooped and stepped inside but hesitated while her eyes tried to see beyond the tidy, orange fire. She hesitated too long. Jake bumped into her. Jess felt herself tilting toward the floor, but then a strong, warm hand gripped hers and gently righted her.

He was always there for her, she thought. She sat down several steps from the door, leaving room for him to sit beside her. He did, and then gave her hand a quick, loving squeeze.

"I am so happy you have come, my sister!" Lily said. "And you as well, Jake. Now, my daughters, what is it that makes you as eager as otters to tell me?"

Lily's hazel eyes rounded in surprise when *both* girls started telling her about the foals at once, then teared as she looked into her older daughter's happy face. She laid a hand on Grace's arm, briefly silencing the girls. "Here, Grace." Lily put away a knife and a large piece of cowhide in a basket, then wound up the long piece of lacing she had cut and pressed it into Grace's hand. "Run to Auntie Nettle's dwelling. Give this to her, and tell her and Auntie Spruzy to come visit as soon as they are able."

Grace beamed a smile and left with the lacing.

Jess found Jake's hand again as Mattie sat on the ground beside Lily and told her about the birthing and naming of the foals. Lily didn't interrupt her daughter, or touch her, or make any movements that would remind Mattie how animated she was being in this moment. Lily simply let her speak and let the child's happy words wash over her. Jess knew it was a sound her friend had seldom heard from her older daughter. Jake pressed her hand again, meaningfully, and she understood well what he silently communicated. This place, this land, was healing another soul.

As mother and daughter spoke, Jess passed her gaze over the interior of the clever stick dwelling. Last year, a fourth sleeping mat had been added when Ho Chen had married Lily. Evidence of his influence dotted the home, from the cone-shaped Chinese sun hats with wide brims to the two gold earrings and two gold bracelets that shone at Lily's ears and wrists—traditional Chinese wedding gifts, Ho Chen had told Jess. *"It is because a couple is always made up of husband and wife, so gifts are in even numbers."* Even the two dolls Jess had sewn for the girls showed their mother's and father's cultural influences, equally cherished. Made of plain ivory batiste, they sat on two rolled-up bed mats, each doll wearing a colorful glass bead necklace and feathers, her head topped with a miniature cone-shaped sun hat.

Jess smiled, feeling contented among her husband and their extended family, listening to the rain spatter a few inches above her head.

Mattie chatted on, pausing a few times to question Jake about the specific birthing process of the foals. Jake graciously accepted the bowl of soup Lily ladled and handed to him, as did Jess. It was a meaty broth made from antelope, one that Lee and Black-Eye had felled during a recent hunt.

Lily ate with them. When they had finished, Mattie finally realized that her own soup was untouched. She fell stonily silent, her eyes downcast, startled at her behavior. Lily merely patted her hand and smiled. "It is *good* that you are happy, Mattie," she said, and Mattie lifted her gaze, hesitant but listening. "It is how the Great Spirit Father wants for us to be."

With the same spare, gentle movements he used when working with skittish horses, Jake reached for a stick and stirred the fire's coals. "When I was a boy," he said softly, "my father told me the same, and I've learned for myself that it's true."

Jess knew that he'd avoided eye contact with Mattie to keep from further startling her, but he glanced at her now, seated beside him.

"That's why the Almighty makes good things like foals, and rain, and family. Bad things come, but He always makes good things come after."

Mattie looked up at him. Her aged, tortured eyes glimmered with hope.

"After a hard winter, He brings foals. After a long drought, He gives us rain."

Jake said nothing more and resumed nudging the coals. In the quiet, Mattie nodded, and that was all that was said. A few simple words that the child understood, examples spoken much like the parables Jesus had used when He comforted the brokenhearted.

Jake was a handsome man, Jess reflected. She loved his appearance, his touch, and his wonderful, deep voice. Above all that, she loved his code of honor and his great faith in the Lord. Without their mutual faith that bound them to each other and to God—which enabled them as husband and wife to fully understand the core makeup of each other—a significant part of who they were would be missing. Vanished. Gone. Without their shared faith, they would be empty shells, skeletons of beasts lost to a desert without rain.

As matters were, Mattie spooned up soup, some of the longstanding tension in her face softened, hushed by Jake's calming presence as much as by his words.

The doeskin hanging over the entrance parted. In came Spruzy, her broad, fleshy cheeks made broader by her grin, with Nettle's solid but petite form close behind... and a look on her brown face like the cat who discovered cream.

Both were looking at Jess.

Jess found she was smiling too. "What?"

Grace slipped in behind them. Her chubby hands covered a threatening giggle.

All the women, Lily and Mattie included, seemed to share some great secret.

His eyebrows raised in mild curiosity, Jake braced his elbows on his knees and watched the faces.

"Come here, my sister," Spruzy requested.

Not sure what to expect, yet fully trusting her Paiute friends, Jess pushed herself up—leaning a hand on Jake's shoulder for support—and did as she'd been asked. She moved toward Spruzy and Nettle, careful to bend her head so that her hair wouldn't be caught in the sticks of the roof. Finally, she stood upright near the center.

Their smiles held in their secret...until they pulled out from behind them one last gift for the Bennett child. Seeing it, Jake slowly rose to his feet.

Jess reached out a careful hand, then pulled her fingers back, not yet daring to touch it. Her eyes took in her Paiute sisters, Lily, Nettle, and Spruzy. "Did all three of you make this?" she asked in awe.

"We all three helped!" Nettle giggled her delight. "Isn't it wonderful?"

Jess nodded, and sank to her knees. The new cradleboard must have taken weeks, if not months, to make. The flat, basketlike oval backing—broader where it would fit across Jess's shoulders, tapering at the hips so she could turn—included a curved shade for the baby's head like a girl's bonnet that would keep the sun out of his or her eyes. The softest of rabbit skins had been stitched together to form two rectangular pieces the length of a year-old baby from chin to feet. These were sewn with strong sinew to the backing's sides beneath the curved shade. The buttery-soft rabbit skins would hold the baby in and cradle him or her in soothing comfort. The long piece of lacing Lily had cut from the cowhide moments before Jess and Jake's arrival was now woven through tiny openings like buttonholes in the two rabbit skin panels, where the pieces would be laced together over the baby once he or she was placed within. On the opposite side of the backing, two straps were affixed, made of strips of buffalo hide, with the hair left on facing inward, so that the meager weight of cradleboard and child would rest comfortably on Jess's shoulders.

Jake was the first to find his voice. "Thank you, all."

"Very, very much," Jess added, and hugged each of the women and girls tightly. She would keep the cradleboard always. No gift she had ever received meant more than this.

❖◈◦◈❖

Jess wore the cradleboard over her shoulders as she and Jake walked back toward the ranch house, already anxious to place their baby in it for the first time. Around them, heavy rain fell and splashed among the budding grasses, the droplets springing upward again like cat toys on strings before dispersing into puddles. In the rising stream beside them, tens of thousands of drops plunged into as many concentric, overlapping ripples... and sounded rather like a round of applause.

Jess felt giddy and was tempted to curtsy in response. Her moccasins were soaked with cold rainwater and squished, and she didn't care at all. She had waited *so* long to become with child. For months she had feared she was barren, unable to conceive. Now, with the gifts the ranch people had given her—

"What are you thinking, love?" Jake glanced at her. Water ran from his hat brim.

"I was thinking that with these gifts from the ranchmen and the Paiutes, I finally feel like I'm truly going to be a mother. Do you know how wonderful that is? It's as if the entire world is celebrating with me."

"At least this part of it is," Jake amiably agreed. "I know that feeling well."

They shared a smile of understanding and love. Then she knew it was time for a confession. "I didn't tell you the rest of my fear when we were talking about such things a few days back," she said over the dancing rain. "I was afraid we would...struggle to keep both the ranch and our family going, and growing." Her hands took firm hold of the buffalo skin straps at her shoulders. Jake's warm brown eyes followed their movements and her expressions. "I'm not afraid any longer. I know that together, everyone here, with us.... Do you know what I'm trying to say?"

"I do. It's like that verse we read in Ecclesiastes. I don't recall the exact wording, but it says that although one person may be overpowered, two can defend themselves, and a rope of three cords is not easily broken."

"Yes, that's it. That's it exactly," she said. Then, "I apologize for having doubted you."

They hurried up the two steps to the porch, and Jake opened the door for her. "Apologize for doubting God," he said, then smiled softly to gentle any sting.

"I just did," she assured him as they entered the main room, where chair spindles and rockers lay scattered across the floor and her loom and rag rug waited.

Jess set the cradleboard against a wall, and Jake dropped the bar over the door. Never had Jess felt this close to him, or known so completely that they had truly become one in mind and spirit. She longed to be even closer and saw that longing reflected in his eyes. She placed her hand in his and let him lead her up the stairs.

Below them, the pieces of chair and strips of rags waited patiently, restfully, while outside the blessing of rain continued to fall.

Chapter Eight

"No, Jess."

"Excuse me?" With what Jess felt was admirable control, she quietly laid the pencil on the desk and turned in her chair to face her husband.

Jake strode back and forth behind the sofa, dark eyes flicking to her, his hands on his hips. Powerful and tall in his cowboy hat and boots, flannel shirt, bandana, and gun belt, he looked an intimidator of men, the successful ranch owner who led a large crew of men who didn't question his orders. Jess knew he was drawing on his considerable strength and honor to remain calm, and she strove to do the same.

Bury the emotions, she told herself, forcing her mind to focus on pure logic. "We need the money, and the path to finding what happened to my father's accounts begins at that bank in Carson City." She thought for a moment. "You and the men will brand the calves today, then you'll drive them where to sell them?"

"To Sacramento City, maybe up to Placerville or down to the coast."

"To Sacramento City? Jake, why so far?"

"Last year's drought was harder on those folks than on us. They lost a lot of their animals. Chop houses there will pay a good price for beef cows."

"They will pay a good price," she mused aloud, "but we don't have many cattle to sell. The profit will cover the men's wages, but it won't get us through next winter." She sighed. Her going to Carson was the only chance they had to keep the ranch going. To keep the ranch, period. "So you'll leave tomorrow, then you'll be gone a month or so before you return."

"I'll stay here until the rest of the mares have foaled and then leave in a couple of weeks. Around the middle of April. The boys and I can't go over the Sierras because the snows still block the passes. We'll head west then south and go around the mountain range as much as we can."

"That'll put you back here the middle of May, maybe a few weeks later than that. I have to go to Carson now, with or without you. If we have another drought to contend with this summer, we'll have to drive the animals into the mountains again, and we won't be back until shortly before the snows come. We won't have time then to go to Carson and search for my father's money."

Jake stopped pacing beneath the painting of him and her, looking so right together, so much a part of each other. "Jess, I already said no."

She stood to her feet, bristling. *Calm*, she thought. *Stay calm.* Jess worked her jaw, trying to ease the tension that had turned it to stone. "Hank mentioned that he wanted to take the remainder of last season's apples to Carson City to sell, and that he needs to buy a new shirt or two. In truth, though, I think that's an excuse, and he really wants to visit with Gusty." Her attempt at mild humor landed like a pancake on the floor, so she went on. "He's taking his wagon, so I could ride with him. I won't even be riding a horse. Both the baby and I will be fine."

Though Jake's face remained passive, his massive arms were crossed and his boots were braced wide apart. Not a good sign.

That riled her. "In the event you haven't heard the news, the Thirteenth Amendment was ratified two months ago. Holding a person against his or her will has been declared unconstitutional."

A muscle twitched in his neck. "You are not a slave, Jess."

"Close to it. I'm a woman. If I were a man, we'd not be having this discussion."

Jake closed his eyes and tipped his head back. A full minute passed before he forced the fierce rate of his breathing to slow. He looked at her again. "Jess, men tend to think and act based on what makes sense. Women tend to think and act on what they feel. This has gotten you into trouble before, and it would get you into trouble in Carson City."

"Yes? What makes you certain of that?"

"Because whoever burned your parents' house wanted all the Hales dead, including you. I don't know why that is. Maybe so they could take your father's savings from the bank, maybe because they had a personal grudge against your father, maybe because you had Southern ties. We don't know why Charlie Shane was hired to burn it down. But we do know that if the person who hired Shane finds out you're alive, he'll almost certainly try to rectify that."

"And you think that this has not occurred to me? Has it occurred to you that if you started asking questions, you'd be in just as much danger? Whoever killed my parents, my sister, and Elsie doesn't want anyone discovering who he is."

Jake's expression softened. "I would take a couple of the men with me to watch my back."

"Hank will already be there, and I'll take Seth as well. Aside from you and me, he's the best shot on the ranch.

And according to Doyle, Hank knows his way around a gun."

"You'd put Hank and Seth in danger, Jess?"

Her eyes snapped to his. "Which two men would you put in danger?"

"I'd ask them to watch from a distance, so they wouldn't be in danger."

"I'd do exactly the same."

"I don't speak with a Southern accent, love. You do. The war is nearly at an end, and the fighting has been worse than ever. If the war ends, things may go badly for the folks in Carson City who supported the Confederacy, or if others think they supported the Confederacy. Unionists may be out for revenge. Or one side or the other may refuse to accept that the war is over. The risk is just too high. We'd do better to wait until the hostilities fade."

Jess braced her hands on her back and shook the hair from her face. "We've already discussed that. We need to be back here to care for the horses by the time the heat of summer comes. And by the time the baby comes. That should be late June. We don't have time to wait."

"Jess, I'm sorry, but you can't go. And I doubt there's anything to find there. The funds are gone. Finding those responsible won't bring the money back."

Since she completely disagreed with him on that point, she didn't bother to argue it. If she found who had stolen the money, she'd almost certainly find out why, and where the money had gone. With the sheriff's help, she'd be able to retrieve it, at least in part. They'd find those who had stolen it and hired Shane to murder her family, and, after two endless years of not knowing who had killed them or why, she would finally be able to leave that part of her life behind.

She knew finances, and she knew that there had to be a record of the person who had withdrawn the funds. Jess wanted the murderer caught, and the ranch needed the money *now*.

"What should I do while you're gone selling cattle? Sit here at the desk and hope the ledger numbers will change?" Though she tried, she couldn't keep the flippancy out of her voice. Perhaps there was some truth to Jake's observation about men and women. Some trifling *bit* of truth.

"The men are anxious to start digging in the mine once the foals have been born. They'll be divided between tasks, so you'll have to run the ranch, see to the scheduling, and oversee all the tasks."

"I can always fill my time, Jake. I meant, how can I help with our financial challenges?"

"By running the ranch, Jess." He gave her a quick smile. "There's a lot of work to be done today. I'd best get to it." He headed toward the door, opened it, and paused in the doorway. "I know you want the men who murdered your family found, Jess."

To avoid his unblinking gaze, Jess shifted her own regard to the ledger. Did the man miss *nothing*?

"A woman who's six months along with child shouldn't be hunting down fugitives. Not even if she has your tenacity. Jess, please trust me."

At this, her eyes locked on his. "What do you mean? What are you planning?"

"I'm planning to sell some cattle and to ask a few discreet questions, is all."

"And you need me to stay caged in at the ranch because I'm not discreet."

The wrinkles at the corners of his eyes softened. He looked as if he wanted to touch her. "I need you to have the freedom of the ranch so that I don't lose you." With that, he ducked his head under the lintel and stepped out.

❖◈❖

Doyle's thickly muscled arms worked the bellows, and Jess backed away from the increasingly hot coals of the forge. Before her, the smithy doors stood wide open. She moved toward the entrance into the morning sunshine. Across the ranch yard, a flood of ranchmen and Paiutes, and even Mattie and Grace, bobbed about the entrance of the stable, where four more foals had been born since sunrise. Two of them while she and Jake had been arguing.

"Why aren't you joining them, Jess?" Doyle asked.

Jess walked back toward the forge and tried to pay attention to Doyle's movements as he picked up tools and began to work. "I've wanted you to teach me the basics of smithery for months," she evaded him. At Doyle's steady look and even steadier silence, she added, "I'm also feeling put out with Jake." Suddenly, she realized what she'd said. "I didn't mean to—"

"It's all right, Jess. We all knows you, and we knows when you're feeling poorly." His mouth quirked a little. "Even when you tries to hide it. Talk if you needs to. You know I ain't one to repeat what's been said."

Jess looked on as he tapped some sort of hammer against the red-hot slip of iron he held with tongs. Rather than reveal her frustrations, she wanted to ask a question. She formed her words with care. This was one matter they had never discussed. "Doyle, how did you survive being a slave during those times you desperately needed to break free of it?"

His hammer blows stopped, and he looked up at her. Then he returned to his work. "I desperately needed to break free of it every minute, Jess. You been to other ranches near here? Then you seen that a lot of ranch workers are black. A lot are Spaniards, too," he added as a side thought. "Most of the black men come here because there ain't nowhere else to go. The white men who hire us know we work hard, and they know we don't complain none."

"You could have gone to the North. Mr. Lincoln issued the Emancipation Proclamation, and in February, the Thirteenth Amendment abolished slavery forever."

Doyle shook his head. "Slavery don't end because of a law or because an important man say so. Only when the war is won will those things make a difference." He slid the slip of iron back into the forge to let it reheat. Standing fully upright and stretching his back, he looked down at her from a height that rivaled Jake's. "Even then, blacks won't know white man's freedom so long as most whites treat us like we're something less. Before I come here, I hid in an attic for six years. Folks brung me food and water when they could, but at times I went two or three days with nothing to eat and nothing to drink. I heard slave catchers search the house below, and I knew that at any moment they would find me, and then I'd be killed for escaping. Finally a preacher come and take me away at night. He was going west in a wagon train, and he hid me all the way across the plains. He fed me what he could, and I could only sneak out for a quick minute or two after everyone else was sleeping. I almost drowned once when the wagon was crossing the Platte River. The bottom flooded and the wagon tipped, and I went under with it. I thought that river was going to be my grave." He pulled the slip from the coals and continued shaping it between the hammer and the anvil. "Yes, I knows what it is to feel trapped and to need to break free. I also knows that the boss loves you and don't wants to see you come to any harm. One of my earliest recollections was my mama screaming for me as a white man pulled me away from her and stood me on the auction block. I was sold, and I never saw her again."

Though tension hardened his face, Doyle remained gentle with the hammer and the bit of iron that was beginning to resemble a pothook, like the one in the cookhouse fireplace. Jess realized Ho Chen must have asked for another hook.

"No one ever cared about me none the way the boss cares about you, except my mama, and I don't remember nothing about her other than her reaching for me and that look in her eyes." He lowered the hook into a bucket of water. The water boiled around it and hissed. Doyle removed the hook and pushed it into the forge once more, then wiped sweat from his forehead with the back of his arm. "I know it ain't worth breaking free if you leave behind the person you love."

Saddened and troubled, Jess braced her hands against a plank table. "You mean you would have stayed a slave if it meant you could have been with your mother?" she asked gently.

With the tongs, Doyle pulled the hook from the forge. "I couldn't stay a slave. I'd find a way to take my mama with me." He cooled the hook in hissing water once more.

A shout from somewhere in the ranch compound drew both their gazes toward the sunlight. Hank jogged past the doorway, then he noticed them and stopped, panting to catch his breath.

"It's over," Hank said, wearing a smile that outshone the sun. "The war is over." With a fatherly squeeze to Jess's hand and then Doyle's, Hank hurried on with the news.

Doyle laid the hook and his tools on the table. He stood, a big, strong man, in his leather apron. And cried.

✦◈◈◈✦

Jake stepped back as the squalling, newly branded calf struggled to its feet and ran back to its mother. "All right, boys. That's the last one. I'm sure Ho Chen has supper ready."

While the other men waved the last cow and calf out of the corral, young Will took long, slow steps over to the watering trough and lowered the branding iron into the water to cool the steaming metal. Jake pulled off his work gloves and tucked them into his belt. Jess had once observed that the spindly, bony-faced youth was tan from hat to boot. He was, Jake realized. Tan clothes, tan hair, hazel eyes, and skin tan as a palomino. If it weren't for his red bandana, Will would blend into the herd of mustangs and look right at home.

"Hey, boss?"

Except for his slow, Tennessee drawl that was never in a rush, much like the youth. "What is it, Will?"

Will filled a bucket from the trough. "You want me to put out the branding fire now, or should I wait until you leave the corral?"

Jake tilted his hat toward the setting sun. "Why not leave it? Some of the boys might enjoy a campfire after nightfall." Just then, Jess stepped out of the barn and into golden sunlight, little more than a round-bellied silhouette against the copper sky. Her endless hair tossed in the wind that also made her skirt flutter behind her. His wife. Jake's heart sighed. Despite their disagreement that morning, he hoped Jess would want to enjoy the campfire with him.

Will let himself out of the corral through the gate, but when he saw Jess walking toward Jake, he left it open. He politely touched his hat as he passed her, leisurely strolling toward the cookhouse.

Jake felt the boyish urge to wash up and comb his hair before he spoke with his beautiful wife, but then she was there, folding her arms across the top rail of the corral fence, lifting her face to his, resting her chin on her hands.

"Hello, Bennett," she said softly.

He rested his boot against the fence. "Evening, Miss Hale."

"Mrs. Bennett will do just fine."

He nodded. "I'm honored." Unable to resist touching, he brushed his fingers along her cheek, beneath her loose wisps of hair. Her skin felt soft as rose petals. The Almighty was wise, he decided, to have created men and women so different. "Quite a day, little lady. Does it seem real to you yet? The war being over in the East."

"Not yet. I've been listening to talk of secession and war all my life. I have no idea what it will be like to live in a time of peace. I imagine it'll take some getting used to."

Jake kept his face passive, giving nothing away. When Hank had brought the news today that General Lee had surrendered to General Grant two days ago, he also told Jake, in private, that the homes of three Southern families were attacked last night—*after* the war news had reached most folks. In the West, the war wasn't over. Good people were still being threatened. Jake hated to keep a secret from Jess, but he had no choice. Her safety was what mattered most. He'd just have to deal with her being put out with him afterward.

He said, "You're wearing Livvy's gowns now, I see. If I recall right, that was the first one she sewed after she learned she was expecting Sadie." It was a china-blue calico with small white roses. With Livvy's black hair and blue eyes, it had been beautiful on her, just as it was on Jess. "The color brings out the Hale Irish in your hair."

"Then perhaps I'll wear it after the baby is here."

"Perhaps you can wear it when we're expecting the next one."

Warm firelight shimmered in Jess's eyes, and gleamed in her thin, silver wedding ring. "And the one after that?" she murmured.

"And the one after that."

"I love you," she said.

Knowing that words were not enough to convey to her what he felt, he leaned down and kissed her.

Jake sighed. He hoped his next words wouldn't spoil this moment. "I think the men will be able to see to the mares and foals."

Jess took a step back from the fence. One hand remained on the top rail.

"I'm leaving tomorrow. At first light."

Jess rubbed her nose, her movements agitated. "Who will you take with you?"

"Diaz and Eli are the best men with the mares and colts, and I suppose that folks who see ranchmen with black skin, or even Paiutes, could get riled."

"It's sad and unfair," Jess acknowledged, "but I expect it's true."

"I'll take Taggart and Will, and leave Seth here with you."

"Why now? You said this morning that you weren't leaving for a few weeks." When he didn't answer, she stepped closer, her expression gentle once again. "Jake, you and I completely trust each other's love and fidelity, and we trust each other to do what's right. I have faith in your judgment. I need you to have faith in mine."

Now, just how was he supposed to answer that?

"I apologized to you and to God for doubting you both," she said. "I feel that you owe me the same."

"You want to go to Carson City while I'm gone."

"Yes."

"Where men tried to kill you and, if they saw you, would want you dead."

"I'll take precautions. Hank and Seth will watch my back."

"How do you know they'll be willing to do that?"

"I already asked them."

Jake removed his hat and thoroughly rubbed his head. *Would you rather have married a simple, demure woman?* he asked himself and instantly knew he'd never be passionate about such a person. "There's still a lot of tension between Unionists and Confederates, Jess. Perhaps more than you know. You'll be walking right into the middle of it, and I won't be there this time to get you out of it."

Jess snorted. "Bennett, I helped break my brother out of a Union prison that was guarded by four hundred sharpshooters."

And she had kept her wits about her, he recalled.

"The Nevada Volunteer Cavalry is stationed at Camp Nye, right near Carson City, should I run into any trouble. Besides, Carson City has nearly as many women as men, and they shop, run errands, and go to church. And children go to school."

"No one wants them dead," he said bluntly.

She didn't flinch. "If I'm a threat to anyone, time won't diminish that threat. I'd rather look that threat in the eye now than one day, years from now, discover a knife in my back."

Jake shook his head. She wasn't going to back down. He'd have to go with her and tell Taggart and Will to sell the cattle without him. But he couldn't send them on the other mission. He'd have to do that alone, and he'd have to do it now, or they might never discover who murdered Jess's family. He *couldn't* go with her. Jake walked a few paces away, then walked back. Never in his life had he been so frustrated, or so worried for Jess.

He couldn't let her go to Carson City. But he knew that once he left on his mission, she'd go there anyway, without him. Jake rolled his head from shoulder to shoulder. A pain in his temples started to pound.

Taggart swaggered over and leaned an elbow on the fence. "The two of ye enjoyin' the night?"

Jake and Jess exchanged long stares brimming with determination. Then Jess's brows curved in the way they did when she gently teased him. Since they now had an audience, he attempted the same mood.

"When we married, you did vow to obey me."

"I don't recall that," she said loftily.

"I was there," Taggart said. "I recall it right enough."

Jess bit her lip to contain a small grin. "I must have been delirious."

Jake chuckled. What a spitfire she was. "You said, 'love, honor, and obey.'"

She grunted, eyes sparkling now. "Honestly, that just doesn't sound like me."

"Perhaps not." Jake laughed and shook his head. "Still, those were your words."

Her eyes gave him a doubtful scrutiny. "You're sure about this?"

"Quite certain, love."

His elbow still braced atop the fence, Taggart leaned his chin into his hand. Jake was sure he was silently wagering on the outcome.

"I don't suppose," Jess said, "you'd reconsider?"

Lord above, he loved this woman. "What, holding you to your vow?" Jake asked.

Jess pouted. Jake had never seen her pout. He hoped she didn't stop.

"Can't we view it as more of a guideline?" she said.

Jake wanted to say, *"For you, I'll make it a guideline,"* but he couldn't. Though they had reverted to teasing and trifling, what she was asking was no less serious than it had been.

Jake glanced at Taggart. "Could you give us a few minutes?"

Taggart chuckled and strolled toward the barn, hands gleefully in his pockets as if thumbing through the phantom coins he'd won.

"Jess," he said, meeting her gaze, sober now. "I have no greater need than to protect you. That need is a large piece of what the Lord put in place when He formed me. Asking me to cut off that need is like asking me to cut off both my arms. Can't you understand that, love? You've made me see that Olivia and Sadie's deaths strengthened that protective part of who I am, and I've strived to weigh all my decisions with that awareness."

Jess threaded her fingers through his. "I know that's who you are, Jake. Most times I dearly love that you care so much, that you love me so much." Her fingers tightened in his. "God gave me the need to fight for what's mine and to see justice done. I know how you feel because my needs burn in me just as wildly, and just as strongly, like there's nobody and nothing that can put them out."

Yes, that was exactly how he felt about keeping her safe.

"Jake, I need you to have faith in me."

She'd spoken the same words this morning, he recalled. Was that the issue? That he didn't believe she was sensible enough or responsible enough to look after herself and to do the right thing?

Her thumb tapped against his, pulling his gaze to hers again. "We can't have this same discussion for the next fifty years. I did vow to obey you. You vowed to love me just as Christ loves the church and gave Himself up for it. Please give up your fears, Jake. Give them up so that I can be free to be who I am." She hesitated, then laid her hand on his arm. "I feel like I have to go to Carson City."

If he hadn't been fully alert, he was now. "A premonition?"

"Not exactly, but a certainty. Do you remember what you told me about those instincts God gives me?" She didn't wait for his answer. "You said, 'Don't let yourself disregard them,' and 'The Almighty lets you know what is coming so that you can help someone else,' and 'Whatever gift we each have, we've just got to do the most good with it that we can.' You were right about that. That's the need God gave me."

Jake remembered the words now, and he heartily resented himself for speaking them. At the same time, he knew he'd been right. Jake felt as if he were physically being torn in two, straight through the core of who he was. Straight through his heart. He *had* to go on his mission. Jess *had* to go to Carson City.

His mind as weary as his heart, he removed his hat and hung it on a corral post.

Jess must have understood what he was feeling, because she let herself in through the gate and came to lean against him so that they were both watching the flames that still danced.

Taggart entered the corral carrying four empty cups. Seth followed, holding a steaming coffeepot with a rag. Seth gestured, and Jake and Jess accepted two of the cups and held them as the young man poured.

"Thank you," Jake said. Seth set the pot in the coals and then wandered back to where they were standing.

Jess looked small, he thought, standing as she was with him and the other two. Taggart was the shortest of the three of them, and the top of her head barely reached the bandana the man wore around his neck. How could he let her go? Yes, she had run her father's business, she could run the ranch, and she could shoot better than most every man he knew. But would that be enough?

Jake realized she was studying his face.

"You once told me that your mother was part of the reason you became a rancher. What was the other part?"

Taggart and Seth appeared to settle in to listen, sipping their coffees and watching the fire, so Jake gave her question some thought.

"When I was just a boy—seven, eight years old—the West…." He frowned a little as he searched for the right words. "The West called to me. My brothers and I would stay out late all summer long, running through the fields, hiding from each other in the orchard. One evening when I climbed to the top of an oak tree, I looked out and saw it. All that land to the west. It lay out there, starting at the edge of the farm, and it didn't seem to have an end. After that, every night when the sun went down, it was as if the sun wanted me to go with it, like it was inviting me to come see where it went."

Seth nodded as if he'd had a similar experience.

"I began to wonder what was out there," Jake continued. "Then I started to hear stories, stories about men who lived on horseback and traveled with the seasons. Visitors would pass through and tell of giant animals like hairy brown bulls, and of mountains that split the sky."

Seeming unable to tear her eyes from him, Jess appeared drawn into his memories, perhaps pulled in, as she'd often said, by the timbre of his voice. If he remembered later, he'd ask her what she was thinking right now.

He took a drink of coffee—yep, Seth had brewed it— and leaned against the corral fence, crossing one boot over the other. "For years I wanted to go to those places, wanted to see every single thing I'd heard about. Trappers would stop for a meal or to spend a night, and I would stay up late asking questions and listening to them tell of how the Indians lived, of mountains they called the Rockies, and of places few white men had ever gone. They said rivers had once been thick with beaver, but now the trapping days were gone. I began to think of ways one might still earn a living in such a place. Then I read about folks in wagon trains going to the Rockies and beyond, some of them driving cattle to raise.

"I read more and more often that people were headed west. One day I simply woke up knowing that I was meant to be a rancher in the land where they were going. Then gold was discovered in California, and nearly every day we heard of folks leaving the East to go west to stake their claims. That seemed to me to be a waste of effort, but I knew they would need supplies, and they would need food. I was seventeen then and had money I'd saved up. I had enough brothers that the farm didn't need me, and my pa knew I needed to get away from all the reminders of ma. So I bought supplies, saddled my horse, and went."

Jess scratched her nose, looking a bit shy, of all things. "You're thirty-three?"

Jake nodded. "Yes, ma'am. I suppose I have a couple of years on you."

"A couple at least. You were riding across the continent when my brother was first teaching me to ride."

He acknowledged her observation, then continued his story for her. "When I reached California, I worked for a cattleman for a few years, learned from him, until I had enough working knowledge and means to continue on my own. I did quite well for a time. Then the mines began running dry. Beef was still in demand, but not like it had been. Doyle was working for me by then, and Taggart."

Taggart saluted with his mug. "Ye see? God was blessin' him, even then."

They shared a chuckle, and then Jake went on. "Things were looking pretty lean when, one day, everyone started running back the way we'd come, wild about the discovery of a silver lode."

"And that's when you met my father," Jess said. "I remember you telling the story to my parents the night you came for dinner in Carson City. That must have been in sixty-one or sixty-two. It seems so long ago now." She tilted her head. "You never staked a claim."

"Never did. Raising cattle was a sure thing. Mining isn't."

Jake fell silent then, reflecting on all he'd told her about those simple days with his brothers. Walt and Ty. Jess continued to lean against him, Jess and their baby. Jake wanted to remember tonight, every detail of it. For now, set his worries aside and lost himself in the peaceful snaps of the fire and the cricket chirrups that rippled through the night.

Finally Jess stirred and stood to stretch her back. Her gentle smile and the subtle gleam in her eyes told him the reason she'd asked him why he'd become a rancher. She wanted to see and experience it all, just as he did. He understood, and hurt, at the same time. Above all, he loved that she was so much like him in spirit.

With his free hand, Jake rubbed her shoulders. "You ready for some sleep, little lady?"

Jess smiled at that. "I suppose I am."

Seth took their cups, then each of them bid him and Taggart good night.

Jess already knew that he wouldn't stop her from going to Carson, so there was no need to say any more. He'd have faith in her, and for her he'd give up his fears that stemmed from what happened to Livvy and Sadie.

They paused on the porch steps of the ranch house. He admired the three weeds she'd planted in front of the porch the autumn before. They had flowered and bloomed. She seemed to be admiring the area of the porch itself that held the two rocking chairs he'd made for them.

As they stood there, Jake prayed for her, more strongly than he'd ever prayed for anything.

❖❖❖❖❖

Jake listened to Jess slip out of bed, pull on one of his flannel shirts, which hung on the wall, then ease out of the room and down the stairs. A moment later, the front door quietly opened and closed.

Coming fully awake, he rubbed his eyes and took in a deep breath. The scent of pine filled him, as it always did. He loved that smell. He remembered placing each log in each room of the two-story house. While he was away, he'd miss it.

Perhaps Jess was thinking the same. She intended to leave at first light, just as he did.

Knowing her, she had gone to the stable.

Minutes later, Jake padded barefoot across the compound, stepping in and out of moon shadows that covered the ground like patches on a quilt. The full moon hung above the sage desert to the east. Out of habit, he glanced at the position of the Big Dipper relative to the North Star. It wasn't as late as he'd thought. About ten thirty.

Rather than light a lantern, Jess had left the stable door open to catch the moonlight. Jake entered, struck now with the pleasant scents of leather and straw and hay. He didn't need to look for Jess. He knew where she'd be. She sat in the clean straw of the only empty stall beside a birthing stall. She leaned against the stable wall, gazing through the slats at the seventh foal of the season and its mother, both lying down.

Jake crouched beside Jess. "Couldn't sleep?"

Her hair was unbraided. Sleepily, she drew her fingers through it, pushing it back so she could look up at him. "It's the moon. It made the bedroom as bright as daylight. It woke me, and I started thinking."

Jake settled in the straw beside her and stretched out his legs. In a natural movement, Jess lay back against his shoulder. Jake lowered his face to her hair. She smelled like desert flowers and woman. "What were you thinking?" he murmured.

"While I was still in bed, I thought of the end of the war, and that last night was only one night before the full moon. Back East, soldiers began riding and walking home, looking into the light of a nearly full moon. It must have felt like a blessing to them, like God was leading them home."

"And then you started thinking of Ambrose."

"Yes. I'm sure he survived the war—you know I refuse to believe otherwise—but it may be weeks or even months before I receive a letter from him, with much of the nation in chaos and ruins. I wonder if he'll come west like he once wrote that he would. In that letter, he also said that he wanted to come here after the war to repair his relationship with Father and to be a comfort to Mother— she worried about him so much it made her ill, more than once—and he wanted to meet little Emma, to get to know her. But they're all gone now, and he has Greenbriar to rebuild. Lexington took some damage at different times throughout the war, and as far as I know, Ambrose hasn't been back to Lexington or Greenbriar in nearly two years. There may be much work to be done. It's even possible all the paddock fences are gone. In one of his letters he said that the Yankees often used wood fencing for firewood."

"If he doesn't come west, perhaps we could find a way to spend next winter with him in Kentucky."

Jess's warm hands took hold of one of his and pressed his knuckles to her cheek. "Thank you for that. I know that may be impossible, but I know that if there's any way to make it happen, you will."

In a few of the other stalls, mares or foals stirred. To Jake, the soft sounds of straw rustling and tails swishing were the sounds of life, and of hope.

Jess turned her head to listen with him. "Look at all of them. Seven babies so far." Then she grinned. "Mustangs—the Thoroughbreds of the West."

Jake chuckled. "That they are, or at least the foals will be. I can't wait to see them run."

Jess sighed, then her smile faded. "I'll miss seeing the birthing of the rest of the foals. By the time we get back, they'll all be following Diaz around like pups."

"Yep, I imagine so."

She looked at the dozing foal. "They'll be all right, won't they, Jake?"

"They couldn't be in better hands. Doyle will be in charge while we're gone, but we've got a lot of good men working with us, Jess, and there won't be any more attacks against the Paiutes."

"Lily, Nettle, and Spruzy are getting ready to plant the garden," she said.

"This year, with the snowmelt and rain, it should grow well. We'll have a lot to can for the winter. Hay should grow well too."

"If the rains hold out."

"If they hold out," he agreed. "What was that?" He knew, but he enjoyed asking.

"The baby's kicking. He does that when I lean back too long." She pulled herself more upright.

"You think it's a he?"

"I don't know what the baby is, Bennett. I just don't want to call it an it. You know?"

They shared a smile. "I understand."

Jess covered a long yawn and then curled into him.

"I have a better idea," he said.

Taking care not to nudge her or the baby, Jake rose and retrieved a couple of saddle blankets, which he rolled together. In the stall, he set the blanket roll in the straw, then lay down and helped Jess settle alongside him, her narrow back to his chest. Together they used the blankets as a pillow.

He could see the glimmer of moonlight in her eyes as she watched the foal through the slats. His hand settled on her hip, his cheek against her hair. Within minutes, she was asleep.

He would add this to his memories of tonight, he thought. Simple pleasures, shared together. Before he drifted off, he found himself wondering how many people had so much as this.

Chapter Nine

O h, dear me, Jessica." Augusta Scott, looking as Irish as a shamrock in her dark green calico, bustled over to meet them as they entered her clothiers shop, a handkerchief in hand. Her blue eyes and pleasantly round face looked red from crying, and several strands of the copper-and-silver hair she usually wore in a twist had fallen loose, unheeded, around her face. "Jessica, how have ye been, dear? Oh, my...." She sniffed but produced a genuine smile as she patted Jess's protruding stomach. "Looks to me that ye're doing just fine. Seth?" She gave him a firm, motherly hug then patted him on the back. "It's good to see ye, lad. Hank." She repeated the back pat. "Ye're looking fit."

Hank reached to remove his hat, then noticed it was already in his hand. His cheeks turned a shade redder than their normal rosy pink. "You're looking well, too, Mrs. Scott."

"Now, none of that 'Mrs. Scott' business, Hank," she declared in her charming accent, which rolled like the hills of her homeland. The only thing Scottish about her, Jess thought with an inner smile, was her late husband's name. "Not a soul has called me that since my husband died years ago, God rest him. No, it's Gusty, if ye please."

Hank smiled. "It suits you."

"There now. What brings ye to town?"

Jess took Gusty's hand in concern. "Gusty, what's happened? You've been crying, and since we rode into

Carson, we've seen storefronts draped in black and people walking about like they're in mourning."

"Oh my! Haven't any of ye heard?" Gusty took in Jess, Hank, and Seth's blank looks, stunned. "President Lincoln was killed."

"What?" The room of fabrics, buttons, and laces swirled around Jess. She felt Hank's broad hands on her arms, easing her onto a sofa. Gusty pressed a clean handkerchief into Jess's hand and sat beside her. Only after Jess fingered it did she realize she was crying. She looked up to see Hank and Seth, two seasoned ranchmen, looking red-eyed and stunned.

"When?" Hank asked. He and Seth pulled over two chairs and sat with them.

"It came over the wire just this morning. He was shot last night right in Washington City, while attending the theater with his wife. Oh, the poor woman!" Tears ran from the inner corners of her blue eyes. She wiped them away. "I'm surprised that ye hadn't heard."

Jess thought of Jake, and how very awful it would be to lose him.

Then, darkness.

An image flashed through her mind—it was Jake, falling. Falling away from her, into empty blackness. Falling, his strong hands reaching, grasping only empty air. He grew distant, then his whiskey-brown eyes met hers once more, apologetic, loving, grieving what they would never have. Then there was only blackness, the hellish chasm, and Jess knew he was dead.

A horrific, deafening scream shook Jess, tearing her back to the present. By everyone's startled expression and the rawness in her own throat, she realized the scream had been hers.

Seth was the first one to move. He was on one knee, gripping her hand. "Jess?"

Lord above, I trust You. I trust You....

Jess closed her eyes and breathed slow and deep for several moments, waiting for the vividness of the images to fade. *Jake is all right,* she told herself. *If he dies, I'm there when it happens. Jake is all right. He's all right...for now.*

A muted whimper sounded from the living quarters on the floor above. Gusty's cool, plump hands seemed flustered as they pressed her neck, felt her forehead. "That's only my...charge. Startled awake, no doubt, and back to sleep in no time. Jessica, ye're as white as starched bloomers, love. What happened to ye?"

Jess's eyelids eased open. Seth, his boyish face hardened in concern, looked ready to do battle. His hat, she noticed, was missing from his head. His mud-brown hair stuck out a little on both sides of his face. It seemed that her thoughts had begun to clear, at least enough to realize that Jake must have had a conversation with Seth in which he'd entrusted the youth with her well-being. She nodded to let everyone know she was all right, and Seth hesitantly returned to his seat.

Gusty hurried across the room with energetic clicks of her heels. Just as quickly, she returned with a glass of water and pressed it into Jess's hand. She gathered her skirts into her lap and sat down again. "Now that was more than shock over Mr. Lincoln's death, m'dear. Tell us what happened," she urged.

"We came here because Hank wanted new shirts," Jess tried to explain, "and I needed bedroom curtains because the moon shines in the window." She shook her head, struggling to grab hold of herself, wishing she could clear away the doubts, the unknowns. Wishing she was able to change her premonitions. She hadn't been able to before, but she wasn't about to give up trying now. Maybe, just maybe, telling the others about it would make the difference. Keeping the visions to herself, or between her and Jake, hadn't done anyone a lick of good.

Jess sipped a little water, then set the glass on a side table.

"That's good," Gusty declared. "Now yer color's comin' back."

"I need to tell you something," Jess said. "Something important that only Jake knows." She studied the three people she needed to depend on. She trusted Hank and Seth with her life, and with Jake's. Gusty had been her mother's dressmaker, and hers, since the Hale family had moved to Carson City. Jess had known Gusty five years and trusted her. It was part of the reason they had come here before going to the bank. She knew Gusty was someone who would help.

As if to confirm her belief, Gusty rose and locked the front door, then turned the sign to 'Closed.' She sat again and met Jess's eyes. "Spill it," she said.

"For years, I've often had strong feelings...intuitions about events, usually events that hadn't happened yet. And they've often been accurate."

"My mother was the same," Gusty avowed. "God rest her."

That was one on her side, Jess thought, but this was where they would start to doubt. She realized she was sweating, and she blotted her face with the handkerchief. "Then about a year ago, I started *seeing* events that hadn't happened yet. What I've seen has been accurate. Every time."

Gusty patted her knee. "Premonitions," she said sympathetically, more to Hank and Seth than to Jess. "Ye poor dear. I've heard of women havin' some terrible ones. That's what happened just now? Ye saw somethin'?"

Jess nodded, and realized she was hugging herself and rocking. Hot tears filled her eyes again, blurring Gusty's face. *Get control,* she told herself firmly. *Get control!* Jess forced her fists to be still among her rose-hued skirts and drew a deep breath. "I've have four premonitions before now. I've tried to change the outcome each time, but that hasn't been possible. A few moments ago, in the vision, I watched Jake die."

Rather than look doubtful, each of them clearly believed her. She sent God a prayer of thanks, then described Jake falling into the blackness. Then she waited for them to react, to respond, in some way.

"Jess," Seth said, and absently she realized he had dropped the "Miss." "The boss told me. Not much, but he said that if you were to tell me that you had a feeling about something, then I was supposed to listen and help all I can. I'd do just that even if he hadn't asked me to."

Jess rocked again, in relief this time, and breathed another prayer of thanks that Jake had had the foresight to mention something to Seth.

"Jessica, dear. Did ye see anything else in the vision?" Gusty asked, getting straight to the business of finding answers. "Was the blackness at the end of a cliff? Or could it have been a lake?"

"A cave? A tunnel? A shaft?" Hank suggested, joining in.

"Aye, there're a lot of shafts in this land," Gusty said. "A miner'll find a bit o' gold and dig a hole straight down under it, hopin' to find more. When he finds nothin' else, he leaves the hole and digs another someplace else."

"Residents around here have learned to be careful of that." Hank rested his elbows on his knees and threaded his fingers together, his ever-present smile tempered with his musings. "I've heard of local shepherds who were watching their flocks see a sheep vanish on a hillside right in front of them. When they go over to see what happened, they discover one of those holes."

"Sometimes it's a dog," Gusty added, "and sometimes a child."

Jess frowned thoughtfully. "But it wasn't a narrow hole. It was a wide space, a chasm. I didn't see any sides. Or the bottom." She bit her lip.

"Then maybe it's a lake," Gusty said. "Perhaps at night."

"There's not many big lakes around," Seth said. "Lake Tahoe. Pyramid Lake."

"Honey Lake," Hank said, "but it's shallow."

"Did ye hear any sounds, dear?" Gusty suggested.

"No. I never hear sounds."

"Any smells?" Hank asked.

"None."

With his thumb and fingers, Seth pinched his bottom lip together, then pulled at it, thinking. "Did you see anybody else there?"

"No. I'm aware only of Jake, and myself."

Seth rubbed his lip back into place and met her gaze. "Do you know when the vision will happen?"

Since the moment she had seen it, she'd been striving to answer that. "I don't know. One of the other premonitions took days to come about, another hours, and another came about within seconds. I just don't know. We'll have to warn Jake as soon as we see him."

Already the two men were nodding agreement.

"Jessica, dear," Gusty began, her blue eyes apologizing for what she was about to say, "is there any chance that ye're misinterpretin' what ye're seein'?"

Jess considered. "I don't see how— Wait." Her insides turned to ice. "I did misinterpret one vision. I thought Jake was going to be shot. I was shot instead." Everyone started talking at once. Jess held up a hand and waited for them to quiet. "I was shot through the hip. I'm fine, and it's just another scar, but...I don't know. I suppose it's possible." She let herself relive the vision. "No. No, I don't feel myself falling in the vision. It's Jake who's falling. I'm certain of it."

Hank took Jess's hand and held it in both of his. They were warm. Comforting. "In the vision," he said gently, "are you still expecting, or has the child already been born?"

"I don't know. I don't know anything more, and it's making me daft!"

"Where is yer man now?" Gusty asked.

Jess sighed. "I don't know. He had something he had to do. He indicated it might take several weeks." Jess wished she could find Jake and warn him, if that were possible. But then, if he was going to die while she was with him, he would be safer if she stayed away.

The baby's weight was making her legs ache. She stood, stretched her back, and walked slowly back and forth near the others.

"Perhaps this vision won't happen anywhere near here," Gusty suggested. "How long are ye plannin' to be in town?"

Jess raised an eyebrow. "That's another matter."

Why do I have to have these visions? she thought. *Why?!* The baby kicked, as if sensing her fears. Jess calmed herself, just as Jake would do if he were here. *Lord, You gave Your prophets visions so that they could help and guide Your people, often to safer places. Now You've given similar visions to me. I know You don't want Your people feeling alone or helpless—that feeling comes from the devil, not from You. So I trust You to help me—to help us—change the outcome of this premonition. I'm not going to ask You to save Jake's life. I'm going to thank You now for already doing so, in case I forget to later.* In that moment, she believed it—*knew* it. Completely. Jake *would* live. She would see to it.

"*How long are ye plannin' to be in town?*" Gusty had asked. Breathing easier now and able to attend to the matters at hand, Jess faced her squarely, knowing the Irishwoman respected the sharp bite of frankness far more than a powdered-sugar-dusting over the truth. "The main reason I came to town is to find the man or men who stole my father's savings from the bank. When I find the man responsible, I'll find the money. Or what happened to it."

Gusty shook her head, her expression one of admiration. "Ye've got backbone, Jessica Hale."

Jess remembered the old Paiute woman's words: "*When you fear what you see, remember to hold on to your strength.*" "Thank you," Jess replied. "I expect I'm going to need it."

Gusty glanced at Seth and Hank. "The two of ye are helpin' her." Her soft grunt was definitely one of admiration. "Which bank?"

"The one here in Carson, on the other side of town. Do you know it?"

"Of course. Why would I bank in Virginia City?"

"Do you know the manager? I would guess his name to be Rafael."

"Why Rafael?" Hank asked, dividing his gaze between Jess and Gusty. It seemed to warm when it touched on Gusty.

"Last autumn, before Edmund Van Dorn—my father's friend and business partner—had to put his wife, Miriam, into an asylum—"

"A tragedy, that was," Gusty said.

Jess agreed. "Before Miriam went, she indicated that she intended to divorce Edmund and marry a man she had quietly taken up with, named Rafael. She didn't reveal his last name, but according to Miriam, this Rafael was wealthy, or he had access to a great deal of money. Miriam was seen handing a large stack of greenbacks to the arsonist who burned down my parents' home."

Everyone let the implications of that fact settle.

"Greenbacks must have come from a bank," Hank confirmed. "Though nearly every bank in this part of the country deals mostly in silver and gold."

"Mostly," Jess agreed. "Still, the bank seems the best place to start looking."

Hank folded his hands over his small paunch. "They should have records of when the funds were withdrawn, and by whom, if an honest man kept the records."

"Yes, that's just what I thought." Images of the vision intruded. Jess pushed them away and tried to concentrate. "Gusty, do you know the manager?"

"That I do, but his name isn't Rafael. It's...Lyman. Yes, Lyman Abbott. Whew. That was no small thing rememberin'. The few times I've heard him introducin' himself, it's always 'Mr. Abbott.' Though I can't imagine him seducin' Miriam Van Dorn. I don't think he's married—though, now that I think on it, I believe he may have been married some years back but lost his wife. I have no recollection how she might have died." She leaned closer, as if about to betray a confidence. "Jessica, ye know I'm not one to gossip. He's always polite, Mr. Abbott is, but he keeps his discussions to business." She lowered her voice even further. "He's not exactly a charmer, though I have seen him take a look at the ladies now and again."

Hank and Gusty glanced at each other, then looked away. Jess was certain both of their pink faces had grown pinker. She would have to see what she could do to help matters along there, she thought...as soon as she asked Gusty this next question.

Jess walked partway across the room and back, recalling the times she'd spent with her mother and Gusty in this very shop, among its long mirrors, bolts of colorful cloth, shelves of laces, ribbon spools, and button jars. Gusty had been one of the few women whose company her mother had enjoyed, as Jess had.

"Gusty, would you permit me to stay here with you—"

"Oh, my goodness!" Suddenly, Gusty was on her feet, rewinding a spool of green ribbon. "Ye'd be most welcome, Jessica, dear, but ye see, I care for a child. For a friend." She flipped a hand in agitation and feverishly straightened jars.

Jess held in a smile. She recalled the year before, the first time she had visited Gusty's store after the fire. Gusty, typically self-composed and collected in a way that made other ladies feel like scatterwits, had been agitated then, as if she had come face-to-face with Jess's ghost. "What is it, Gusty?" she asked softly. "Surely you're no longer overwhelmed that I survived the fire?"

"Overwhelm, I'm findin', comes in many guises." With her handkerchief, she vigorously rubbed nonexistent smudges from a button jar. Her brusque movements caused her pouf of copper-and-silver hair to resemble a fitful pincushion. "I'm afraid I just don't have the space for another long-standing guest, love." She glanced apologetically at Jess.

All at once, Jess understood her confusion. "Gusty, I'm not asking to stay here every night, perhaps even not at all."

Gusty's polishing slowed. "Ye're not?"

"No. Hank knows a woman who runs a boardinghouse here in Carson. I'll be staying there. What I'm asking is, will you permit me to stay here with you for a few hours, perhaps one night, in the event things go badly and I need to leave Carson City in a hurry."

"That won't be easy," Hank reminded her. "Because of your condition, it took us four days to get here instead of two."

"You're right. Gusty, I'd just like to know I have a place to hide if need be. Believe me, I wouldn't ask if I didn't have to, and I won't put you at risk in any way, as long as I can help it."

At that, Gusty waved away any further explanation. "I understand. If ye need to hide, I have a place where I can hide ye. But Jessica, love." She paused and folded her hands together. "Ye're expectin'. Couldn't the sheriff look into this for ye?"

"He already has, Gusty, to a small extent. That was months ago, after Edmund Van Dorn went to withdraw the money for me and learned that the account had been emptied. The sheriff just doesn't have the resources to do what needs to be done." She glanced at Seth. Though he looked relaxed with his elbows on his knees, he was paying close attention.

Gusty tilted her head and appeared to listen for sounds. Perhaps she expected the child she was caring for to awaken from the morning nap. Then, "Will ye be goin' to the bank today?"

"No, I need to rest up so that I have my wits about me. Four days was a long journey. I'll go meet Mr. Abbott tomorrow."

Huffing out a sigh, Gusty brightened. "Well, now, if that was all ye wanted to tell me"—Hank and Seth chuckled appreciatively at the Irishwoman's unflappable humor—"perhaps ye'd like to browse the fabrics? Ye said ye needed curtains."

❧◈❧

That night, too hot for a blanket, Jess stretched out in bed and curled the single fresh sheet under her chin, a sheet that smelled of soap and the outdoors. Within moments the sheet became too hot. She pushed it off and lay atop the covers in her nightgown. She thought of home, and decided she envied the mares who were pregnant through winter.

Even so, she'd happily be pregnant through a thousand summers if it meant she would have this child. The baby shifted. Jess turned gently onto her side and pulled the white cotton fabric of her nightgown tight against her stomach. With the hazy town lights that sifted through the threadbare curtain, Jess could just see the slightest movements. Her hands pressed lightly where the little nudges had been. Patiently she waited, longing to feel the tiny flatness of a foot or the bend of an elbow. Gradually the baby relaxed, but Jess left one hand there to let him or her know that Mama was still near.

Absently, Jess's unoccupied fingers tugged on the bottom of the curtain. The bed sat lengthwise under a small upstairs window, and the room was so tiny that Jess wondered if the builder had had to construct the room around the bed. Thankfully, the room was affordable, and the boardinghouse keeper was a good cook. However, the saloons down the street were open at all hours, raising a discordance of laughter, shouts, and occasional gunfire that echoed up the street and would likely make sleeping a challenge. As would the thousand or more stamps that pounded silver ore incessantly all over Mount Davidson, from its high line of peaks to its canyons far below.

Canyon. She had to change the outcome of this premonition. Again and again in her mind, she saw the image of Jake falling, saw him look up at her as he grew distant. She lifted her hand, splayed her fingers, as if she could take hold of his hand and keep him from plummeting beyond reach. Jess realized what she was doing and dropped her hand. She thought through every moment, searched the edges of every image, and still learned nothing more. Her hand moved to her forehead and pushed back her hair. At least now she knew where Jake was. Or, at least, what he had gone to do.

While she'd looked at fabrics for curtains, Gusty had taken Hank over to the shelves of premade goods an aisle away and shown him new shirts. They'd talked a little more about President Lincoln, and the war being over, and Gusty had expressed dismay that the bullying against Southerners in town hadn't let up at all. That, if anything,

Unionist resentment over four years of war had made harassments more frequent, and worse. Gusty had met Jess's eyes over the shelving and had raised her voice to be sure she heard her when she'd cautioned that Jess, with her accent, should be most careful about where she spoke in public, and to whom.

In response, Hank had commented that before he'd left home, he'd learned that after General Lee had surrendered to General Grant, attacks against Southerners in Honey Lake Valley and beyond had escalated and grown even more violent. Several people south of Lake's Crossing who were suspected to have Confederate sympathies had been murdered. *"Ye mean, Knights of the Golden Circle?"* Gusty had asked. *"In the West, they generally call themselves the Order of the Golden Circle,"* Hank had replied.

Then Jess had known exactly what Jake had gone to do. Though he'd married her, a Southerner, he was from Illinois, and he had no Confederate sympathies. But those opposed to the Golden Circle, and to all local Southerners, had escalated their terror tactics, from burning houses and driving away Southern families to outright murder. Either those radicals felt a need to further punish people from the South for their part in the war, or they didn't see the war as being over. Jake wouldn't permit innocent people to die, or allow a new war to begin if Southerners in the territory reciprocated with similar tactics.

It seemed that a band of Union loyalists had a secret organization of their own, and that Jake had gone to find them and stop them.

Jess had heard rumors of the Golden Circle, but as she'd listened openly to Hank's conversation with Gusty, she had learned more. Much more than she'd cared to.

Hank had said that a businessman relative of his late wife's, who had commissioned Hank to paint a portrait of his own wife, had tried to bring him into their organization. The man had privately told him one evening that Jefferson Davis, while he was still President of the Confederacy, had personally commissioned new governors and military officers and sent them to the leaders of the West Coast Golden Circle, to install them in state and territorial government posts currently occupied by men loyal to the Union. Their headquarters were in San Francisco, but their plans involved the entire Pacific Coast, as well as other states and territories, as many as they believed they could either persuade to join them or conquer. The man had told Hank that the federal authorities watched their known members very closely, and they had yet to succeed with installing Davis's commissioned leaders into significant posts, but he had warned that Hank did not want to be on the wrong side if hostilities broke out.

He'd said the West Coast Golden Circle boasted nearly 30,000 members.

Jess had been stunned to hear that a conspiracy on such a scale existed all around her, and she'd finally understood why so many forts like Fort Churchill had been established throughout Nevada and California.

Though federal loyalists and establishments vastly outnumbered and outweighed even the Golden Circle's 30,000 men, the conspirators remained a threat. Now those people—or innocent Southerners—were being murdered, and Jake had taken it upon himself to stop those responsible for the killings. To stop those whose actions could bring about a new large-scale conflict.

For once, Jess almost resented Jake's code of honor. Almost. If it weren't for good men like her husband— small people, individuals, who worked to right the wrongs of a nation—that nation would fall into chaos and crumble.

She knew it was the few, the anarchists, who now threatened the precious, tenuous peace that hundreds of thousands had died to bring about during these past four years of war. No, she couldn't resent Jake's honor. Couldn't begin to. If he were able to halt the drop of a pebble before it formed a ripple, then no wife alive would know greater pride.

Jess curled her hand around her wedding ring, and knew that was already so.

Still too warm to sleep, she knelt on the mattress and pushed the window open. Below, the streets of Carson City felt familiar to her, yet strange. She had lived here for three years and worked with her father at Hale Imports, and over there, at the end of town, she had stood beside a stagecoach as her brother had climbed in and left to fight in the war.

In the same wide streets, she had met Jake, the streets where supply wagons and pedestrians and drunks and courtesans hurried past in every direction, as they had then. The same place where miners pulled mules piled high with pickaxes, tools, rifles. The same sounds of crude laughter, the same pounding of the ore stamps.

On the other side of town, which she could not see from the window, her family was buried in the cemetery. She had lived here, and her family had died here, but this town had never become a part of her.

Preferring heat to the reminder that she was compelled to be so far from the ranch, she closed the window and lay down with her back to it, pulling her hair away from her neck to cool the skin there.

Jake had done the same with her hair as they'd lain in the straw that last evening they'd spent together in the stable. They'd listened to the quiet sounds of horsetails nearby, and the occasional lows of cattle out in the night, Jess recalled, and yawned, long and deep. They'd been surrounded by wide-open spaces. They'd been caressed by the calming, cooling fingers of the wind.

Chapter Ten

Jake looked up from his campfire when he heard two sets of footsteps approach. He took up his Henry rifle in his right hand and cocked it, then drew the Remington revolver with his left and thumbed back the hammer.

His instincts told him to rise, to be prepared to dodge bullets. His need to find the Unionist radicals, all of them, compelled him to remain where he was—his back leaned against a tree trunk, his boots crossed insolently atop his saddle, the Remington aimed, the Henry rifle laid across his legs—a man undaunted by the odds.

About twenty paces away, two shadows took shape. Starlight touched on the lighter color of their faces and trousers and gleamed off the buckles of their gun belts. Jake heard only the press of rock beneath their boots, but no jinglebobs. Neither one of them, then, was a cattleman. They neared, and the yellow flames of his fire picked out details. One stood a few inches taller than the other, had a slenderer frame, and was dressed in subtle style designed not to stick out as either a dandy or a rogue. In a city, he would be invisible in the midst of any crowd on the street. By his stance, he was the man in charge. Despite the bore of the Remington moving apace with him, his face, intelligent and cleanly shaven, showed no concern.

The man who came up beside him was burly beneath his lightweight cotton shirt and rolled back sleeves...with sheep's-wool sideburns. Instantly, Jake recognized him as one of the nine men who had attacked Jess in the streets of Carson City two years before.

Jake's finger hovered lightly alongside the trigger guard, ready to shift to the trigger should either of the men's hands flinch in the direction of their holsters.

Apparently they knew it. The somewhat dandified leader smiled in unconcern and lifted his hands away from his gun. "No harm intended, friend," he said. "We just saw your campfire and thought we'd stop by and be neighborly."

The man wore no lawman's badge, and by his plain, crisply spoken English, he was not a Southerner. Jake had seen him before dusk that day near the outskirts of Galena. He was the precise man whose eyes he had met, whose attention he had intended to draw.

Jake lowered the Remington and laid it across his knee.

The man eyed him, and Jake knew what he'd see—a man dressed much like him, though perhaps a bit more roguish, with no jinglebobs or other evidence of being a ranchman, a man who hadn't shaved in the greater part of a week, and who wouldn't take kindly to being reminded of it. Cielos stood nearby, a muscular, long-legged black stallion of obvious breeding and speed...a horse the man with sheep's-wool sideburns had seen two years before, and eyed again now. Jake moved his finger to the side of the Remington's trigger and watched the man's face for a look of recognition. His small eyes returned to Jake's face, and Jake saw no twitch, no recognition dawn in it. The leader glanced at Jake's saddle—the scuffed, cracked leather that bespoke a man down on his luck, in need of employment, and likely not choosy what that employment entailed.

The leader smiled again, calm and friendly, and unhurriedly seated himself on the length of a fallen tree on the opposite side of the fire. The man with sideburns rested a boot on it and continued to watch Jake's face and movements.

Heat lightning flashed high in the night sky, momentarily brightening the clouds above.

The leader appreciated it until full darkness returned, then leaned his forearms on his knees. "My name's William Bodine. This fellow is Matthew Malone. We saw you earlier in Galena. Is that a Henry repeater? I've heard of them, of course, but never had the occasion to see one until now."

Jake remained motionless, his gaze steady. Bodine seemed pleasant, and that surprised him. When he'd left the ranch to find the radicals, he'd been expecting men of overbearing arrogance, or troublemaking drunks, but not this individual of good manners and natural command.

"We intend no harm to you. We'd just like to talk," Bodine assured him.

Finally, Jake spoke. "I'd find that easier to believe if you'd call off those other three that I hear creeping up the canyon behind me."

Bodine tilted his head in acknowledgement and respect of Jake's observation, then called out for the three to back off and wait by their horses. "You're an interesting man, Mr.—" He waited for Jake to put forth his name.

"Kane." Donovan Kane was Jake's best friend growing up. They'd gotten into and out of all kinds of trouble together.

"You're an interesting man, Mr. Kane. You're also more than you appear to be. A fair shot with either hand, I'd

153

wager, and a man who'd wanted to be found, and found by me, or else you would not have given me the appraising look you did in Galena, and you would not have built a campfire and left a trail I could find. Why did you want to meet me?"

To remind them of its presence, Jake rubbed the Remington's barrel along his pant leg, as if idly polishing the steel. "I have need of employment, preferably in a place where I won't be asked personal questions," he said, keeping his voice low. "You looked like a man who has friendships and connections."

Heat lightning flashed again, as if threatening to expose all that Jake needed to keep hidden. He forced himself to breathe evenly.

Almost imperceptibly, Bodine's eyes sharpened as they passed over Jake's bedroll and saddle, but his face gave away nothing of what he thought, and Jake was a man well experienced with reading others' faces.

There. He saw it around Bodine's mouth. Two thin lines deepened there, a change Jake might not have seen without the play of firelight and shadows. Bodine was mildly distrustful, but he also wanted something from Jake. If he didn't, or if his distrust at first glance had been greater, he wouldn't have come. He'd have simply had his men silence Jake in the early hours, after he'd gone to sleep. Now Jake waited to see which of Bodine's two reactions would prevail—distrust, or the decision to reveal what he needed. Again the man eyed the Henry rifle, and Jake knew what he wanted. A man who could shoot straight and then disappear.

Jake uncrossed and recrossed his boots atop the saddle in a wordless show of impatience. The gesture drew no reaction from Bodine.

These men had killed before, Jake thought, without provocation or conscience. He had to find the group or groups of Bodine's coconspirators—all of them—before they killed someone else, and before their leader, if indeed they had a leader above Bodine, discovered that Jess was alive and only a few short miles away in Carson City. Normally, Jess was the Bennett who sensed future events, but Jake felt strongly that they had to bring these attacks against Southerners to a rapid end.

"I'm sorry, Mr. Kane," Bodine said. "I cannot help you."

Bodine sat upright and placed his hands on his knees, as if he intended to stand and take his leave. Malone did stand, his eyes sweeping the narrow canyon and the Sierra foothills on either side, as if searching for onlookers. Witnesses.

More firmly, Jake gripped the Remington.

Heaving a sigh of feigned disappointment, he played the card he had saved for now, and prayed that it was the one he needed. "That's too bad. Shane Porter suggested I find you."

Shane Porter, also known as Charlie Shane, had been killed at the ranch, but no one except the sheriff and Edmund and Miriam Van Dorn knew that Porter was dead. He hoped.

Bodine hesitated. That was the confirmation Jake had needed.

"Again, I apologize," Bodine said, and he produced an almost-warm smile. "I don't know any Shane Porter."

Jake lifted a shoulder in indifference. "You probably know"—he'd almost said *knew*, which would have given away that Porter was dead—"him as Charlie Shane. At least he told me to call him Charlie."

Both Bodine and Malone fully relaxed now. "Ah, yes, Charlie Shane," Bodine said. "He was sent on a job last summer. I haven't seen him since. How is that ol' rascal?"

With effort, Jake overlooked the warm sentiment behind Bodine's words, biting back the response that the "ol' rascal" tried to murder his wife. Instead, Jake focused on the rest of what Bodine had said. *"He was sent on a job."* Not, *I sent him on a job.* Bodine had a superior. Given the audacity of the men's actions over the past few days, the superior who sent them out to commit the murders either was not afraid of the law, or was far enough removed from the men who pulled the triggers that he had little fear of being caught.

"It's been months since I've seen him," Jake said, forcing the tension out of his chest and shoulders. "Said he was heading across the state to Austin to see if he could buy into a couple of the silver mines. I reckon he figured that if one didn't pay out, another would."

Bodine chuckled. "Yep, that's Charlie. Always eager to turn a profit. He never did like living rough."

"Not as long as I've known him," Jake agreed. Taking his hand from the Henry, he tossed another log into the fire. It landed with a gentle hiss and a flare of sparks that quickly settled. "Charlie would want justice done to the man who shot President Lincoln," Jake said in an attempt to redirect the conversation.

Malone nodded soberly, and Bodine, for the first time, looked coldly capable of murder. Never before had Jake seen such a look in a man's eyes, as if sanity—and all self-control—had left him.

Bodine fixed his wild eyes on Jake. An owl hooted, and the sky lit up, then darkened. In that short space of time, Jake decided to press the matter and trusted that he wasn't wrong to do so.

With his fingers, Jake caressed the barrel of the Henry repeater. "Some folks think that the war isn't over yet," he said, keeping his attention on Bodine, "that the rebels"—he knew Jess would forgive him for that—"will attempt to fight back out of rage that they lost."

Bodine's expression eased once again, and most of the madness left his eyes. "'Attempt' is the appropriate word, Kane."

"I hear the Knights of the Golden Circle had a western branch."

"They still do." Bodine drew his knife, snapped a slender branch off the downed tree he sat on, and began scraping off the bark. "The Golden Circle, which some call the Order, intended—and still intends—to replace loyal government officials with their own men, traitors," he spat.

"But you won't let that happen," Jake said.

Bodine glanced at him with a guarded grin, then resumed peeling wood. "Loyal federalists all over the West and the States won't let that happen."

Jake uncocked the Remington and assumed a look of irritation and boredom. "Then I have no need to request employment from you."

The knife stopped its cutting. Bodine exchanged a look with Malone, then both eyed Jake with a measure of newfound respect. "You've managed to surprise me, Mr. Kane." He blew the wood shavings from the gleaming blade and tucked the knife away. "Up till now, I've anticipated your actions as well as your responses. You could have heard Charlie's name anywhere, but no man who knew me would dare to show annoyance in my presence unless he truly was annoyed."

Malone placed his hands on his gun belt. "If you haven't seen Charlie in months, how did you know where to find us?" he demanded.

With a raised hand, Bodine quieted Malone, but he too awaited Jake's answer.

"I've had a couple of tough weeks," Jake answered flatly, "and I haven't eaten in more than a day, but there's nothing wrong with my knowing how to pay attention."

Malone's hand dropped to the butt of his gun. "He's lying. He's a lawman, Will." Malone squared himself, and unsnapped the flap of his holster.

"That must be why you're in charge," Jake facetiously complimented Malone. "You're under arrest."

Bodine glanced at Malone. "A sheriff wouldn't lead us to a desolate canyon only to arrest us, unaided, three or four miles from Galena." He turned his attention to Jake. "How did you know where to find us, Mr. Kane?"

The man was polite and patient once again, Jake noticed. He no longer wondered why these radicals hadn't been caught. When judging by mannerisms, Bodine seemed, for the most part, open and friendly. Outwardly, there was nothing radical about him, and he kept the men beneath him well in hand. "A man who intended to become judge and another aspiring to be sheriff were killed a few weeks ago in Genoa. Both were known to have strong Confederate sympathies." Jake knew he was likely staring into the friendly, smiling eyes of the killer, and inwardly he felt the precariousness of the position he was in. "Days later, north and east of Genoa, in Dayton, an employee of the saloon and billiard parlor there who frequently spoke against federal government control was killed. It was in the papers. Perhaps he was a suspected member of the Order. After that, the day the war was declared over, a newspaper reporter with secessionist ties was found dead in Washoe City, to the north and west of Dayton. Then yesterday morning, north of Washoe City, in Galena, a few miles from here, a man who intended to enter the state legislature was killed. From what I read in the papers, each man died a different way, but each was suspected of having Southern connections, and most aspired to positions of influence. What's more, no one who might have done the killings"—*murders*—"remained in town to be found, that anyone could tell, no one boasting their achievement, no one getting drunk celebrating, or else those who did the killings would have been found, and it would have been in the newspapers. That meant the men responsible were smart and either could fit neatly into a crowd or were men who know how to live rough in the mountains for days or weeks at a time without drawing notice." Jake glanced at the men across the tongues of red-orange fire. They were listening, alert yet amused. Neither would show amusement if he still suspected Mr. Kane was a lawman, unless they intended to kill him.

"All I did was go to the last known location and place myself where I could watch the comings and goings, and where anyone who needed another set of eyes, ears, and guns would see me in return. Since all this has taken place within a short amount of time and in one area, it seemed the men I wanted to find would be here."

"Some of the men are here," Bodine said, "and others work in different locations. San Francisco, Sacramento City, Placerville, Carson City. Men watch, and listen, and see to it that loyalists remain in control." He pulled a stack of greenbacks from his vest and tossed several onto the ground near Jake. "You are now employed," he announced with the warmth of an older brother, and Jake found himself tempted to like that part of the man who openly gave friendship. "Come on, Mr. Kane. Let's put out this fire, and I'll take you to meet the three who couldn't sneak up on a man with hearing like a hound's."

Jake holstered the Remington and stood. Malone's gaze followed his rise, then recognition snapped in place. His cheeks beneath the wool sideburns flexed. "I know you, and that horse."

Bodine stopped kicking dirt onto the fire. "How?

The Henry nearly slipped as Jake's hands began to sweat, and his forehead above his hat brim prickled with the hot dampness of fear. *Lord Almighty, keep the sweat from rolling down.*

"About two years ago, a couple of my buddies and I tried to rid Carson City of a traitorous Confederate woman."

"A couple?" There had been nine, Jake inwardly raged. He bent his expression to one of tolerant amusement.

"Kane interfered," Malone declared, "and four others with him. They were dressed like ranchmen."

Jake laid the saddle over Cielos and slid the Henry into its sheath. "My job, at the time."

Bodine ground out a live coal with his heel. Silent lightning flickered again above him. "What happened to the woman, Kane?" he asked, his own hand near the butt of his gun. "Did she go free, or did she suffer?"

"I promise you," he said, imagining how his flippant, spitfire wife would answer in his stead, "the woman lived to regret it."

Jake wished he had Jess's clear-as-day premonitions, because he had a feeling that the situation was about to go terribly wrong.

They were south of Washoe City. The five men riding horseback near him loped by moonlight as naturally as wolves and similar four-legged, clawed predators of the night. Jake didn't recognize the three men who'd attempted to approach him from behind when Bodine had first appeared at his campfire, but he was unable to feel thankful for that. Though Bodine accepted his presence, albeit with reservations, Malone and the other three remained openly distrustful. As they continued south, Jake thought of the ranch, and how he preferred to keep company with cattlemen who were men of honor, whom he could turn his back on and trust. He looked forward to getting Jess away from Carson City and returning to Honey Lake Valley, where they would have the unknowns behind them.

Jess. Did she miss him? Had she started any battles on the streets of Carson? Had she experienced another premonition that she felt compelled to act upon? Was she all right?

He imagined her, pregnant and standing toe to toe with thirty men who intended to harm or drive off a small village of Paiute people. He saw her with a mug of that bitter tea in hand, cheerily determined to force the brew down his resisting gullet. He felt her, in the baby's room, letting the broom fall to the floor as she stretched up against him, her fingers doing wonderful things in his hair, her mouth warm, eager.

A hard wind swept down from the mountains, whipping tree leaves and slamming into him with such might that his hat flew up, but he caught it and tugged it back in place. Jake nodded silent thanks to the Almighty for returning his mind to his current situation. If he wanted to hold Jess again, he must keep his attention sharp.

All five horses maintained an easy gallop along the well-worn road. Cielos must have sensed his rider's trepidations, because the animal was plenty willing to hold the pace but fought Jake over the direction they headed. High clouds flickered with hot, white bolts of heat lightning, and Jake began to feel the same sizzling heat pulse through his own veins.

He couldn't see the Big Dipper through the clouds. More than an hour had passed, he figured, perhaps an hour and a half or better. He'd ridden this way only a few times, but he was fairly certain the town they just passed was Franktown. The road began to curve, but instead of following it to the left, Bodine led them to the right, along a rough trail up into the Sierra Nevadas.

They hadn't stopped to water the horses at the creek north of Franktown—that alone told Jake all he needed to know about the character of these men—and the horses, thirsty and tired, began to stumble. Jake didn't rub Cielos's neck or murmur assurances to him. He couldn't afford to. He had to appear just as indifferent as his companions who watched his moves.

They climbed for nearly an hour. Sagebrush gave way to juniper, and juniper gave way to pines. In places, the pines closed in over the path, and increased his certainty that trouble was coming.

The path topped a rise, then descended into a small clearing below. Bodine whistled a signal, then led them on. Men's voices drifted up, laughing, howling. The voices should have sounded pleasant. They didn't.

Jake's eyes identified four different lookouts. They were no more than shadows crouched between pines or watching from the far side above the hollow, but the waning moon cast down its gleam onto their rifle barrels.

As Jake and the other men reached the hollow, other horses came into view, eleven or twelve of them, standing saddled, tied to trees or rocks. Shanties and lean-tos stood to one side, their far walls lit by a blazing fire. Two men approached, smelling of ripe sweat and unwashed clothes. They loudly greeted Bodine and their compatriots and eyed Jake with curiosity and amusement.

"He's new," Bodine explained. "Mr. Kane." He stepped down from the saddle and led his horse toward the sound of trickling water, which followed the far side of the hollow. He glanced back at his men as he disappeared into the shadows. Among the shadows, Jake thought he saw a cave. "Take care of him."

Malone jumped to the ground. His startled horse took off. Malone ignored it. He eyed Jake as he raised his head in the direction of the bonfire. "Hey, boys!" he called. "We got us a new one!"

Hoots erupted from the direction of the fire, then boots pounded the ground, advancing in his direction—the riders of the eleven or twelve horses plus the four he'd ridden with.

Jake firmed his jaw. He turned Cielos and smacked his rear. Cielos broke through the enclosing circle of men, his eyes rolled white.

Jake turned, his expression blank as he took the measure of the sixteen men who, in turn, took his.

Here were the men of arrogance, he thought, the toughs, those who loved to kill. Their eyes were alight with it. Their hands curled into fists, and six or seven of them moved in.

So this was why God had given him two brothers and neighbor boys who'd loved to brawl, he thought. He'd known such a moment would come. Jake stretched his arms and shoulders. And grinned.

The biggest one struck first. Jake shifted to one side and used the man's momentum and a thrust of his boot to send him face-first into the dirt. The second one jumped him from behind. Jake bent, sending him over his head, which knocked off his hat. Someone landed a hard punch to his ribs. Jake struck back, snapping the man's head around as the man stumbled off balance. Another man struck, and another, bruising Jake's upper body, leaving his lower body free. Jake shook off a small man who'd grabbed onto his arm, and he drove his elbow into the man's nose—he heard the crack—and pulled another man down by his shirtfront as he thrust a knee into his chin and then rammed a boot heel into the side of still another tough's knee.

Jake had the advantage of height and cattlemen's brawn, and used it. Within three minutes, four men lay on the ground in clouds of dust, the fight gone out of them. Twelve more to go.

He glimpsed Bodine leading his horse back from the stream. When he paused to watch, the smile on his face was that of a man entertained and confident. The proud owner of a new prizefighter.

A few of the others had also backed away to look on. Jake ducked and came up under one who was still swinging, and he lunged with his shoulder to successfully knock the wind from him. One of the big men grabbed

Jake's throat with two hands and squeezed. Jake gripped his hands together and rammed them up through his attacker's arms, breaking their hold, then rammed them upward again into the base of the man's neck, cutting off his air.

Men began to chant, "Kane! Kane! Kane!" Jake was winded and occupied, but not too much to recall his alias and to realize that they were cheering for him, that all this was not an attack but a test of his worth.

Seven men lay groaning. Three of the chanters helpfully dragged them out of the way to give Jake and the others room to fight. Four were unwilling to stop, Malone among them, his eyes darkening beyond the need to test Jake. They went feral in his need to kill him.

Malone jerked his knife from his sheath. The men who had remained in the fight backed away. The chanting had stopped.

Jake glanced toward Bodine. He stood holding his horse's reins, his face mildly questioning Jake in return. The fight, then, was between him and Matthew Malone.

Jake could have drawn his own blade but didn't. Malone circled him, not slashing at him out of temper but waiting for an opening with forbearance, breathing hard, his face between his sideburns rigid.

Pain from rock-hard blows stung Jake's face and almost every part of his body. He wiped his forehead on his sleeve, aching to be done with this, to be alone with a comforting piece of ground. But first he would have to disarm Malone while keeping his own skin from being slit apart.

Malone was shorter than Jake, the top of his head coming to his chin. He would aim low, then, probably for his gut—

The blade slashed upward. Jake moved forward rather than back, encircling Malone's clenched fist with his own hands, bringing Malone's wrist down, and, with sudden force, breaking his wrist over his knee. Malone's grunt of pain was brief. Jake heard the knife strike the ground.

With his good arm, Malone clutched his broken wrist against him, face taut with pain, but showed begrudging acceptance in his eyes. He nodded to Jake, then picked up the knife and walked away to tend his arm.

Jake felt the fiery burn of a deep cut along his forearm where Malone's blade had connected during its downward swipe. Blood oozed down, and Jake pulled a bandana from his pocket, wrapped it tight, and knotted it. The cut on his stomach was minor, blocked mostly by his arm and the thick leather of his gun belt, which, he saw, bore a shallow groove.

Around him the men shouted, cheering and clapping and hammering him on the back. The ones closest to the bonfire began to walk and hitch their way toward it.

Bodine, chuckling over some private joke, tipped his hat in Jake's direction, then turned away and led his horse toward where the others were tethered.

Perhaps he'd been wrong to fear some impending danger, he thought.

In the next instant, pain exploded through the back of his skull, and everything went black.

Chapter Eleven

J ust fell like a cow on slick mud."

"Who'd have thought a body could raise so much dust?"

The two pretty young women giggled together across from Jess at the boardinghouse breakfast table. The bench they shared afforded them close enough proximity to hunch companionably as they gossiped, and to punctuate their giggles with nudges to the taffeta-clad shoulders of each other's morning dress. While they relived with relish the unfortunate spill that had befallen some woman, their slender, tapered fingers picked daintily at their sweet pastries like vultures' talons feasting on the heart of a kill.

Jess missed the quiet Paiute women of the ranch, and the way they were raised to build people up rather than to tear them down. Right now Nettle, Mattie, and Grace would be carrying buckets of fresh milk into the cookhouse, where Ho Chen and Lily would be making breakfast for the ranchmen. Nettle would be preparing to churn the milk from Hank's cows into butter. And the men would be feeding the cattle and horses, and checking on the well-being of the new calves and foals. The new calves and foals whose births she and Jake had not been there to witness. Those very foals were the first of the new breed they were developing, the breed that could make the ranch thrive and succeed for years to come. She and Jake were missing it, and they weren't even missing it together. It was a first that they would never get back.

She didn't even know where Jake was. Often of late she'd wished her senses or instincts or whatever they were would go away. Now she wished they were highly acute. She wished she knew for certain that Jake was all right.

Softly, Jess smiled at what felt to her like an impatient jab within her protruding middle. The place, just beneath her ribs, continued to echo the sensation. An elbow, she imagined. She pressed her palm against the calico fabric of her dress, hoping the baby would nudge her again in the same place. Moments passed, then another jab landed near her ribs. She felt it with her hand, the rounded elbow of a baby's arm. Jess pressed harder, already aching to touch him or her, to see impossibly tiny, sleepy eyes gazing back, to hold the baby close against her, soft and warm. Dutifully fulfilling the unspoken request, she bit into a steaming biscuit spread with strawberry jam and sent it on its way down to her occupant. Knowing Jake's affinity for bacon, and that his child may have inherited it, she also ate a slice of the fragrant, crispy meat, then added a swallow of coffee for good measure.

Across from her, the taffeta twins tittered about the ball gowns pictured in the latest edition of *Godey's Lady's Book*. They tossed a few imperious, covert glances at her pale blue calico, then bent together laughing, so close that their neat coiffures nearly collided. Jess was sure that such an event would have ended in gasps of astonishment and a flight back to their rooms with looks of devastation akin to those that might coincide with the Lord's second coming.

They switched topics to discuss the benefits of a new face powder. *Face powder?* Jess desperately needed to talk to someone normal. *What time does Gusty open her shop?* she wondered.

Jess forked fried potato wedges into her mouth with more practicality than grace, thanked the boardinghouse owner for breakfast, and excused herself. The older businessman seated at the far end of the table stood in a show of good manners. Jess offered him a brief, polite smile and went upstairs to her tiny room.

There she neatened her already neat bed, fluffed the pillow with repeated punches, then brushed particles of dust from the clean dresser top.

She'd been in town less than a day, and already she was losing her mind. Before Hank, Seth, and she had left Gusty's shop the evening before, they had agreed that Hank and Seth should watch the bank throughout this morning and midday, and observe Lyman Abbott if they could, to become aware of comings and goings, schedules and patterns, and anything unusual they might glimpse, before she went to meet the man. Hank was watching now, and Jess wished that Seth had been willing to stay at the boardinghouse near her rather than camp at the edge of town. Seth was young but sensible, and she very much needed someone sensible to talk to. Perhaps then, if she spoke her thoughts out loud, she would understand why she was feeling so anxious.

From her saddlebags she pulled a ball of green yarn and a slim crochet hook; then she sat in the room's single, stiff wooden chair, propping one arm on the dresser. This crocheting was a fairly new concept, though she preferred it to knitting, a process during which the yarns fought with her and slipped rebelliously off the needles. She was in no mood for obstinate yarn.

The top few rows of a baby bootee took shape. She unwound a few arm's lengths of yarn from the ball, then resumed hooking the yarn into the form of a sock.

How old was Lyman Abbott? What would he look like? He was the manager of an important bank and likely not easy to intimidate, though she was Isaac Hale's daughter, and she had learned intimidation from the foremost authority on the matter.

Jess smiled brokenly and stabbed the hook into the next loop of yarn. Her father had died trying to save his wife and baby daughter from the fire that consumed their house. Had he lived, he would be ten short weeks away from being a grandfather. He hadn't always been a tender or gentle man, but he'd desperately loved his "girls"— Jess's mother, Georgeanne, baby Emma, and Jess, too, whose ideas and opinions he'd often consulted and always respected.

What would her father think of her actions now? Would he approve of her risking herself and his unborn grandchild in the hopes of retrieving an inheritance that had been stolen, or would he rather she keep herself and the child safe and get by as best she could? Uncomfortable with the answer that came to mind, she tugged additional yarn from the ball and continued crocheting. Her father had given his life to try to save his family. She would merely ask questions, and watch a man, and, if God willed, find records revealing that the funds had been transferred to Abbott's personal account, or had been withdrawn by him or by another employee of the bank. No harm would come to her or to anyone else. Hank, Seth, and she would simply conduct a little unauthorized records check. The bookkeeping skills she'd learned while working at Hale Imports might very well lead her to the man who had stolen her parents' savings. Even her father would have called it poetic justice.

Isaac Hale would no more agree to her actions, she admitted, than Jake had been willing to do. Fully agitated, she jerked more yarn free, sending the green ball bouncing across the small floor. Rather than ply the hook, she stared at the bootee. Why was she even making it? The baby would be born in late June or early July. Why would any rational mother put bootees on a baby when the temperature was one hundred degrees or more? The soonest he or she would wear bootees would be months later. How big would his or her feet be then? How was she to know? If the baby was a boy who would grow to be as big as Jake, he would outgrow the stupid socks before he would ever wear them. Why did sane women knit bootees? This child would wear moccasins anyway!

Jess stood, then stooped to retrieve the ball. She rewound the yarn and stuffed it, the green sock, and the crochet hook back into the saddlebag, then buckled the leather flap shut. She would very much love to throw it all instead, but she knew she would get too little satisfaction from it.

Hands braced against her lower back, she began to pace. Perhaps she should search out her old friends while she was in town and had time to spin. It had been a few years since she'd seen them, but certainly they weren't as narrow-minded as the taffeta tarts. At the mean-hearted thought, she apologized to God and strove to check her mood. Those girls were God's children, just as she was, and just as much in need of godly love and patience.

Patience—why hadn't God given her more of that virtue when He'd known the kind of life she would have? Sure, she had patience for the people and animals who depended on her and who were close to her, but she had none for happenings that went askew, or for injustices, or for those who pursued actions that were flat wrong. She and Jake were different in that way. Jake had patience in nearly all things, though not for injustices. Patience was one of the many attributes she wanted to learn from him, if God blessed them with a lifetime together.

Her old friends, she recalled, returning to that idea, still thought she was dead, and Gusty had nearly succumbed the first time she'd slapped eyes on Jess a year after the fire. No, she would pace this floor the size of a griddle cake and wait for the bank's closing time so she could get several minutes alone with Lyman Abbott.

The pins holding her braid into a bun were poking her scalp and the back of her neck. Jess tugged the pins out and let her braid fall comfortably down her back, then tossed the pins onto the dresser and rubbed away the ache where they had been. Perhaps she would again coil her hair into a neat bun or twist before she went to see Abbott.

Abbott, she realized, was the source of her vexation, her fear. He was why she'd been impatient with the two girls during breakfast, why she'd wanted to throw the ball of yarn through a window and listen to the glass shatter and crash into the street below.

She had rarely been afraid of confrontation—a pity Jake didn't always find her outspokenness charming— but in this instance, she would confront a stranger, one who may have helped Miriam Van Dorn hire the arsonist who'd killed her family. One who'd intended for Jess to lie buried beside them beneath six feet of Nevada desert, and who would almost certainly still want the same the instant he saw she wasn't dead.

With shaky fingers, Jess pushed back loose hairs that began to slip free of her plait and that began to brush her cheeks and chin, tickling unpleasantly. Moisture on her fingertips captured her gaze. They were glistening, damp with sweat. With her forearm sleeve, Jess wiped her face.

After she confronted Abbott, she would have to watch her back, and Hank's and Seth's as well. But how should she approach Abbott? What would serve her better—Hale intimidation and tenacity, or Bennett patience?

The baby, Jess realized, was not moving, and hadn't moved since breakfast nearly an hour before. For an instant, her fears that she would miscarry, like her mother had, shot to the surface, and she gently prodded her abdomen to evoke a response from the baby. There was none.

Again she prodded. Again, nothing.

Sleeping, she told herself. The baby had to be sleeping. Right?

Jess unbuckled and then lifted the leather flap of the saddlebag and removed the yarn, miniature sock, and crochet hook once again. In the chair, she resumed her work, adding loops to form a heel, *willing* the child to live. She'd just make the things big, so they would fit all winter, even if she had to tie thongs of sinew around the baby's ankles to keep the bootees from sliding off.

Are all expectant mothers so emotional? she wondered. *How many mothers-to-be have to confront their parents' killers when they are nearly seven months pregnant?* another part of her asked. Whether or not Lyman Abbott was that man, her goal was to track down the one responsible.

Jess had always been a person who stood on her own, but now, in this moment, she wanted Jake beside her to share her burden, to keep her from going through her confrontation with Abbott alone. But since she had to go through it alone, she would let her anger over that fact give her strength—her anger over that, and her anger that he had gotten away with murder for so long.

Jess would be clearheaded when she approached Abbott. Determined too. She and the baby would both get through everything that lay ahead, even though her senses told her a whirlwind was forthcoming.

She just wished she could sense whether Jake was all right.

⬥⬦⬥

After watching the bank manager for a day, neither Hank nor Seth had reported much more than what Gusty had told them about Lyman Abbott. Of course they both had come and gone from the bank throughout the day to avoid drawing notice, and neither had entered the building, but Jess trusted Seth's cattleman's hearing and lucid observations, as well as Hank's artist acumen. Completely. Lyman Abbott was polite but strictly kept his discussions to business.

It was up to Jess to rattle the man.

Hank had told her details about Abbott's appearance that she might not have noticed, though Jake would have, she was certain. They were details that now led her to draw further insights about Abbott, which she might use to her advantage in her imminent discussion with him. She recalled them as she followed Abbott's movements from where she stood, her shoulder to the outside wall of the bank, just at the edge of the window, seeing but not being seen.

He worked at the teller's window nearest her, weighing gold dust for a wiry man—a miner, if the black soot that layered his hands and clothes was an accurate indicator—

and speaking pleasantly with him. Abbott's fingers, in contrast, were clean as new linen as they deftly bagged the gold dust, tightened the leather strings of the pouch, set the gold aside, and then counted greenbacks in precise tempo. Had Abbott been a musician in command of a guitar, his strums would have been perfect, methodical. He tapped the greenbacks into a thin, neat stack, then counted them for the miner a second time.

Abbott wore clothes of quiet good taste, though his gray clerical waistcoat appeared slightly worn at the side seams where the white sleeves of his elbows brushed, and the ivory cravat tucked into the vee of his waistcoat collar looked in need of updating. The chain of his pocket watch was dull silver, not shiny gold.

Otherwise, he was dapper, almost handsome, for a man of fifty or so. His graying dark hair had been cut by a barber of admirable talent. It was trimmed short above his small, round ears, parted on the left, as precise and tidy as the rest of him. His nose was large—thin from the front, and in the shape of a nearly perfect triangle from the side—and gave way to a prim, curved mustache the same gray-brown as his hair. His low brow and oval eyes—an almost clear, pale gray—together with the nose and mustache nicely concealed the fact that Abbott had little in the way of jaw or chin.

The miner asked a lengthy question, legs spraddled, gesturing broadly. Abbott didn't smile, but his face was constantly pleasant. Though Jess couldn't discern his reply, the tone of Abbott's voice hummed a little higher, a little quieter, than she had expected.

In all, the bank manager was nothing like what she had expected. She had imagined a large man, one who was self-assured, jovial perhaps, and mildly condescending. Hank had been right. Abbott was a man of contrasts. By his mannerisms, he appeared to insist upon a certain level of decorum and respect. Yet Jess also detected uneasiness in him, as if the bank was his domain, but other places and circumstances might leave him uncertain of himself.

Apparently, he was not the Rafael whom Miriam Van Dorn had been talking about when she'd said, "He's important, and he's going to give me everything I ever wanted, and we're going to be happy!" That is, unless Miriam was as nearsighted as she was mentally unbalanced.

The miner pocketed the greenbacks, and he and Abbott exchanged departing pleasantries. Jess stood upright and shifted her gaze away from the window as she mentally prepared herself.

The outside of the bank, like other businesses in Carson City, was draped with swags of black in deference to the passing of President Lincoln. With her fingers, Jess eased down the thin, black netting of the hat Gusty had given her and moved along the bunting toward the open door of the bank. The net would lightly shadow her features from hat brim to chin, but it would not obscure her peach-toned skin and green eyes. Georgeanne had occasionally visited the bank with her husband. Jess would rely upon her close resemblance to her mother and, she hoped, startle and confound Mr. Abbott.

She moved through the door into the dim interior of the bank. The words God once spoke to Joshua settled in her mind. *"Be strong and of a good courage; be not afraid, neither be thou dismayed: for the LORD thy God is with thee whithersoever thou goest."* Jess stood tall, lifted her chin, and strode forward as the last patron walked out.

Abbott had taken the gold dust into the back room. Jess heard the safe's door thump closed then the dial spin to lock it. The two other tellers, she knew, had left minutes before. Abbott would close up the bank alone.

Effecting an image of determined calm, Jess folded her hands in front of her, shielding the small roundness of her middle from view. She was undersized for a woman so far along, just as her mother had been with Broderick and later Emma, and that would suit her purpose. The raised waist of her camel-brown wool hid her condition even further. The appearance of an expectant woman didn't intimidate. The ghost of a dead woman did.

Abbott appeared in the doorway, thin shoulders slumped with the hour of the evening, unfolding his shirtsleeve toward his wrist. His gray eyes lifted at the presence of another patron, then his pupils shrank to pinpoints as the pallor of his face whitened to chalk.

Jess spoke in a low voice as she continued toward him. "Do you remember me, Mr. Abbott?"

"O-of course. M-Mrs. Hale! I thought— There was a fire, and you—well, your family, that is—" Abbott abruptly composed himself and stepped into the teller window. "How may I assist you, madam?"

Jess leaned close to the thin bars that separated them, as close as her hat brim would allow, and pointedly slid her folded hands toward his beneath the bars. Abbott's fingers, folded neatly together mere inches from hers, trembled.

"Fires are terrible things, Mr. Abbott," she said smoothly, then pulled up her right sleeve to reveal the faint, puckered scarring there. His wide eyes seemed to draw back into his head, and she pulled her sleeve down once more. "Too bad about Shane Porter. The kerosene he poured on the house must have doused his sleeve. He struck the match, and—" Jess softly, soundlessly snapped her fingers. "No more Shane."

Confusion flashed in Abbott's eyes, almost instantly replaced by his pleasant banker's mask. Whether the confusion was due to his knowledge that Shane had survived the fire because he had hired him again for another murder, or due to the fact that he didn't know Porter at all, was impossible to tell.

"What may I do for you, Mrs. Hale?" he asked, outwardly maintaining control.

His composed behavior was practiced more than natural. The man's entire surface, Jess determined, was a mask. She suspected that great depths existed beneath the mask, but were those depths harmless, or evil? Whoever Lyman Abbott truly was remained a mystery.

"Such happenings," she remarked with an exaggerated shake of her head, intentionally ignoring his wont to focus on the matter of business. "And now, Miriam Van Dorn, in an asylum for the insane."

The corner of Abbott's mustache twitched, and a silvery thrill shot through Jess. He was Rafael. He had to be.

"The hour is growing late, madam, and it is time to close the bank. Perhaps you can tell me in what way I may assist you?"

Jess slid her hands marginally closer to Abbott's. "Isaac Hale kept his account here. I have come to withdraw funds from that account."

Around his face, Abbott's immaculate haircut grew damp. "I—I believe the account has been closed."

"Now, what would give you cause to think that, Mr. Abbott?" she asked, echoing his pleasant tone.

"Quite some time has passed since the fi—since the tragedy. Nearly two years, hasn't it been? Wouldn't his solicitors have seen to Mr. Hale's personal affairs?"

"Now why would you ask me such a question when I come to you for answers?" He was stalling, Jess knew, and attempting to confuse or outwit what he believed must be an inferior woman's mind. He had just made his final mistake. "His solicitors would not have seen to his affairs because, as you can see, I am very much alive. And since I am, the account is still open. Now, will you kindly assist me in making a withdrawal?"

A thin drop of sweat trickled from the neat part in his hair, while the gray in his eyes turned, almost imperceptibly, to steel. "Of course. Do you have the account number?"

Jess tilted her head in feigned regret. "The fire...you understand. However, you recognized me, Mr. Abbott. I'm certain you can look up the account record. Hale. It's spelled H-A-L—"

"Yes, I'm familiar with the spelling." He turned to the shelves that lined the wall behind him and searched the records, which were arranged alphabetically. He pulled a file from a shelf just above his triangular nose and partly faced her as he opened it and scanned its contents. He flipped a few pages, then frowned. "Hm. It appears, madam, that Mr. Hale closed his account with us February second of eighteen sixty-three." His eyes lifted to Jess. "The record gives no indication as to his reason. I'm sorry, Mrs. Hale. Might I suggest you try the bank in Virginia City, or San Francisco, perhaps?"

Her father had closed his account? Jess's certitude wavered. That couldn't be. Abbott had to be lying. He *had* to be. After all, hadn't he suggested she try the bank in the heart of the Comstock, over the top of the mountain to the east, in Virginia City?

Jess drew her hands back and slid her left hand behind her skirt. She splayed out her fingers wide, then closed them into a tight fist. Then she repeated the movement. Forcing the tension from her shoulders, she blew out her breath. And prepared to go to war. "Hand me the account record, Mr. Abbott."

Abbott snapped the file shut. The steel in his eyes was flinty. Dangerous. "Again, my apologies, madam," he said stiffly. "Mr. Hale did not include your name as one who should have access to his bank records. You are not permitted to view it."

Abbott had just snagged the wrong stitch. *No one* told Jessica Hale Bennett what she couldn't do.

Behind her, the bank door closed, shutting off the street noise and leaving the room eerily silent. Heavy, booted footfalls struck the plank floor and stopped just behind Jess. She heard a hollow scratch against firm leather, then the loud double click of a hammer pulled back. The gun barrel eased forward over her shoulder. And took aim at Abbott.

"I believe you should listen to the lady," Seth said.

Abbott's hands rose, though he didn't wear a gun belt, then stretched out the file toward Jess.

She removed her hat and set it on the countertop beside her. Entrusting the bank manager's movements to Seth's capable guard, she opened the file and eyed columns and dates, ignoring both men.

"You're not Mrs. Hale," Abbott said.

Jess was astounded at the erasures that had been made. She flipped pages. All but three had been removed. The original page remained, detailing the establishment of the account when the bank had initially opened for business, as well as the final page, which noted the withdrawal, just as Abbott had said, and was signed with the bank manager's first and last name and initials. In the upper half of the final page, and on the page that preceded it chronologically, deposits had been logged—deposits with amounts totaling hundreds of dollars, not the thousands she knew must have been there. Care had been taken to disguise the erasures and the new numbers that had been added, but the person responsible had not been able to remove the indentations of the initial numbers logged.

Lifting the ledger, Jess tilted it toward the window and the fading evening light. Barely wasting a moment on that useless attempt to read the erased numbers, she hurried around the counter, her skirt nudging Abbott aside, and found a clean sheet of paper and a pencil. Laying the ledger flat, she covered it with the blank paper and lightly rubbed the edge of the pencil lead over the column of totals—a practice she'd adopted while working as a bookkeeper at Hale Imports when she'd occasionally erased a number by mistake that she'd needed to recall.

From right to left, numbers began to appear amid the gray pencil rubbing. Two thousand. No, twelve thousand. She moved the pencil left and rubbed again. Eight hundred twelve thousand dollars. The pencil stilled in her hand, and her abbreviated corset suddenly felt oddly tight around her ribs.

Her father had deposited more than eight hundred thousand dollars in this bank account. Where had he gotten all that money?

"You're not Mrs. Hale," Abbott repeated, his quiet voice accusing.

Jess faced him. He lowered his hands to his sides in a way she found menacing. She took a step backward. Seth took a step of his own. Forward.

The ledger lay in a single patch of fading golden sun. On the top edge of the page she had laid over it was Abbott's name, penned with curling flair. The name included a middle initial. Staying clear of the space between revolver and target, Jess pulled the record toward her, slid the loose paper aside, and, with what felt like weighted hands, turned to the original page detailing the establishment of the account, praying that it would be there.

Her eyes found the signature, that of Lyman Abbott. They rose to meet the glare that threatened her, the twin slits of gray, just beneath a forehead slick with sweat. "I'm not the only one who is more than what she seems, Mr. Abbott. Miriam Van Dorn was insane, but she surely liked to talk."

Jess turned the ledger toward him and pressed a fingertip to his name. Lyman Abbott. Lyman *Rafael* Abbott.

"You hired Shane Porter to murder my family, Mr. Abbott." She stepped toward him, seeing the man through a red haze of fury.

"Jess," Seth warned her.

"Miriam hired Porter," Abbott avowed.

"I watched burning bits of wood singe my father's coat," Jess said.

"Jess!" Seth warned her again.

"I watched my father run up a burning staircase to save my mother and sister. I watched the house fall on him."

She took another step toward the banker. Her hands ached to squeeze his neck, to squeeze until he turned blue. "My mother and sister were burned alive. Do you know what it feels like to be burned, Mr. Abbott?" She was inches from his face now, her eyes nearly level with his. "The burn feels like white-hot coals pressed to your skin. The white-hot coals stay pressed to your skin for weeks while you heal. They burn like the fires of Satan's furnace." Jess felt his cravat in her fingers, felt her hands tightening their grip, heard Seth mutter a curse. "Satan's furnace doesn't go out, Mr. Abbott. God keeps the fires stoked for all eternity." Absently, she heard her voice go shrill, fierce. "Do you know how long eternity is, Mr. Abbott?"

Gradually Jess became aware that she was breathing hard but that Abbott wasn't breathing at all, and Seth was standing over her, prying her hands from the cravat just beneath the pale blue face and curving mustache. "Eternity is one year for every dollar you've stolen!" Forcefully, Seth folded her arms across her ribs and yanked her backward against him. "Eternity is eight hundred thousand years. You'll burn because my family burned!"

Abbott pulled at his cravat and braced his hands on his knees to regain his breath. "Miriam hired Porter!" he insisted. "I found him, but Miriam hired him. She meant for your father to live."

Jess jerked a hand free of Seth's grip and reached back for his gun. She tugged it from his holster, raised it. With his free hand, Seth used her arm's momentum and raised it higher, snatching it from her grip. "You knew my father would go back into the house for my mother, didn't you? You knew it! You knew how much he loved my mother, that he would never turn his back and leave her to die!"

Seth had holstered the gun and regained control of Jess's right arm. He pinned it with her other arm and dragged her away from Abbott, around the counter, and toward the door.

Jess knew she couldn't fight him, or she'd risk harming the baby. "Admit it, Abbott!" she roared.

Seth tugged open the door and yanked her through. She kicked at it, sending it crashing open with enough force that it then swung closed, shutting off her view of Lyman Abbott.

The last emotion she saw in the banker's face was fear. His expression didn't flicker, and it didn't fade. The door swung closed on a guilty man who could already feel the noose of justice around his neck.

Miriam had hired Shane Porter, but Abbott had found him, and he had known that Isaac Hale, that all the Hales, would die by fire.

When she and Seth rounded the corner of the building, Jess's knees gave way as she relived the agony of two years of waiting to learn the identity of the man who had arranged for her family to die. Great, painful sobs clawed her from throat to heart to soul, tearing forth all the memories, the nightmares, the desolation. She sank into the dust of the dark alley, the edge of the walls shredding her hands. Then she was being pulled up, lifted in a pair of firm, wiry arms, and carried to an unknown place, while her own arms longed for Jake.

Chapter Twelve

Jess watched from inside the window of Hale Imports as Lyman Abbott strode from the bank in a topcoat and hat the same shade of gray as his waistcoat. And his face. Hank pushed away from where he leaned against a storefront wall near the bank and casually followed the bank manager at a distance.

While Edmund paced, Seth knelt before her chair and followed her gaze, a clean, soapy rag waiting in his rough cattleman's hand. "Mr. Hank's following him then."

"Mmm-hmm," Jess agreed, drying the last dampness from her cheeks with her shoulder. "Like he was born a Pinkerton rather than an artist." She turned back to Seth. He carefully dabbed at the raw lines across her palms, these cuts the only visible evidence of her encounter with Abbott. All other wounds she had tucked away inside.

Not willing to relive all that had just happened, she focused her eyes and her mind on Seth's ministrations. In past years, Seth had been shot, gored by a cow, and more, and he knew a good deal about healing, as a result. He considered himself a master brewer of cowboy coffee, but of his two abilities, Jess preferred his doctoring. She had tasted his coffee.

He glanced up at her. "You all right, Jess?"

How was she to feel about his dropping the "Miss" from the name he had always called her? He made no overtures except those of a friend, and she supposed they had been through too much together to stand on formality. Seth had been shy around her when they'd met, but his carved leather hatband and boots, and the stance of the person in them, were those of a man. Apparently he had overcome the nerves of youth. "The soap burns a little, but it's fine, Seth. I'm grateful for your help."

His tan hat tipped in acknowledgement. "Oh, no problem."

"Seth." Jess waited for his whiskered face to lift to hers. "What I mean is, I'm grateful for *all* your help."

Seth grinned a little. "For a minute there, I thought you were going to pop his head off like a cork from a bottle."

They shared a reluctant smile, and she allowed the events to reappear in her mind. "I wasn't in the mood to contain myself," Jess admitted, "and I'd already decided before the meeting that I would turn up the heat under him and see what bubbled to the top. I want you to know that I drew your gun in full control of my person. I wouldn't have shot him. I just had to have an answer." She sighed. "And now I have the answer. Unfortunately, it's made matters worse for everyone."

"How so?"

"He confessed to helping Miriam hire Shane Porter to commit murder," she said softly, having a care for Edmund's feelings, since he was looking on, listening, grieving. "With that information, the sheriff could have arrested him, and then the bank and his home could have been searched for my father's bank records or for the money itself. Then I attacked him, and if I have him arrested for murder with only my word as evidence—"

"And mine," Seth added.

"You're biased. It won't make much difference. And I've discredited myself by my behavior. If I have no additional evidence to present, Abbott would likely have me arrested for assault. Now we'll have to watch him for days, maybe weeks, to see if he reveals anything definitive and tangible that we can use against him." She looked to Edmund for his thoughts.

"I agree, Jess." He brushed back his thinning hair with pale hands. "Without tangible evidence, Abbott could go free. Better we wait and watch and give him a chance to become comfortable and make a mistake."

Jess shook her head. "I'm sorry, both of you. Seth, you didn't plan to be away from the ranch for so long. Edmund, I know you want justice done and this whole business behind us, just as I do. I had to know if Abbott meant for my father to die too. His intentions simply can't be the same as Miriam's were, unless he's just as unstable as she is. Oh, what a mess."

Seth glanced at her. "Jess, if Abbott's vindictive, he'll come after you."

"If he's vindictive, he'll come after us both. We'll have to watch each other's backs, as well as our own. We'll have to be careful to not be seen by him."

"Which is why you both will be staying with me in my home," Edmund announced. Beneath the 'Closed' sign, he locked the door, then headed toward the stove.

Seth set aside the cloth and rinsed Jess's hand in a basin. With his thumbs he gently wiped the soap away from her cut. Fresh blood from her palm turned the water pink.

Edmund Van Dorn had been her father's closest friend since they were children, and he had been like an uncle to her and Ambrose for as far back as she had memories. At times, he had been as close as her father. His clothes, though elegant, hung from his stooped shoulders, which bore the heavy burden of his wife's betrayal and her permanent confinement in the asylum. He had dearly loved his wife, and no other woman but her. He was nearly bald now, the last strands of mud-gray hair above his ears and shirt collar fading to white. He had lost his best friend, his best friend's wife and daughter, and, most recently, his wife. Jess was the only family who lived near him that he had left. She didn't want to stay with him because doing so could put him in danger, but she couldn't say no. He needed the closeness of family as much as Jess needed him. They would watch out for each other.

"We'll be grateful to stay with you, Edmund."

Edmund smiled softly as he added water to a teapot, then turned back to place several sticks into the stove.

Seth dried her hand without comment, but Jess could see he didn't agree. "We'll watch out for him," she murmured, keeping her voice low.

Seth began work on her other palm. "No, you should stay in his house and keep that baby safe, but I should stay someplace else," he said. "If Abbott sends out men to look for us, they'll be looking for you and me together. And Hank should keep to the boardinghouse."

"Baby?" With a haggard but genuine smile, Edmund closed the window shade, lighted a lamp for Seth to see by, then settled into a sofa opposite the window.

"Gusty—Augusta Scott, the seamstress—has rare talents with a needle and thread," Jess answered. "Though she altered my dress to conceal it well, I'm nearly seven months along. Jake and I will have a child around the first of July."

In his homely, round face, Edmund's smile broadened. "That's wonderful news. Jake will be a good father."

Automatically, Jess nodded and smiled. She didn't know why, but she had begun to worry for Jake.

"You've remained small, like Georgeanne always did," Edmund went on. "Because of that, both you and Ambrose arrived sooner than either of your parents expected." A chuckle shook his narrow shoulders. "Both times, Isaac sent a servant for me so I could pace with him while the doctor or midwife was with Georgeanne upstairs. You remember how his hair stood on end? It did even more so during those times. Until then, I'd never seen a man who looked like he'd swallowed a hurricane."

This time, Jess's smile was genuine. She could well imagine her father looking just as Edmund described. "So you paced with him?" she asked.

"No, I simply moved the furniture out of his way and stayed clear while he thundered. Your mother was so tiny, he was afraid for her. Rather than show fear, he grew more determined that she would be fine. At times he seemed almost angry." Edmund considered Jess. "I've seen that in you on occasion."

Seth grunted his agreement, and Jess was tempted to lift her moccasin and toe him backward into the bowl of water. "On occasion," she echoed.

Seth tore a clean bandana in half and knotted one part around her palm. While he bandaged her second hand, Jess told Edmund about Jake's mission, and her own here in Carson City. Then she told him about the amount that had been erased from her father's bank ledger.

When she was finished, Edmund shook his head, looking dazed, grim. "I never would have suspected Mr.

Abbott capable of murder," he said. "He used to be a family man, married once, if I recall correctly. I believe his wife passed on some years ago, perhaps shortly after he moved here. I'm not certain. He's kept to himself mostly." Steam billowed from the teapot on the stove, and Edmund rose to attend it.

Jess thanked Seth, then leaned forward and stretched her back. "Edmund, do you have any idea where my father's money could have come from?"

Edmund dusted a silver tray and lifted teacups from a display, leaving the price card behind. "Greenbriar always did very well. Young men around Lexington were willing to pay a good price for horses before the war, and your father's were among the best. When he moved your family here, he would have closed his account at his bank in Lexington and withdrawn the balance, and that must have been a substantial sum." Edmund glanced at her while spooning tea leaves into a piece of cheesecloth. "We never discussed dollar amounts beyond those of the store, mind you, and he made a number of investments once he arrived in Carson City, though I don't know how many or of what kind. I don't believe for a moment that he stole the money, so if that's what you're thinking, you can rest your mind."

She hadn't been thinking that. Well, not for more than a moment, anyway. Her father had worked hard and invested wisely. People who worked as hard as her father weren't thieves.

Could he have saved a large sum over the years in Kentucky and earned the rest here? The imports store had profited very well while the economy complied. Yes, taking Greenbriar into account, and her father's inclination to store up rather than to spend foolishly, he could possibly have amassed a comfortable fortune. Even so, Jess had the feeling that there was another contributor or contributors.

Edmund placed a china tea set on the end table beside Jess, interrupting her thoughts. He sat again and served neatly, with barely a rattle of cups on saucers. Seth sat on a hard wooden chair and stretched out his legs, receiving the cup of tea. Had Jess not been watching for his frown, she wouldn't have seen it. No doubt Seth wished the steam was rising from a mug of thick, hearty coffee rather than tea. To her surprise, she realized that she felt the same.

"I wired Isaac's solicitor in San Francisco once more, less than a month ago," Edmund said. "He never found your father's will."

Her heart sinking, Jess lowered her cup. "So we'll never know where else he invested."

"I'm afraid not," Edmund said.

Jess felt a jab from within. In response, she drank half of her tea.

What a conundrum she was in. And her emotions were about to split her in two. Lyman Abbott knew where the money had gone, yet before she could contact the sheriff, she had to wait for Hank to return and tell her whether the banker's actions revealed where the money had been moved. Because of her love of the ranch, she needed to wait for the arrest of the man who had contributed directly to her family's murders. The income from her father's other investments would almost certainly have been sufficient to support the ranch, but his will was gone, and now she would never know what those investments had been.

The baby jabbed. She drank more tea.

"How does one go about hiring an assassin?" she asked.

The quiet discussion between Seth and Edmund ceased. Both pairs of eyes turned to her. Seth appeared to be gauging her sanity with considerable concern.

Rolling her eyes, Jess sat upright and set the empty cup aside. "I'm not looking to send someone after Abbott," she said. Just how badly had her emotional seams unraveled at the bank? "I'm wondering how a man like Abbott found a man like Shane Porter."

Seth seemed to relax, albeit marginally, and to give thought to her question.

Edmund crossed his legs and eyed the lamp, though Jess doubted he truly saw it. "A saloon? No," he answered his own question, "people would have seen him. Outside a saloon, long after dark. Hmm, that doesn't fit either. Perhaps through another connection?" he suggested. "A mutual acquaintance?"

Seth leaned his wrists on his knees. "Jess, that's as near as no matter. Porter's dead already, and you'll have your justice on Abbott."

"He's right, Jess," Edmund said, his voice as gentle as it had always been.

Jess nodded and decided to let the matter go, though she wasn't certain she agreed with Edmund about the saloon. Someone as disreputable as Abbott might be found anywhere. The fabled wolf in sheep's clothing. The devil hidden within the smooth skin of a snake. She was glad she hadn't strangled him, for he needed the chance to find God, but she wouldn't shed tears when the man hanged.

❖⊱◈⊰—⊱◈⊰❖

"Please don't argue with me, Hank," Jess said firmly, then sought to soften her request with a little Southern charm and humor. "It'd be a shame to watch a strong man like you wear yourself out attemptin' the impossible."

Hank gave her an amused sidelong look as he gently helped her down from the wagon. When she stood beside him, his chuckle shook his belly—about the same size and shape as hers, she realized with a chuckle of her own. Then their amusement subsided, and they were left with a brilliant May sunrise slanting down, the Carson City cemetery stretching out beside them in soft light and shadow, and the long night of her standing watch at Abbott's many hours ahead.

Hank lowered his pink face to give her his best fatherly frown. From him, it was the look of a doting cherub recommending a child not eat cookies before supper. "Seth and I will continue to watch Abbott, Jessica. You and that baby need sleep."

"Then you shouldn't have shown me where he lives," she said. Hank's mouth almost curved into a genuine frown, so she patted his arm to reassure him. "I'll sleep all afternoon. You and Seth need rest too. You both came to Carson with me more than a month ago as a favor to Jake, to see to my well-being. All that's happened since we arrived, this watching Abbott's movements, neither of you agreed to that...nor should you continue to do so," she went on when he opened his mouth to speak. "This is a matter that *I* must attend to now."

Jess had meant to help keep watch right from the beginning, but then she'd gone to stay at Edmund's, and he'd immediately insisted he would be most appreciative of her help at Hale Imports. He had clearly needed it. She had sat in a comfortable chair, her feet elevated, updating books that had gotten behind when customers had crowded the store after the winter snows had cleared. Then she had been too exhausted each night to awaken and slip out of Edmund's house. But no longer. She had finished updating the records last evening, and Edmund had been able to rehire his assistant for the spring, summer, and autumn. She was no longer needed at the store.

Only hours ago, shortly after midnight, Hank had observed a man ride up to Abbott's home, talk with Abbott for a brief minute, and then ride off the way he had come, away from Carson City. Such a meeting was not the kind a mere banker would undertake, especially at that hour. It had been the first divergence from Abbott's otherwise predictable routine. Jess would not miss the second.

"Now, Jessica, Jake asked us to be here for you and for whatever you might need. That includes"—this time Hank raised his voice to cover her objection—"whiling away a perfectly leisurely day or evening playing cards or checkers with other men in front of the mercantile, or sipping lemonade and watching the moon cross under the stars while keeping one eye on Mr. Abbott. Now, both young Seth and I know just how strongly you and Jake and the good people of the ranch depend on what we learn from this bank man." He patted her arm much as she had his. "We'll tell you if he speaks to anyone, and where he goes, if he goes anywhere but to the bank and home, just as we have done."

Jess smiled. Apparently, Hank didn't yet know her well. This moment was not the one in which she would enlighten him.

Lifting the hem of her lavender skirt, she took his arm and let him lead her among the cool, damp green grasses that brushed her calves, that bowed then rose between the grave markers as the fingers of the breeze caressed them like harp strings. Jess nodded in the direction of her family's marker, and Hank, with his customary patience and leisure, strolled toward it, rounding other headstones and taking in the peaceful morning sensations with her.

Above them, the red rocks of the western slopes of Mount Davidson lay in morning shadows, a broad cascade of burgundy earth flowing from the mountain's peaks down into the rich green grass and gray-green desert sage that pooled humbly at its feet. The green and gray-green sage, vibrant beneath the sun, spread out northward and southward for miles, a valley between the high spires of Mount Davidson to the east, and those of the Sierra Nevadas to the west, interrupted only by the town of Carson City, which huddled between them.

The West was a land of extremes, Jess reflected. Desert and Eden. Harshness and beauty. Rugged and rejuvenating. A wilderness God had created, and then had sprinkled with treasures. It wasn't a place for those who preferred what was easy. Surely He meant it for those who thrived on challenge, and who loved what was rare.

A pair of hawks rode the wind above, wings glinting like topaz in a gilded, diamond-blue sky. One turned its head and called to the other, and the canyon walls echoed its sharp cry. The people of Carson City, who rushed to get more, buy more, have more—did they stop to look up, to take in the wonder of sound and flight, of color and warmth and wind? Since she had been back in town, Jess had seen none of it, only quick paces and heads bent over lists of tasks, barely sparing the emptiest of smiles.

Her family had once amassed wealth and belongings, and then she had lost it all. Then, at the ranch, she'd discovered that beyond four walls containing a horde of possessions, there existed a world outside, one filled with riches. The cool, musky scent of sage. The sharp, fresh tang of pine. Soft purling sounds of a stream gliding through time-smoothed stones. A rabbit's feet whispering over grasses. The sweet smell of hay. The bristly swish of a horse's tail as it swings. The touch of a foal's nose as it shyly nudges her hand. Jess tipped back her head, thrilling at the feel of the zephyrs wending through her hair. She had received cold glances of disapproval in town for leaving it unbraided, but who could bind her hair on a day such as this?

This was the reward God gave to His children for accepting His love—more of His love in return, poured out in moments like these. Problems came and always would, and sadnesses came and always would, but to ensure peace amid them, the Almighty provided treasures like these. One need only condition oneself to step out of the rush and experience all that existed within every beautiful moment.

"What are you thinking, Jess?" Hank asked.

Jess realized they had already been standing before the grave marker for a minute or two, and she was surprised at the question. She had become accustomed to ranchmen, who, by nature, never asked personal questions since they didn't care to have personal questions asked of them. But Hank was not a ranchman. He was a farmer, a painter. A cherub.

"I was just enjoying the peacefulness here."

Hank hooked his hands around his suspenders. His smile as his gaze probed her face was one of gentle concern. "This place hasn't always been peaceful for you, though."

Jess tried not to look away but couldn't help it. She stared out toward Mount Davidson, where the sun crept higher and the shadows crept back. She had learned that Hank, as a man, didn't always understand women's motivations, but as an artist, when he paid close attention, he noticed even the finest details in a person's expressions and translated them well. "Of course, this place hasn't always been peaceful," she answered softly. "Jake and Edmund buried my family. Did you know that? I wasn't even here. I didn't visit here until months after they died." She risked a glance at him. "It's the one sadness of my pregnancy, other than that I haven't seen Jake in weeks. They'll never know their grandchild."

Hank made a sound of understanding and looked over toward three wagons filled with people that had just arrived. The men and women were all dressed in black, in mourning. One man lifted down a child-sized wooden coffin, then set it on his shoulder. He carried it to where a dusty man waited with a shovel near a newly dug grave. The pastor separated himself from the small gathering and opened a Bible.

Jess listened to the pastor's voice rather than his words, soothing, compassionate, rough with sorrow. When the time came to lower the box into the ground, the man who held it, the child's father, Jess surmised, cradled it in his arms, head bowed over it, his sobs carrying on the wind.

No one tried to hurry the man. No one tried to make him let go. The others stood, crying quietly, in the dappled shade of the tree above them. This was the last time the man would hold his child until Jesus returned to bring them together again. Jess knew how desperately he wanted his child back, even for a moment, just to hug that wonderful person once more. He just stood, and cried, and held that box. And Jess realized she was crying with him. This was one of those moments that God gave, one more moment for the father and family to live in, before the child was buried and they began a life without him.

The breeze stilled, and Jess heard one of the women speak, asking a friend or sister for a handkerchief. Her voice lifted with the warm, soft lilt of the South. "She sounds like she's from Georgia," Jess murmured.

"They're from Alabama," Hank said. "I heard about it yesterday at the mercantile. One of those bands of crazed Unionists attacked the father's home, north of here, and began shooting. A woman was shot—the child's aunt, if I heard it right—and the young boy there was killed."

"The casket is small. He couldn't have been more than a year old."

Still clutching the casket to him, the father knelt, then laid the box in the grass beside the grave that patiently waited. A woman knelt beside him and placed her hand on top of his where it held to the lid of the narrow box.

Hank turned to Jess, wiping sweat from his pink face and bald head with a bandana. He blotted his eyes too, then his gentle smile was back in place. "I know you miss your family, the same as I miss my sweet Mary, but is that all that you brought me here to tell me?"

Jess avoided his gaze again and turned her face into the wind to let it brush strands of chestnut hair back from her cheeks. "I wanted to share the sunrise here with you, but I also wanted to ask you a question," she confessed, "and I had to ask you away from Edmund, so that he wouldn't be sad because of it."

"I see. Would you like to sit down?"

"Thank you, but I'm fine. What I wanted…what I need to know is, how much time must pass before…. Well, you lost Mary before I lost my family, and…."

"You want to know how much time must pass before the pain of it fades."

"No. I need to know how much time must pass before the rage of it fades."

"Oh. Well, I lost Mary over months, to disease. You lost your family all at once, to murder. That changes things a bit." He walked around her and looked into her face. "You're still troubled by how you tried to choke Abbott when we first arrived in Carson."

Jess threw up her hands in frustration. "Yes! I was so furious that I wasn't even aware of what I was doing!" The mourners peered in their direction, and Jess forced herself to quiet. "Look at these graves. Look at what Abbott did to my family and to Miriam, and to Edmund and me. Do you think these are the first people he has hurt? Do you think they'll be the last?" She waved to indicate the mourners. "When a murderer strikes another family, we may feel empathy toward the survivors, but the attack wasn't against us. It wasn't personal. We may feel empathy, and we may want the man responsible hung, but we don't feel compelled to pursue the matter until the noose is wrapped around his neck. I know what it feels like to want to knot the rope at his throat, and I've lived with that feeling since my family died." Jess pushed back her hair, vexed with it now, and with the wind.

"You're frightened because you could have killed a man."

"No, I've killed men before, in self-defense. It was a clear choice—either an innocent person dies or a murderer dies."

"Only you didn't attack Abbott out of self-defense. You attacked him out of revenge."

"I'm not certain. I haven't worked that out yet in my mind or heart. Partly it was out of anger for my family, and partly because I'm furious that he's had two years in which he may have hurt someone else. If he continues to walk about free, who else will he murder?"

Hank began to lead her toward the wagon. "Then what's troubling you, Jessica?"

"I don't know! I think it's because of the rage that I lost control. He wasn't wielding a gun. It wasn't a choice of who was going to live. He deserves to hang, but if an innocent life isn't in imminent danger, then he also deserves the chance to find God and forgiveness, doesn't he? I would want that chance, in his place."

"Ah, I finally understand what all this is about. You feel rage at what Abbott has done, and rage that he is still free to harm others, but you also realized, after your confrontation with him, that there might be a thread of decency in him that would allow him to turn to God."

"Yes. Yes, that's it exactly." They paused beside the wagon, and Jess petted the horse without thinking. Feeling the smooth warmth of its side comforted her.

"That's why we have laws and judges. Well, much of the United States does." Hank chuckled. "A trial is a fair form of justice—at least it is if the judge is honest—but the trial process also gives the defendant the chance to turn to his Father, and to be blessed with His forgiveness. Jesus told the man on the cross that he would be with Him in paradise. It's never too late to turn to God." He nodded toward the cemetery. "It's also never too soon."

"Now Abbott will have that chance," Jess reflected. "Though he doesn't deserve it."

Hank helped her up into the wagon seat, then climbed in beside her and took up the lines. "I expect none of us deserves it," he said. He released the brake and clucked the horse into motion.

The cemetery slipped away behind them. The Hale grave marker eased from view, and the father was finally lowering the small casket into the earth.

"I may want Abbott to have the same chance to find God that I've had," Jess said. "But I still feel rage."

Hank glanced over at her, then turned his attention back to the road. "I know you do, Jess," he said. "It should begin to fade once justice is done."

Chapter Thirteen

The ride into Carson City calmed Jess, enough that she didn't miss Hank's subtle look down the side street they passed, where Gusty's shop was located. He stared forward again and blinked as if to clear his vision. His eyes latched onto the street ahead, but Jess suspected he didn't see so much as a wheel rut.

She wasn't sure whether to laugh or growl. Men in love were denser than iron.

"Hank, why is it that we've been in town for more than a month, and you haven't gone back to see Gusty once?"

He glanced at her, a manful attempt at a blank look, which was nonetheless peppered with panic. "W-whatever would bring her to mind?"

"Well, I suppose the fact that we crossed her street back there, and your eyes all of a sudden seemed welded to her storefront."

He lifted his chin as if to loosen his collar's grip on his throat, then struggled to answer.

The cherub, it seemed, had taken two rounds at point-blank range from Cupid.

"Hank, how long were you and your wife married?"

"Thirty-two years."

He breathed easier now, though Jess had no idea where the wagon was headed. She hoped they stopped before they reached the rim of the Grand Canyon.

"Surely you courted her?"

A shoulder lifted. "Not so much. She was the neighbor girl. I asked her to marry me, and she said yes."

Jess's heart sighed. It sounded so sweet. So right. "How old were you?"

His cherry cheeks darkened. He rubbed his nose with a knuckle. "Seven, and she was four." He slanted Jess a look of pure delight. "Her mud pies were something really special."

Jess laughed and raised her eyebrows. "I'm sure they were."

"After she learned that I preferred mine without rocks, she'd sit there right in the mud in her pink pinafore, picking the nuggets out of mine."

"You were right to marry her," Jess said, and she knew that he had been. Any young lady or gent who'd do so much for another person would be worth holding on to. "Did you do something kind for her in return?"

Hank tilted his head in mild embarrassment. "I borrowed my mama's metal vegetable strainer, tipped it upside down over a chipmunk, and slid a plate under it." Another boyish glance. "I thought she'd be impressed."

Jess was smiling so wide that her cheeks hurt. "What happened?"

"Well, little Mary, she looked through those holes at the chippy, and the chippy looked back through those holes at Mary, and I thought for certain my bride-to-be had just given her heart to another. But then the chippy shrieked, and then Mary shrieked, the two of them startling each other, and I yelled because they'd both startled me, and when I did, my hand holding the vegetable strainer jerked, knocking the strainer from the plate, and the chippy scampered off into the woods…right across Mary's lap, and that scared her more, and she screamed like a whole tribe of banshees. Of course, being seven, I thought the whole thing was hilarious, and I laughed until I nearly split my britches. Mary was so mad she didn't talk to me for nearly an hour, and I thought my heart would break."

"But then she forgave you?"

"She had to. She wanted to be pushed while she sat on the rope swing, and since she was the oldest child in her family, I was the only one around to push her." Hank shook his head. "So I pushed. I thought my arms would fall off from aching before she'd decide to talk to me again."

Jess recalled the many paintings Hank had done of Mary, most of them set outdoors. She knew, with hearing Hank speak of her, that they had loved well.

"Hank, tell me, why is it that you can be so comfortable talking about Mary and mud pies, yet squirm like a worm on a hot road whenever talk turns to Gusty?"

The bandana was in his hand again. Patting, patting.

"I…didn't grow up with her."

If he turned much redder, Jess was afraid the poor man might burst.

He tucked the bandana in the direction of his pocket, kept tucking. Couldn't connect with the pocket. Finally he just gripped the bandana in his hand. "I didn't grow up with Gusty," he repeated.

"No," Jess said gently. "But you could grow old with her."

The shoulder lifted again, and he sighed. "She lives here."

"Yes, she does," Jess agreed. "Because she has to. She might not want to stay here. Would you?"

He thought about that. "I would if she wanted to," he admitted.

Jess breathed in deep and let the air rush out with a peaceful smile. Hank was already in love with Gusty. That would make her job simpler.

"Hank?"

"Hmm?"

"Do you suppose we could turn around and head back toward Carson City? I don't know enough Spanish to continue riding much farther south."

He flushed again, in regret. "I'm sorry. You're almost eight months along. This wagon seat can't be comfortable for you." With a practiced hand, he turned the horses and headed back, sparing her another glance of concern. "How do you feel?"

"Like an ox."

He frowned. "You mean you feel big?"

"No, I mean I'm so hungry I could eat an ox. Promise me you'll take me to lunch."

His chuckle was as warm and hearty as the sunshine and the Sierras combined. "I'll take you to lunch. Seth is on watch until five."

Good. That left them the whole afternoon together. Jess hoped that business poured through Gusty's shop as slow as maple syrup.

Hmm. Now that she thought of it, she hoped maple syrup tasted delicious poured over roasted ox.

❖◦◈◦◈◦❖

"Jess, dear! It's wonderful to see ye," Gusty, never one to quibble over formality, called out to her from the back of the shop where she was helping a customer. She patted the woman's shoulder, murmured an excuse, and hurried around tables of fabric to grip Jess in a hug. "Now, don't ye be tellin' me ye came here alone."

"No, Hank will be here in a while. I sent him back to the boardinghouse where he's staying for his canvas and paints. If it won't be a bother to you, I asked him to do a painting for me of the inside of your store."

"No trouble at all," she assured Jess. "Though why would ye want a paintin' of the dress shop?"

Her face alight with curiosity, Gusty clasped her hands before the indigo skirt at her plump waist. The shade of blue, Jess observed, deepened the blue of the shopkeeper's eyes, as well as complemented her copper twist of hair, which was swept with silver strands like fine filigree. Gusty was perhaps five to ten years younger than Hank, and her pretty face was youthful still. Already, Jess could see Augusta Scott as a painting on Hank's wall…and as his wife. A blend of joy and warmth and jewel tones that fit so perfectly with the man himself.

Jess smiled and sighed as she smoothed a hand over a bolt of velvet on display. "I have memories of visiting here with my mother," she answered, delighted to share part of the truth and perhaps help bring two good people together, and delighted that doing so helped her to feel closer to Jake. "It's nice to be able to remember a special place, don't you agree?"

"Aye, that I do."

Hank appeared in the window of the door to Gusty's shop, framed like one of his paintings by the wood that held the window glass. His eyes settled on Gusty. He looked nervous and happy, and just then Jess wished a tree existed nearby, one with softly shadowed privacy and a romantic rope swing where he could push Gusty and the two could be alone. Jess determined to make do. In his arms Hank carried a fresh canvas, an easel, a much-used painter's cloth to cover the floor, and a sack of what Jess knew must be paints and brushes. Shifting the canvas, he pushed open the door.

"And a painting," Jess continued, "provides color, something a photograph can't do."

"Sure, and it sounds lovely. Hank, it's a pleasure to see ye, and it's kind of ye to paint a picture of the store. Where would you like to set up?"

Clearly he had given it thought, for he nodded toward the sofa. "There, if it won't be a bother." He blushed, but his voice shook only a little. "From that back corner, I'll be able to see most of the store and the front windows."

"It won't be a bother at all!" Gusty bubbled with laughter. "Imagine, my shop bein' painted, as if it were one of those fancy castles in Ireland!" She elbowed Jess and winked one twinkling blue eye. "Now, dear, ye'll just have to do with callin' me 'yer ladyship.'"

Her giggles followed her as she returned to continue assisting her customer and, knowing Gusty, to share, with her contagious effervescence, all the to-do about the painting.

Hank's worm-on-the-road jimjams diminished as his artist's side came to the fore. Almost unself-consciously, he laid out the paint-speckled cloth, set a wooden chair and the easel atop it, then propped the canvas in its place on the easel, casting only occasional glances at Gusty, who twittered gaily with her customer over the fabric she had chosen. His eyes connected with the shopkeeper and his mouth twitched each time Gusty tossed her head and giggled. Jess knew he was probably unaware of his reaction. Humming softly now, Hank settled into the chair beside the sofa, arranged his paints on the floor cloth within reach, adjusted the angle of the easel, and then studied the room, a fist propped on his thigh as he contemplated. Finally, he scraped a pencil tip along a blade to sharpen it, then began.

All this Jess had watched from the soft yet weathered sofa, where she had collapsed in satisfaction, ready to give her feet a rest and well positioned to nudge the sprouting romance along, should conversation falter. The sofa's placement offered an additional benefit: it sat behind Hank and to one side, where she could watch the drawing, and later the painting, emerge.

For nearly half an hour, while Gusty took her customer's measurements in a dressing room, chatting with her all the while, Hank's pencil skimmed over the canvas in arcs, lines, and whorls. In the upper left, he outlined the stacked shelves of fabrics and lace that reached nearly to the ceiling, though he kept a section free of lines nearer the center of the canvas. The upper right showed the tall, rectangular mirror in its frame, and the baskets of remnants and ribbons that lined the wide front window. Gusty's potted plants in their small clay pots huddled on the wood plank floor at the bottom of the drawing to the far right, and on the lower left, the tables appeared beneath more bolts of fabric, and finally the plush ottoman with its display of sofa pillows. Still, each time Gusty laughed, the corner of Hank's mouth twitched. He rested his drawing hand on his knee and eyed the canvas, then the room, and back again.

An oval in the upper-left center of the drawing remained curiously blank.

Jess's feet had begun to throb. She pushed herself up, taking Hank's hand when he offered it. Hoping she wouldn't cause him too much trouble with his drawing, she lifted the display of sofa pillows, tucked them onto a shelf, and pushed the ottoman over to the sofa, where she sat again. When she lifted her feet, Hank kindly positioned the ottoman beneath them.

"Thank you," she breathed and sent him a grin. "An odd tribute to history, isn't it?" she said. "The Turks build an empire, and we name a footstool after them."

Hank's smile reached nearly to his ears. "So, what do you suppose history will say of our times?"

"Queen Victoria will be remembered for fashion," Gusty sang out from the dressing room.

"I'm sure King George will be remembered," Jess said. "And Napoleon."

"Napoleon?" Gusty scoffed. "The way history is taught, he'll be lucky to have a pastry named after him."

Focusing again on his craft, Hank eyed the room once more, then the canvas. Next, he selected brushes, readied his palette, and applied a smooth strip of red-brown along the edge of the shelf he had drawn.

Jess looked around behind Hank to the sofa pillows she had removed from the ottoman. Their covers were sea-green liquid silks and cool, rose-petal-soft satins in varying shades of reds and pinks. Jess leaned down. Arranged artfully on the floor beside the sofa were more pillows of velvets, linens, and wools in purple, blue, nutmeg. Most of the pillows were embroidered with interlocking diamond shapes in gold or silver thread, or edged in lace with tassels at the corners. Each pillow was unique, and each a masterpiece of crafting.

"Gusty?" Jess called. "Where did you find these pillows?"

Gusty stepped out of the dressing room, jotting notes, and paused to see what Jess was referring to. "Find? I didn't find those, m'dear. I made them!" Her customer hurried to meet her, and the two verified the pattern the woman had selected. Gusty rechecked her math, received a deposit on the sewing work she would do, and assured the woman of the day she should return for the fitting. After they bade each other a good afternoon, the woman left amid the jingle of the tiny bells affixed to the door, and Gusty set the fabric the woman had selected on her worktable, along with the woman's pattern and measurement information.

"Gusty?"

The Irishwoman made a few additional notes, then dusted her hands triumphantly and bustled over to view Hank's progress. "How are ye comin' along, then? Well now, that's just beautiful. Already the colors are goin' on. Oh, Jess, dear. Ye had a question, I believe. Do ye see how beautiful he's paintin'?"

Gusty's admiration for his work was unmistakable. The fact that Gusty seemed, for the moment, more intrigued by Hank's presence than her own couldn't have delighted Jess better. Gusty rested her hand on the back of Hank's chair, just behind his neck, as naturally as if it belonged there. As she watched deft flicks of the brush add vivid depth and dimension, Gusty bent her fluffy orange head near to Hank's bald, pink-red one, and Jess bit her lip to hold in her ill-timed sense of humor. *The carrot and the radish,* she thought. In every way, these two truly were a perfect blend.

Offhandedly, she wondered if the restaurant across the way was still serving dinner.

Gusty abruptly spun and slapped a hand to her forehead. "Great Scot, Jessica, dear, ye had a question." Attentive now, she lifted her indigo skirt aside and plunked down beside Jess.

"The pillows." Jess grunted softly as she bent to lift one, pressing her free hand to her stomach, as if that would help hold it in place. "How long have you been sewing these? I don't remember seeing them the last time my mother and I came here to have our ball gowns made."

Gusty's exuberance dimmed like the flicker of a flame under a sudden wind, then bobbed back nearly to its full brilliance, though a new tightness around her blue eyes told Jess the enthusiasm had somehow been strained. She thought back over her words. Her mother...the ball gowns. Last year, while Jess had been in Carson City and had seen Gusty for the first time since the fire, Gusty had told her that she'd brought a finished gown to the Hales' neighbor for her final fitting that night, and that she had seen the blaze overtake the house. Jess recalled how upset Gusty had been when she'd told Jess about the fire as she had seen it. Gusty may have seen her mother in the upstairs window. She may have seen her succumb to the flames. All too ready to leave their mutual nightmare behind, Jess turned the pillow in her hands to draw Gusty's gaze to it.

"You must have been sewing these for years," Jess added softly.

"That I have!" Gusty hooted, apparently as eager as she was to fasten hearts and minds onto something whole and lovely. "When I was just a small colleen—no greater than six or seven—my mum—she was Katherine, Katie, my father called her—she owned a shop just like this one at the edge of the town where we lived in Ireland. She

211

had more woolens, of course—ye find sheep there the same as ye find cows here—dottin' the green hills thick as fireflies dottin' a summer's night. Anyway, I was six or seven, as I said, and as my mother sewed gowns for the hoities—"

"The hoities?"

"As in hoity-toities," she said, her humor and rolling accent adding a light whisper over the *t*'s. "Wealthy folk, women of consequence, who had more gowns than a poor man's pallet had bedbugs. Few patrons had use for the fancy remnants, so my mother, bein' Irish and abhorin' waste, told me I could have the remnants and the profits from whatever I set my hand to in the use of them."

She paused to look over Hank's shoulder at his work. As if he could sense her interest, his neck grew a full shade darker, though his paintbrush never wavered.

"She had ribbon cuttings too, and lace, and embroidery threads. This very sofa sat in her shop—it was all I brought with me when I sailed from Ireland—well, this and a trunk of my clothes and whatnot—and the sofa's been recovered since, but I used to sit right here and stitch those fabrics and laces into pillows, which sold rather nicely, once Mum helped a bit with offerin' ideas for designs."

"Did you ever make mud pies?" Hank asked, his attention on his painting.

"Mud pies, no, but to some of the children who lived there and about, sheep droppin's made for fine enough plates and cups, I recall bein' told, until they dried, that is. I expect then they crumbled. Why would ye be askin' about mud pies?"

Hank's head bowed, and his shoulders shook. He held the paintbrush away from the canvas. Startled, Jess sat upright, thinking fast, desperate to salvage the precious bonds that had threaded their way between them.

Then Hank's bald head tipped back, and he howled in laughter, gasping for breath as tears ran from his eyes.

Gusty tilted her head as if offended, but her blue Irish eyes shone in amusement, not that Hank could see, sitting, as he was, with his back to her. "And just what are ye laughin' at, Hank Beesley? Is a fine man of the arts like yerself above sculptin'?"

Gusty was laughing with him now, and Jess joined in, partly cringing at the absurd turn the conversation had taken.

"I didn't say as I made plates and cups with the other children," Gusty explained, "but I could see the sheep in the hills out my mum's shop windows, and the children told me of their adventures, true enough, but I couldn't stop myself from the makin' o' pillows."

The bandana was out, and Hank was wiping his eyes. Rather than pick up the paintbrush again, he lifted the pencil and lightly sketched cloud shapes beyond the store's window where Carson City's shops should have been. Then he added a few arcs like the tops of rainbows, and Jess realized the cloud shapes he was adding were sheep, and the arcs hills, helping to bring Gusty's happy memories of her mother's store into the painting.

Gusty smiled her pleasure and softly patted Hank's shoulder in gratitude.

"In time," Gusty went on, "I became nearly as well-known for my pillows as my mum for the gowns she sewed." Looking thoughtful, she rose and collected blue squares of cloth for a pillow she had begun, along with scissors, needle, thread, and gold embroidery thread, then sat again beside Jess. She took Jess's hand, flattened her fingers comfortably together, then began winding the embroidery thread neatly around Jess's hand, loop after loop after loop. "Then when I was nearing fourteen or so, a lady entered the shop whom Mum had sewn for, and who had bought two or three of my pillows. She asked if I could make cushions for her carriage seats and offered to pay an astonishing sum, in gold."

Jess held her fingers still as Gusty ceased winding and cut two new pieces of gold thread from her spool, each piece several inches long. When Gusty didn't immediately continue the story, Jess prodded, "So, what did you do?"

Concentrating now, Gusty produced a slender crochet hook, slipped it carefully between Jess's top finger and the loops of embroidery thread, then pulled one of the new gold threads halfway through and knotted it on top, securing all the loops together at one end.

With a small nod of accomplishment, she continued. "I had no idea at all how to go about makin' a carriage seat." Gusty speared Hank and Jess with a conspiratorial gaze. "But she didn't know it, so of course I said yes!" She laughed at the memory. "Then all at once, my brain became mired, mud-like, and my mum had to quietly tell me to go measure the carriage seats so as not to leave the lady standin' there doin' nothing more than holdin' down the floor."

She gently nudged the crochet hook between Jess's first and second fingers, then pulled half the second piece of thread through. With it, she loosely tied the cluster of loops. Jess could see now that Gusty was forming a tassel.

"After she left and I started sewin', I was so excited that I kept makin' mistakes and sewin' the wrong places, so I had to remove thread and start again, a dozen times or more. Finally I got it right, and they fit into the carriage just perfect." Breathing a sigh of happy reminiscence, Gusty eased the loops off of Jess's fingers and tightened the second knot she'd made, about an inch below the first. Plying the scissors, she cut the bottoms of the loops down their middles, then trimmed the bottom threads even.

Jess stared, enchanted, at the tassel Gusty had so easily made.

On the canvas, Hank sketched a woman's shape into the oval he had left empty, the back of a woman's shape. Then, in the mirror, Gusty's pretty face began to appear beneath his talented hand. Jess knew that the painting she had originally asked Hank to paint for her would likely be finished for Gusty. As the Irishwoman began sewing the tassel to a corner of the pillow, Hank gave Jess a private wink, then held her gaze with a look of heartfelt gratitude. Jess gave him a hint of a nod and a soft smile in return.

"My father—Colin was his name—he was another artist, like yerself, Hank. A glassblower he was. He made that blue vase in the corner there—that's what I managed to bring from Ireland to remind me of him. I watched him make that one Saturday afternoon when—"

Tiny feet thumped down the stairs from the living quarters above, and Gusty was instantly out of her seat. Jess saw the skirt of a pale pink dress that brought to mind Hank's story of little Mary's pinafore. Then Jess glimpsed shoulder-length dark blonde curls, and one blue eye peeking curiously around the corner of the stairway…gazing at the pretty room, at Hank and his painting, at Jess. Jess smiled and waggled her fingers. The girl smiled and waved back, her hand still plump with babyhood. When Gusty reached the bottom of the stairs, she scooped up the girl in her arms and briefly hugged her tight, pressing her face, then a kiss, to the child's hair. Gusty's gaze was deeply apologetic, but Jess smiled easy assurance and waved her on to see to her charge. With the toddler settled on her hip, tiny fingers absently splayed against her back, Gusty headed upstairs, her attention on the child.

A needle of pain speared Jess's heart as she was reminded of her baby sister, Emma, and of Broderick, who had died years before, as a baby even younger than Emma had been. Losing Broderick had been horrible for her and Ambrose both, but Jess knew that for Ambrose, losing Emma had been even harder, even though he never got to meet her. She knew he would always carry that with him as one of his most difficult regrets.

Jess realized that her morose thoughts had her protectively clutching her stomach with both hands, and she gentled her hold. Yet, her thoughts continued to harrow her. Two of her siblings had died as infants, and her mother had miscarried twice besides. Jess had been unable to conceive for more than a year, and she often feared when the baby within her stopped moving for long periods of time.

She trusted God, she reminded herself. She *had* to trust God. *"Be strong and of a good courage; be not afraid."* Holding tight to the strength of those words from the book of Joshua, Jess silently prayed for her and Jake's baby, and for her husband's safety. Then she prayed for the boldness of a lion for what she must do in the hours ahead. Finally she prayed for Gusty, in the event the child was more than merely her charge. Clearly Gusty had strong feelings for the child, and the young girl's eyes, Jess recalled, were blue, like Gusty's.

From upstairs, Jess could hear the woman's cheery voice murmuring enthusiastic responses to whatever the child said. Her heart lighter from having left her concerns with God, Jess used her feet to push the ottoman aside and sat forward to warmly squeeze Hank's arm. "The pillow Gusty's making is of the same fabric as the curtains she made you last year," Jess told him softly.

"Is it?" he said, his tone light, intrigued. Near the top center of the canvas, he added color to the drawing in the oval. The back of Gusty's hair took shape; then he dabbed the same yellow-orange to the reflection in the mirror. He switched brushes, picked up a new paint color with the bristles, then Gusty's dress started to take shape, first the back of her, then the tinier image reflected in the mirror.

Gusty slowly descended the stairs, gripping her hands as if in dire need of prayer. "Jessica, dear...how can I even begin to apologize?"

"It's fine," Jess assured her. "Perhaps not all customers understand a shopkeeper who must also care for a child, but I certainly do. A Paiute woman friend of mine at the ranch—Lily—has two daughters, and she undertakes many jobs that keep her busy. Besides, I don't need any special care. I'm the one who intruded on your time...for a good cause. What do you think?"

Gusty, the normally effervescent professional seamstress and shop owner, seemed at a loss for words, so she moved beside Hank to take in his progress.

Jess saw Gusty's eyes soften as she recognized the face in the mirror, and then she bit her lip. "It's like seeing my mother," she said. "I'd never realized I look so much like her."

Hank drew back the brush and smiled up at her, then picked up more paint and continued with the dress.

"That's not the dress I'm wearing," Gusty commented, her voice lilting in question.

Hank smiled up at her again. "It's the dress you were wearing the first time I saw you," he said.

Gusty tilted her head as if to say something flippant but then said nothing, only laid her hand on Hank's shoulder and kept it there.

Careful not to disturb them, Jess lifted her handbag, pushed herself up from the sofa, and slipped silently out the door. When she glanced back through the window glass, Hank was painting again, looking happier than Jess had ever seen him. Gusty sank into a chair beside him, her shimmering eyes fastened on the canvas, even as she leaned over and softly kissed his cheek.

Chapter Fourteen

"Jessica? Are you up here?"

Hearing Edmund climbing the stairs, Jess rapidly tossed her bulky package onto the dresser in his guest bedroom. She pulled the door shut, then produced an expectant smile as he topped the stairs.

"Ah, there you are." His smile was that of a man who had put in a long day's work...and who'd had an exceptionally good day, Jess decided.

"I'm missing you at the imports store already," he declared with a glimmer of his old humor in his plain but endearing face. "It's dull as a spoon there without your wit to keep things lively."

She doubted that, given the excitement he obviously held in check. Crossing her arms, she lifted an amused brow. "All right, out with it. You have news you're just itching to share."

"Have I?" Though age and dignity prevented his feet from moving, he seemed to Jess to be practically dancing in place. "What prompts you to think that?"

Beside her, the door, which she had failed to latch tightly, eased open. Jess forced her eyes to remain on Edmund, to resist the pull to the package on the dresser, hoping desperately that Edmund couldn't see it. Her smile felt like the sham it was. "What prompts the thought is that I know you. What is it?"

"Would you like to sit in the parlor?" he invited her. "You'd be more comfortable off your feet."

"Thank you, I'm fine. Edmund, what is the news?"

"All right. I received a telegram today from a man who may be interested in purchasing several of your horses. He'll arrive in town in a couple of days, and he wants to meet with you."

That was good news. After the baby was born, she and Jake would have little time before winter to find a buyer on their own. Selling a small number of horses now would save them the trouble and give them the funding to see the ranch through till next spring. It would buy them time, which, she was reminded, she had very little of at the present moment. "Edmund, that's wonderful. I'm looking forward to meeting him. Unfortunately, I must beg your forgiveness, but I'm very tired, and I think I'd best get to bed early tonight."

His forehead wrinkled in concern. "You're not staying up for dinner?"

"No, I'm afraid not. I did enjoy a rather large luncheon. It's been a long day." It had been, she realized. Had she and Hank visited the cemetery only that morning? "I'm certain I'll sleep the night through, so don't trouble Martha to check on me."

"Oh. All right. Shall I send her up to help you dress for bed?"

"I'm not that big yet, Edmund," she said, attempting to alleviate his worry. "I'll be fine."

"Are you sure? I can send for the doctor. You have only six weeks until the baby's due, and it could come early."

Jess laughed and took his arm, guiding him away from her door. "Expectant women become tired, Edmund. Nothing else is wrong." Of course, everything was wrong, but not with her physically.

"All right then." He looked doubtful and gazed at her long enough to nearly make her wince. Then he finally took his leave. "I'll see you at breakfast."

"I'll see you at breakfast," she affirmed.

He descended the stairs, and Jess silently let out her breath. Inside the guest room that had been her room for the past month, she closed the door firmly and locked it. The package, wrapped in brown paper and secured with string, lay atop the elegant, polished dresser like a dirty accusation. She had told Edmund part of the truth—that she needed to get some sleep—and she was also keeping her promise to Hank and Seth that she would rest.

Jess removed the string, then unfolded the wrapping. A man's ragged clothes that smelled of dirt and use lay atop a battered hat and a pair of old boots.

She was keeping her promise, she reflected. She would rest. Then, come nightfall, she would make her way to Abbott's house, wait for the man to fall asleep, and find a way in.

She had intended to stand watch, but she had had enough of waiting. A month had passed while Hank and Seth observed Abbott's unchanging routine. Abbott might see them at any moment and hire another Shane Porter. Jess was not waiting any longer.

If the banker kept records or money hidden in his home, she would find it. Tonight.

⬥⬥⬥

Feeling fully rested after four hours of sleep, Jess thrust the last pin into her braid to secure it atop her head, then pulled the old hat on. It sank down nearly to her ears, covering much of her forehead and nearly all her hair. It would work well. In the yellow glow of an oil lamp, the mirror reflected the shirt, vest, and britches of a potbellied drunk. The face, however, remained that of a young woman. Jess pressed her fingers into the cool fireplace soot, then rubbed the black onto her face and neck. Better. Her nose was still slender instead of bulbous, and her cheekbones and lips fine instead of fleshy, but she could do no more. Still, the sot to whom she had given new clothing in exchange for these, she mused, had gotten the better half of the deal. With the long shirtsleeves, heavy vest, and denim pants, she'd sweat a pond before the night was over.

The baby kicked, already protesting the heat. Jess patted it lovingly through the shirt and vest. "Don't fret, little one," she murmured. "You're not alone. We're in this together."

She cupped her hand over the lamp's chimney glass, blew out the flame, then mentally steeled herself against her fears.

"If an expecting mother will not work, then she will give birth to a child who is idle," Jess's Paiute friend, Red Deer, had once told her, repeating what Jake's wife, Olivia, had initially said. If that were true, Jess thought, then this child would be a fighter. He would never quit. He would never give up.

As Jess opened her bedroom door and peered into the deep evening shadows of the hall, the baby began practicing the leaps he would take as soon as he learned to run. She had no idea how pregnant women rode in *or* walked alongside their Conestogas as the wagon trains rolled west. She knew only that if they could survive it, then she would survive this.

The stillness of Edmund's home gave way to the night sounds of Carson City as she closed the back door behind her. Seth had taken to sleeping under the trees near Edmund's carriage house. She made out his form, boots still on his feet, his hat over his face, but she was unable to see his chest rise and fall in the darkness. Since the moon had set hours before, and since clouds stretched across the sky, she considered grimly, she would have to rely on breaks in the clouds and lanterns lit inside of homes to find her way to Abbott's. As far as finding her way around his house in the blackness, she'd have to devise a way once she was inside.

With the boots clutched in one hand, Jess felt with the toes of her moccasins for the edge of Edmund's porch, her empty hand grasping the rail for steadiness. Four steps down, she'd counted earlier, and she took them without a whisper of movement to alert Seth to her passing. Hank was standing watch, and she'd have to evade them both. She couldn't risk being stopped, and she refused to allow any harm to come to either of them.

She rounded the house now, pausing to look back. Seth hadn't moved. Pleased that she had accomplished her first goal that night, she started north on Mountain Street. Once she was certain she was beyond Seth's hearing, she pulled the boots on over her moccasins. A better fit, she couldn't have hoped for.

Wanting to hurry so that she had sufficient time, yet needing to mind her comportment so that she wouldn't raise anyone's curiosity if she was seen, Jess ambled north at a slow pace.

For the middle of May, the evening felt overly warm, humid. Because of that fact, nearly all the homes that she passed stood with windows open and curtains drawn back to air out the heat of the day. Unfortunately, the hour was late, ten thirty by her estimation, and most people were asleep. Only two homes had lanterns burning—one behind, one ahead—shedding mere wraiths of pale glow on the grass beneath their windows.

Rather than turn onto the road where Abbott's house was located on the far edge of town, Jess walked slowly past the turn and continued into the desert. A drunk with no sense, to anyone watching.

From an alarmingly close distance, a coyote yipped then howled, the sound plaintive, savage. An entire pack then gave rise to the cry. One keen after another pierced Jess's spine like cold spears.

Sweat began to dampen her face and trickle down her neck, whether from the heat or the threat of the coyotes, she didn't know. Fearing an attack, she angled east, easing her way between stands of sagebrush as she moved in the direction of Abbott's house from the rear.

When it came into view less than a quarter of a mile away, she crouched down as far as her girth would allow and crept forward, bracing her hands against her knees for support.

For once, the pleasant, musky fragrance of the sage leaves failed to calm her. The coyotes still howled, thankfully no nearer than they had been. She prayed the light wind wouldn't change direction and carry her scent to them.

In the sky, the clouds stretched into thin webs of gossamer, then broke apart. Jess dropped to her hands and knees. In the shadows beneath Abbott's front porch, a darker shadow had moved, a shadow the size of a man. She waited for Abbott's high, cold voice to call out, to acknowledge that he had seen her.

When he didn't call out, she realized that, had he seen her, he could be advancing toward her.

Rejecting the notion that she would be caught or would fail, she crawled southeast as quickly as she could, away from her previous position. Her heart thrummed with uncertainty, but she didn't dare raise her head to look up.

A tiny screech erupted beside her. She felt a thump against her wrist and resisted the urge to scream. A scrambling sound, then she glimpsed a small rodent scurrying away. Jess shuddered and forced herself to remain in place. She determined to be exceedingly careful where she placed her hand.

Though she heard no human footfalls, she could no longer bear the wait. She had to know whether Abbott had left his porch to search for her.

Jess bowed her head, then eased the hat off and lowered it to clasp it to her middle.

She gazed between clusters of sagebrush toward the house. She had come farther than she had thought. Abbott's back porch was no more than one hundred paces from her. And, he still stood among its shadows.

A quiet sigh of relief escaped her. Though she couldn't see his face, his frame seemed leaner than when she'd last seen him, a little more than a month before. Something in his stance told her his purpose outside was more than to enjoy the pleasure of the night. She sensed he was alert. Tense.

Slowly, she sank again among the brush, and crept closer. If he remained in back of the house, she reflected, then she would take advantage of it. She would enter through a side window and wait for the man to fall asleep.

As she came even with where she calculated the back porch to be, she turned toward the house. Then stopped.

The ground beneath her hands began to tremble. The coyotes fell silent.

Knowing that Abbott's attention would be drawn to the growing rumble, Jess risked a second glance near the tops of the sage. She was less than ten feet straight east of the porch. She could see Abbott now, bending to lift an object from the boards near his feet. His hand turned, and Jess saw that he held a saddlebag with pouches distended, straining with their contents.

In another month, she mused offhandedly, she'd know just how that felt.

Loose stones danced near her hands now as the rumble grew to a roar. Horses were approaching. A large group of them. Though Jess knew that no houses had yet been built near Abbott's, she looked frantically for a place to hide. Abbott's porch was too low; she'd never fit under. A cluster of three sage bushes a few yards away was her best option. A man standing on the porch wouldn't see her among the leaves, but for a man seated on a horse, the view might be clearer. She had no choice. She scooted among them.

A pair of grouses boomed and rattled their wings, flying at Jess's head. A scream tore from her; she instantly silenced it, knowing that the thunder of hooves and the grouses' loud whoops had almost certainly downed out her alarm. The grouses fled past her out of the brush as the horsemen reined in their mounts.

Jess stared into the sage, seeing nothing beyond. What sounded like twenty or more men dismounted, and one stepped up onto the porch.

"Evening, Abbott," the man said rather pleasantly, surprising Jess. "We received your message, so here we are. Nice evening for a ride; you couldn't have picked one better."

"I have a few jobs for you," Abbott said.

Had she heard a slight quaver in his voice?

"That's what the message said," the man noted amiably. "I trust that's our payment you're holding? Thank you."

Several seconds passed with a few of the men talking quietly or chuckling among themselves. Coldly, Jess thought. Like men who shouldered no burden of concern, who had no fear at all.

"It all seems here," the eerily pleasant man noted. "What do you need done?"

"In Dayton, a newspaperman by the name of Walter Simms. In Washoe City, a man running for the legislature—"

"Another man running for the legislature?" the man asked Abbott in mild amusement.

"Yes," Abbott's voice replied. "The man's name is Dustin Keet. Do you want to write this down?"

"There's no need."

Jess's stomach turned, sickly, to ice as she realized what she was hearing. Abbott was ordering these men, paying these men, to kill certain people. *Lord above*, she prayed, *help me find some way to stop them.*

"But first, a woman here, in Carson City," Abbott directed. "Initially, I hired Shane Porter for the job, but it needs to be completed. The woman is married now, so her name will have changed. Previously, she was known as Jessica Hale."

Shock like cold lightning ripped through Jess. The sage, the night, the very air around her, turned white as she stared outward, her mind, senses, and hearing going numb with the impact of what he'd just said. Abbott was speaking again. She had to hear him.

"...and any companions whom you see with her," Abbott said. "Her father was close friends with Edmund Van Dorn."

No!

"The owner of that imports store?" the pleasant man asked.

Jess tasted vomit, forced it down.

"Yes," Abbott confirmed. "She may be staying at his house. If she is, take care of Van Dorn too. I want this woman to be your priority."

"You want?" the man queried. A quiet threat had seeped into his voice.

"Those are your orders," Abbott said—defensively, Jess was certain.

What's happening? she wondered. *Why would Abbott's men threaten him?*

Clouds eased by overhead, darkening the desert around her. With a careful hand, Jess moved a single branch to one side, giving herself a partial view of the man who stood facing Abbott.

Abbott's hand snatched the saddlebag away from the man. "If you feel yourself incapable of the task, I'll hire someone else who will do it."

The man snatched the bag back and dangled it, laughing, before Abbott. Turning his back to him, he opened the flaps, pulled out a stack of what could only be greenbacks, and tossed it to one of the men, who caught it amid loud cheers. More stacks of bills were thrown until both sides of the saddlebags were empty. Then the man tossed the bag to Abbott and gave the banker a rather stylish salute.

"We'll take care of it," the man assured him.

The branch slipped from Jess's grasp. She moved it aside again. The men she could see were in high spirits as they returned to their horses and mounted up.

Only a few feet above her, a boot slid into a stirrup, then saddle leather sighed with sudden weight. The animal's large, eager front hooves drummed the ground, trampling sage, and nearly struck her hand.

Jess darted backward, reacting without thinking. Her heel snapped a branch of sage; the sound startled the horse, a buckskin, and drew the rider's suddenly angry eyes to hers.

"Hey!" he called to his mob, hand already drawing his gun. "There's a man here who just overheard everything!"

The revelry ceased as more guns were drawn and cocked. Jess tugged her hat onto her head, her veins burning as if her blood had turned to fire.

One member of the mob jumped down from his horse and yanked her to her feet beside him. Swiftly, Jess looked from the dirty shirt stretched over a broad chest, up to the unshaven face, and into Jake's furious eyes. Her chin trembled.

"Go on," he called over his shoulder to the men. "He's just a drunkard. I'll take care of him and meet up with you."

Jess strove to act like she was drunk—not difficult given her weak-kneed reaction to Jake's fury. His grip on her arm was the only thing holding her up.

"You know where to find us, Kane," the leader said.

Jake drew his Remington while the others rode out. Jess knew a verbal battle was coming, but she also knew they needed to deal with Abbott first.

His gun uncocked and aimed safely to one side of her, Jake propelled her up onto the porch and over to Abbott. Jess kept her head lowered and let the hat hide her face.

"You have rope?" Jake asked.

"Yes, in the cellar," Abbott said. "I'll get it."

Jake gently pushed her through the door after Abbott, then stepped in behind.

Abbott turned. "Wait, you're not bringing him in here!"

"If he stayed outside, he could have gotten away," Jake countered. "You have that rope?"

Abbott left, then Jake backed toward the door and whistled a birdlike warble out into the night. In reassurance, his hand briefly pressed her arm.

Quick footfalls returned. As they did, Jess glimpsed a pair of hands reach in from outside the living room window and take hold of the sill.

Abbott thrust the rope at Jake. "Here. Tie him."

The front door slammed open at the same instant Seth vaulted in through the window. Hank drew his own gun, thumbed the hammer back, and pointed it at the stunned bank manager, while Seth disarmed the man.

"What—?"

Jake holstered the Remington and made swift use of the rope. While he did, Jess closed the front door and tossed her hat onto a table.

Abbott's eyes widened in recognition. "You!"

Jake shoved him into a wooden chair and tied him to it.

"You're Golden Circle!" Abbott exclaimed, looking like he wanted to spit on Jess. "I should have known that the instant I heard your filthy Southern accent. Know *this*," he instructed her, his tone steadier, one of threat. "The war isn't over. Offensive Southerners like you will be *buried*."

Though she felt a prickle of apprehension at his words of hate, she also sensed, strongly, a fear of something imminent underlying his declaration. That didn't make sense. People of the Order didn't murder, so if that's who he believed her and Jake to be, he should have no immediate fear of them.

Jake secured the knot behind the chair, then immediately pulled Jess into his arms. The great love he felt flowed through him and into her as she pressed her face against him. He smelled hot and dusty...and wonderfully of horses, leather, and man. Tears pricked her eyes because she was overjoyed he was safe and holding her, and because she feared what she had seen in her premonition.

Jake pulled away and drew her with him toward the back door, lifting her hat from the table along the way. "Stay with him?" he said.

"We'll be right here," Hank told him, while Seth settled himself onto Abbott's sofa.

Outside, Jake guided her away from the house, past Cielos, and into the desert. Finally, he released her. Never had she seen him so enraged that he looked like he could break a railroad spike in two. Though she knew he'd never strike her, she backed a step away. "You promised to trust me," she reminded him.

"How could you do such a thing?" he shouted, ignoring her words. Jake never shouted. Ever. "How could you give so little thought to yourself and our child? How many wives and children do you think I can bear to lose? Haven't there been enough coffins buried in the ground?

You, Jessica Bennett, will return to the ranch at first light. You may not care about this baby, but I do!"

Jess recoiled as if she'd been slapped. "I have taken good care of the baby!" she shouted back. "If that horse hadn't sidestepped, I never would have been seen! How was I to know twenty armed assassins were going to show up at Abbott's house? I have had enough of your controlling bent. We've been through this. God did *not* intend for a wife to be a puppet on strings. If He had, He wouldn't have bothered sticking a brain in her head."

Jake's face was fierce. "This is not about me being controlling."

"Yes, it is. He created you and me both to protect others. My instinct is just as strong as yours. Hank and Seth have been spying on Abbott for a month. If he had seen them, he could have hired another Shane Porter. Abbott was the one who helped Miriam to hire him—*he's* Rafael, the manager of my father's bank, just so you know—and I wasn't going to allow him to hire another Shane Porter, especially after Hank reported seeing a stranger visit Abbott's house late last night."

"He sent a message to Bodine, the leader of that group back there."

"I realize that now, but I couldn't risk doing nothing. I had intended to get into his house while he slept and try to find solid evidence that the sheriff could use to arrest him—he knows what happened to my father's savings. The baby and I have gotten some exercise. That's all."

"And if Abbott had caught you inside his house?"

Jess pulled from her trousers' pocket the derringer she'd borrowed from Edmund's maid, who had it to keep her persistent and dangerous former husband at a distance. Jess had come to know she could trust the maid during the weeks she'd stayed as Edmund's guest.

"So, you'd be alive," Jake seethed, "but you'd be giving birth to our child in prison."

Jess pushed the gun back into her pocket. "Would you have had a better idea?" She waited.

Jake stared at her, hands on his hips, as he appeared to weigh the options. "No," he finally admitted. "Though I'm not controlling," he said, his tone a little softer. "I'm protective, just as you are."

Since he had, Jess gentled her words, as well. "If we search Abbott's house, we may find out what happened to my father's accounts. We may even find some of the money here."

"No, love, we won't find anything," he said gently. "Bodine and his men have been getting paid to attack Southerners since shortly after your pa died."

"You don't understand. I saw my father's account record at the bank. He had more than eight hundred thousand dollars in it."

Jake's hands lowered as if he had lost the ability to hold them there. "Where would your pa get that kind of money?"

"I don't know. I was hoping to find out. We can search his house now. We heard him giving the orders to kill those people...to kill me."

"No. We're going to bring the sheriff into this now, and Tom Rawlins, if we have to," he added. "We're going to follow the law. If we break it, then we're no better than Abbott or Porter or Bodine and his men."

Jess knew he was right. "Whatever we do, we'll have to act fast. Those men will come after Edmund and me tomorrow night."

Jake bristled with frustration, considering. He made a noise like a bear growl.

"Do you want to shred leather, Bennett? Chew bullets?"

He growled again.

"When you're done growling, will you tell me how you came to join those men?"

Jake took her hand and walked farther from the house until he found a large rock. He sat on the ground and leaned his back against it. Jess sat down beside him and stretched out her legs. The throbbing in her feet faded.

He told her about meeting Bodine and about the fight with the men and being knocked unconscious. "A reminder," he said, "should I ever decide to break with the group or inform on them." He said they had travelled to Placerville and Sacramento City, and around to Susanville and Honey Lake, then back to Lake's Crossing and down to the towns south of Carson City. They knew the position of every military outpost and knew of dozens of places to hide. They'd bullied folks, burned a house and a barn, which Jake had had to allow so that he could hope to find a way to snare Bodine's entire mob, but they'd killed no one, nor attempted to, until a group had broken away a few days before and killed a young woman and a small boy. "There was nothing I could do."

"Hank and I were visiting my family's grave at the cemetery this morning when the boy's family buried him. It was awful," she recalled. "His father couldn't let go of the casket."

"I know how that feels," Jake said quietly.

The baby kicked, and Jake laid his hand along her stomach. A coyote yipped near where the pack had been before. Jake must have noticed her grow tense. "It's all right," he murmured in that gentling tone he used to calm horses, then pressed a kiss to her temple. "I'm here."

Soothed, feeling cherished, she reflected that Jake noticed everything. "How did you know it was me in the sage bush?"

"I'd know that mouth anywhere. A little dirt can't hide so perfect a shape."

Jess felt herself blush—something she hadn't done in ages. "Soot," she corrected him and then lifted her mouth to his.

He kissed her warmly. Then passionately. Finally he lifted his head, though his hand still rested against her side. She'd had no idea how much she would miss his nearness, his handsome face, his touch.

"How did you know Hank and Seth were nearby?" she asked. "I didn't even know Seth was here. He was sleeping outside Edmund's carriage house when I left."

"Seems like maybe he wasn't. I noticed Hank when we rode in, though I almost didn't see him. He was half a block to the south, sitting on someone else's porch."

Jess smiled at that. It seemed Hank could be brazen when he wanted to be.

"I heard Seth's signal when we went inside," she told him.

"Jess, I'm sorry for what I said…about you not caring for the baby. I know you want the baby as much as I do. I'll always regret having said it."

"You can just forget about having said it, and I'll do the same," she said, caressing the soft beard he had grown. "I don't ever want anything to stand between us, not even words we didn't mean."

The clouds pulled apart again, letting through enough moonlight so that she could see the intensity in his eyes.

"I want to take you away from here," he said.

"Tonight? But, Jake—what about Hank and Seth? Edmund?"

"Just for a little while. I need to be alone with you."

She wanted to go. Desperately. But, the premonition— "We can't."

He tilted his head down to study her. "Why can't we?"

Clouds drifted over, once more deepening the night. If she told him about the chasm, if he knew she had seen him fall to his death, would he let her remain in Carson City and help to stop Bodine and his men? *Should* she stay? Was that what would cause the vision to come true?

"Jess?"

She couldn't live out the rest of her years within the confines of the ranch. She also couldn't leave Hank, Seth, and Edmund to their fates while Bodine's men hunted them down. Jake would know that. He wouldn't force her to go. But would keeping the premonition from Jake help him or harm him? Thinking of the possible outcomes, nothing could harm him more than the fall she had seen.

"You had a premonition," he said.

"It's bad," she whispered, unable to speak the words aloud. "Really bad."

His hand left her stomach and the frolicking of the child within her to curve gently around hers. "Tell me, love."

Jess leaned her head against his shoulder and told him.

"I wanted so badly to see you again," she said, "but I'm also afraid to go anywhere with you." The crinkles at the corners of his eyes had deepened in concern, she decided, though not alarm. "I was with Hank, Seth, and Gusty when I first saw the images, and they suggested the chasm could be anything—a cliff, a lake, a cave. All I know is that the place is dark." She looked at the cloud cover above and trembled.

"The place I had in mind for tonight is the hot spring. You can soak your feet, and the warmth will ease your aches away. The spring isn't far, about a mile or so east. I'm sure you know of it. There's the quarry, but no cliffs are near it, and no caves."

"Bodine's men could see us. Anyone could see us, and our plans could be changed without us being able to stop it."

"It's the last thing we should do," he agreed with an unusual inflection.

Jess worked to puzzle out his meaning. "You think we should do what we normally wouldn't do," she said slowly.

"Mmm-hmm."

"You think *that* might change the outcome."

"Maybe."

Recalling the images of him falling terrified her.

"Darlin', tell me what's the matter," he murmured.

That was all it took. The dam that had stabilized her heart broke. Jess found herself kneeling before him and clinging to two fistfuls of his shirt. "Jake, I love you *so* much, but ever since you had pneumonia, I've been afraid that I'm going to lose you, and that I'll have to continue the rest of my life without you. Then the vision I saw of you dying made that fear a hundred times worse. As Paul wrote in First Corinthians, if I can prophesy and understand all mysteries and fathom all knowledge, if I have all faith, enough to move mountains, and yet have no charity—no love—I have nothing at all. I can't lose you, Bennett, or I'll have lost what it means to love."

Jake's big, warm hands caressed her own, relaxing their grip. "What about the part about having all faith? You had faith that the Almighty would get me past the pneumonia, and He did. In Hebrews, it talks about great men who through their faith subdued kingdoms, brought about justice, escaped the maws of lions, and evaded the sword."

"That's what I kept praying right after I had the premonition: 'Lord above, I trust You.'"

"Then let's not stop trusting Him now, love."

"Is going to the hot spring faith in the Lord or a foolish risk?"

"No cliffs," Jake repeated softly. "No caves. Would it be foolish to return to Abbott's house?"

"No, it wouldn't be."

He leaned forward and pressed his mouth to the soft underside of her jaw, just below her ear. "Then come to the hot spring with me," he entreated her, his voice husky. "Let me be alone with you."

Jess felt her insides dissolve into liquid. Her head tipped to the side of its own accord as his mouth did spectacular things.

Absently, she thought that even a woman carved of stone would melt into vapors when pursued by a man with the touch and tenacity of Jake Bennett.

"Hand me my hat," she said.

Chapter Fifteen

I f Hank, Seth, and Abbott were not waiting for them, and if the threat to her and Edmund did not exist, Jess thought ruefully, this might very well be the most beautiful night she and Jake had ever spent together. Cielos, for once, was content to stroll, as if he knew the hazards and the unknowns that tomorrow would bring and wanted to gift them with these next few hours. His black mane and head seemed part of the night, part of the amalgam of earth and wind and life, and they were disappearing into it with him.

Jake was solid and safe as he held her on his lap. His right arm cinched her firmly to him; his left occasionally brushed her midriff as he reined the horse. She was surrounded by him, his thighs beneath her, his bearded chin resting lightly atop her head. A breeze stirred; Jess turned her face to welcome its contact with her skin. Why was it that a simple wind felt like it could whisk away the day's cares and labors, she wondered idly, as if God had intended for it to do so? Perhaps He had, she mused.

Jake passed the reins into her hand, then reached back toward the saddlebags. A moment later, he gave her a bandana wrapped around a small bundle. She returned the reins to him and began unfolding the bundle.

"Fresh biscuits and beef jerky," he explained.

"Food?" Jess's fingers dug into his hair and pulled his face down for a brisk kiss. "Yes, I'll marry you," she said, then bit deep into the fluffy, buttery bread.

"You already did marry me," he said.

She gobbled the smoky, salty meat. "Once was not enough."

Laughter rumbled in his chest.

In the bandana was enough jerky for three people. The man was a saint. "You want some?"

"Uh, no."

A *saint.*

Jake held a hand to her stomach where—she was certain of it—the baby was leaping with joy. Jake murmured into her hair, "Does he like the jerky?"

Jess nodded and swallowed. "He says if you have lemonade in your canteen, you'll be his hero."

Jake handed her the canteen. "No lemonade, I'm afraid, but tell him I'll get him all the lemonade he can handle once the authorities have Abbott and Bodine's gang in custody."

The canteen was full, and the water was wet. It was enough for now. Jess sighed and handed the vessel to Jake. He took a long swallow, then held it for her to cap. Jess finished the biscuit while he shifted her and rehung the canteen on the pommel.

Not ready to think about tomorrow yet, Jess listened to the grasses whisper and the crickets tweet—sounds that reminded her of childhood, which she and Jake would soon relive with their son or daughter. She imagined wearing a hoopskirt again—wide, like women wore in the South— so that the hot fabric was held away from the skin, and breezes could slip under and cool her right up to her waist. She'd shorten her pantalettes, cut them off at the knees... and weave her petticoat into a rug.

"What are you thinking about?" Jake asked softly.

Lovely. Fine time to ask. "Uh, clothing."

"Where did you get yours?"

Jess laid the bandana and second biscuit in her lap. She tucked loose hairs behind her ear, mildly embarrassed that the first time Jake had seen her in weeks, he had to see her like this. "From a man, outside a saloon."

Out of the corner of her eye, she saw Jake grin. "Oh? And is this man especially enjoying the breeze this evening?"

She smiled with him. "I bought him new clothes to replace these. What about your clothes?"

He glanced down at her. "I bought them new."

With barely a pull on the reins, Cielos slowed to a stop. Jake's right arm stayed at Jess's back, and his left caught her under her knees. He stepped down from the horse, carrying her with him. If he intended the move to be romantic, Jess reflected, he succeeded. He didn't even drop the biscuit.

She folded the rest of her snack into the bandana and anchored her arm around Jake's neck as he lowered her feet to the ground.

A few hundred paces away, the former Warm Springs Hotel squatted like an aging, plank ranch house, a dark shape under a dark sky. The building, such as it was, now housed the territorial prison. Jess had never been here before, so she hadn't known what to expect—certainly not this shack of a place. "Will there be any guards or prison...occupants about?"

"No need to worry, Jess," Jake said. "If we're asked to leave, we leave. If we're asked to hand over our money and our horse, we introduce them to the Remington."

Jake loosened Cielos's saddle and tied him where he could eat his fill of bunchgrass, slipping the Henry rifle from its sheath before giving the horse a final pat. "Hold on to my arm, wife," he said warmly. "With this cloud cover, we'll have to feel our way with our feet."

Jess sniffed as they walked, trying to smell the sulfur that would lead them in the right direction. "Why can't I smell the hot spring, do you think?"

"This one doesn't smell of sulfur. There. There it is. Do you feel the heat on your face?"

"Yes, and with my long-sleeved shirt, vest, denim trousers, bloomers, corset, and chemise."

She felt Jake's glance. "Ready to shuck a layer, are you, Jess?"

"The baby makes me hot," she explained.

"And cuter than a button."

She smiled. "Just for that, I'll let you kiss me."

"Let?" he teased. "Did you think you were going to stop me?"

Jess employed a little sultry Southern charm. "I had no intention of stopping you, Bennett. What was that sound?"

Jake cleared his throat. "Uh, I dropped the rifle."

"Oh. Good."

They paused as he retrieved it, and Jess bit her lip. She hated being apart from him, but reunions, it seemed, were so very pleasant.

"We're at the edge," Jake said. "Have a seat, and I'll help you with your boots."

Jess held his hand as she settled onto the ground. Yes, she could feel the heat now. She shrugged out of the vest and rolled her sleeves up. Jake was a shadow beside her, propping the rifle within reach, then kneeling. His hand lifted her calf, and then she felt a tug, and her ankle was free.

"What's this?" he asked. "You're wearing your moccasins too? I see now why you feel so hot."

His hands felt for the ties, and then he was easing her moccasin off. Helpfully, she lifted her other foot.

"I neglected to mention my footwear. How hot is this water?" She removed her hat and tossed it aside.

"Oh, about a hundred fifteen, hundred twenty degrees, I reckon."

Her other foot was free, and she wiggled her toes, loving the feel of having fewer constrictors. Jake folded back her pant legs until her calves were bare.

"There now," he said. "Put them in, but go easy. The temperature may take a little getting used to."

Heels first, Jess decided, and lowered them in. She almost jerked in response. Almost. The water was hot as chili peppers, but it also melted the aches away. Gradually, she immersed her legs right up to her calves. "Ohhh, this is so-o-o wonderful."

Jake sat down beside her, trouser legs rolled up, and eased his legs in. Jess slumped against him. This was bliss. "What, no boots?" she teased.

He slanted her a look. "This is a special occasion."

Jess was grinning. She wasn't sure when it started, but sure enough, a smile was there. "Bring me back here in the winter," she moaned.

"It should be pretty here then," he said, as if imagining it. "Snow on the ground...."

"Like a picture," she agreed.

"With the winter chill, the air will be thick with steam."

"Hmm. Sounds nice."

His arm shifted slightly against her cheek. She supposed he was looking down at her.

"You getting sleepy, little lady?"

"Hmm? No, not so much. Just relaxed." She no longer felt pain in her feet. She wasn't sure she still had feet at all. They seemed to have drifted away with the current. "There are small ripples on the surface. I can feel the rise and fall of water against my knees."

"That's the nature of most springs around here. The Washoe Indians and other tribes have been coming to this one for centuries. White settlers only discovered it in the last ten or fifteen years. There're other hot springs near the ranch. Next winter I can take you to Shaffer's Station. That won't be so far to go."

"I can already imagine it," Jess said. "You and me, up to our necks in warmth. As long as you don't get pneumonia," she added.

"Won't happen," he assured her.

"Good. We'll throw in some sage and have cowboy soup."

Jake's arm encircled her, pulling her closer against him. "Are you missing the ranch, Jess?"

"Yes," she admitted. "I imagine the garden's been planted and is already growing. Honey Lake must be getting rain. We've had plenty here."

"The horses should have plenty of grass. Enough to get them through until winter."

At the mention of the horses, Jess remembered something she'd wanted to tell Jake. "Edmund knows a man who may be interested in buying several of the horses. Edmund said he'll be in town in a day or two and wants to meet with me."

"We could sell him five or six," Jake said thoughtfully. "The income will buy us enough supplies to get us through the winter." He nodded. "That's good to hear. Five or six. Any more and we won't grow the ranch as soon as we'd like."

"I calculated the same." She drew circles in the water with her feet. Liquid warmth swirled around them and between her toes. "I wish I could see better. I have the irrational sensation that some spring-dwelling creature is going to come up under me and nibble my feet."

Jake leaned down and brushed his warm lips to the corner of hers. He lowered his voice to a murmur. "Would you mind if I nibbled, Mrs. Bennett?"

"Have I ever minded?" she responded. Then, "Jake, what do you think about sheep?"

He leaned away a little. "Sheep?"

"Yes. Hank and Gusty—you remember her, the seamstress?—they seem so right together. You should have seen them earlier today—or maybe it was yesterday now; it must be close to midnight."

"Have you been knitting hearts together again, love?" he asked.

Jess shrugged. "I put them together and started them talking. They're both alone, and caring and kind and funny. They would so enjoy being able to spend moments like this one together, the way you and I do.

"Hank and I visited Gusty's shop for part of the afternoon. He was painting a picture of her store, and she spoke about how she designed it to be like the one her mother had in Ireland when Gusty was a girl. Her mother's store was on the edge of town, and through the store's front windows, Gusty could see sheep grazing on the hills. When Hank heard that, he began to draw the hills and sheep onto the canvas."

"Well, in a painting, I suppose sheep are fine, though they don't belong on a cattle ranch. Or a horse ranch. You think Hank and Gusty belong together?"

"Maybe."

"Well, then, we'll see what the Almighty has in mind for them."

Jess heard the door close on that subject and smiled. She wasn't sure if it was because of his gender or because of the cattleman breed, but he never cared to talk about other people's matters for long. She usually felt the same, unless it came to matters of the heart.

The temperature of the water began to make her uncomfortable. She pulled her feet up on the bank and let the wind dry them as she leaned back against her hands.

Jake turned and braced a hand on either side of her hips. Judging by his manner, he was no longer interested in talk. Jess's blood heated, and she was no longer interested in teasing.

He leaned toward her. She met him halfway.

With his lips, he gave, and cherished, and stirred her. Her fingers eagerly refreshed their memory of the hard bulk of his arm muscles and the broad expanse of his back. Images of the vision surfaced; she forced them away.

Right now, in this moment, they had each other. For now, they were alive.

❖⊰⊱❖

Jess lay snuggled against Jake's side, the baby kicking Dad's ribs through Mama's belly. Jess rested her head on Jake's shoulder. Overhead, the clouds thinned enough to tell the time by the position of the stars. Two in the morning. They had nuzzled and rested for about two hours.

Dawn was only three hours away.

"Jake, what do you suppose we'll do after? After Abbott and Bodine and his men have been caught?" she clarified.

Jake inhaled deeply, as if to waken a voice that hadn't been used in a while. "You mean, what'll we do now that we have no Indian haters to battle, no drought to fight, and no militant radicals to capture?"

Jess heard the wryness in his tone and smiled. "Exactly. How will we fill our time with only horses and a child to look after?"

He knuckled the sleep from his eyes and laughed. "We could finally name the cat."

"Or put wallpaper in the outhouse."

"Or build a canoe."

Jess giggled. "A *canoe*?"

"Sure, why not?"

"Where would use it? We live in a desert."

"That didn't stop Noah."

Jess laughed harder. "Please"—she gasped—"please tell me you'll shave the beard before you look like Noah."

"We'll build a canoe, put it in the creek, and paddle downriver."

Jess pressed a hand to her stomach, as if that would stop the ache she got from giggling. "We could build two and race."

Jake looked at her, grinning the crooked grin that she loved. "The creek isn't wide enough for two."

"Easily solved—I get the lead boat."

The wrinkles at the corners of Jake's eyes were damp; she could see it in the starlight. He wiped the moisture away, still chuckling.

Jess smoothed her fingers over Jake's shirt. "We could go look for the fabled lake of gold," she said. "Perhaps we'll even find it."

He laid his big hand over hers. Squeezed. "Maybe we already have."

High above them, clouds glided past. The sky stretched over them like a huge, upside-down bowl, from horizon to horizon, a bowl of blackest hot cocoa, and the clouds were the cream that swirled on the liquid surface.

"Bennett? I think I'm hungry again."

He sat up and handed her the second biscuit and the canteen.

The night had finally cooled, she perceived as she ate. A fine mist rose from the spring. A mile away, she thought, Carson City awaited.

She finished her biscuit, drank from the canteen, and stared at the gently purling spring. "I wish we could begin the whole night over again," she said.

"I know." Jake pulled on his socks and boots, then rolled his pant legs down. "Jess, what can you tell me about Abbott?"

She sighed, resigning herself to what had to follow. "Not much more than you would have observed. He's perhaps fifty—Gusty thinks he was married once, but that his wife may have died. He's polite, as a bank manager should be, and well-spoken, but he's careful to keep to himself, to discuss nothing personal—his own business or anyone else's. His clothes are a little dated, but they were stylish when new. He's thin, thinner now than when I first saw him. Neatly trimmed hair, clean fingers. Pale skin—he doesn't work outside."

Jake was listening, and closely.

"I sensed uneasiness in him, as if he was comfortable within the bank but knew he didn't fit in well in other places or circumstances. When he first saw me a month ago, his hands shook. He hired Shane Porter, knowing, of course, that my father would die." She clamped down on the rush of bitterness. There would be time for it later. "Abbott didn't want to let me see my father's account record, as you might expect. He knew about the money—the amount that had been there, as well as where it had gone. The last I spoke with him a month ago, he was afraid, like a man who was staring into his own casket."

He processed that.

"Jake, how did you locate Bodine? No one else has been able to, neither the soldiers nor the law."

"Before we left the ranch, Hank mentioned attacks against Southerners that had happened in three different towns that sat far from each other. To many folks, those attacks in those places would seem random. To me, they sounded like a coordinated effort. So, the day I left the ranch, I went to see Tom Rawlins at Fort Churchill, because he's been investigating for some time. He learned that each of the Southern men who were killed had a mid-level government job and was within reach of moving higher. Tom's a Union captain. He was in no position to put a man on the inside."

"But you were able to be that man," she said coolly. "To mingle among the murderers."

He looked her over and grinned a little. "You don't look like you're going to drag me behind Cielos, so I suppose that means you're handling this well so far."

"So far."

"So, the men who were murdered were members of the Order of the Golden Circle. That verified my suspicion that the killings were a coordinated effort. Someone planned them. Someone who would have access to the Order's meetings, who posed as one of them to find out who was in a position to cause the Union trouble, a man who could coordinate the killings and pay other men to carry them out and stop the GC from gaining power."

"Abbott."

"Right. To coordinate another attack, the gunmen would need to meet the man who hired them, and the next targets would be specified and the information passed down. By becoming that inside man, I would be able to go with them and find out who was issuing the orders. Tom and I made plans, then I left Fort Churchill and headed toward Galena, the town in the middle of the three where the most recent attacks had taken place, to try to find a few of the gunmen."

With a moan, Jess rubbed her eyes, guessing what he had done next. "Don't tell me you went into saloons, drank whiskey, and listened to conversations."

"Of course I didn't. What good would that do?"

"You didn't?"

"No. I had to look like a gunman for hire who needed employment. I took the Henry rifle, stood in plain sight at the edge of town, and blasted holes through the centers of tins at fifty paces."

"That would have done it," she agreed, then flicked the black sleeve of his shirt. "You certainly look the part."

"Most people hurried to avoid me, and no one looked me in the eye. Except Bodine. I set up camp that night nearby."

"You let him find you."

"Yes, ma'am."

Jess was furious at the danger he'd placed himself in, but, oh, she ached with pride that that body was attached to that mind, and that both were married to her.

"Why did Bodine call you Kane?" she asked.

"They think my name is Donovan Kane. A childhood friend," he explained. "One of the gunmen—a man with sheep's-wool sideburns—is one of the nine men who attacked you in the street in Carson City the day you and I met two years ago."

"He still hates Southerners, I see." She sighed. "This whole time I've been back in Carson, I've had to say very little in public because of my drawl."

Jake kissed her forehead. "I like your drawl."

Jess caressed his cheek with her thumb. "I've noticed."

They sat quietly for several moments, listening to crickets, and Jess contemplated all that Jake had said about Abbott and Bodine.

Jake stared into the darkness, one elbow resting on a bent knee. "There's one more piece to all this that we haven't found yet. A big piece. Abbott isn't the top man in charge. He's taking orders from someone else."

"What? How?" Stunned, Jess tried to put words to her careening thoughts. "Hank and Seth have watched him for a month. The only man they saw Abbott contact was the messenger last night."

"He must be someone who occasionally visits the bank, or he occasionally sends a man to visit the bank."

"And then he passes Abbott his orders," she said, her thoughts still in a whirl. "The hydra has another head? Jake, why would you think so?"

"Because Abbott was afraid. Of you, and of Bodine. And Abbott's in a position where he might get caught. A man who's the head of the secret Unionist organization and wages a private war against Southerners would make certain he won't be found out or stopped."

"Why, then," she asked slowly, "would Abbott allow himself to be in a position where he might get caught?"

"That, my love, is what we'll need to find out. Now we just need to figure out how we're going to go about that."

"And we'll need to do it in the next few hours, before anyone else is killed." *Abbott is the man who should get dragged behind Cielos,* she thought. Then another idea came to mind. "Abbott believes us to be members of that Confederate Order, and he believes that he's been found out as an imposter."

"I'm listening."

"The manager of an important bank would have to be coerced, threatened in some way, to be forced to comply. Abbott certainly hasn't been paid to do what he's done; he doesn't live at all like a man of means."

"Agreed."

"So we, supposed members of the Confederate Order, coerce back. Abbott's superior in that organization must be threatening him, perhaps threatening his life. I think we need to threaten him in the same way, and hope he reveals the name of his superior. Or perhaps the sheriff will agree to offer a deal—as much as I hate to suggest this—and Abbott would face prison rather than be hanged."

"Sounds like a couple of good options. Now all we do is pray that one of them works. Let's go do it."

"You? Shouldn't you get back to Bodine's mob before they become suspicious?"

"No, it'll be all right. I'll return to them after we get the information out of Abbott. Then we'll figure out how to catch all of them and finally put an end to this war." Jake began to help her into her moccasins and boots.

"You will have been gone all night, and perhaps part of the morning. What will you tell Bodine?"

"The truth," he said. "That I saw a woman who caught my fancy."

❖◦✦◦❖

Jake lifted her into the saddle as the first gray light of dawn edged the high peaks of Mount Davidson to the east. He settled on Cielos behind her and pulled her close, but this time, Jake's touch failed to comfort her the way it had during their ride to the hot spring. It failed to make her feel safe.

She had agreed to come here tonight because of the hope that taking a path they normally would not might change the outcome of the premonition. The images of Jake plummeting had neither altered nor faded.

The only comfort she felt was due to the fact that Jake would fall in conditions of darkness, and now the sun was rising. They had another day, another chance to bring about a different future.

"When you fear what you see," the Paiute woman had said, *"remember to hold on to your strength."*

Jess gave thought to exactly who her strength was— God.

Then, deep within her, Jess heard another voice speaking to her. *"Be strong and of a good courage,"* He said. *"Be not afraid, neither be thou dismayed: for the Lord thy God is with thee whithersoever thou goest."*

Chapter Sixteen

Oh my," Edmund said dazedly for the third time. He sat in Miriam's formal parlor on the sofa across from Jake and Jess in his night garments, his eyelids heavy with interrupted sleep, his eyes vacant.

The parlor, Jess saw, hadn't been changed at all in the many months Miriam had been gone. The dainty tea tables stood where they had always been, not a single lace doily out of place. Edmund had kept it the same, Jess felt certain, as a memory of his wife and of what he had once thought of as happy times. He had deeply, blindly, loved her. He had not known at that time the depravity his wife was steeped in.

Jess wondered if Edmund would be able to bear keeping any of the furnishings now.

Shakily, Edmund rubbed his face and looked up at her and Jake. "All this has happened since last night?" he asked.

Jake sat forward, his face tense. "Edmund, Jess is going to change her clothes and then leave. Abbott ordered Bodine's men to find her. Once she is gone, she'll stay somewhere else, so you'll be in no real danger."

"Neither will your house, nor any of the servants," Jess added. "Since those men won't see me coming and going here or at the imports store, or see me anywhere with you, they shouldn't cause you any trouble."

"You can go to work like always," Jake told him. "In fact, it would be safest for you if you did, though you should carry a gun with you until Bodine and his men are caught and all this is past. It's possible that when they can't find Jess, they'll come ask if you know where she is."

Jake was intent on keeping her and Edmund and everyone safe, Jess knew. He was also intent on getting back to Bodine and his men before his absence raised questions...and they still needed to get answers from Lyman Abbott.

Abruptly, Edmund sat upright, his expression fierce. "The servants can have a paid leave and my house can go to blazes," he declared. "I will not concern myself with my own fine health while murderers are searching for Jess!" Edmund looked only at Jess now, and she saw in his eyes the firmness of his mind, and the great weight of regret. "Because of me, you lost everything. Your family, your inheritance, your home. You must let me help in any way I can, and I must ask for your forgiveness."

Anger shot through Jess. "Nothing that has happened was your fault, Edmund. While my parents were alive and Ambrose was at war, you did everything in your power to help me hold my family together. I refuse to accept your apology, because you weren't responsible. Besides, you suffered losses too—your wife and your best friends."

"I should have seen some indicator in Miriam," Edmund said, "some inconsistency in her behavior, but I didn't. I just didn't realize who she truly was."

Jess reached her hand out to Edmund, who took it. "Of course you didn't, Edmund. None of us did."

Edmund gave her hand a fatherly pat, then released it. "Jake, Jess, I'll make up for the harm Miriam helped

Abbott cause in any way I can. We still have an hour before dawn. Let me take Jess to the imports store," he implored them, "and hide her there."

"I appreciate that, Edmund," Jake said, "though I know of another place where she can stay where she will be safe, and that will also keep Bodine from causing further trouble for you. We may need your help later."

"Anything. I won't leave the store today, so I'll be there when you need me. I'll tell the servants to be aware of possible trouble here."

All three of them stood. Edmund shook Jake's hand, then briefly, tightly, embraced Jess.

"God be with you both," he said.

Jake said, "God be with us all."

❖◈◈❖

Jake settled into a chair facing Abbott and casually crossed his legs, intentionally giving Abbott the impression that he had all time. Abbott, however, looked miserably as though he had precious little time. Even by scant lantern light, the man's eyes showed agony, some rage, and desperation.

His knees were pressed tightly together.

Seth took up position directly behind Abbott, just beyond the banker's line of vision, a silent threat, an unknown. Hank and Jess stood watch at the bedroom windows, out of Abbott's sight.

"I searched the house, boss," Seth told Jake. "Every inch of it. There were no bank records at all, and no money."

Jake merely nodded and kept his gaze on Abbott. He hadn't expected Abbott to have them here. Isaac Hale's bank record could have incriminated him, and Abbott's superior would have possession of the money.

He and Jess had planned to use Abbott's belief that they were members of the powerful Confederate Order to intimidate him so completely that he would reveal information in exchange for leniency. The fact that an empty water glass and two empty coffee mugs sat beside Abbott, and that the man hadn't once left the chair he was sitting in during the five hours he and Jess had been gone, Jake reflected, would work even better.

Rather than waste time asking questions that Abbott didn't want to answer, Jake leaned back in his chair and pulled his hat down over his eyes. Abbott would let him know when he was ready to talk. Until then, Jake would get a little rest. He was sure he'd need it.

"What do you want?" Abbott demanded, a little plaintively, Jake thought, though not plaintively enough.

About five minutes passed. Then Abbott swore. "Tell me what you want!" he yelled.

No, Jake mused. He wasn't quite there yet.

Jake's breathing had just begun to deepen when Abbott's voice became a plea. "What do you want to know?" he wailed.

Jake pushed his hat back and sat upright. "Simple. I need to know who hired you."

Abbott stared at him, as if debating his answer, then emphatically shook his head, dislodging the neatly combed-back hairs so that they now fell over his forehead. "No one hired me. I command the men. I have the power!"

Less than two feet away, a coffeepot sat on a small cast-iron stove. Jake poured himself a mugful, then steadily drank about half of it down. The rest he balanced on his knee between him and Abbott, idly swirling the contents. Abbott glanced at the motion of the liquid, then quickly looked away.

"How far from here is the outhouse?" Jake asked.

Abbott's eyes darted toward the west side of the house.

"Hmm. Not far, then," Jake said. "It wouldn't take us long to untie that rope. You could be there in less than a minute."

To Jake's surprise, tears sprang to the man's eyes, though not tears of anger or desperation, he realized. They were the tears of a man who was haunted by a terrible secret.

"I can't tell you anything," Abbott said, leaning back in agony. "*Please* believe me."

Jake believed him. Whatever secret he held was apparently more than that of a man waging a private war against people he viewed as the enemy. Abbott was horribly, completely afraid, though not for himself, Jake was certain.

Jess appeared in the doorway behind Seth. Soundlessly, she held up a toy sailboat. It was basic, Jake saw, one main piece made of wood with one sturdy mast and sail. Somewhere, Abbott had a small son.

Jess pointed to herself, Jake, and Abbott, then with two fingers pantomimed walking. When she saw his acknowledgement, she left again.

"Hank?" Jake called.

His neighbor appeared, looking a little tired but fully alert. "What do you need?"

Jake looked to Abbott. "You have a buggy?"

Clearly as uncertain about the change of events as he was terrified and in distress, Abbott nodded.

"Hank, will you hitch up Abbott's buggy?"

"Sure will."

Setting the coffee mug aside, Jake drew the Remington and cocked it. He did not want to shoot the banker, but neither would he let him get away. Abbott was the key to everything.

"Seth? Untie him."

Seth did as he'd said, then drew his own gun. Abbott looked down the two barrels, obviously afraid to stand.

Jake rose to his feet. "We'll take you to the outhouse, Abbott. You need to know that if you give us a reason to stop you, we will."

Abbott nodded once, then stood and walked with prudent self-restraint toward the outhouse.

◆────◆

Most of the sky had lightened to gray when the buggy stopped at the Carson City cemetery. Jake reined in Cielos behind it, uncertain why Jess had brought them here but trusting her reasons. He stepped down and looped the reins through the ring on a post, then unsnapped the flap of his holster. Abbott had sat carefully still during the brief journey, and he climbed out of the buggy after Seth now, and waited for Hank to help Jess down, clearly no less aware of their intentions should he attempt to call out or run. The man had dignity, Jake mused, just as Jess had said he did. He hated Southerners vehemently, that was obvious, but that didn't make the man a leader of murderers. Whatever had drawn him into the position of issuing orders to kill people had been no small incentive.

Jess headed toward the far side of the cemetery. Abbott, flanked by Seth and Hank, followed a few paces after her, and Jake trailed behind them, eyes peering into the heavy shadows for movement ahead of Jess or behind them all. So far, he had detected none of Bodine's men watching or following.

Though Jess's motives for bringing them here remained a mystery, she walked tall, with boldness, despite the threat against her. Jake burned with pride. Jess was slimmer than Olivia had been at this time in her pregnancy, but Jess hadn't gone soft, hadn't lost an ounce of her tenacity, though she knew that before the day was over, Bodine would try to kill her. She wore dark blue, almost black, underscoring the impression she gave, intentionally or not, of the angel of death, moving over the dark earth among the burial places of the dead.

Jess stopped beside a new grave, not yet revealing what she held bundled in her cloak. Hank, Abbott, and Seth stopped across from her, Abbott unable to pull his gaze from the freshly turned earth. The grave, Jake saw, was small. An infant had been buried there.

"This child was buried here yesterday morning," Jess told Abbott, her voice reflective. "I was here, visiting my family's grave, when the burial party arrived." Pale morning light encircled the whites of her eyes as she spoke solely to the banker, their depths compelling and not condemning. "The coffin was small, no bigger than a twenty-pound sack of sugar. The child's father carried the coffin from their wagon and held it while the pastor spoke. But when the pastor was done, the father couldn't let the casket go. He stood there, right where you are, holding it against him, as if someone were asking him to leave his heart behind."

What fear and water and coffee hadn't done, Jake saw, emotion just might. Abbott had begun to crumple.

"Members of Bodine's group," she went on, her tone just as compassionate, "burned Southern settlers' homes in an effort to drive them away, Southerners who came west to escape the war, like my family did. Some brought their political feelings along, and I don't intend to discuss the right or wrong of that with you, but I am certain that none of them, at least none I'm aware of, has hurt anyone, or gunned down the children of those whose beliefs he didn't share."

Jess glanced down to the grave at their feet. "This baby had no political leanings at all, and yet he was shot dead the day before yesterday by Bodine and his men. I know what it is to lose a child, Mr. Abbott. I lost a newborn brother and a baby sister. I suspect you know what it is to love and to lose a child too."

She pulled back a fold of the cloak she held, took out the toy sailboat, and held it out toward Abbott. He pressed his knuckles to his face, crying openly now.

"Who does this boat belong to, Lyman?" she asked softly.

"My son!" Abbott burst out. "The boat belongs to my son. Oh, Lord above, help me!"

Jess had done it. The defensive walls within the banker had begun to topple. Jake continued to watch the darkness, but he kept one eye on Abbott.

"You said 'belongs,'" Jess said. "Is your son still alive?"

"I didn't mean for this man's son to die! I don't want my son to die either!"

"Who has him, Lyman?" Jess asked.

"I can't tell you," Abbott sobbed. "Believe me, I can't."

"You can tell me," Jess replied. "We will not harm him."

"No, you don't understand. If I tell you anything, the man who has him will kill him."

"No, he wouldn't kill a child."

"He killed my wife!" Abbott shouted. "Before Porter burned your house, this man killed my wife."

"Why?"

"To force me to help him. He needed a banker, because he needed money."

"To fund his private war," Jess said, the boat still held aloft in her hand.

"Yes." Abbott's fingers were dug into his hair now. "He killed her, then told me he'd take my son if I didn't do as he asked. He was in the bank one day, and we started talking about our mutual hatred of Southerners, then, when he started to walk out, Miriam came up to me. There was no one else in the bank, and she thought she and I were alone. I knew who she was, of course, though we hadn't spoken more than civil pleasantries until then. She told me about your family and said that you had Confederate ties, that your father was a member of the Order."

Isaac hadn't been, Jake knew. Isaac had disowned his son for choosing to fight for the South.

"Miriam said she wanted to kill them to protect our noble cause, and she asked for my help to do just that, and told me who they were. R— the man who has my son overheard everything. I told Miriam that I shared her hatred, but that I wouldn't help her to kill anyone. She became angry but left, and the man came back and told me he wanted to build a secret army to fight the Confederates who had come west. He asked me to help him raise it and fund it. I refused, and he left without another word. But the next day…. The next day, my wife…."

"The man killed her," Jess murmured. "Is that what you mean to say?"

Abbott nodded and pulled out a handkerchief to wipe his eyes. "The man came to her funeral. To her funeral! He walked up to me afterward and saw me holding my son. He said that if I didn't want another grave dug, then I'd reconsider his request. He knew who Miriam was and knew that she had a lot of connections. He told me to get close to her and to stay close to her, and to find a man to do as she'd asked, who would see to it that all the Hales were dead.

"Shane Porter."

"Yes. I told Porter to burn the house, because that way your family would have a chance of getting out. The man said to be sure the man I hired left a Confederate flag behind, because he wanted everyone to know that a new war had begun. By then I knew that Miriam only wanted your mother dead, so that she could pursue your father. You were right about what you said to me in the bank. I had met your father and your mother, many times. I knew he would try to save his wife."

Jess's chest slowly rose then fell, but she said nothing.

"Porter helped me to find Bodine," Abbott continued, "and both of them helped me to find all the other men Bodine now leads. At first, the man gave orders that they terrorize Southerners—any Southerners who were known to have Confederate sympathies—to drive them out, and he paid Bodine's men well to do it. Despite his efforts and intentions, few of the Southerners left. Then he heard that Jeff Davis had passed out commissions to members of the Order of the Golden Circle, and he told me to infiltrate the Order, to find out who was working themselves into positions of authority among the local government. The first time I presented him with names, he told me to issue orders to Bodine to kill them. I refused. I told him I was perfectly willing to intimidate Southerners and drive them away, but that I wouldn't help him to murder. Before

I reached home, my son had been taken. I went to confront him, and he said that I would issue the orders and let the Southerners see to their own problems, or I would bury my son. That was two months ago. I haven't seen Wirt since." Quaking violently, Abbott fell to his knees. "He's only four! He must be so frightened! I don't know where he's taken him."

Jess lowered herself to her knees across the grave from Abbott. The lightening sky cast a faint yellow over the toy boat. "The man wanted my family dead, so that he would have access to father's money?"

"Yes." Abbott looked up at Jake. "I expect you know the rest, if you've been riding with Bodine."

Jake did, but he didn't know what events would cause a man to murder an innocent woman, to kidnap and hide behind a small child, to lose all sense of honor. If a man lost his honor, what was left to respect about himself?

Jess grasped the banker's hand. "We'll help you get your son back. We'll stop that man, and we'll put an end to all of this. Please trust us. The sheriff can help."

Abbott looked at her as if she were mad, then threw back his head and laughed, the sound of utter hopelessness. "You just don't understand, do you. You think this man wouldn't have thought of that? You think he wouldn't have ensured his own protection? He has other men around him who have their orders. If the sheriff or anyone else asks a single question, if anyone tries to find Wirt, or if this man is shot, my son will die. It is impossible to outmaneuver this man, and it is impossible to stop him."

Heat shot to Jess's eyes. "I don't believe anything's impossible, Mr. Abbott. You asked for the Lord's help a moment ago. It's standing all around you."

"You're insane," he scoffed. "Why would you, of all people, help me?"

Jess's jaw went rigid. "Two people's lives depend upon us, though neither they nor their families know of it—the two men you ordered Bodine to kill. In Dayton, the newspaperman Walter Simms, and in Washoe City, the man running for the legislature, Dustin Keet. I don't know the men or their politics. All I know is that it's wrong to do nothing and let them die. The war is over. What's more, whatever you've done, God is waiting for you to ask forgiveness so that He can forgive you, and so that He can bless you again."

Jake loved her intensely in that moment. His wife was a woman of honor, worthy of great respect for her faith and courage. The Lord had blessed him mightily.

Abbott's hair, his mustache, his clothes—all of him—looked limp, beaten. The man had caused all his own agony and loss himself, Jake reflected, because of his hatred for his fellow man. He hated, and he suffered for it.

Jake had also suffered—for loving—but his love hadn't caused the suffering. Love never did.

"How can you stop this man?" Abbott asked Jess dubiously, almost seethingly.

"I don't know yet," Jess said, "but that doesn't mean we quit. We'll see to it your son lives a full life, Lyman. It's up to you whether he lives those years believing his father is a murderer, or believing that his father turned against that evil in the end to save innocent men's lives.

"I honestly don't know how we'll stop this man, but I do know this: There is no record of the withdrawal from or alteration to my father's bank account. There is no evidence of stealing or of any wrongdoing on your part.

You found Porter, but Miriam hired him. You haven't pulled any triggers, and you haven't struck any matches. When you passed this man's orders on to Bodine, you did so under coercion, after your wife was murdered, and when you fingered the members of the Order, you did so fearing for your son and hoping the men would survive.

"I also know that I'm the only witness to all that has happened. I'm the only one who can testify against you on every point. As that person, I can also ask a judge for leniency."

Jake knew otherwise. Abbott had helped to commit multiple murders. Duress or no, the man was going to hang. There was no avoiding it. "Jess, he'll get life in prison, at the least."

Jess acknowledged that. "Abbott, that's thirty years of being a small part of your son's life, and not just a memory." She reached across the grave and pressed the toy boat into Abbott's hand. "Who has your son, Lyman?"

Abbott didn't answer. His eyes lifted to Jess, then his brows arched in a way men's did when a long-searched-for answer came to them. "The man's name is Ross. Please understand that I'm afraid to trust you with more. You or the sheriff could interfere with my only chance to get my son back."

Already Jake didn't like whatever Abbott had in mind. Nevertheless, he asked, "What chance?"

"Ross has arranged to buy four crates of new guns, through me, and me through Bodine. Bodine knows many people," he explained. "The man who's selling them will deliver them to Ross at ten o'clock tonight, at a place where Ross will be vulnerable, a place where Ross has the payment and room to store them until we can get them to Bodine. Ross planned to get them to Bodine by including the crates among other goods that he's sending by wagon to San Francisco at the end of the week. Bodine and his men will then 'steal' the freight and obtain the guns."

Abbott stood up and faced Jake directly. "The password I use for conveying messages to Bodine is 'Old Glory.' Tell him that information about the weapons shipment came in just after he left last night, and that I gave you the password and told you to send his man to the bank, and I'll provide his man with the location of the new meeting place, so that they can pick up the weapons personally. Tell him that the time will be at ten o'clock tonight. He'll need to know that to send his man in time to deliver the message."

"No, tell me the place, and I'll tell Bodine."

"I can't. I must know that you and the sheriff won't be able to interfere before I have the chance to get my son back."

Jake grunted in anger, but in Abbott's place, he would have insisted on the same. "Your plan will get Bodine and his men and Ross in one place, and our goal will be to capture them there—wherever "there" is—but how will that get your son back?"

Abbott appeared to brace himself. "It won't, unless I take Miss Hale, posing as a hostage, and offer to trade her to Ross for my son."

Jake thought little of Abbott's humor. Then he saw that the banker meant it, and he involuntarily leapt at the man.

Seth thrust himself between them with a shouted warning, clearly prepared to physically stop Jake from harming the man.

"Never before," Jake growled, "have I had to force myself not to strike a man for what he said." Gradually, Jake eased his stance and spread his fingers to let the tightness in them subside. "My answer, Abbott, is no. We will not put a woman in danger."

Jess, he saw, hadn't reacted at all. She'd gone motionless, deathly stiff. "There has to be another way," she said. Her hands moved then to clasp protectively over the baby.

Jake rapidly considered options. "The sheriff—"

"Would endanger Wirt," Abbott insisted.

"Then trade me to Ross," Jake said. "Tell him that I can testify about Bodine."

Abbott shook his head, keeping Seth between them. "You pose no real threat to him. Miss Hale is the one who would inherit Mr. Hale's money. She's the only one whose very existence jeopardizes his plans."

"Then we'll capture Ross in his home," Jake barked, "or on his way there."

Abbott clasped his hands together, as if begging him to understand. "Ross has men around him—I don't know how many—and they have their orders regarding my son. Ross will *not* let himself or his plans be surmounted."

Jake rubbed his face. "Abbott, how do you even know that your son is alive?"

"Ross had brought me a few pictures that my son drew. I know he's alive."

The sun had begun to rise. For once in his life, Jake deeply hated it for ending the night. They were running out of time. Bodine and his men would soon be coming for Jess.

"Jake?" Jess said, and Hank helped her to her feet. "Jake, we have to do this."

Jake rolled his head on his shoulders, then eyed the graves around him and thought of other burial mounds just like them. His mother's, whom he'd helped bury when he was just a child. Livvy and Sadie's. The Hales', after he'd picked through the rubble left from the fire and gathered their remains. For two years, he'd protected Jess with everything he was, until he had let her come here to Carson City, and now her life, and that of their child, was at risk from the men Bodine led. If he rejected Abbott's plan, his son, Wirt, would remain in the hands of a killer, and Jess would still be in imminent danger. But to put her into the grasp of that same killer, to trust a man like Abbott, who'd let others die for his own weakness...he couldn't do it.

Jake lifted his eyes from the grave before him. Hank and Seth both met his gaze, but it was Hank who spoke. "If needs be, I'll give my life to protect Jess," he vowed, to Jake's astonishment, "as if she were my own Mary. Enough people have died, son. We have to end this."

Seth cleared his throat. "The other men from the ranch will want to be here, boss. Every last one will find work elsewhere if you let Jess and the three of us face all those men without them."

Though he was a small man, Abbott now stood like a confident one. "We can do this. Miss Hale need only get Ross to confess to ordering the murders so that the sheriff can overhear, or so that Miss Hale can testify. She's already proven herself fully capable of that." He cast a respectful glance at Jess. "All you need to do," he said to Jake, "is to be there in time to keep her safe, should Ross be unwilling to trade my son for her. I can only hope he'll see it to his benefit and send a man to bring Wirt. When my son arrives, the sheriff's men and yours can move in, and we'll all fight to keep Wirt and Miss Hale from harm."

How can I possibly prepare for this? Jake wondered. He had no notion of who Ross was, or of where Abbott planned to take them. When he looked down, Jess was standing beside him.

"Hank, will you and Seth stay with Mr. Abbott?" she asked. At their nods, she took Jake's hand and led him several paces away.

"Jess, I don't trust Abbott to keep his word. I know that grieving, vengeful look in his eyes. He wants his son back, and he wants the man who took him destroyed. I'm afraid for you, love, and I'm afraid for the baby."

She stared up at him. "I'm afraid too, but you already know that I have to be the one to go with Abbott."

"We're testing God, Jess."

"We're not testing Him. I'm not jumping off the roof of the temple, wondering if He will catch me. We're not doing this without reason. We're trying to save a child and two men, and countless others. Ross's actions are not war—there is no justice in them—and they've already gone on for more than two years. Hank is right. We can bring about the end of this tonight." A breeze lifted a slender lock of her hair, and the curving brown strand drifted in front of her eyes. She brushed it back in a gesture that was as familiar to him as the movements of his own hands. "Because we know the Lord, we can trust Him, even in this. Jake, your love for me, and our mutual love for the West, which is being attacked, has driven us both to want to make things right. You and I have to finish together what each of us individually started alone, to end the attacks against Southerners, and then we can finally go home and just *live*."

Lord Almighty, help us, he prayed, then walked with Jess back to the men. "Seth, I'd like you to escort Abbott straight to the bank and watch him today. See to it that he doesn't talk to anybody he shouldn't. I'll visit Sheriff Smith on my way to join Bodine. I'm sure he'll send a man to stand guard with you."

Seth nodded.

"Go straight to the bank?" Abbott blustered. "I won't be able to change clothes!"

"That's right," Jake said flatly. "You won't. Other than that, you're to make matters appear normal in case any of Bodine's men show up. Hank, I'd like you to take Jess to stay with Miss Scott—"

"Jake," Jess interrupted him, "I do not want to put one more person at unnecessary risk."

"Understood. Then take her to your boardinghouse room so she can sleep until tonight."

"I'll do it," Hank said. "What else?"

"Plenty. As soon as you leave Jess, send a telegram to Shaffer's Station, and keep sending it every ten minutes until you get a reply. Shaffer knows me. Have him send a rider to the ranch to tell all available cattlemen to come immediately and to meet Edmund at the imports store. Taggart knows where it is." Jake looked to Abbott. "I trust this place we're going tonight is within an hour's ride of here?"

"It is—within half an hour, on a respectable horse."

"Good."

"Jake?" Jess was shaking her head. "The ranch is sixty miles from here. To make it by tonight, the men would have to run the horses nearly all the way. The horses won't survive it."

"We're placing our faith in God, right?" he said gently.
She closed her eyes, then finally answered. "Yes. We're
placing our faith in God."

"Hank, next I'd like you to wire Captain Rawlins at
Fort Churchill. Tell him everything that's happened and
what we have planned. If he can send men to help, have
them meet Edmund at the imports store. When you're
done sending telegrams, go stay with Edmund and watch
his back until tonight, just in case Bodine attempts to find
Jess through Edmund.

"In the same vein that Abbott here doesn't trust us
with Ross's full name or where we'll meet him, I don't
trust Abbott with knowing where Jess is, so, Seth, don't
reveal Jess's whereabouts to Abbott until tonight when
he leaves to get her. At that time, Abbott, you'll tell Seth
where you're taking her. Agreed?"

Abbott hesitated, then nodded. "That's acceptable.
Miss Hale and I will need to get to Ross before ten o'clock
so that we can confront him, and he can send for Wirt,
before Bodine's or your men arrive. If we arrive by nine
forty, that should give us the time we need. Ross has
boasted that Wirt is only a few minutes away from...
where we will meet him. He frequently tells me"—Abbott
smoothed down the front of his shirt, apparently trying
to get his next words out—"that it entertains him to have
lunch with Wirt." He cleared his throat. "I surmise the
boardinghouse is here in Carson City. Miss Hale, I'll
come for you one hour before, so that we can travel slowly
and have a care for your condition." At her look of inquiry,
he explained, "I finally realized that you're expecting, and
that the two of you are married."

"All right," Jake said. "Once Abbott tells Seth where
the meeting with Ross will take place, Seth will go to

Edmund's store and tell everyone there. Whoever's there will shadow Jess and Abbott to make sure Jess stays safe and to round up Bodine's men when they arrive. Try not to be seen following Abbott and Jess, in the event Bodine's men are watching. You'll want to bring all the iron you can carry. I don't expect they'll give up easily. I'll arrange for the sheriff and his men to follow Edmund, Hank, and Seth.

"Jess, after Bodine's messenger tells him where we're going to meet, I'll try to get the information, then slip away from the men and get to the place early so that I can keep an eye on you and see to it Abbott doesn't go against his word."

"And you'll be there to bring down Bodine's men," she said.

"That's right, love, I will. Abbott, we'll try to save your son, but remember that *I* can testify against you about everything I've heard you say, and I will if you let any harm come to Jess."

Once again, Jess's fingers linked tightly over the baby. "So many things could go wrong," she murmured.

Jake gathered her in his arms and held her close. He whispered into her hair, for her hearing alone, "You have the derringer, should you learn that Abbott lied to Seth about your destination and you find yourself in need of it. Almighty God," he prayed with her, "we trust that You will make us bold as lions, and that You will enable good to prevail tonight, that the war in the West will finally end." Then he pressed his forehead to Jess's. "How did I ever allow us to get caught up in all this?" he wondered aloud.

"Because this is the man God made you to be. I love you, Bennett."

Jake kissed her lips, her temple, her hair, and, feeling his heart ripping in two, hurried over to Cielos.

As he mounted, the first rays of sunlight steamed over the top of Mount Davidson, and bathed Jess in a pool of gold.

❖❖

"Seth?" While Hank headed to the buggy with Abbott, Jess pulled the young man aside. Cold fear tightened her throat until it was nearly choking her. "I have to ask you one more favor."

"What is it?"

"That you give me your promise." Her voice shook, but she couldn't help it. "Promise that you will not allow Jake to come near me tonight, no matter where we are, no matter what happens."

In consternation, Seth lifted his hat and dragged his hand through the mud-brown thatch of hair. Above his bandana, his Adam's apple bobbed. "This is about what you saw, about that premonition, isn't it?"

"Yes. I haven't been able to change the outcome of any other visions. You know that I have to stop this one. If Jake isn't near me...."

"Then he can't be in a place where you see him fall," Seth finished.

Jess gripped his sleeve. "Please promise me."

Seth looked out over the desert for a long moment, considering, his mouth grim.

Then, darkness.

An image flashed through her mind—empty blackness. The chasm. Her skirts swung out over it, her feet dangling. A weight was pulling her down. Her hands, clinging to a chain, began to slip. Across an expanse, Jake looked straight at her and called to her. He called to her, but he couldn't get to her. Someone wouldn't let him. Then she was weightless, falling. Falling away from him, into empty blackness. The square of light above grew smaller, fainter. She ached to see Jake just once more, and to tell him that she loved him...and then she realized that he already knew.

Then, there was only blackness.

Blinding light speared into her eyes. It was sunlight. She was gripping someone's sleeve...Seth's. She knew she already had his promise.

Jess looked up into his young brown eyes, which were rimmed with silver. She released his sleeve as the film of shock faded from her mind. *Jake would live.*

Chapter Seventeen

Jess settled into the buggy seat beside Abbott, her insides churning to butter. The banker studied her face, then lifted the reins and set the horses into motion. Neither of them spoke. There was nothing left to say.

The buggy rolled down the street, which vibrated and rang with absurdly cheerful piano music and laughter. *The idiotic sounds of the merrily inebriated*, Jess thought brittlely. Sometime late tomorrow morning—Saturday, she realized—the inebriated would wake from their celebration-induced stupors. They would stretch and grin and look forward to a day of leisure, with no notion of what a small group of strangers had gone through this night to ensure them safety from a man's personal war, that they might enjoy hundreds of more chances to celebrate and make merry.

Already regretting the jealous, waspish thought, Jess folded her hands together, her grip painfully tight. This mess with Ross was not their fault, she reminded herself. If she had a choice, she'd be singing and laughing right alongside them.

Abbott guided the horses beyond the edge of town, then snapped them into a trot, heading northeast toward Dayton. Two horses, Jess noted, instead of one. Two to ensure Abbott's fast escape with his son, or perhaps to pull the buggy up into the mountains. Jess looked around behind them, hoping to see a glimpse of Jake, or of Edmund, Hank, and Seth…and apprehensive that she would instead see a horde of Bodine's men, rifles drawn, come to carry out his order. The road that parted the desert behind them appeared empty, desolate, save for the last gray light of evening that lay like a mist above the upper curves of the Sierra Nevadas and left the lower slopes shrouded in night.

She couldn't believe that she had come to be in such a situation. Only hours before, the man beside her had ordered her demise, and now she was voluntarily going with him so that he could attempt to trade her life for that of his son. How true it was that circumstances often made unusual bedfellows.

The two buggy lamps, which scattered light on the backs of the horses and on the road ahead, grew more pronounced as the sky turned black. Already the last-quarter moon had begun to sink behind the western Sierras. Already the mountains she loved were fading from sight.

Abbott turned the horses onto the grade leading up toward Silver City and Mount Davidson. The buggy began to rattle as they drew nearer to stamp mills where hundreds of stamps pounded and crushed gold and silver ore into sand-like slurries with percussive, jolting thuds.

The increasing noise battering her eardrums irritated her. *Ground* on her. Apace with the clamor, her anger burgeoned for having allowed her own dread to cripple her, until now. Flashes of heat shot beneath her skin. Jess silently thanked God for her anger. In the sky ahead, heat lightning mirrored the torrid sensation, as blazes of purple and blue stabbed through thin stretches of cloud.

They didn't halt in Silver City, yet she didn't ask their destination. The twinge of helplessness she suffered at not knowing fed her rage, and rage fed her strength. The words Jake had spoken streamed through her mind, but in a voice other than his. *"...who through their faith subdued kingdoms, brought about justice, escaped the maws of lions, and evaded the sword."*

Thank You, Lord, she responded, then forced her attention beyond herself.

Jess eyed the sharp turns in the road for possible ambush. They winded their way up the steep, narrow streets of Gold Hill, past immense mining operations that she had heard about in Carson City but had not seen, with signs that declared them the Crown Point mine, the Kentuck, the Yellow Jacket, and others. Then the horses lowered their heads and quickened their pace to pull the buggy over the divide into Virginia City. In no way could she fathom why Abbott had brought her here, though she knew this was their destination. No other large towns existed beyond it, until one came to Lake's Crossing, miles distant. What had her father, an imports merchant, had to do with the businesses of the Comstock?

With perhaps ten times the population of Carson City, Virginia City bustled with activity, even at this hour. The city itself trailed from the high peaks of Mount Davidson, steeply down its eastern slope to Six Mile Canyon far below, reclining indolently as a lady of the evening, her curves spangled with silvery squares of light.

Jess was as surprised to see the thousands of points of illumination as she was to find herself among the buildings from which they shone.

Then her heart sank down through her ribs. Abbott pulled up in front of a mine office. The tall sign that spanned the front over its entrance read "The McKinney Mine." McKinney had been her mother's maiden name.

"Lord above," she breathed. Heat lightning flashed silver-blue above the mine.

Abbott slanted her a look as he set the brake and secured the reins. "You didn't know about this, did you?" he marveled, as if a great mystery were suddenly making itself clear. "Until this moment, you never knew that your father owned a silver mine." He chuckled. "A pity."

Then he drew a revolver from his coat, cocked it, and aimed its bore at her.

"Get out of the buggy," he said. "Now."

Rather than step down on his side of the buggy, he followed her across the seat and climbed out after her, his gun unwavering.

This was not a part of their plans. Jess seethed. She had been a fool to trust him. He'd meant to turn her over to Ross all along. His story about having a son had been a lie. Her fingers twitched as she fought her desire to draw the derringer. She had to help round up Ross and all his men. Tonight.

Abbott took her elbow in a painful grip and pushed her toward the door to the mine office. Jess's gaze swept the streets behind them once more, yearning for a glimpse of Jake or Seth or Hank. Heavy ore wagons rolled by, their wheels following the ruts carved into the street by countless other wagons that had gone before them, but she saw no familiar figures, sensed no protection forthcoming. Then she realized the full extent of Abbott's duplicity—he had sent Bodine's men to trap Jake and the others.

Her hands trembled on the railing as she climbed the steps to the mine office. Never had she felt such rage.

She pushed the door open, and they stepped into a large room that was two stories high and felt twenty or more degrees hotter than the air outside. Thick smells encircled her, smells of dust, kerosene, and machinery. Shirtless miners, their chests streaked with dust and sweat, cast curious glances in their direction but kept moving. At a small table, they seemed to be signing off from their shift. Other men, bare-chested but clean, carried lanterns and buckets of water and ice to elevating platforms that whirred and had begun transporting them downward in twos.

At least now, she mused, she knew where the eight hundred thousand dollars had come from.

Abbott consulted his pocket watch. Apparently, he had tucked the gun away before they had entered, so that none of these men would see a need to come to her defense. "Right on time," he commented, then snapped the timepiece shut and tucked it away. He took her arm again and steered her through an open door into an office. A large man in a tailored vest and shirtsleeves stood between them and the desk, his back to them. Abbott slammed the door.

The man turned. He held several sheets of paper in his hand.

The banker lifted his free hand to indicate the man. "Galen Ross," he said snidely to Jess, though she detected an underlying nervousness, "manager of the McKinney Mine."

Ross's heavy, black eyebrows lifted in question. Jess's breath caught. The man was perhaps thirty, and nearly as devastatingly handsome as Jake. His straight, black hair was roguishly finger-combed, his eyes deep-set and broody, and his mustache dashing. His shoulders were broad, his legs long and trim. He was the kind of man whom young women battled each other for, in the hopes of being the one selected to attend the theater with him so they could waltz in, draped on his arm.

His eyes assessed her with passing interest, barely pausing on the outward curve of her middle, then hovered on Abbott with mild amusement, like someone scrutinizing a colorful insect. From her father, Jess had learned to recognize the mask a man wears when he plays poker. Within Ross's guise of patience, she saw a soulless man one did not cross, one who was furious to see Abbott. Of the two with her in the room, Jess instantly knew this was the man to be wary of. Apparently Abbott knew it as well. His grip on her arm wavered.

"To what do I owe the honor of this visit?" Ross said, his voice mellow. His eyes returned to Jess, openly probing, as if trying to place her.

Lord, be with me.

"I want my son, Galen," Abbott declared, "and then I want out. I'll give you this woman in exchange."

Ross's expression instantly darkened, and then he chuckled. The chortle escalated to rich laughter and ended in a smirk. "No," he said.

Jess glanced toward the window, willing herself to see a familiar shape in the darkness beyond the glass. Heat lightning briefly seared the night and gilded the tops of buildings on the mountainside below, then vanished into unbroken night.

"I'm surprised you asked me, Abbott. Very surprised. She's extraordinary, indeed, but next time—if I allow there to *be* a next time—try bringing a young woman who isn't with child."

Ross glanced at a wall clock, then tossed the papers onto the desk. He strode around Jess like a man inspecting a trophy. "Who is she?"

The mine office rattled from pounding ore stamps. Abbott lifted his chin. He said each word distinctly, so that Ross could hear over the din, "Jessica *McKinney* Hale."

In sudden anger, Ross grabbed Jess by the chin and forced her face toward the oil lamp bracketed to the wall. "That's how I know you." His fingers dug into her jaw, his face mere inches from hers. "I saw Isaac walking in Carson City once with his wife—a beautiful woman I shall never forget. No wonder Isaac cherished her." Ross smiled slyly in the banker's direction. "My gratitude, Abbott, for bringing her to me."

Perhaps Abbott hadn't lied or betrayed them, Jess thought desperately. Perhaps the gun had been a prop for Ross to see if he had glanced out the window. For a judge to hang Ross, she reminded herself, he would have to admit what he had done. Jess jerked her chin free. "You forced Abbott to hire a man to murder my family. You kidnapped his son to gain his cooperation. How can you hide behind a child and call yourself a man?"

Ross's dark eyes flickered, then he folded his arms over his chest and gazed at her warmly, his feet spraddled. He moved toward her in the rolling gait of a sailor, then stopped when the length of his body was a mere inch from hers. She could feel his breath on her face. "Actually, I meant for you to die too, Jessica. Ah, look at that; your eyes turn to green fire when you're riled."

"How much of my father's money did you steal from Abbott's bank," she hissed, "so that you could fund your sick little war against Southerners?"

"I took all of it," he said breezily.

He was a man too rich, and too powerful, to be troubled by what she knew, or by their presence here. It was then that she knew he didn't intend to let either of them leave alive.

Jess feared she would throw up. Beyond the door, a bell clanged and gears ground, the sounds of more of the night crew descending shirtless into the hot mines. The unnatural metallic noise pounded, drowning out the chaotic thrashing of her heart.

Her fear fueled her rage. This man was going to hang.

Ross followed her expressions, his amusement genuine. "What are you thinking, Jessica McKinney Hale?" he murmured.

She tilted her face to meet his gaze directly. "I was just wondering if you'll foul your trousers when you hang."

Before Ross's fist could connect, Abbott shoved his revolver into Ross's face, briefly startling the man back. "Send a man for my son," he yelled, "or I'll escort her to the sheriff myself!"

The pendulum of the wall clock swung idly back and forth. Two minutes left until ten.

Abbott backed toward the door, his gun hand shaking as he placed himself between Ross and Jess. He reached his empty hand back and pulled open the door. "Send a man!"

Lightning pulsed. The window glass glinted white.

Ross advanced almost lazily toward Abbott. "I've considered your offer. However, I still need you to continue as commander and paymaster in my war, and I believe I would lose your services were I to reveal the location of your son."

Abbott screamed in rage and shoved Ross through the office door into the main room. He struck the bigger man with hand and gun, thrusting him bodily toward the mine shafts. Ross stumbled backward then regained his balance. He grabbed fistfuls of Abbott's coat and spun, throwing Abbott viciously into the wall. Abbott's gun struck the floor as he struggled to check his fall. Ross kicked the gun toward the office door.

Momentarily stunned, Abbott pushed himself upright.

When the last two miners turned toward them, Ross barked, "This is under control. Go do your jobs."

Jess wanted to ask them for help but stopped herself. She did not want the innocent miners getting hurt in the battle to come.

Abbott edged around Ross in the direction of the gun. The two miners glanced at each other dubiously but stepped onto the elevating platform and began their descent.

The moment they were out of sight, Abbott charged Ross, grabbing the bigger man around the ribs and pushing him farther from Jess. Realizing that Abbott did so to give her a chance to flee, Jess moved toward the revolver herself. Ross easily recovered and shook off the banker.

Ross then stalked forward, forcing Abbott back to where simple wooden gates were all that barred a fall into the gaping, black throat of the mine shaft.

The gun was still about twenty feet away. There was no time to retrieve it. Jess snatched a flickering kerosene lantern from the wall beside her. She darted around Ross to join ranks with Abbott and held the lantern high. "You come any closer," she vowed to Ross, "and you'll know what it is to burn."

Beside her, Abbott quaked. "I'm sorry, Jessica," he cried out, "for trying to trade you for my son, but I had to try! God, help me!"

"Come on," Jess said. She started to move away from the open mine shaft and Ross. Behind the big man, heat lightning flashed gold-white in the open doorway to the outside, throwing into silhouette the progression of men who entered.

None of them was Jake.

The men were not dressed like miners but wore guns and riding boots. Ross's secret army. Jess's feet, suddenly heavy as anvils, wouldn't move.

Five men entered, ten, twenty, more. Abbott nervously wiped the sweat from his face and stepped forward, beaming a captivating smile. "Ah, thank you all for coming. We were just about to begin the meeting."

The heat in the room became unbearable. Beneath her half corset, Jess's skin prickled with sweat.

Beyond Bodine's men, the open doorway and the building's many windowpanes winked light.

Ignoring the threat of the lantern, Ross grabbed Abbott by the lapels, his face contorted and eyes blazing. "You brought the men here? Why? To expose me? Bad move, Abbott. Now I no longer need you!"

A deafening blast shook Jess as window glass shattered inward and crashed to the floor all around them. The sudden wind sent the lantern flames bowing and fluttering as Jake and the cattlemen landed in a circle around Ross and the militants. Each of their guns was aimed at a different man.

Jess's eyes stung with tears of pride as they took in Jake, Hank, and Seth. Her gaze continued around the perimeter of Bodine's men, who looked uncertainly, and angrily, at the trap they found themselves in. Jake's other men stared back, unflinching—Doyle, Diaz, Taggart, Will, Payton, Ho Chen. She saw three burly men with stars on their vests—lawmen—then cloth of federal blue that winked menacingly with military brass. Captain Tom Rawlins and soldiers from Fort Churchill. Though Jess couldn't see all the men who had come to her aid and to stop Ross and Bodine, she was heartily thankful for every one of them.

Seth glanced at her, his promise to her steady in his eyes. He would keep Jake away from her.

The hot moisture brimming between her lids spilled over; with both hands, she hugged the child within her, knowing what Seth's promise would mean.

Jake and Tom Rawlins's thirty or so men stood almost evenly matched against Ross and Bodine's twenty-five. Bodine's men ignored the flailing Abbott, who was clearly not the man in charge, and looked to Ross for orders.

"Kill them!" he roared.

The room erupted into a swirl of men and determined fists connecting with jaws. A few guns were fired, the rest were holstered; no one wanted to mistakenly shoot his own men. Jess recognized three Paiute men—Lee, Black-Eye, and Black-Eye's son Natchez—in the thick of it, their gleaming knives slashing.

Seeing that he had been found out and that all would be lost, Ross's handsome face contorted in insanity and vengeance as his eyes fixed on Jess. He threw Abbott backward toward the mine shaft. Abbott's weight fractured the two wooden bars of one of the gates. He grasped for the wall, his eyes frantic as the top bar snapped fully in two. In reaction, Jess hurled the lantern at Ross and leapt to grab on to Abbott's jacket. With all her weight, she pulled him forward, and he grasped the doorway then pitched onto his knees, his breath heaving.

Like a rabid wolf hunting prey, Ross dodged the lantern; one of his men rolled over it, breaking the glass with a howl of agony and extinguishing the flame. Before Jess could run, Ross hauled her up against him with a snarl, his arm crushing the upper swell of her stomach.

Despite her struggles, he dragged her toward the open maw of the mine shaft—capturing the queen to assure the win. The floor ended, and she looked down into bottomless blackness.

The chasm.

The heat surging up from the mine shaft became intense.

Jess searched wildly for Jake, but she knew what was coming, knew she couldn't call for him or he would be the one to die. Refusing to give up, she lunged forward, throwing Ross off balance and herself with him, but it didn't loosen his hold.

She saw Edmund in the doorway, momentarily lit like an angel by a flash of lightning. She cried out his name. He looked in her direction, then started toward her. Fighting men abruptly blocked him from her view.

Ross's stance was solid once more.

Over the heads of the fiercely fighting men, Jake's gaze landed on her. He began throwing men from his path as he charged in her direction. Seth looked up, saw Jake's destination, and kept his promise. He jumped his boss from behind and wrapped his arm around Jake's neck. Seth held on, despite Jake's considerable attempts to throw him.

Ross whipped Jess around, toward the chasm, then let go.

She grabbed on to the chain that had held the top bar in place and landed on her hip on the edge of the blackness. Her skirts swung out over it, her feet dangling. The platform cables disappeared more than a thousand feet below.

Ross's heel rocked backward near her hip as he lost his balance. Knowing what would happen, she gripped tighter to the chain. His sudden, immense weight was pulling her down.

Her hands, clinging to the chain, began to slip. Several links slid through her fingers. She screamed, her arm muscles straining against the pull on her skirt, clenching the chain to her chest. She felt her stomach and the baby being pressed into the floor, and she shifted onto her backside. Ross's weight dragged her closer to the edge.

Across the expanse, Jake looked straight at her, and called to her. He called to her, but he couldn't get to her. Seth wouldn't let him. Then Seth looked up and saw her... and let Jake go.

Jess shrieked, "Seth, *no!*"

Ross was too heavy. Jess looked down, kicked toward his hands. Another chain link slipped past her hands. She couldn't hold on. She felt Abbott's sweaty hands on her arm, trying to pull her from the edge. Just as she glanced up at Abbott, he lost his grip and fell backward into three other men, toppling two of them.

Jess slid another link and screamed, out of rage. The scream gave her added strength.

She heard the rip of cloth above the clamor. She looked down and felt Ross thrashing, heard him yelling obscenities.

Now she was crying. Her arm muscles quavered as their last vestiges of strength dissolved.

Two rough, brawny hands clamped firmly to her left wrist. Her gaze shifted to the man who held her. Jake! Another pair of hands anchored her other arm. She stopped sliding, and looked up into blue eyes—her brother's. "Ambrose?"

Jess's skirt tore again. The top of the skirt gaped away from her bodice. Between Jake and Ambrose, she saw a knife descend toward her middle, held in Doyle's coffee-colored fist. With a smooth movement, he slit her tightly stretched overskirt further.

Ross's thrashing turned wild. The knife cut again. More tearing. Then more. Suddenly Jess felt light, and she heard Ross's fading screams echo back up the shaft.

Jess cried in relief as Jake and Ambrose pulled her carefully into the room. Edmund and Seth pushed a table that was on its side and maneuvered it to bar the way to the shaft. Shaking violently in nothing but her petticoat, Jess clung to Jake, one hand digging into his shirt. With the other hand, she wove fingers with Ambrose.

Ambrose had survived the war, and Jake had survived the chasm. Because Seth had seen that she was going to fall and broke his promise to her, Jake had survived.

Jake laid his free hand lightly against her stomach, feeling for contractions, she surmised, and watching her face for pain. "Is the baby all right?" he asked.

"I think so," she said, "but I don't believe we should move until I'm certain."

Beyond where Jake and her brother knelt, she saw Seth and Doyle keeping Bodine's men back.

At least two dozen men lay on the floor. From their dress, she knew that most of them were Bodine's. In the midst of them, she saw Bodine jerk his knife from its sheath and face Tom, who then circled him, drawing his saber. The fight continued around the two men, dwindling as ranchmen, soldiers, and lawmen dealt hard blows and added to the heaps of unconscious militants piled on the floor.

Ignoring them, Tom and Bodine circled. Each patiently waited for an opening. The knife swiped wickedly toward Tom's body, again and again. Tom, clearly a highly trained swordsman, calmly stayed inches beyond Bodine's reach. The next time the blade swept past, Tom struck.

The saber pierced Bodine's heart and went deep. Very deep. Jess saw blood seep into the back of his shirt. The evil man slowly fell to his knees, pulling the end of the saber down with him. He looked up at Tom in astonishment, then all emotion faded from his face. His knife struck the floor, and he fell over on top of it, dead.

The few murderers still standing raised their hands, ending the fight. Tom's men and the three lawmen forced them to a corner of the room. One of the lawmen hurried out the door and quickly returned with a crate. He set it on the floor, then drew out several iron shackles, which he and the other two lawmen affixed to the murderers' wrists while the ranchmen kept their rifles trained on them. It was over.

Lying on her side, Jess dropped her forehead to her arm and cried again, this time in great relief. She felt no contractions, and her water hadn't broken. The baby kicked, demanding sustenance.

Jake had survived, Jess thought again, her quiet sobs turning into soft laughter. All of them had survived. And she and the baby were all right.

Inwardly, she praised God.

Beyond the windows, heat lightning flashed once more, faintly, then all became still.

Chapter Eighteen

The sheriff of Virginia City, Sheriff Howard, heartily shook Tom Rawlins's hand like a man who probably even slept with gusto. "I've seen to it that one jury consisted of all skinny men," he announced, "and another of all fat men with their chairs crammed together." He guffawed, his eyes twinkling merrily. "After all, what citizen would want to attend a trial with no spectacle for entertainment? This time, I think we'll have a jury of all ugly men."

Jess smiled from where she sat leaning against the wall. Sheriff Howard turned aside to talk with Carson City sheriff Tim Smith and his deputy Thomas Bedford as nearly twenty men in dark blue uniforms, brass buttons, and gleaming sabers began to lead Ross's men out.

Tom Rawlins stepped close, reached out a hand, and, with Jake's assistance, gently helped Jess to her feet. "Are these all the radicals?" Tom asked his friend.

"All the ones I know of," Jake told him.

Grinning, Tom slapped Jake on the back. "You may have just gotten me promoted to Major. I believe I owe you."

Like Tom did, Jake whacked his friend's shoulder. "You'll know who to come to when Fort Churchill needs more horses."

"It's a deal."

Jess held a hand to her middle, but the baby seemed to be fine. "Captain?" Tom's gaze lowered to meet hers.

"I'd like you to meet my brother, Ambrose Hale. Ambrose, Captain Rawlins is the man who helped get Jake and me in to see you at Camp Douglas prison during the war."

"I'm truly grateful," Ambrose said sincerely and shook Tom's hand—the Confederate soldier and the Federal, establishing the first of many bridges that would be needed in the coming years to span the residual hatred and damage of war.

"I rely upon my conscience to determine right and wrong," Tom said, "not my uniform."

Jess bit her lip to keep back the fresh threat of grateful tears. Silently, she thanked God once more, this time for giving them hope for their nation. She knew they would all need it in the years to come.

Behind Ambrose, Edmund rocked on his toes, looking particularly pleased with himself, and a delightful suspicion took root in Jess's mind. She met the gaze of her family's longtime friend. "Edmund, by any chance, is Ambrose the man you said was coming in to town to meet with me about the purchase of several of our horses?"

Edmund's plain face turned red as he nodded. "I wanted you to be surprised," he confessed. "We would have arrived here at the same time Jake and the ranchmen did, but my horse spooked at the lightning and threw me." He indicated the rip in his pant leg. "Ambrose had to chase down my horse."

Ho Chen was circling the wounded, assessing injuries. He paused beside Ambrose and patted the younger man's arm warmly. "It is good to see you again, Mister Ambrose. It has been very long time," he said. He flashed a quick, fatherly smile, then hurried on to see to the wounded.

Hank and two other men did the same. By their late arrival, their clean appearance, and the black bags they carried, Jess realized they were doctors. Someone must have planned for them to be here now. Hank's brief, knowing smile in her direction told her who the man with the foresight had been.

Jake hugged Jess to him. She lifted her hand to rest it against his ribs. Beneath, she knew, he bore the scar—to her, a mark of valor—from the night he'd tried to save her father. "I can't believe all the ranchmen made it in time," she said.

Jake glanced down at her. "Jess, my horses were bred to be used by the Pony Express. Of course they made it. And last I saw, all of them were fine. You can see for yourself once we get outside."

She would, she acknowledged silently, but the men came first. Steady enough now to stand on her own, she moved away and began to check on the men herself. Jake and Ambrose remained near her side. Taggart knelt in front of Diaz, knotting a bandana over the remaining stub of the Spaniard's pinkie finger. Jess felt sickened as she realized he had lost it in a knife fight.

Diaz's teeth gleamed white between his silky black mustache and goatee. "The other man fared not as well, I assure you," he said, both his spunk and his charm neatly in place. "This will give beautiful woman yet another reason to dote on me, eh, *Mariposa?*"

Ambrose glanced at her. "*Mariposa?*"

"It's Diaz's name for me. You remember him and Taggart from Chicago, yes?" she said, and the men exchanged nods and tired pleasantries. "*Mariposa,*" she explained, "means 'butterfly.'"

Ambrose's look was one of older-brotherly love. "Seems fitting to me."

Jess's heart felt lighter than it had in more than five years, since the day her brother had boarded a stagecoach and left for the war. Ambrose had called her his butterfly ever since they were young. Now he was here, thin, aging, but alive, and she was married to the best man God had ever made. Jessica Hale Bennett felt complete.

Jake pressed his own bandana to the gash on the side of Diaz's head and held it to stem the bleeding. "Ambrose, did you know that your father owned a mine?" he asked, apparently understanding the implications of its name, McKinney.

Ambrose lifted his hat and pushed his sandy-gold hair back from his face. "No, I had no idea." He looked to Edmund. "Did you know?"

Edmund shook his head. "No, but I think I know why Isaac never uttered a word about it. He must have staked the claim right after he arrived in fifty-nine, before your mother, Jess, and you arrived with your household belongings. At first, he didn't know if it was going to pay off," he reasoned, "then when it boomed, I expect he didn't want me to know that my success didn't match his."

Jess gently rested a hand on her brother's arm. "I think he didn't tell Mother or me, because he knew a portion of its profits would go to the federal government to support a war against you, which he must have feared would destroy his relationships with Mother and me."

Ambrose patted her hand. "Father left me Greenbriar, Jess, something I don't believe he would have done if he'd stopped loving me. He knew it was all I ever wanted."

Abbott spoke up from where he had been quietly listening. "After your parents died, Ross withdrew Mr. Hale's savings from the bank in gold, little by little, until he had possession of it all. He nearly broke the bank more than once. Ross was amused," Abbott continued, his voice heavy with remorse, "at the irony that a Southerner's investment was being used to fund his war against Southerners."

"There was an amount exceeding eight hundred thousand dollars in the account," Jess told Ambrose. "We don't know where the money is now."

"Perhaps we'll find it," Abbott suggested, "when we find my son. Please"—he looked at Jake, and at Sheriff Howard as he returned—"please, help me to find my son. I don't know how much time he has before one of Ross's men finds out what happened here and goes to...to find Wirt and hurt him."

"We just caught a man," Sheriff Howard said, poking a thumb in the direction of the door, "who was trying to deliver a shipment of guns to Ross." His eyes sparkled. "We just thanked him warmly and arrested him." He shifted his gaze to Abbott. "Ross has your boy?"

"He kidnapped him," Jess said, "to force Mr. Abbott to comply with his demands." Abbott tossed her a look of profound gratefulness. "According to Mr. Abbott, Galen Ross killed Mr. Abbott's wife for the same purpose."

Sheriff Howard rubbed his chin as he glanced around at Jake, Jess, Edmund, and the others. "I'll have to question all these folks about everything that's happened," he warned Abbott, "but I'll see to it that the judge takes Ross's means of force into consideration. Now let's see what we can do about finding your son."

Jess thought rapidly. "Mr. Abbott has been to Ross's home. Wirt isn't there. That means Ross has been paying someone to look after the boy. Ross was a manager, so he would have kept his account books in order. There would be records of payments to an individual, most likely a woman."

"But the records wouldn't be kept here," Jake put in, his words more of a question.

Edmund nodded. "That's right. If he made notations of payments in the mine's records, someone might have seen him make an entry and asked about it."

Sheriff Howard looked at Jess and Edmund. "You two know something about keeping books, do you?" At their nods of acknowledgment, he made a decision. "Then I'd like you two to come along. Abbott, you know where Ross lives, or lived," he corrected himself, "before he took up residence in the bottom of the mine shaft?"

"Yes."

"Then you can lead us there. I won't shackle you yet, but if you try to run for it…." He rested a hand on the butt of his gun and left the remainder of his words unspoken but clearly understood.

"I can go with you," Ambrose suggested. "I kept books before I left for war." He shared a knowing look with Jake. "Jess should stay in one place and rest."

"My arms and stomach muscles hurt fierce," Jess said to her husband and her brother both, "but the baby and I are all right. Jake, I need to help find him."

Jake gave her a long look of frustration, then shifted his gaze to Ambrose. "You ever win an argument with her?"

"Not since she was about five."

"Then I reckon she goes with."

Taggart pulled Diaz to his feet, and around the room downed ranchmen also gained their feet, lending each other a hand or a supportive arm. Eli Payton was the only one whose wounds looked serious, Jess saw. Jake must have seen him at the same time, and the doctors bending together over him, because he left her side to go kneel near Payton amid broken window glass.

Jake gripped the older man's hand and spoke softly to him. Payton replied, then said nothing more. The two doctors glanced regretfully at Jake, then moved on to others whom they could help.

Jake continued to hold Payton's hand as the man's back arched and his boots kicked against the grasp of death. And then Payton lay still.

Jake removed his hat, and around the room the other ranchmen did the same, a silent, respectful tribute to one of their own.

While the sheriff and Abbott preceded Edmund and Ambrose out the door, Jess held Jake beside her until the others were beyond hearing. "What did Payton say to you?" she asked softly.

Jake settled his hat on top of his head. His voice was gruff, but his brown eyes were steady, as he replied, "He asked that I bury him at the ranch."

❦

"Too bad Ross went down the shaft with his key," Sheriff Howard commented. "Anyone know how to get through a front door as solid as this?"

Jake lifted a boot and drove the heel into the door just below the lock. The edge of the door splintered as it flew wide.

"Ah, you found the spare key!" the sheriff exclaimed. "Well done."

Moments later, the mood turned somber as they stepped into the tomb-like house. Since Abbott knew his way around the front room, he entered first and lighted a lamp. Tomb-like had been an apt first impression, Jess saw as Abbott turned the wick higher. If the front entry was any indicator, Ross's house was more sparsely furnished than Hank's. No hall tables or sconces broke the empty space of the walls. Not a single painting existed to add color to the bare plaster. Not one rug warmed the floors.

It felt like a place where nobody lived, where nobody had ever lived.

"Ross's study is down this way," Abbott said.

Only one chair sat in the study behind the desk. Jake helped Jess into it, and Abbott, Edmund, Ambrose, and Jess immediately dug though the desk for Ross's account books. Edmund found several books in the bottom drawer. Each of the foursome took one and began flipping through.

Ambrose stood nearest the door. Sheriff Howard stepped close to him as he lit the two lanterns that sat on the desk. "Mr. Hale, may I trust you to keep Abbott in this room?"

"Of course."

"I appreciate it," the sheriff said. "Mr. Bennett, perhaps you can help me search this sarcophagus for the boy, just in case?"

"Glad to."

Jake followed the sheriff out, both of them holding lanterns, and Jess bent over the dates and entries in her ledger, absently listening to the men's boots stride from room to room and up the stairs to the floor above, and praying that they would find Abbott's son alive.

As if hearing her thoughts, Ambrose innocently asked, "Why are we hurrying as if the boy is in danger? Surely he's safe if Ross has been paying someone to look after him."

Abbott's eyes were bloodshot as he scowled at Ambrose, and Jess realized that the banker truly hated Southerners with everything that he was. Her own accent had faded over time, but Ambrose had been in the South for years, and his drawl was as pronounced as ever. Even so, Abbott answered politely enough. "Ross has men around him to whom he had given orders, though I don't know their names. When they hear about the trouble at the mine office, they will go straight to my son and kill him." His voice broke. He clamped his lips together and lowered his face to the records in his hand.

"We'll find him first," Ambrose said, then bent again to his own ledger.

Abbott, who seemed to focus more closely on each entry than the others, was still reading near the middle of his ledger when Jess closed hers and reached for the last one in the bottom of the drawer.

"I found it," she said, holding open the front cover for the others to see. In tall, smoothly penned cursive were the words "Ross's Brigade."

Abbott tossed his own record book onto the desk and snatched it from her. His eyes shifted from side to side over each line, while a loud pounding shook the floor overhead.

Jess looked up to the ceiling—one of planks rather than plaster—as a piece of wood gave way in the room above with a clean snap. From the ceiling, particles of dust drifted down, forming a thin layer over hats and shoulders and the desk. She heard Jake's and the sheriff's tones of discussion yet could not discern their words. A moment after the discussion ended, the pounding resumed, until a board broke directly above. Lantern light shone down though the hole in the ceiling, and Jake's crooked smile appeared, cast in a white-yellow glow.

"Here, catch," he said.

Surprised by the request, Jess held out her hands just an instant before a small cloth sack landed rather heavily in them. She closed her hands around the sack and felt the corners of small rocks inside it.

Stunned, she looked up through the hole and saw Jake looking down with an odd expression on his face. "Sheriff Howard is pulling greenbacks out of the floor near the bed," he said with a tilt of his hat in that direction. "Jess, the whole floor up here has been pried up and nailed down again. Almost all the nails are new."

Jess's heart fluttered in hope, afraid to believe what that must mean. Feeling Ambrose's warm eyes on her, she tossed him a quick, hopeful smile before laying the sack on the desk and tugging open the drawstring.

Rocks and dust spilled out onto the desk, drawing the astonished gaze of every person in the room.

The lantern flame gleamed through the sparkling glass chimney, flooding its light over the mound of gold nuggets that lay there.

Jake's deep voice floated down, much as the dust had done only moments before. "Ambrose will now have the means to rebuild Greenbriar," he said, "and the ranch...."

She breathed the remaining words with him: "Will survive."

❖◈❖◈❖

"Here!" Abbott shouted, probably not aware just how loudly. He held out the record book to no one in particular and scanned the faces, clearly not seeing them. "I found my son," he said shakily. "I found my son!" He yelled this time, the words a basic but effective communication to Sheriff Howard.

The sheriff thundered down the stairs and into the study. "Where?"

Abbott swallowed as if he'd just crawled across a parched expanse of desert, unable to answer.

Edmund took the book from him, read down the page, then met the sheriff's gaze. "The entry says 'Mrs. Fitch, for assistance rendered.'" He skimmed the rest of the page, then the next. "The entry reappears at two-week intervals."

"I know a Mrs. Fitch who lives down on the edge of the bordello district. She runs a lodging house," he said defensively, then cleared his throat, "though I was asked to investigate her a time or two, when a few women of the town complained of her being a fraudulent fortune-teller. Mr. Van Dorn, Mr. Hale, would the two of you stay here and keep an eye on the place until we get back? I'd like Mrs. Bennett to come with us to have another woman present, so Mrs. Fitch can't accuse me of wrongful behavior, and I'd like Mr. Bennett to come with us, in case I need assistance with another door, or if Ross's men arrive ahead of us."

Sheriff Howard's burly fist kept pounding on the door until Jess could hear the tired drag of slippers approaching it from the opposite side.

"Who in blazes is there?" a woman hollered. "It's the middle of the blasted, bloody night!" A lock bolt clicked back. "Galen, that had better be you," she muttered.

The instant the handle turned, Sheriff Howard shoved the door open and used the back of his arm to press the stunned woman to the wall. "Where's the boy?"

Her eyes grew large and round in her head as she recognized the sheriff. Her mouth opened and closed like a fish's as she tried to form words that wouldn't come.

"Mr. Bennett, go with Abbott as he searches the house," the sheriff ordered.

Jake was already on Abbott's heels, and Jess was only a step behind.

Downstairs were a small parlor, dining room, and kitchen. Abbott hurried up the stairs. Jake paused, swept Jess up in his arms, and took the stairs after him two at a time. On the upstairs landing, he set Jess down again and pressed a fast kiss to her hair.

A long hallway stretched out from the back of the house to the front. Jake began opening doors to the left while Abbott opened the ones to the right, both men calling for Wirt.

Jess, however, eyed the stairs that rose behind her to a small, square door in the ceiling. An attic. She knew with certainty that the boy was there.

"Jake?"

Abbott didn't hear her, but Jake immediately spun. A question formed on his lips, and she answered it by simply nodding to the flight of stairs.

"Abbott."

The banker—*former banker*, Jess mentally corrected—heard her husband. Once he saw the object of their interest, the door in the ceiling, he pushed past Jake and ascended the stairs. In the darkness, Jess saw his fingers push against the door, then feel around the edges. "The woman's locked him in! She's locked in my son!"

Jake was already beside him. "Stand back," he said. Jake lifted the heels of his hands to the door and shoved as if he intended to lift the ceiling. The lock held, but the two hinges didn't. The door flew upward and clattered.

Jake climbed two more stairs until his head could see into the room. "Hi there," Jake said softly. "You must be Wirt. I'm a friend of your father's. We've come to get you. You're safe now."

"M-my father's here?"

"He's right here," Jake assured him. He reached his arms through the opening. "It's all right, I've got you."

He lowered his arms, and a pair of small, bare feet appeared, then a pair of tattered pants. Chubby arms wrapped around Jake's neck as he ducked again into the stairway.

The boy's head turned, and two lines of tears glistened on Abbott's cheeks as he reached out and gently took his son.

Jess watched from below the balustrade as Abbott clutched his son to him and sobbed.

Abbott was trying to thank them both, Jess was sure, but with his son's choking hug and his own tears, he couldn't quite say the words. Jake gave Abbott a nod, letting him know that his and the boy's happiness were thanks enough.

When they went downstairs, the sheriff spoke to Abbott and said he would arrange to have his deputy stay the night with him and his son at Abbott's sister's home in Carson City, though, having a care for the boy, he didn't add that Abbott would be arrested in the morning.

Abbott nodded over his son's shoulder, clearly thankful for the unexpected consideration the sheriff was showing to him and his son.

Jess curled her hand into Jake's. In her heart, she found herself praying that this man, who had ordered the murder of her family, would be spared an executioner's noose and would instead be sentenced to life in prison, so that his son would grow up knowing his father.

Chapter Nineteen

J
ess wasn't certain how long she'd been standing under the archway of Edmund's carriage house or how long she'd been currycombing Luina's soft palomino hide. She was, however, certain that the sunrise she had just witnessed had been one of the most beautiful she had ever seen, and that this precious moment was one she would never forget.

She smoothed the currycomb, then her hand, along the warm, satiny fur underneath Luina's butter-yellow mane while the horse stood contentedly, one hind leg bent in repose, the tip of its black hoof resting against the earth. The horse's mood couldn't have matched Jess's better. In the earliest of Jess's memories of when she was a small child at Greenbriar, she reflected, their neighbors had spoken of war, and threatened war. Then states around them, one by one, had seceded from the Union. Her family had come west to avoid the conflict but instead had been pursued by the ever-expanding ripples of war. She had lost her family to it, after all. At the ranch she and Jake had faced threats against the Paiute families she had come to love as her own. In the past months, they had rid Honey Lake Valley of the miscreants who had lived to drive the Paiutes away, and now the men who had terrorized and threatened people like her family were no more. Even the drought that had for three years threatened the ranch was past, and grass grew thick and high everywhere. Never before had she faced a day completely free of concern for what it might bring. The horse hair felt silkier, the sunrise looked more vivid, and the sound of loudly snoring ranchmen, who lay strewn under trees across Edmund's yard, had never delighted her more.

The sunrise, still golden, lay on Ambrose's hat and shoulders like a blessing as he dismounted near the street. He quietly led his horse around the ranchmen and toward the carriage house, plainly taking care not to wake them. At the trough alongside the building, only a few paces from Jess, he watered the horse then tied it to rest. Spying her skirt and face on the opposite side of Luina, he smiled, found another currycomb, and joined her.

"You were out early this morning," she observed softly, so as not to disturb any of the men.

He kept his tones as quiet as hers. "I wanted to see the place where our house had stood, and to visit Mother and Father's grave at the cemetery. I like the headstone you chose." He brushed Luina's chest with the rhythmic, gentle touch that had always drawn horses to him. Luina turned her head curiously, then lightly rubbed her nose along Ambrose's sleeve. Seemingly unaware of the horse's affection, Ambrose smiled sadly at Jess. "I was finally able to say hello to Emma, to introduce her to her big brother. Ah, Jess, I wish I'd known her. I wish I'd been here for you and Mother, and for Father."

"If you'd stayed, you might have died in the fire with them. You had to follow your heart, Ambrose, just like we all do. God put it in your heart to go where He needed you to be, and because of that, you're alive. You know that you never could have lived with yourself had you ignored that calling and stayed here and left all the others to fight."

Ambrose nodded but didn't answer. She surmised that his being away when their parents and sister died was one regret, perhaps one of many, that he would need time to overcome.

Jess followed his gaze as he studied the wagon that was, strangely, parked in the middle of the yard among the ranchmen.

"The men must have placed it under that tree before they went to sleep last night," she said, answering her brother's unspoken question. The tailgate was down, and in the wagon's bed they could see a long shape wrapped in horse blankets. "The body of Eli Payton," she murmured. "It's the men's way of giving him one more night among them, of paying him honor."

Ambrose considered the ranchmen, young and old, white, black, and Indian, who lay dirty, tattered, and bandaged, and his hands stilled on Luina's side. "This looks like the aftermath of a battle," he mused.

Jess saw that beneath Diaz's sombrero, his head was still wrapped, and a bandana remained knotted over the stub of his pinkie. "That's exactly what it is," she said. "Last night may very well have been the last battle of the War Between the States." Not willing to dwell on sadness any longer, or to tarnish or dishonor all that the cattlemen had fought for and won, she sought to turn the conversation back to the good of the morning and the reasons to find joy. "I never once believed you wouldn't survive the war, you know."

His sky-blue eyes sparkled with teasing, and in them Jess glimpsed the Ambrose she had always known. "You know Hales are too stubborn to die," he said.

Jake chuckled softly as he dismounted Cielos behind Jess. "Hales are too stubborn for a lot of things," he said, then leaned to press a sound kiss to Jess's temple.

"Such as taking no for an answer?" Ambrose suggested with a grin as he combed Luina once again.

Jake tied Cielos. "And allowing anyone to tell them that something can't be done."

"Or that they should marry." Ambrose's sandy-gold brows lifted at Jess in a not-so-subtle reminder.

"Or that they should stay at the ranch until trouble passes," Jake added.

The two men shared a quick smile. Jess wanted to flatten them both.

An Irish voice spoke from under a hat where Taggart lay. "Or to allow that a marriage vow to obey might be more than just a guideline."

Diaz's lazy voice replied, "One should not expect so much of *la Mariposa*, amigo. Only *Dios* is able to do miracles."

"It gives Jess something to strive toward," Doyle put in.

Jess speared each of the shamelessly laughing men with an exaggerated smile. "My, I just can't tell you how glad I am that I have all of you to help me correct my faults."

"Ye *need* all o' us to accomplish that," Taggart avowed.

Briefly, Jess debated a sparring of wits, but then decided on a more effective means to deflect their banter. She loudly breathed in, sniffing the air in exaggerated bliss. "Is that fresh biscuits and coffee that I smell? And strawberry jam as well? Edmund's cook must have left the kitchen window open. I wouldn't be at all surprised if she fixed enough for twenty men."

Moments later, the yard had cleared as the appetites disappeared into the house, and Jess stood alone with Jake and Ambrose under the archway of the carriage building.

"They care about you," Ambrose observed.

This time, Jess's smile was genuine. "Yes, they do. They're good people." She glanced warmly up at Jake. "Every last one of them."

Ambrose's mustache lifted in a grin. "So, when am I going to be an uncle?" he asked.

Jess gave the horse's rump a pat. "Five or six weeks. Will you stay until the baby's born?"

"If you do, snow will block the roads over the Rockies by the time you get there," Jake noted, "but you'll have your pick of horses to take back to Greenbriar come spring."

"Well, that's too many good reasons to pass up," Ambrose said brightly.

Jess could already imagine it: her brother and her husband, talking horses and in their glory for an entire winter. Suddenly she realized that they had begun doing just that; Jake was telling Ambrose about the horse breeds at the ranch. Those two, she mused, were already as comfortable and as well matched in their new friendship as a pair of old leather boots.

"What about this palomino?" Ambrose asked. "Is she for sale?"

"Not Luina," Jess said, grinning. "She thinks she belongs to Diaz."

Jake asked, "What do the two of you want to do about the management of the McKinney Mine?"

"I thought about that while I was riding this morning," Ambrose said. He looked to Jess.

"Edmund?" she said.

Ambrose nodded. "Seems right to me to offer it to him."

Jess hung her currycomb on its nail on the carriage house wall. "Father always shared half his business profits with Edmund. If Edmund is willing to take on the work to oversee it, I think we should do the same, though mine production has dropped off over the past year, all across the Comstock."

"Half to him and half to us," Ambrose agreed, "whatever that may be, for as long as the ore holds out. Jake?"

"Edmund's a good man," he said, "and he might appreciate the change in surroundings."

"He might indeed," her brother said. From his face, Jess thought he must be recalling what she'd written about Miriam in her letters. "Is Edmund here?"

Jake leaned his arms on Luina and waved a hand toward the middle of town. "No, he went with me this morning to answer the rest of the sheriff's questions. Jess, the sheriff said he'll write to us if he needs either of us to testify, but with Edmund available to testify, and with all the information we've provided, he doesn't think he'll have to trouble us.

"Edmund went to the imports store afterward," Jake told Ambrose. "We can stop and talk to him about the mine on our way out of town today. If he chooses not to manage it, he'll likely know someone trustworthy who will want to."

"What about the money you found in Ross's house?" Jess asked.

"The sheriff's men have collected all the greenbacks and gold," Jake answered. "He has to go over all the papers to legally confirm ownership, then he'll turn it over to the two of you."

"To the three of us," Ambrose corrected him.

Jess playfully tossed her head. "Do what you want with your half, big brother, but don't offer to share my half with anyone." She sighed regretfully. "Eight hundred thousand just doesn't go as far as it used to."

Jake squeezed her shoulder and went to join his men, apparently aware that she and Ambrose wanted a few more minutes together before they packed up to leave.

"Do you still have the ribbon I gave you?" she murmured.

Reflectively, Ambrose removed the pin holding his shirt pocket shut and withdrew the green satin cording. It was ragged and bloodstained—from when Ambrose was shot, she knew—but he'd never lost it during four years of war.

Jess smiled as he pinned it back in place. A warm breeze stirred, rustling the leaves over her head. This moment was indeed one she would never forget. She had managed to change the outcome of her visions, Eli Payton was walking with God, and the Lord had blessed her with a new family and a ranch that she loved. She couldn't wait to show it to Ambrose.

At long last, they were going home.

❖❖❖

Tall, green bunchgrass rippled across the gentle rises and falls of Honey Lake Valley, more densely packed than the solid gold that paved the streets of heaven. Jess shaded her eyes from the setting sun as she swayed easily atop the wagon seat beside Hank. As he guided the horses, she thrilled at each new piece of the ranch as it came into view, and marveled at how completely different all of it was from the barren stretch of desert that had become familiar to her during the years of drought. Jake had seen it like this, probably when he'd bought the land, and most of the ranchmen would remember it as well. But to Jess, this was a whole new region.

No wonder stories of it had enticed a generation of people to uproot and move west.

Hank looked over at her, his smile bright as ever. "Are you doing all right, Jess? You and the baby ready to be firmly on the ground again?"

"We're just fine. How about you?" She brushed back loose hairs from her face, which the wind blew right back. "You didn't say good-bye to Gusty yesterday morning before we left Carson City. I'd thought you would."

His smile turned pensive. "Perhaps I'll go back and visit her when work allows."

Jess wanted to give him a little verbal nudge in that direction, but then they rounded the last mountain, and the slanted roof and pine logs of the two-story ranch house appeared at the far end of the valley, and she could no longer remember what she had wanted to say.

Other ranch buildings gradually appeared—the bunkhouse, cookhouse, smithy, barn, workshop, and stable—as well as the rest of the three hundred and twenty beautiful acres those buildings sat on, all of it encircled by thin wire fencing like a silver lining around a dream.

As Jake, Ambrose, Ho Chen, and the ranchmen approached the north gate ahead of Hank's wagon, several Morgans, mustangs, and Thoroughbreds within the paddock lifted their heads to gaze in their direction. As if they sensed the return of their friends, a group of about twenty adult horses and young foals broke into a gallop and rounded the inside of the fence nearest them, their hides gleaming like polished quartz, onyx, and topaz as they stretched out under the last copper rays of the day.

Seth opened the gate. The men rode their horses onto the Bennett Mountain Ranch and continued through the waving grasses toward the ranch compound. When Seth closed the gate and Hank guided the two wagon horses in procession after the others, Jess felt regal, a sensation that grew as the wheels whispered across the simple bridge that led over the stream.

Before Hank set the brake, Mattie and Grace were climbing aboard and welcoming him and Jess home. Lily, Nettle, and Spruzy hurried out of the cookhouse only a few moments behind them. The three women greeted the men and beamed at Jess, their round faces elated.

Jess hugged the two girls to her. *I was right to insist that we return home as quickly as possible,* she thought, and they had made it in less than two days. Yes, they had to bury Payton, but Jess also couldn't have borne to stay away another minute.

❖•❀•❀•❖

Ho Chen and Lily's rooster crowing at the sunrise, Jake decided, sounded as if it had a sock lodged in its throat and was determined to expel it. Had Jake lacked all recollection of returning home the night before, that sound would have erased his doubts.

He sat upright in bed, rubbing the sleep from his eyes with this thumbs. The first thing he noticed, besides the pleasant fact that the rooster had stopped crowing, was that the sky beyond the window was dark gray—it couldn't yet be four in the morning—and the second thing he noticed was that Jess wasn't in bed beside him.

He'd find her in one of two places: the baby's room or the stable. He listened. The soft movements coming from the other side of the wall told him that she was in the baby's room.

Out of habit, he pulled on his shirt and trousers, but, after brief reflection, he lifted his boots and carried them. He eased open the bedroom door, which she had pulled closed, then stepped out into the upper hall. The door to the left was cracked open, and a narrow strip of lamplight spilled out onto the ceiling, floor, and railing. Rather than disturb her, he leaned a shoulder against the doorjamb and simply watched. His wife.

She passed in and out of his line of vision as she rearranged objects and dusted them. She wore a robe over her nightgown that floated around her when she moved, as did her endlessly long chestnut hair, which glowed soft as angel's dust in the low light cast by the flame. He saw the side of her face as she reached a cloth up to dust away a spider web, the green of her eyes and the thickness of her lashes, the angles of her nose and cheeks, the redness of her full lips. As she stretched upward on bare feet—which he found tiny and adorable—she unconsciously pressed a slender hand to the robe where it slanted over the baby.

Lord above, he loved her. He loved them both.

She moved to Hank's painting on the far wall and dusted the top of its frame. She dusted out the tin cup Seth had given her and rehung it on its nail, then adjusted the child-sized lasso Will had woven, giving it a gentle pat. From the bassinet that rested on the rug Jess had woven from old strips of cloth and yarn, she lifted the black and red flannel blanket, the remnants of Taggart's winter shirt, and gave it a shake to free it of any dust, then carefully placed it back within the bassinet. She picked up the small wooden horse Diaz had carved and blew particles of dust from its back. Replacing it, she fingered the tiny moccasins that Lily had given for the baby, then turned the tepee-shaped lantern Doyle had formed, as if she enjoyed the differences she discovered on each side. Her eyes moved to the only book that stood atop the dresser, the Brothers Grimm fairy tales Eli Payton had purchased in town. Jess lifted it, opened the cover, and gently turned pages, caressing them as if they held meaning of greater worth to her than the stories and illustrations printed there. Jake knew that they did, for both of them.

Nearer the door, Jake saw part of the cradleboard that all the ranch Paiutes had labored together to make, and he realized that he was just as impatient to see their baby in it as Jess had said she was.

Rather than intrude on her special time alone with their child, he left her to her nesting and moved away and down the stairs with his boots in hand.

He eased open the front door and walked out onto the porch. There he leaned against the wall and pulled his boots on, admiring the pair of rocking chairs beside him, and the three flowers that bloomed in front of the porch, which, he saw, someone had kept watered during the weeks he and Jess had been gone. A soft purring pulled his attention to the rocking chairs. Between them, the orange cat that Sadie had loved stretched out on its side, fully expecting Jake to give her a scratch. He complied.

Out in the ranch yard, starlight blanketed the ranchmen who hadn't been disturbed by the crowing rooster. Jake was certain that Ambrose, who had politely refused to stay in the guest room in the main house, was resting companionably among them, as he certainly must have done among his fellow soldiers during the war.

Jake eyed the compound and realized he was seeing it as through the eyes of Jess and their child, who would grow up here. Would he sneak out of the house and cross this compound to sleep out in the stable with the foals, as Jess and Ambrose had done when they were children? Jake realized he had stepped down from the porch and was walking toward the stable, as if already searching for his son. He kept walking, living out what he knew was his dream for a few short years from now. During the night, Jess would sleepily ask him to check on their son, or daughter, and he'd whisper to her that he would, and he'd leave her to sleep, but he'd find the room beside theirs empty. Outside, Jake would quietly pass the same or similar men sleeping out in the cool air, listen to the restful song of crickets as he was now, and swing open the door to the stable, where moonlight would follow its retreating shadow across the floor, and fall on—

Mattie and Grace.

Jake chuckled softly. The two sisters slept beside the nearest stall, much like Jess had done before she'd left for Carson City. His knees creaked as he bent to pull their blanket up over them from where it had fallen to one side, then he remained there, forearms on his knees, his heart brimming. He realized it was also churning with dread. He was worried for Jess.

According to Jess, her mother had miscarried twice. One of those times, it had been late in her pregnancy. He was afraid of losing the baby, especially after what had nearly happened to Jess and the baby both only three nights ago in Virginia City, but he was also afraid for Jess. She was slender and had fine bones, and he knew that for some women, childbirth could be very difficult.

The thought had drifted through his mind ever since she'd first mentioned her fear, and now he knew it had become his fear too. They were so close to the delivery, a little over five weeks away. Already he loved the child and dreamed about finding him, or her, here with the horses. He wouldn't let anything happen to either of them, he determined—Jess or the child. He would keep close watch over Jess and perform any heavy tasks for her.

Feeling the need to work off the tension of his doubts, Jake closed the stable door behind him and walked along the river in the direction of the garden. He recalled Jess teasing him about the canoes they would build to race and estimated that with the height and current of the stream, having a canoe or two might not be such a bad idea after all. The thought of a future with Jess, he found, reassured him, and he let his mind continue along that path as he approached the garden—many of the plants were nearly as high as his boots, he saw—and turned south along the fence to the gate to Hank's land. He was closing it behind him before he even realized his intentions.

He was going to visit Olivia and Sadie.

After rounding Hank's small orchard of apple and cherry trees, Jake continued west along his neighbor's southern fence line and past the abundant hay that needed cutting. This land had once belonged to him, but he didn't regret Hank's ownership of it. Hank was the best neighbor he'd ever had. He hoped the man stayed on for years to come.

Nearly ten minutes passed before he stopped at the foot of the three small hills of earth. Beneath one were Livvy and Sadie. Jess's Paiute friend, Red Deer, lay beside them. Next to her, the newly turned earth covered Eli Payton, whom the ranch people had buried the evening before. Subdued, he greeted each one, then sat down in the grass beside Livvy.

He prayed he'd never have to bury another wife and baby here.

"Hello, Livvy. It's been a while since I last visited you, but you know I'll always stop by when I can." He smiled softly. "I'm going to be a daddy again, so tell Sadie that she's going to have a little brother or sister that she'll get to meet up there one day." *Please, Lord, let that be years from now.* "You know me well enough to know that I'm feeling sad again that you and Sadie haven't been here with me these past few years, and I know you well enough to know that you'd have a thing or two to say if I let anything get in the way of me being happy, just as I would have wanted for you if I'd been the one to go first. I also know that you're happy walking up there with the Almighty, you and Sadie, and Red Deer, and Eli Payton—he's the new man you may have already bumped into—and I'm sure you've met my mama by now. I'm sure she's crazy about Sadie."

Jake's sorrow began getting to him. He imagined what Jess would say to him if she found him here. She'd remind him that their child was in God's hands, and that there was no better place for him or her to be.

The thought settled comfortably in his mind. He felt his fears lift, though they didn't vanish entirely.

"Five weeks to go," he told Livvy with a shake of his head, "and already I'm a nervous father."

He also felt closer to God.

Unwilling to leave that sense of nearness, Jake lay in the grass beside Olivia and Sadie and rested until the sun rose.

"I imagine that if Jess is still awake, then she's getting hungry," he mused aloud and then, after a stretch and a yawn, stood to his feet with a smile. "You should have seen her eat chili peppers last night, Livvy. She loves them just as much as you did when you were expecting." Bright orange sunlight blazed into his eyes, and he realized he'd forgotten his hat. His grin widened. "Jess won't let me forget this one," he mused. "I'll say my good-byes for now. Look after each other; I'm sure it's a big place up there. Red Deer." He nodded respectfully. "Payton."

Minutes later, Jake closed the gate behind him once again, and spotted a traveler coming up the road along the base of the Sierras. The man was driving a covered wagon—an immigrant, Jake reckoned. His gray horse was thin and moving with effort, like it had pulled the wagon two thousand miles by itself. When the man slowed the animal near the south gate, Jake headed there instead of to the house.

"Good morning," he called out.

The man looked to be twenty or more years older than Jake, with gray hair to match his horse, and his smile was friendly, if a little tired. "Good morning," he called back. "I wonder if I might trade this horse for one of yours. He's a good animal, just needs a rest, is all."

"I'd be glad to trade him," Jake said, the Western code coming as naturally to him as grass came after a rain. If a man had a need, a ranchman provided for it. "You're welcome to stay for breakfast," Jake offered. "I have one of the best cooks there is."

"Thank you, but I ate less than an hour ago. Yours is the first ranch I've come to," he said as he stepped down from the wagon and began unhitching his horse.

"It won't be the last. A lot of good folks around here. I'll go catch you a fresh horse."

When Jake led the buckskin through the gate, the gray was already tied inside the fence, its eyes half shut as it rested. Jake made a mental note to water it and rub it down as soon as the man left. It had had a long journey and would enjoy getting coddled some, as Jess had once put it.

Jake helped the man to hitch up the horse, then the man shook his hand. "I'm obliged," he said. "Truly obliged."

"Where are you headed?" Jake asked.

"The northern California coast. I heard there's some good farming land up that way."

"There is indeed. Beautiful country."

The man seemed to recall a matter and reached under the wagon seat. He pulled out a box of dishes and dug through it until he found a small object in a calico bag. The man handed the bag to Jake. "I'd like you to have this, to thank you for your kindness."

Jake made no move to take it. "I can't accept anything. I'm trading a good horse for a good horse. Nothing more."

The man stared at the pink calico in his hand, then lifted his sunburned face to study Jake. "I found these at a trading post before I left Missouri. They're earrings I'd intended to give my wife once we arrived in California, to welcome her to our new home. My wife died along the way," he said, "so I'd be happy if you'd share them with your missus instead. I'd like some special lady to have them." He smiled then, a little sadly. "You're the first man I've met since I crossed into California, so I think they should go to you."

With his visit to Livvy fresh in his mind, as well as his love and concern for Jess, Jake knew just what the man was feeling, and he took the small pouch with a nod of thanks. "At least let me trade you something more for them."

The man's smile lost its edge of sadness as he gazed contemplatively at Jake. "Son, during my years, I've learned that when one of God's children has done good things for others, He sometimes gives special blessings to let them know that He sees. Maybe you could think of this gift as such." He added, "I very much appreciate the fresh horse."

"Then I'll very much appreciate the gift for my wife, though I wish yours had made it here with you."

The man climbed up into his seat and gathered the reins. "She's in a better place," he answered with certainty, and started the buckskin on its way.

Jake untied the gray horse from the fence and began to lead it toward a water trough. Then curiosity compelled him to shake out the earrings into his hand. They were squares of silver filigree, with tiny green stones the same color as Jess's eyes.

He looked up to watch the kindly man drive off. The road was empty.

The man, the wagon, and the horse had vanished.

Jake looked to the lead that he still held in his hand. At the other end of it stood the buckskin.

Jake gently curled his fingers around the silver earrings. They were there. They were real.

He rapidly searched his memory to recall what the man had said. *"When one of God's children has done good things for others, He sometimes gives special blessings to let them know that He sees."*

Peace and awe flowed through Jake as he realized he'd just been visited by an angel.

"Why are you standing out here with this horse?" Jess asked.

After what had just happened, Jake wasn't surprised that she was there. With the silver earrings tucked in one hand, he removed the lead from the horse. The buckskin walked a few feet away and ate grass.

Jake smiled down at his wife and laid the pink calico sack and earrings into her hand. "A...traveler gave these to me. He wanted me to give them to my wife."

"Jake, they're beautiful." Her bright green eyes looked up at him. "But what are these for?"

He bent to kiss her nose. "For you, to wear." He'd tell her all that had happened later. Right now he was inspired to say something else. "All you have to remember your family by is a couple of pieces of jewelry in a drawer upstairs. Seems to me that it's time for new keepsakes, so that you remember now."

His breath left him. In part because of the look she had given him, in part because she had just thrown herself against his chest and was nearly strangling him in gratitude.

"I love that idea," she murmured, then lifted her rosy mouth to lock with his. "And I love you."

Her green eyes sparkled, as if with a secret of her own. "I have one of my feelings," she said, "and it's very strong."

"What is it?" The Almighty would keep her safe, he knew. She and the baby were in His hands.

"I'm sensing that something wonderful is going to happen. I wondered if it might be twins— Just why are you looking choked up?" Her enchanting grin practically outshone the sun. "You're not looking forward to being a father again, are you?"

"You think you're having twins?" What an awesome blessing that would be!

Jess lifted a pert shoulder. "I don't know. All I know for sure is that it's going to be wonderful, and I'm fairly certain the timing of it will coincide with the birthing."

She hadn't been wrong about her intuitions before, Jake recalled, and now five weeks seemed a longer wait than ever.

As Jess attached the earrings to her lobes, her feet seemed to be dancing.

"Something wonderful," she had said. Whatever it was, Jake had no doubt that it would be.

Chapter Twenty

I can't believe Hank isn't here," Jess muttered as she breathed and paced. "Two days before the baby's due, and he decides it's a fine time to go on vacation. Doesn't he know yet that he's family?"

"Of course he does," Jake assured her gently. "He needed supplies that couldn't wait."

"This baby isn't going to wait." Jess leaned on his arm and gestured for him to begin another lap around the compound. "Everyone else is here. This child will know the names of every person at the ranch...he'll be saddling his first horse...then along will come Hank at long last, and the boy will ask, 'Who are you?'" She stopped walking and panted as another contraction wound her stomach into a painful knot, and then finally eased. She looked helplessly up at Jake. "Am I supposed to be this cantankerous?"

"Yep."

"I feel as big as one of the mares. Believe me, I'll have even greater compassion for them after this."

"Love, you won't even remember this once you have the baby in your arms."

Jess squinted up at him. "You think so? Then you deliver the next one." They continued walking. "You keep reminding me that I'm in God's hands. I'm honestly grateful for that, but I do wish He'd quit squeezing so tight."

Jake walked her past the corral where Meg nibbled hay from the platform feeder. Jess wanted to pet her—petting horses was always so soothing—but she didn't want to react to a contraction and startle Meg. They kept walking.

A hard, forceful contraction built, and Jess groaned as she waited for it to peak. This one wasn't stopping. "Jake!" She was half bent over and gasping before it slowly, slowly began to ebb. Sweat rolled from her face, and Jake blotted it with a bandana.

"Do you want to go inside, love?" he asked gently.

"Not until I have to. Why is it so hot today?"

"It's nearly July, love," he reminded her.

A little shaky, Jess gradually stood upright, still clinging to Jake. She hoped the apple Eve picked had been a mighty good one.

"We haven't come up with any names yet," he offered.

Jess slanted him a glare. "I can think of a few."

Then Ambrose was there, removing her hand from Jake's arm and placing it in his. "Jake, go have some supper," he suggested. "I'll walk awhile with Jess."

Jake waited for her nod. "I'll eat fast, love. Ambrose, call out if you need me before I'm through." He gave her the bandana, then hesitantly started toward the cookhouse. He looked back once more before he ducked inside.

"You shouldn't be so hard on him, Jess," Ambrose murmured as he began walking with her.

Jess refolded the bandana to reveal a dry spot and pressed it to her neck. "People don't appreciate things that come easy," she replied. "I know that's why the Lord gives women pain in childbirth—so they'll love those little babies they labored for. But maybe that's why He also makes us so cranky—so the fathers will appreciate it too."

"Jess, that man is suffering plenty. You're in pain, so you can't see it, but he's worried terrible bad."

"He is?" she said weakly.

"So am I. We all are. One of the worst feelings for a man is to be helpless. We see someone we care about in pain, but there isn't one thing we can do about it. Jake is in terrible pain, just a different kind." They rounded the workshop and headed toward the stable. "I can't imagine how hard this is for you already, but I believe he'd feel even more respect for you if you...." He seemed to be searching for the right words.

"Took this like a ranchman?" she said helpfully.

Ambrose smiled a little. "Something like that. It'd be a good way for him to look back in years ahead and remember you." He pulled out his own handkerchief and wiped her forehead. "Try to love him through it, butterfly."

Jess stopped to pant through a contraction. "Why did you have to pick now to appeal to my heart? Now," she gasped, "when I want to hit something?"

Ambrose laughed softly. "Should we find you a tree to fell?"

"As long as it's a big one."

"Gold!"

The holler came from across the ranch to the southeast. "I found gold!"

Seth came running, one hand clamped on his hat and the other raised high in the air. If he'd ridden a horse to the mine, he'd just left it behind.

"I found gold!"

He ran up to Jess and Ambrose, face beaming blissfully, eyes unfocused. His hand was shaking as he pushed what he held toward Ambrose. "Please tell me it's gold! It has to be!"

Ambrose opened his fingers. Both he and Jess stared closely at the lumpy rock of white, silver, and gold, nearly as big as his palm. The bits of gold were shaped like large slivers, and they lay within circular clusters of silver.

Jess looked up at Seth's excited smile and realized men were running toward them from the cookhouse and the Paiute women and Mattie and Grace were racing from their village. Jake, Ambrose, and several of the others exchanged open-mouthed gazes. Taggart was the first to find his voice.

"Well, how do ye like that?" he grumbled. "There Seth goes off, enjoyin' himself in Carson City, while we're diggin' day after day, and here you come back and just pull a nugget, nice as ye please, right out of the ground!"

"Out of a wall," Seth corrected him. "Is it real, boss? Is it gold?"

Jake slapped him heartily on the back. "It's gold, Seth. Like I told you men, you get half of whatever you dig up."

The men stared at each other, and then in a roar they ran toward the mine tunnel, Seth leading the way.

Jake dusted his hand, grinning at a private joke. Seth had taken back the stone.

"What?" Jess asked.

"I didn't know those boys were capable of moving without a horse under them."

Ambrose chuckled with him, but Jess doubled over in agony. When Jake tried to help her upright, she shook him off and knelt on her hands and knees in the grass.

"Jess!"

That quickly, the gold discovery was forgotten, and her husband was lifting her with great care into his arms. With long strides, he carried her toward the house with the same gentleness that she'd seen him use to soothe mares while they were delivering their young.

"What can I do?" Ambrose asked, keeping pace alongside Jake.

Jess heard Lily answer him. "Come with me. We'll need buckets of water. Mattie, Grace, you girls tell your father that Mother Jess's time is here."

Feet hurried away through the grass, and then Jake was climbing the porch stairs. He turned sideways to ease them both through the door, which he'd left open to cool the house, and Jess saw the anxiety in his face.

She reached a hand up to his cheek and turned his face to hers. With her thumb she caressed the crinkles at the corner of his eye, his skin brown where years of sun had darkened it, with tiny white lines where the sun couldn't reach when he was squinting or smiling. He held her just inside the door, and she knew better than to be concerned about his being troubled by her weight; it was meager compared to the cows he lifted. She wanted this moment with him, for both of them to cherish always.

"After this, you and I won't be alone anymore," she said softly.

His eyes locked warmly with hers. "I'll find time for us to be alone, little lady. Never doubt that."

"I love your crooked smile," she said.

"Crooked?"

"Did you know that your eyes are exactly the color of whiskey?"

His crooked smile broadened, but faltered when she grimaced through vehement pain.

"And," she panted, "how you smell like horses and leather—all good things."

"Did you know that you have four tiny freckles on your left cheek in front of your ear"—he kissed the place— "shaped like a backward *c*? It's always reminded me of the stars."

"I love that," she said. She knew how very much he loved the stars. The comparison was precious, and she was absurdly thankful for those four little freckles.

Jake kept holding her. "I don't expect you can give birth here, can you."

"That's all right. I don't want to go upstairs yet. Can I just sit on the sofa for a while and enjoy the breeze?"

It felt nice inside, she thought as Jake lowered her to the leather cushion. He'd opened the doors and windows upstairs and down, and the air flowed through, cooling the perspiration on her face.

"Poker?" he suggested.

Jess laughed. He knew her too well. "If you don't mind helping me pass the time."

He lifted a deck of cards from the mantel. "I don't mind losing a few hands," he said.

Lily, Nettle, and Spruzy entered with wooden buckets of water. Ambrose stepped in behind them, frowning as he watched Jake deal.

Jake glanced at him. "Care to play a hand?"

Ambrose frowned, then chuckled, then frowned again. He was still holding two buckets when Jess had mercy on him. "Things here are not like they were in the South," she said. "Here, folks deal with matters as best they can with what they have on hand, and they don't trouble themselves about what proper society dictates as acceptable. A game of cards is a distraction, and right now, that's exactly what I need."

"Shouldn't we send for a doctor?" Ambrose set the buckets on the hearth. He didn't seem to notice when Lily rolled up Jess's sleeves and washed her skin with the fresh water to cool her.

Jake started to speak, but Jess gave him a look that said, *"Better let me."*

"Ambrose, the nearest doctor would take a day to fetch and bring here. Lily's given birth to two girls and been a midwife to many women, Jake helped Olivia with her birthing, and there isn't a man on this ranch who hasn't delivered a hundred calves and foals, even with complications. I don't need some stranger clearing the room of the people I love and barking out rules and making me miserable for however many hours of labor I've got left. I'm comfortable, and I'm surrounded by people who know what they're doing. Does that make sense?"

Ambrose scratched his sandy-gold hair like a man who didn't know what to think. Then he pulled up a chair beside her and gave her a reluctant wink. "Deal me in, Jake."

❖❖❖

Around midnight the pains intensified, but Lily told Jess it would be a few hours more at least and suggested Jake take her down to the stream. The cool water, she said, would ease the pressure of the pains and give Jess some relief from the heat.

It did both, but Jess was restless and found she constantly wanted to be somewhere else, doing something else.

A few hours later she was resting on the sofa again, with her bare heels propped on the coffee table. Jake kneaded her shoulders, and Nettle massaged her feet.

Jake hadn't left her side, Jess thought, and he'd eaten only once. After the child came, he was going to be as tired as she was.

The ranchmen began poking their heads through the doorway, keeping watch on her with as much care as if she were one of the mares. When Taggart's blaze of orange hair poked in, she asked him the time. He stepped to the window and bent to look up. "Two thirty. Ye about done yet?"

The pains were very close together. She tried not to scream as one clamped down on her. "I'm sorry," she ground out, "to be inconveniencing *you*." Her head fell limply back against the sofa, and Spruzy mopped the trickles of sweat from her face.

"I don't think she has much longer to go," Lily said.

Taggart strode out onto the porch. "Hey, boys!" he called to the slumbering forms across the compound. "We're almost there!"

A round of cheers went up, and absently Jess wondered what she had done to these men that had changed them from the quiet, withdrawn cattlemen they once had been. Then she thought that perhaps they weren't the only ones who had changed. Three short years ago, she never would have imagined she'd be sitting inside a ranch house while gangling and burly men wagered on the outcome of a birthing.

Tall men began to fill the room, gazing eagerly at her like she was the two-to-one favorite and was several lengths ahead as she neared the finish line.

Ambrose gave her a gentle look that reminded her to be nice.

She felt like a spectacle. She also knew they were here because they cared about her.

A pain gripped her. Taggart settled on the coffee table, took her hand, and let her squeeze.

When it was over he glanced at the men, then returned his Irish blue eyes to her. "I have good news, Jess." He laugh-coughed into his fist. "There're nine of us in the room, but only one of us is in pain."

Jess stared at him. "I was hoping for other 'good news.'"

Will gave her a jaunty smile. "The corn is knee-high, and it's not even July."

So this was what it was like to give birth on a ranch.

Lily had mercy. "All right, everyone out." She shooed them out the door, then returned to give Jake a pat. "I think it's time to take her upstairs, Father Bennett."

Jake settled her on their bed, and Nettle and Spruzy propped pillows between her and the pine log wall. Lily lit then blew out a smudge stick that continued to smoke. It smelled wonderfully of juniper.

Jake folded back his sleeves then washed his hands in the basin while Lily checked her progress. Lily's confident, motherly smile assured her it was finally time.

"Let's bring your baby, Jessica," she said.

Jess nodded, then turned her eyes to her handsome husband...his unshaven jaw, that wonderful mouth she loved to kiss, the crinkles at the corners of his eyes, his ridge of dark eyebrows, and that thick, black hair. The mattress sank as he sat beside her. She forced herself not to shriek through the next pain, panted for a moment, then managed a smile. "You'd best put your hat on, Bennett. You want your child to recognize you after today, don't you?"

He chuckled, and then she couldn't see him at all. Horrible pain ripped through her as her stomach hardened and began to push the child out.

"It's coming fast," Lily said.

"It's about time!" Jess screamed. She gripped Jake's big hand, which steadily held hers, and Nettle and Spruzy encouraged her as she used the next pain to push.

All at once, she felt tremendous relief, and slumped back against the pillows as a cry broke the stillness.

❖〜❖〜❖

"He's blond."

Taggart peered doubtfully over Jake's shoulder into the tiny face that peered doubtfully back.

To Jess, the baby was perfect. Jake held him wrapped in the black and red blanket, colors that matched the curious muddy-brown eyes within the small, pale face and contrasted almost comically with his dusting of white-blond hair.

After Jess had slept a few hours, she'd asked Jake to help her downstairs to the main room sofa. Everyone wanted to see the baby, and she didn't want to miss a moment of it.

Midday sunshine slanted in through the window like a blessing. Jess had chosen to wear the silver filigree earrings as a memento for them both—to remember the birthday of Jake's first son, and as a reminder of how the Lord had been and was always with them.

Jake held her hand in one of his and held their son in the other. He didn't seem able to let go of either of them.

Diaz gave Taggart a look. "You think he should have hair the color of yours, amigo? People will look at him and think the boss's cat exploded."

Mattie and Grace giggled. Both of them knelt in front of the baby, gently feeling the soft, blond hairs, plainly fascinated with him.

"Ambrose was blond when he was born," Jess said, "and so were Emma and Broderick. Ambrose's hair darkened as he grew older."

From where he sat on the arm of the sofa, Ambrose leaned over to admire his nephew. "Our father was blond," he said. "So was our grandfather. It's always been common among the Hales." Ambrose gently hugged Jess around her shoulders, and she felt the tremor in his embrace.

Jess knew he must be missing their family. He was thrilled to be here for this birthing, she knew, but his heart was also burdened with the absence of those who should have been here.

"What're you going to name him?" Doyle asked.

Seth gazed imperiously down at Taggart. "I think you should name him something Taggart can't pronounce. Like *dent-de-lion.*"

Taggart tore off his hat and made a show of thwacking Seth with it. "It'd be heartless to name him Spindleweed."

Seth set his gold and silver rock in the center of the table as a means to get the last say with Taggart. "I think I'm just going to call the boy Nugget."

The ranchmen glanced at each other, briefly considering, then began to agree that Nugget was a fitting nickname.

"What are you going to do with your gold?" Lily asked Seth.

Seth sobered and stuck his hands into his back pockets. "Well, ma'am, there's a large vein of it. I'm going to buy the land to the east and start my own ranch like this one." When everyone stared at him but said nothing, he grinned in Ho Chen's direction. "You didn't think I'd buy land someplace where I couldn't enjoy Ho Chen's cooking?"

Hearty congratulations followed, and much backslapping and hand-shaking, as the young man's face reddened at all the attention.

Jake leaned close to Jess. "It looks like that feeling you had was right," he murmured warmly. "You sensed that something wonderful was going to happen around the time of the birth."

A hand reached in and knocked on the open front door, and Hank's pink, smiling face appeared behind it. He lifted his brows to look over the crowd at the baby, then his expression faltered between joy and hesitant expectation as he gazed at Ambrose and Jess.

"Hank?" Jess called out. "Won't you come in?"

He stepped inside but remained in the doorway.

"Hank?" Jake asked.

The men grew quiet and parted so that Jake and Jess could see their neighbor.

"Jess, Ambrose," he said, "we need to explain something to the two of you."

"We?" Jess asked. She had sensed that something wonderful was going to happen, but Hank's behavior was beginning to scare her. "Hank, what has happened?"

From the porch, a slim hand reached for Hank's, and Gusty joined him in the doorway, in tears and looking equally as hesitant as Hank had been.

"Gusty?" Jess gave a half smile. "It's good to see you. What brings you here?"

"Jessica?" Gusty's fingers twisted together as she remembered her manners. "I'm sorry—I'm glad to see ye again, Ambrose." She began again. "A year ago in Carson City, the first time I saw Jessica after the fire, I told her that I was there the night yer house burned down, deliverin' a dress I'd sewn to one of yer neighbors."

336

"To Mrs. Nolan, for her final fitting," Jess recalled as her insides sank. *Please, Lord,* she prayed, *please, don't let Gusty be involved with Galen Ross and the fire.*

"Do ye remember that I told ye I rounded the corner and saw yer parents' house blazin', and I thought hell had risen right up through the streets of Carson?"

"I remember."

Gusty produced a handkerchief and wiped her nose. Jess felt Ambrose stiffen beside her.

"I—" Gusty closed her eyes briefly, as she had the first time she'd told Jess about that night, and Jess knew she must be reliving it once more. "I was alone, near the back of the house, and fire was rollin' up the walls toward the upstairs windows."

"You saw my mother," Jess said woodenly. Georgeanne had gone to help Elsie, the nursemaid, put Emma to sleep. "You saw my mother in the nursery window."

"Aye, that I did." Gusty's tears came faster now.

Oh, please, Lord.

"Last year, so much was happenin', and then ye left my shop so fast I didn't have time to tell ye." She wiped her nose again. "And then, two months ago, ye came back, and ye had that premonition and all, and I knew ye'd be in danger doin' what ye needed to do, so I didn't tell ye then, either. In truth, I wanted to tell ye, desperately, but at the same time, I couldn't bear to tell ye." She looked at Jess and Ambrose both. "Please, *please* try to understand."

Jess felt her hand go limp within Jake's grip. "Understand what?" she breathed.

Gusty pressed her lips together in a teary smile. Then she looked down at something out on the porch. "Come on, love."

Jess heard light footsteps, like those of a small child, then glimpsed shoulder-length, dark blonde curls, and one blue eye peeking curiously out from behind Gusty's skirt. The little girl from Gusty's shop. She looked about three years old…the age Emma would be if she had survived the house fire.

Both Jess and Ambrose stood. Jess looked between her brother and the child. They possessed exactly the same blue eyes, the same nose and chin.

"Lord above," Jess whispered, her heart praising God when the words wouldn't follow.

Ambrose sank slowly to his knees before the girl. Clearly, he already knew who she was. She was the sister he'd always wanted to know, whom they'd believed had died in the fire.

The girl stepped out from behind Gusty and eyed him with a buoyant, fascinated tilt of her chin that made her blonde curls bounce. She looked at his handsome pose and his golden hair and leaned closer. "Are you a knight?" she asked.

Knowing that she would have years to spend with Emma, Jess stayed back and allowed Ambrose to finally meet their precocious sister.

"I'm Ambrose," he told her throatily. "Your brother."

Apparently untroubled by all the people looking on, Emma stepped forward and hugged Ambrose.

Ambrose reached back for Jess's hand. "And this is your sister, Jessica."

Jess leaned a hand on Ambrose's shoulder and knelt to touch, to hug, Emily Frances Hale. "Emma." Jess pressed her cheek into her sister's hair, and cried.

"Jake?" Jess asked a few minutes later.

"When I searched the rubble, I found few remains, and no little ones at all," Jake said, and Jess heard the grief, the regret, in his voice. "The fire was fierce. I'm sorry I didn't tell you; I never once thought she might have survived."

Ho Chen, who had searched the rubble with Jake, spoke up. "Only find bone fragments, Miss Jessie, Mister Ambrose," he quietly confirmed. "We believed nothing left of child to bury."

Jess wasn't hurt by the mistake. She was all too happy to order another name removed from the Hale gravestone. They had Emma back.

This, she realized, was the "something wonderful" that she had sensed was going to happen. If such happenings were a part of sensing future events and experiencing premonitions, then she would always trust God with the bad and look forward to the good.

Emma stepped away from Jess and looked past her to the portrait of Georgeanne on the wall. Beside it hung a cluster of tiny dried flowers with a faint purple hue. Lilac blossoms Ambrose had sent from their mother's hedge at Greenbriar.

"Who is that?" Emma asked.

Jess looked through hot tears to Gusty and left the explanation to her.

Gusty sniffed. "Emma," she said, "that is yer mother."

Emma's pale blue eyes shifted to Jess. "She looks like you."

Jess smiled for her benefit, then looked to Gusty again, wanting to understand. "You saw my mother in the nursery window," she repeated.

"Mrs. Hale had brought Emma into the store after she was born," Gusty said, "so when I saw her through that window with flames surroundin' her and a bundle in her arms, I knew it was Emma. She'd opened the window before I arrived, but she had no way to climb down. I held out my skirts, and she kissed the baby, then tossed her down. A moment later, yer mother was consumed. I saw that the baby's hand had been burned, so I took her away to tend her. When I heard that all the Hales had been killed in the fire, I raised her as my own. Jessica, dear, I'm so sorry. The first time I saw ye in my store, I didn't know what to do. When Hank here came to visit me in Carson two days back and told me ye were all right now and that all the trouble is past, I knew I had to bring her to ye. I love her, I want ye to know that, and it's tearin' me apart to lose her, but ye are her rightful family. She has to grow up with ye."

Jake handed the baby to Lily. He gave Jess a gentle, meaningful look.

Jess thought of the two years that Gusty had raised Emma as her own child and had showered her with love. Gusty was the only family that Emma knew. Taking her away would frighten and devastate Emma.

Then she saw Hank tenderly pull Gusty close to him. Jess envisioned his Spartan house next door and smiled. She was fairly certain that Hank didn't intend for it to remain Spartan for long. Like Jake and her, Hank and Gusty were meant to be together.

Emma wouldn't have to lose anyone, and none of them would lose her.

"I think we have a name for the baby," Jess announced. "Don't you think it's right, Gusty, that Emma know both sides of her family?"

Gusty slowly nodded, apparently uncertain what Jess meant.

Jess took Gusty's hand in hers. "Wasn't your father's name Colin?" she asked softly. "If we name our son Colin, then one day Emma will ask where that name came from. We'll tell her he was named after Aunt Gusty's father."

⋅⋅⋅◈⋅⋅⋅

Jake laid Colin in Jess's arms and led her out onto the porch. Below it grew colorful flowers she had planted there the year before as a sign that she would always remain at Jake's side. Jess cuddled her son close, loving his blond hair, loving the sleepy, mud-colored eyes she was sure would one day turn the same shade of whiskey-brown as his father's.

In the compound, Mattie and Grace hurried toward the stable amid girlish giggles, ranchmen went about their chores, and Ho Chen and Lily walked toward the cookhouse to prepare dinner.

In the corral, mares stood resting while spring colts and fillies leapt about, and Mattie and Grace quieted and enticed the foals closer to the side of the corral with pieces of long, green grass.

Ambrose and Emma stepped out of the house to join Jake and her on the porch. Jess could hear Hank and Gusty in the house behind them, talking softly together, and by Gusty's elated sob, Jess knew that Hank had proposed, and that Gusty had accepted.

At Ambrose's whisper, Emma smiled up at Jess and took her hand.

On the far side of the brook, several horses galloped for the simple pleasure of running, the wind in their manes, the afternoon sun gleaming off their coats like satin. One broke from the others, went down on its knees, and rolled onto its back, hooves high as it thrilled in the feel of the grass.

She had found the Lord in this place, Jess reflected. Since then, He had strengthened her faith, encouraged her with hope, and blessed her with love.

Jess felt her sister's hand in hers and her brother's arm along her shoulder, and she looked up at her son and her handsome, wonderful husband.

God had greatly blessed her with love.

❖❖❖

About the Author

Tammy Barley's roots run deep and wide across the United States. With Cherokee heritage and such ancestors as James Butler "Wild Bill" Hickok, Ralph Waldo Emerson, and Henry David Thoreau, she essentially inherited her literary vocation and her preferred setting: the Wild West. An avid equestrian, Tammy has ridden horseback over Western mountains and rugged trails in Arizona.

Tammy excelled in her writing studies at a local college, where she explored prose, novel writing, and nonverbal communication. She even enrolled in acting classes to master character development.

In 2006, she published two series of devotionals in *Beautiful Feet: Meditations for Missionary Women* for the Lutheran Women's Missionary Society. She won second place in the Golden Rose Contest in the category of inspiration romance, and she serves as a judge for various fiction contests.

Faith's Reward concludes her first series with Whitaker House, The Sierra Chronicles. The trilogy also includes *Love's Rescue*, which begins the saga of Jake and Jessica in a story of loyalty, heroism, and the depths of love, and *Hope's Promise*, a tale of patience, perseverance, and the power of faith.

In addition to writing, Tammy makes a career of editing manuscripts, ghostwriting, and mentoring other

writers. She also homeschools three children. Tammy
has lived in twenty-eight towns in eight different states,
but the family currently makes its home in Crystal Lake,
Illinois.

Lassos-N-Lace
Newsletter

Enjoy the latest from author Tammy Barley,
delivered right to your e-mail inbox! In addition
to receiving special giveaways and surprise
goodies available *only* to newsletter
subscribers, be the first to be notified of
new releases, book giveaways, contest news,
appearances, media events, and more!

Lassos-N-Lace Newsletter
Always something new.
Always inspiring.
Always great with chocolate.

To subscribe, simply visit
http://www.tammybarley.com
and look for the yellow Subscribe box.

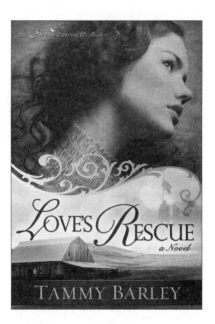

Love's Rescue
Tammy Barley

To escape the Civil War, Jessica Hale flees Kentucky with her family and heads to the Nevada Territory, only to lose them in a fire set by Unionists resentful of their Southern roots. The sole survivor, Jess is "kidnapped" by cattleman Jake Bennett and taken to his ranch in the Sierra Nevada wilderness. Angry at Jake for not saving her family, she makes numerous attempts to escape and return to Carson City, but she is apprehended each time. Why are Jake and his ranch hands determined to keep her there? She ponders this, wondering what God will bring out of her pain and loss.

ISBN: 978-1-60374-108-8 ♦ Trade ♦ 368 pages

WHITAKER
HOUSE

Hope's Promise
Tammy Barley

Jake Bennett is finally wed to the love of his life, Jessica Hale—but he isn't convinced she won't leave him. Life is a constant struggle for the Bennetts as they battle drought and live in fear of raids on Southerners, and he is not sure that Jess knew what she was getting herself into when she married him. Jess, however, despairs for another reason—she is unable to conceive a child. While trying to prove their unconditional love for each other, the Bennetts must stand in faith through betrayal, danger, and barrenness, trusting that God will reward their hopes for a better future.

ISBN: 978-1-60374-109-5 • Trade • 336 pages

WHITAKER
HOUSE

Beautiful Bandit
Loree Lough

Having escaped a gang of robbers who forced her to participate in a bank heist, Kate Wellington adopts an alias and decides to flee to Mexico. Lost and hungry, she stumbles upon the camp of a man named Josh Neville who offers to escort her across the border. But when she injures her ankle, the kindly cowboy takes "Dinah" home to his ranch to heal, instead. As the two grow closer, Josh realizes he's fallen in love, even as he learns the truth about Dinah. But does he know the whole story? And, after the truth comes out, will he put his life at risk to keep her with him?

ISBN: 978-1-60374-225-2 ✦ Trade ✦ 400 pages

WHITAKER
HOUSE

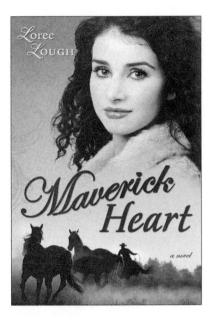

Maverick Heart
Loree Lough

When a coincidental meeting brings the tragically widowed Levee O'Reilly and rancher Dan Neville—a confirmed bachelor for reasons of his own—together, they're awakened to a long-ignored desire for love and acceptance by the realization that they might have finally found it. Can these two mavericks accept the plans God has for their lives?

ISBN: 978-1-60374-226-9 ✦ Trade ✦ 400 pages

WHITAKER
HOUSE

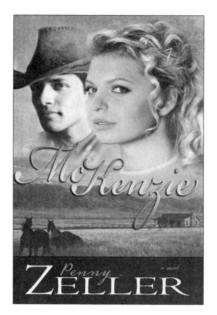

McKenzie
Penny Zeller

Desperation to save her younger sister from an abusive husband prompts McKenzie Worthington to run away from the comforts of her Boston home as a mail-order bride for a rancher in the Montana Territory. She takes comfort in knowing she can have the marriage annulled when she rescues her sister. Desperation is also what prompted Zachary Sawyer to post the ad, and he eagerly awaits the woman God has chosen as his wife. When they meet, McKenzie tries to keep her distance, but she can't help feeling attracted to Zach and his selfless, godly ways. What will become of her plan?

ISBN: 978-1-60374-216-0 ♦ Trade ♦ 320 pages

WHITAKER
HOUSE

Kaydie
Penny Zeller

Since the death of her abusive husband, Kaydie Kraemer's life has been easier, but she remains wary of men. Staying with her sister and brother-in-law at their Montana ranch as she awaits her baby's birth, she builds a protective wall around herself that won't be easy to tear down. Ranch hand Jonah Dickenson had a painful childhood and never wants to marry, but there's something about Kaydie that makes him question his decision to remain a bachelor. When an old friend of Kaydie's comes to town, an unforeseen prospect of marriage arises. Will she settle for a safe union with someone she knows well, or can she trust God to guard her heart in the arms of Jonah?

ISBN: 978-1-60374-217-7 • Trade • 304 pages

WHITAKER
HOUSE

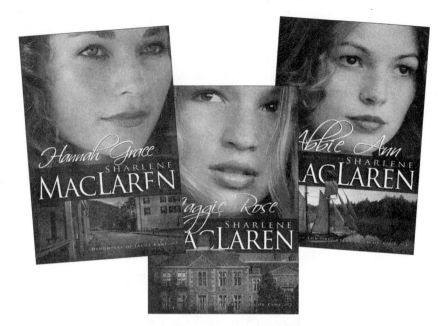

The Daughters of Jacob Kane Series
Sharlene MacLaren

Welcome to Sandy Shores, Michigan, where there's never a dull moment with the witty, winsome Kane sisters. In *Hannah Grace*, the feisty, strong-willed eldest Kane sister strikes up a volatile relationship with the new local sheriff, Gabriel Devlin—a relationship that turns to romance, thanks to a shy orphan boy and a little divine intervention. In *Maggie Rose*, the middle Kane sister moves to New York City to work at an orphanage, falls in love with a newspaper reporter, and discovers God's greater purpose for them. In *Abbie Ann*, Jacob Kane's youngest daughter is a busy woman with little time for frivolous matters, including romance—until a handsome, divorced shipbuilder comes to town, his young son in tow, and God changes their hearts.

Hannah Grace ◆ ISBN: 978-1-60374-074-6 ◆ Trade ◆ 432 pages
Maggie Rose ◆ ISBN: 978-1-60374-075-3 ◆ Trade ◆ 432 pages
Abbie Ann ◆ ISBN: 978-1-60374-076-0 ◆ Trade ◆ 528 pages

WHITAKER
HOUSE